DARK MATTER PRESENTS

MONSTER LAIRS

A DARK FANTASY HORROR ANTHOLOGY

Other Books in the "Dark Matter Presents" Anthology Series

Zero Dark Thirty: The 30 Darkest Stories from Dark Matter Magazine, 2021–'22

Human Monsters: A Horror Anthology

Monstrous Futures: A Sci-Fi Horror Anthology

Haunted Reels: Stories from the Minds of Professional Filmmakers

Haunted Reels 2: More Stories from the Minds of Professional Filmmakers

The Off-Season: An Anthology of Coastal New Weird

Little Red Flags: Stories of Cults, Cons, and Control

Edited by Anna Madden
Proofread by Maddy Leary
Book Design and Layout by Rob Carroll
Cover Art by Olly Jeavons
Cover Design by Rob Carroll

ISBN 978-1-958598-08-5 (paperback)
ISBN 978-1-958598-58-0 (eBook)

darkmatter-ink.com

DARK MATTER PRESENTS

MONSTER LAIRS

A DARK FANTASY HORROR ANTHOLOGY

EDITED BY
ANNA MADDEN

DARK
MATTER
INK

For my Beast, who keeps the wolves of life at bay.

—Anna

Contents

Content Warning

This anthology contains content that may be unsuitable for certain audiences. Stories include foul language, disturbing imagery, and graphic depictions of sex and violence. Reader discretion is advised.

Introduction

By Anna Madden

I have a confession to make. When I was first asked if I would edit *Monster Lairs*, despite my excitement and the faith of others in my capabilities, I doubted myself. I was afraid. Who was I to be worthy to hold the keys? I looked into that fear with wide eyes and saw a tall tree grown in shadow. Its roots were a cage for my bones. My marrow was its milk.

This project was a lair, and the monster was my own shadow. I can't say that I defeated it. Can you defeat your own shadow? But I accepted its existence, and I didn't stop stepping forward.

Monster lairs are places to face our truest selves. Places where dresses are stitched into skin, where sisters say goodbye and children are given to winter's embrace. Where light-woven braids dangle from the sky and candles are lit with the knowledge they will eventually flicker out.

Even a god can fear the dark.

To be afraid is normal. It is human. It is what we do when we're afraid that defines us.

When I wrote the guidelines for this anthology, I asked writers to take me on journeys to places only they could imagine. In return, they showed me worlds previously unknown. I walked a moonlit path down into the valley of the night, where monsters prowl. I listened to the power within a scream, believed in the formidable nature of trees and deep water, stared into the beauty of a nettled smile. With eyes turned to diamond and shimmer, I met travelers with thorn-sliced cheeks, found a red scarf, buried an embroidered slipper, and I learned what it's like to forget my own name.

In this volume, the reader will ride on horseback until the sands of desert turn to ocean waves. They will breathe in the scent of wood and cloud-damp and whiskey, step between snow-clad trees, watch the blue disappear from the sky, wield ironwood blades, visit a garden rooted by love, find hope in the light of a firefly, like a kiss turned to an ember, staving off a harsh November wind.

This third monster-inspired anthology from Dark Matter INK is filled with tales of decidedly inhuman monsters. There are guardians, demons, gods, great fish, nine-tailed foxes, ghosts, angels, vampire descendants, giants, and more. They are dangerous, for sure, but most are simply trying to survive, to love, to find purpose, to protect their young, the same as any of us.

And if that's not relatable, it's certainly reasonable.

There are thirty-one stories here. Thirty-one doors to creak open and enter. I can tell you with certainty one is crimson within a black frame, crisp lines outlining the shape of a web across it. Another is narrow, its hungry splinters nipping at your clothes. Others are abraded by sand and dirt and bleakness, salted with brine, moonlit and clawed, overgrown, sun-bleached, stained from tears and blood and soot and gunpowder, matted by white and nut-brown fur.

For every door, there is a lair, and those who travel beyond will find sacrifice, obligation, loss, but also love, transformation, and light all the brighter for the contrast of the surrounding shadows. They will feel the weight of copper promises, taste flesh, find new clothes to replace blood-stained ones, learn to sew and to preserve, and wrap sharp knives with bramble.

These are stories that persist. That will consume until only ash remains.

Sincerely,

Anna Madden

Has Someone Ever Dared To Scream?

By Victor Forna

Of Sight

I first saw in the dark when I was eleven years old. A vulture—featherless, huge and gray. It hacked through the night. From the palm forest behind the snoring town it came, easing into our hut through a damaged window Papa wouldn't fix.

My sister, that gentle sleeper, that naughty baby we all loved so much. The vulture hovered over her, flying circles. It opened its ragged beak. No teeth. No tongue. I saw its raw, red throat.

About to scream, to wake Mama, to wake the neighborhood, tales in my head warned me to remain quiet…tales Granny used to tell us by the fireside, before she died.

They warned me to not scream.

Unless you want to die, my daughter.

They saved me.

I clamped my mouth with sweaty hands. In the corner, by gourds and clay pots, I shuddered.

The vulture flew off—done with what it had come to do.

I saw it change outside. Into a man. Wings became hands. Claws became feet. Crack, crack, as its skeleton morphed from one thing to another. The vulture became Pa Basi, advisor to our chief. I almost gasped at his bony face. Chunky liquid smeared his naked body, from bald head to calloused toes. I pinched my nose. He landed on the ground and lumbered homeward through the night.

When he disappeared into his house down the road, behind the twisted orange grooves, I let myself breathe, at last.

I let myself whimper.

That morning, as Mama bawled over Yebu's body, I did not tell her I had seen in the dark. I did not tell her I had the eye. I did not tell her I had seen what happened to my baby sister. I did not tell her Pa Basi was a witch who had swallowed her daughter's life.

In silence, I wept.

Unless you want to die…

Guilt and grief filled me like pus in boils, but I kept my mouth shut.

Of Silence

Time passed.

In the sun, when Abu told me he liked my breasts and cupped them by the river, I said nothing. His hands went where Granny said no hands should go.

In the sun, when nightmares of my sister rained on me, I said nothing.

In the sun, when Papa asked why I had not been eating these days, I wanted to tell him there was already too much inside of me that needed spitting out. I said nothing, only losing weight.

In the dark, when I saw kurfi leave my aunty's hut, I said nothing. I watched from beside our latrine, shaking. It nodded to me—no eyes, no nose, tiny holes all over its face—showing its respect for my silence.

In the dark, when I saw thebu, naked, short, mischievous, frolicking under a tamarind tree, I said nothing. I closed my eyes. I saw through my lids.

In the sun, to Foi, that beautiful boy I liked, I said nothing. When he started loving one of my friends, I cried. But I said nothing to them.

In the sun, when my father's sisters ganged up against Mama and called her a witch, I said nothing. I played gɛgɛ beside an orange tree.

In the sun, when Mama paid little attention to me and my siblings as she mourned, I said nothing, although I wanted her to hold me.

When I saw my dead sister wandering the dark with rotting feet, I said nothing. I did not tell her she must follow that rhythmic pounding, pestle in mortar, to find our foremothers in Fouta Djallon. I watched her become a restless spirit.

When I saw Pa Basi eat the life of his own mother, I said nothing. When he came over the next day, he smiled at me. I smiled back. I flashed cassava-white teeth, hoping they eclipsed my hatred for him.

When I saw a group of men in the deserted village of Mosenge kill a girl to feed their Bɔrɛ Fima, cut her portion by portion, stomach opened and flapped to her chest, I said nothing. I watched them eat the girl as though she were a deer. My lips pressed, containing the sound of my terror.

The night I told Mama about what Abu had been doing to me was the same night I smudged my eyes with spit and mud. I was seventeen. Maybe Yebu and all the dead would forgive me if I shut my eye. Maybe it would heal me of my guilt. My eyes flicked open. Between the stripes of mud on my lashes, I saw. I saw in the pale-lit forest, among the palm trees, a calm family of kurfi kut-kin hopping through the fog. Spit and mud had not shut my eye.

What was the point of this gift, this curse—to keep the secrets of monsters for the rest of my life?

Weeping to myself, I heard a tussle inside our hut. My parents simmered in a quarrel over me.

Papa told Mama that I must remain silent about Abu, not to bring attention to our household, that we were all family in this town. Mama insisted that we must tell the chief, for my safety and that of the other children. Papa said it was not our place. Papa said I should just stay away from Abu, just stay away from the river when he went there. Mama said no, that was not correct,

Abu always went to the river looking for me. Papa screamed that Mama never listened to him, that maybe his sisters were right. Mama wanted to say something, she sobbed instead. The child must remain quiet, Papa said. I hoped Mama would keep screaming for me. Mama stuttered. Her voice dimmed like a lamp in need of kerosene. When Mama became silent, I knew I must do the same, in the sun and in the dark.

Of Destruction

On that day we burned the woods to sow rice in the aftermath of destruction, tɔngɔ came to town.

They had heard of the deaths and disappearances in our region. They had come for the discovery of witches, no stone unturned, no leaf unshaken. They blew their horns. They summoned us from our farms. They rang their bells. With a go-ahead from our chief, they gathered us in a circular clearing by the grave-yard behind town. They made us stand in lines, by family. To see in the dark was not witchcraft, but what will the tɔngɔ call my silence? Our people did not believe in good witches. My stomach cramped.

Pa Basi led his line, the head of his family, unafraid and bold. Other witches mirrored him in countenance, laughing and making jokes.

If only I could scream their names.

Buamɔ Nepɔ, the leader of tɔngɔ, spoke from behind the flaps of her leopard skin cap. "If you know you have witched before, step out of line." Her voice was soft. It sounded musical.

No one moved.

"What I mean is, if you have eaten the flesh of another person, step out. If you have fed your medicine with human blood, make yourself known. If you have gathered in a forest in the dark, singing to bad fires, come here. If you have chewed and rubbed shit on your body to shapeshift into an animal, leave your family's side. If you have eaten the life of another—"

My eyes landed on Pa Basi. He did not flinch at the words.

"When our play begins, we tongɔ will not show mercy." With our chief's approval, Buamɔ Nepɔ signaled her followers to begin.

My heart kicked against my rib cage even though Buamɔ Nepɔ had not called those with the eye.

Tongɔ, twenty of them, wailed in unison like mourning mothers at the gravesteads of their children. They danced like joyful brides. They stabbed into the lines with their arrow-headed tongɔra. When we tried to move, we could not. We were at the mercy of their spirit spears.

They approached my family's line. They jabbed Papa. Tongɔra bounced outward. Papa was unharmed. Mama, too. All my siblings.

When they reached me, my chest almost flamed. They pierced into my ribs. I grunted. Sunlight beat my brow. Was this punishment for letting my sister die? For leaving her alone in the dark? For all the evil I had seen and never spoken of? Maybe I deserved to perish here. Maybe I wanted to perish here. But the spirit spear bounced outward.

I was unscathed. Free.

My breaths returned in rushes.

Pa Basi was writhing in the distance, worm-like, when I lifted my eyes.

I found myself smiling.

Human faeces and the skulls of vultures had been found in his gown pockets, and other small sɛbɛ, his failed charms for protection and hiding. Tongɔ stabbed him on the ground, over and over and over. He screamed. Tongɔra plunged into his stomach. Gray innards followed when the weapon was pulled out. Pa Basi died with his eyes open, almost ten years after eating my little sister's life.

Up to fifteen witches were discovered in our town on that day we burned the woods to sow hope in the aftermath of destruction. None were shown mercy.

Buamɔ Nepɔ slithered up to me. She had taken off her cap, revealing a girl not far from my age. She donned a leopard hide jacket. Her wrists and elbows and ankles were also adorned with strips of animal skin. Unlike me, she was tall. She had muscles where I had bones. Tattoos of leaves arrayed her face. With all our differences, she still reminded me of myself, of someone I could have been in another life. We stared at each other, a familiar hush sizzled between us. She opened her mouth as if to scream. I spotted a coal-black ball floating and spinning over her tongue. It caught the tired evening light just before she closed her mouth and, in that glow, I glimpsed it was an irisless eye. She walked away, as if her silence was a secret shared with me.

Of Sound

After tɔngɔ, the dark of our town Nerekora turned into a less scary thing.

I no longer saw witches or animal-attired cannibals. I no longer saw people feeding their medicine bags with human blood. Most had been slain by tɔngɔ, and those who survived did not dare operate anymore. The things I saw in the dark became easy to turn away from, and the silence of my tongue did not load me with guilt as much as before. In the dark, I saw mostly kurfi. Kurfi kut-kin that lived with the palm trees. Lonesome ronsho, resting and whistling underneath banana trees, duffels on their backs. I saw the red-skinned man-woman who lived in River Ma, I saw them pull Abu into their depths one night, and for once I was proud of how versatile I had become in voicelessness. I also saw the dead searching for Fouta—most found those mother mountains in the end, while others lost their paths and stayed behind to haunt the winds with their wails. I forgave those silences. May the dead forgive them too.

When I was twenty-three, Papa died one afternoon. The smoke season had filled his lungs with cold. He coughed and coughed. There was crimson on his lips when we found him. Mama cried over his body, but not as much as she had cried over Yebu. My siblings cried. I cried, in my heart. Papa had always been good to us, provided for us…but that memory of him telling Mama to choose silence…but in the end, I forgave him. Forgiving my silences made it easier to forgive the ones others kept. On the seventh day after his death, across citrus-dotted planes, I saw him run toward Fouta Djallon.

My siblings left soon after Papa's forty-days. All three of them. They left for New London, the town foreigners were building by the sea. They left me with Mama. They were ambitious. Unlike me. I did not mind spending all my days in Nerekora—was I not named after that pink flower that only grew on its soil? I did not mind plowing farms until my death. I did not mind living as my parents or grandparents had lived. I did not mind wasting my nights singing or telling stories around a fire. I longed for a simple life. If I had ever left this town, it would have been because of the dark—but even the dark did not scare me anymore. It was familiar. And who knew what the dark of other places held? I did not want to know.

I found the voice to tell Foi I liked him after I turned twenty-four, after my friend left for New London. Maybe it was the miles between them, or a small miracle—he said he liked me too, said he always had. His parents met Mama and my uncles, and we were married with song and dance. Soon, we were blessed with twins, boy and girl, both as beautiful as our love.

All was well in the sun. All was well in the dark.

Six months after the birth of my Gbeshe, the child who came after the twins, the child who had my smile and Mama's name, I saw a white bat flapping in the direction of my home.

The bat entered our hut.

It circled my sleeping daughter.

I stared at the creature with widened eyes. My hands, for the first time in a long time, shook as they clamped my mouth closed.

The bat morphed into a man covered in faeces. Chief Sumanɔ. I almost gasped on seeing his familiar and perpetual smile. I had known this man all my life. I had never seen him in the dark. His sɛbɛ hid and protected him well, from my eye and from tɔngɔ that had come here. Wasn't it he who had given them the go-ahead to play?

His movements were jerky, as he found his way toward my child.

I thought of Yebu. I thought of all the others I had watched killed over the years. Would I ever forgive my silence, if I let him swallow my daughter's life?

He crept closer.

Stay silent. *Unless you want to die, my daughter.* I felt myself become a child again.

He opened his mouth.

I saw his—

Maybe, years from now, tɔngɔ would return from their bush and slay Chief Sumanɔ.

But grief had turned Mama into a shadow. Grief for one child skewed her love for all the others, skewed her love for herself. Did I want that?

Against every instinct, against every story, I screamed. I woke the town up. I called for everyone to come out. I screamed again. I did not want to die…but what else could I do when I wanted my children to live, to dream, to blossom?

I waited for lightning to cleave the reed roof and strike me down…

Chief Sumanɔ turned his head backwards, to face me. His front, like his back. His back, like his front. He stared from sallow eyes. A hiss rose through his teeth. He began stumbling toward me.

I screamed, afraid. I screamed, angry.

He paused.

He exploded.

Blood and guts and bones splashed on me and the mud walls. Stench of flesh. Stench of meat. His remains crawled down the bricks like palm oil.

I hammered my mouth closed.

But the sound of my scream had taken on a life of its own. It dragged through the night, dragged through the air, a shapeless killing thing.

On and on it went, for miles.

I heard more screeches, witches meeting their ends in their dark lairs. They all perished at the touch of my voice—fathers, mothers, daughters, sons—a purging.

Did they know of this power at the tip of our screams? Was this why they spread those stories? To scare our tongues into silence?

I felt a sudden pain in my head. I winced. In my eyes. Pain unlike any I had ever felt before—rats chewing through my skull, worms eating into my temples—the world went pitch.

Liquid dripped down my face.

I traced the streams with unsure hands. Where my eyeballs should have been, my fingers dipped into endless holes.

I shuddered, but I was no longer afraid.

Witchroot

By R. F. Anding

They called it the Watchtower and it stood almost at the center of the forest, the tallest thing in the wood, erring a little west on the swamp side. It was older than our village, perhaps older even than our country.

No one knew what manner or species of tree it was, only that it was strong and no saplings ever sprouted around it, no matter how vast its canopy or how prolific its acorns.

The nuts fell once a year, around the Spring Equinox. They were shaped like fat raindrops with a horned cap at one end. The nut itself was an odd lacquered crimson, while the cap was matte gray with spikes so sharp it was not uncommon for them to draw blood when collected. Yet there was very little point in gathering them. In earlier, more sparse times, women had tried crushing up the nut meat for flour. The result was a powdery red substance like brick dust that would not commingle with other ingredients no matter how much it was kneaded. Those that tried were rewarded with inflamed palms and a rash which lasted for days. The flavor was acrid and when ingested in any form it produced at best a sour stomach and at worst several days vomiting blood. Any attempts to use the acorns for culinary purposes was abandoned and the women of the village cautioned their daughters and granddaughters to keep them well away from the kitchen.

There was only one reason an acorn would be collected, and that was for the *bloedgeld*. But we shall come to that by and by.

Everyone has a story about the tree. This is mine.

• • •

As a girl, I never understood why anyone would fear the tree. To me she was a protector, offering shade in the blistering summer and I would often steal away after my chores to lay beneath her crown of star-shaped leaves and read a book stolen from my father's library. Mother, who came from across the ocean and once boasted three private tutors before her family fell on hard times, had taught me to read on the long days Father worked the fields. It was our little secret.

I was the only girl I knew who could read, setting me even more conspicuously apart from the other village children. They already thought I was odd with my exotic mother and the features I had inherited from her. My hair was dark as a crow and my skin was coppery and they said I smelled of strange herbs, though I always associated the fragrance proudly with the flowers my mother dried and placed in my locket or wove into my hair. Either way, I had no one I could call a friend but that suited me well. I would rather read or wander the woods than play with the other children.

Sometimes I left gifts for the tree. A lemon drop, a shiny pebble, a castoff ribbon from Mother's sewing box. I don't know why I did this, but I always felt the tree was lonely somehow. She was like me, a unique specimen in a forest of ordinary trees. I never quite understood how I knew the Watchtower was a *her,* but I did.

Sometimes, it seemed she also left gifts for me. I noticed them just after the Equinox. It was a holiday in the village and we all attended a religious service together, then the Elders and the eldest girls continued festivities into the night. I was too young to know much more, only that the holiday kept me dressed formally and forbade me from playing in the forest. I thought the tree must have missed me and that is why she gave me gifts.

Once I found a scarf tangled in her lowest branches. It was diaphanous and white, an oddity amongst a group where women wore mostly coarse fabric dyed dark hues. It was streaked red, likely from brushing up against the acorns, I thought. I remember bringing it to my mother and the way her face turned pallid, almost as pale as the fabric, when she saw it. She grabbed it from my hand and hurried it off to the shed where, to my amazement, she dug a shallow hole and buried it hastily. I was too startled by her actions to ask any questions and had the feeling she was not about to answer them even if I had.

A year later I found a lone slipper. It was satin and embroidered with little pearl beads. Curiously, the beads were sewn in the shape of an acorn. It was the sort of thing I had seen the older girls wear at the Equinox the previous day, though I did not understand at the time. Again, I presented it to my mother, assuming a girl had lost her shoe in the forest and my mother would return it to her. But this she also buried in the shed. When I worked up the courage to ask her about it, she looked me up and down as if measuring me.

"It belongs to Greta," she said simply, her voice barely above a whisper, "and you shall not mention it to anyone."

I didn't mention it. Partially out of a sense of obligation to my mother which I did not wholly understand, but also because I never saw Greta again. Her desk was empty at assembly the next morning as was the corner of her family's bench, three rows ahead of us, in church the following Sunday. My mother noticed me noticing and I can recall the way she pressed her lips together and held my gaze. She reached out and grabbed my knee and I expected her to be cross, yet her touch was gentle. I did not understand it then, but I do now.

I shall add just one more memory of childhood to my tale. On a late spring day when my father left early for market, I took a book and made my way to the Watchtower, curling up in the curve of her many roots. I placed a beetle-black button, which I had found trampled between two floorboards in the meetinghouse, into one of her knots as a present. I smoothed my dress beneath me and felt an alarming jab, realizing I had carelessly pressed my palm onto one of the fallen acorns. I withdrew as if bitten and watched a crimson stream of blood flow down my wrist and pooled on the ground. Immediately, darkness began to blur the edges of my vision. I was not a squeamish child, living on a farm and no stranger to butch-ery or the sight of blood, but I felt a lightheadedness unlike anything I had experienced. Gooseflesh broke out across my arms and my scalp prickled. I watched crimson drops soak into the moss and disappear like they were being absorbed, like they were being *swallowed*.

The sensation dissipated as quickly as it began and I nestled down and opened my book. The air was thick and warm, fragrant with pollen and nectar, and the song of cicadas lulled me into dreaming. It seemed to me, though I felt foolish in thinking it, that the root was slowly wending its way around my body, cradling me. I heard a voice whispering to me of far-off places. I had strange dreams of castles made of thorns and blooming ruby-red flowers, pulsating as if they had a heartbeat.

When I woke, twilight surrounded me. I panicked, racing home, certain I would receive a beating from my father who would have returned from market while the sun was still in the sky. I was in such a hurry it only occurred to me later how the roots must have shifted in the darkness so that I wouldn't trip as I sprinted away.

That would be the last time I saw the tree for many months, for the following day my mother took ill and never recovered.

A handful of years went by uneventfully. My father had me give up school as he thought it a waste of time. It was just as well because the village children were even less kind after my mother's death. They called her names I will not repeat and told me I would also die young because of my *witchblood*.

I tried my best to assume my mother's work around the farm, but I was a poor replacement. My stitches were haphazard and the goats kicked when I milked them. The butter was always lumpy no matter how long I churned it and all of the flowers in the front garden wilted the first spring following her death. The only thing I had any aptitude for was making her salves and tonics which my father sold at market each full moon. I found it curious that the very people who called us witches were the first to snatch up bottles of our cures to soothe their sore muscles and weeping sores.

I spent less and less time beneath the Watchtower, but I felt the pull of her in my dreams and it was not uncommon for me to fall asleep humming lullabies to myself, songs my mother had brought from her homeland in a language I did not speak nor understand. In that liminal space between waking and dreaming I would hear another dark and lilting voice join the chorus. It was then the words would translate to me, tales of maidens sacrificed, thrown to the sea only to swim into the depths and return with mouths full of needles and revenge in their water-logged hearts.

It was the day after my thirteenth birthday and I was carrying a pail of milk into the kitchen when everything changed. I had been preoccupied with what I could do to allay my father's rage when he saw just how little milk there was. The goat had kicked the pail and most of it spilled onto the ground. I had been planning on making cheese, which was his favorite, but it would have to wait a few days. If I made one of my mother's specialties perhaps he wouldn't notice. I was trying to remember the recipe for my mother's stuffed squash when I felt the dull ache of something jabbing me in the gut and a warmth spreading down my thighs.

I froze.

Mother had cautioned me that someday this would happen, but thus far I had put it from my mind. I was not in the company of any other womenfolk and as such had nearly forgotten the inevitability of womanhood.

I did not know why it terrified me so. There was a latent fear of my father knowing, of *anyone* knowing. It felt like a dark secret, like items belonging to missing girls hidden in the shed.

Immediately, I stripped off my petticoat and stockings and threw them in the washtub to soak. I grabbed the scouring brush and rubbed the small blossoms of red from the stones and returned to the tub with the strongest bar of lye soap we owned. Frantically scrubbing, I did not notice when my father's shadow fell across the doorway.

I heard him holler close behind me. Father had seen the scarcity of the milk pail. I felt him bearing down on me and braced myself for the blow I knew was coming but then he stopped, arm suspended in mid-air. He was staring over my shoulder at the wash tub, the water now a muddy reddish hue, and at the stained petticoat in my hand. He was not an overly intuitive man, my father, but I could see he understood.

I tried to stutter, to apologize, but hadn't the vocabulary. He did not strike me, but it was not an act of mercy. Rather, he recoiled as if I had suddenly turned to some lowly disgusting thing like a weevil in his bread.

"Very well," he said under his breath, more to himself than to me, "I see what must be done."

"What do you mean?" I asked, my voice feeling small and foreign in my own ears.

My father sighed. For living alone as long as we had, few words passed between us and we had grown accustomed to spending evenings in silence.

"I know you are aware of…" He trailed off. I didn't know if it was the actual talking or the subject matter which pained him.

I turned to face him, my back pressed against the edge of the washtub.

"Certain customs dictate that girls…*womenfolk*…after their first blood, must add their names to the tithe, the *bloedgeld* at the Equinox."

"Well, that's good, isn't it?" I don't know why I said that, except I wanted it to be true. In my heart I knew it wasn't. It was always portrayed as a joyous event, but there was no denying the missing girls. Some of them, it was rumored, were given in marriage. But that could have been a lie.

"It is an honor, really," he stammered.

I remembered the gossamer scarf, the beaded shoe left at the base of the Watchtower. Gifts the tree had given me. Gifts the town had first bestowed upon the tree.

"You could get married," his voice cracked. "That is one way to abdicate. I could speak to the Elders."

My mind reviewed the village boys whom I hadn't seen in years. Their pale, cruel faces and the sound of their mocking laughter. I then heard a subtle whisper at the back of my mind, the voice which sang to me at night, the voice of the Watchtower.

Listen.

I knew I had no reason to fear her or the monster which lay at her heart. Better to make a swift sacrifice of my blood than submit to the slow, wearisome sacrifice of working my fingers to the bone in a backward village that valued crops above women.

Listen.

An idea began to form, unbidden, in my mind. It formed like the dreams beneath the Watchtower, both slow and bright, like moonlight sliding between clouds.

My father could not read my face and turned away. He left without explanation, saddling his mare and riding toward town.

I don't know what possessed me then, but I took my garments, wrung them as best I could with my bare hands, then threw them in a basket and made for the woods. I stumbled toward the Watchtower, comforted by her familiar silhouette, the knots and grooves of her trunk like the moles and wrinkles on the face of a wise grandmother. I hung my clothes in her branches, both the wet ones in my basket and the dress I wore over them. I lay naked on the moss, curled up like a younger child than I was, and watched the remaining blood slowly disappear from my garments. At first the stains moved slowly across the fabric, like diluted ink, toward the branches from which they hung. The rusty stains collected against the bark then faded, leaving behind perfectly cleansed petticoats. I saw this transpire as if in a trance.

I curled my limbs around the roots of the tree and pressed my feverish forehead against the soft, cool moss. I lay there until the shadows lengthened and crickets began to chirp. All the while I cried and I bled beneath her branches. I gave her my sorrows and my fears and I listened to her subtle voice as it soothed me. Yes, there was a monster there, but she was now my kin and my only companion. And after I told her my deepest thoughts, she began to tell me hers.

Listen.

She wove for me stories of ancient powers, of a giantess who slumbered in the ground, her veins turning to red, red roots. I heard tales of revenge and sacrifice, of small-minded men and desolate towns and the passing of time.

I listened.

When I arose, I knew what I would do.

The boy my father chose was not the worst I had met. I hoped he would prove more of a dullard than of malicious temperament. I realized my hopes were in vain when he whispered close to my ear, "I will abide you having your mother's witch hair, but if you become willful I shall cut it all off whilst you sleep."

I sweet talked him, batted my lashes, and let him slide his arm around my waist, feeling the blood boil in my veins with each beat of my heart. I led him into the wood under a crescent moon and lay down with him beneath the Watchtower.

"I think you were right in calling me *witch*," I murmured as our limbs entwined. The ecstasy I felt was not of his doing.

Blood spilled beneath the tree that night, but it was not mine.

I had no explanation of where my betrothed had gone. I told the Elders in all honesty that he suspected me of witchcraft and perhaps that caused him to change his mind and flee rather than own his dishonor. My father said nothing but his eyes held both sadness and suspicion as we rode back from town with not a word passing between us.

That night I dreamed crimson dreams.

The Equinox approached and those festivities which had seemed so cheerful to me as a child now took on a sinister cast. The red banners around the town square, the hand-me-down gowns and beaded slippers which had been worn by countless girls and were too big for my feet.

I stared down at the slippers, wiggling my toes and watching the embroidered acorns twitch as if worm-infested, while the Elders gave dry, pontificating speeches about harvest and gifts to the earth, thinking of that long ago day when my mother buried a shoe in the shed.

The circle of faces around me stirred unpleasant memories of vicious teasing, but impending doom was a great equalizer and no one smirked at each other now. School days were behind us. We were all scared in our way, all reduced to the value of what our untainted femininity could buy for our village.

The most primary Elder, a man so ancient he looked like an animated corpse, presented a leather pouch tied with red ribbon. His age did not hinder a lascivious look as he pulled the edges open with his long fingers and presented it to the first girl.

I could see her hand trembling as it disappeared within the pouch and fumbled about. She winced in pain and then her face relaxed as she pulled out a smooth, simple oak acorn.

The ritual was repeated by the next girl and the next until at last it was presented to me. It occurred to me then that this game was rigged. I already knew what my hand would find inside the bag. Of course they avoided the horned acorn and withdrew the others one by one. It was not a random draw. There was only one left.

I didn't flinch as I wrapped my hand around the acorn. I withdrew my clenched fist and heard the collective gasp as those clustered closest saw blood running down my arm. Whether they were gasping at the blood, my brazenness, or in relief that I had been chosen over their beloved sisters and daughters, the matter was nothing to me. It had been decided.

In this way, I grabbed my own fate. Yet I also held theirs, though they did not know it.

Listen.

This is how the story ends, or at least how mine does.

I was brought to the tree, I was bound to its trunk. The Elders circled around me, dark and forbidding, though I knew some of them were afraid.

Much that followed is a blur to me. I remember the bark pressing against my back but it was not sinister, it was like the flesh of a friend. I clung to the tree like a child clinging to her mother's skirts. I dug my fingers into the scabby lichens around her base as I felt the earth tremble beneath my feet and saw the surprise in the Elder's faces. I remember it was dark and their widened eyes shone pearl-like in the shadows.

I heard roots shift and limbs crash in the tempest of her rage. I heard both prayers and curses from the lips of the Elders, but mostly I heard screams.

The world went soft and black for me as I drowned in her thirst. I thought of the sacrificial maidens who ventured to the bottom of the sea and were reborn. I wondered if I would return, what I would become.

Listen.

I don't know if it was only the Elders who slaked the thirst of the great tree that night, or if she took the entire village. I saw images of great limbs twisting between stones, between bones, but that is someone else's story to tell. What I do know, beyond the shadow of a doubt, is that her red roots run deep.

A Matter of Grace

By Zachary Rosenberg

Our village burns as the monsters drive us into the sea.

These beasts dress in iron, clutching steel. Twilight fires reflect upon their metal coats, their laughter ringing out through the dying day. My sister holds to me, a prayer in Hebrew tumbling from her lips. Though she implores and beseeches the heavens for help, no aid is forthcoming. We are forsaken.

We are the women of Khen, a Hebrew word that means "Grace." Our only crime is our heritage and faith. For it, we are pushed to the seas. The marauders from the west lift their crosses, speaking of crusades and holy justification. Lush and fertile fields are burned and upturned, livestock and kin lifeless in the homes we once called our own. My brother Yakov is among the dead, his kind smile forever stilled and his flesh chewed apart by steel teeth.

We have been pushed toward the sea to drown. Any other women, men, or children have been left in the midst of the ruined village. Doubtless, the invaders mean to make sport of them: a way to amuse themselves on their Crusade.

"Rivka," my sister, Chava, whispers. She pulls me with her, a sorrowful tug as the cold waters lap at our feet. We stand at the base of the rocks. To descend further is to give ourselves to the ocean's cold and drowning depths. To return to Khen is to face the fire and the blades, a quicker and certain death.

Praying for forgiveness for my cowardice, I resign myself with the other women of Khen to the sands below. The cliffs are high and steep behind us, impossible to climb. This small plateau will soon be consumed by the rising tide. The heat from the flames behind us cannot scorch away the onrushing winter chill.

"We will not last the night," Chava whimpers with all the grief of a woman who has seen her life burn to ash.

"We cannot yield." Naomi is a young woman my age. So alike to me, yet she still has hope. The Crusaders want our despair, but our lives will suffice if they cannot have that. If not at the point of their blades, perhaps the freezing waters will do the job.

The sun abdicates its rule, the moon assuming the throne. The chill is sharp and biting as the blades that slew our brother. I picture Yakov's smile in my mind, the warm and caring hand he would offer to any in need. He even extended it to the invaders, only to see it lopped from his wrist.

I force the mourner's Kaddish through chattering teeth, clutching my garments to me. Chava huddles closer to me for warmth, the elder sister meant to keep her safe. I look at the dark seas, the tides burying shards of ice within my feet. I look at the waves, expecting only smooth and glassy waters.

Instead, a rainbow burns within the depths. A shimmering light illuminates the sea, vermilion and sapphire streaks shifting just below the surface as though something glides there. I stare, wondering if sanity has abandoned me, opening my mouth. I prepare the Shma, the prayer for my own approaching death.

"Do you see it?" Naomi's voice bears wonder. The murmurs from several dozen throats echo the emotion; there is no room for terror. Not for those who have already faced the worst of nightmares. All for our faith and heritage, all for being who we are.

The light burns brighter, moving to the east. It waits there, the colors dimming. On some mad instinct, I take a step to follow it, trying to keep it in my sight. Our legends tell of creatures within the seas, beasts such as Leviathan and Behemoth. Whales that can swallow a man whole. Living near the sea, I have never seen such a creature until now. Death by cold or drowning, death by the teeth of what lurks in the cold depths. It matters not to me. I hear Chava moan softly, the women talking among themselves about what it can be, must be.

Monster is the word they use. Demon. Sheydim. Lurking in the eternal sea from which there can be no escape. I hug my sister to me, pushing her head to my shoulder so she doesn't see.

The water comes forward slowly. I turn away, to the smooth rocks behind me. What I see there is not stone, but a cavernous maw of darkness above a small ledge. A cave just behind me that was not there just minutes before.

"There!" I shout and point. The rest see and I do not need to elaborate. The mad rush begins, acceptance of death fading the moment a chance for life opens. The strangeness of the circumstance is not considered and I abandon hesitation. Perhaps it is a blessing from the almighty, a passage to lead to higher ground and escape the rising tide. All I know is it is a chance. Jewish history is full of miracles.

Guiding Chava with me, we go, pushing one by one into the cave before us, hoisting up on the ledge. I am the last, looking out over the sea and the strange glow therein.

It dims, fading, as though the cause of that radiance is sinking into the depths. I turn from the sea and follow the others into the cave. The descent is quick, the passage narrow. We walk ahead, uncertainty our companion.

"I've never seen this, Rivka." Chava reaches a hand to the cave wall and my hand follows her own. The walls are warm, pulsing to the distant rumble of the waves outside. They move, like the drumming of my heart in my breast.

"It feels like it's alive," Naomi says, fear in her eyes. Hope has been dangled before us like a twitching fish on a barbed hook. Now I wonder if we should have remained to face the tide and the glow within the water.

The cave floor slopes down and with no recourse, we proceed. One by one, until I stand in a cavern. Wide and vast about us, a towering ceiling studded through with pointed rocks and blue light casts a plaid shadow upon my sister's face. The floor is pockmarked with jagged holes, pools of gleaming seawater heavy with the scent of salt.

My foot touches something hard, the floor of this cavern a ghostly white. I whisper a prayer in Hebrew for strength and courage. The cave shivers, as though in response. I look about us, taking it in.

The passage through which we emerge gapes in the shape of a mouth, the narrow way leading to me built like a neck. All around us are formations of bone white, jutting about in bizarre shapes and patterns. The walls pulse, bone white with dark ridges between them. They move, seemingly breathing.

Naomi stands tall and proud, even as other women quail, saying their prayers. Light illuminates this hidden place. The entrance is a pale skull, a face set in the bizarre facade of humanity. Upon the roof of the cave, the ridges are not rocks at all, but the grooves of a spine. Curling down over what can only be ribs, we are ensconced within the embrace of bent wings.

This is no cave.

It's a corpse.

The remains of something vast and chthonic. I stand within something buried and forgotten. It is naught but bones and scraps of flesh, the pools like ragged wounds in its ancient hide, the seawater like congealed blood. And yet this thing moves, and breathes.

And from a pool of water something emerges.

The body is winding, serpentine and draconic all in one. The shimmering scales reflect all colors of human perception and some I have no name for. Upon each scale is an eye, lidless and burning with lights sapphire, turquoise, emerald, and all the sea's colors. Arms extend from its body, a multitude of wings made of pale coral sprouting from a back dripping seaweed. The face is beautiful and terrible all at once. A combination of shark, squid, human, and more, the coalescence of all life of the sea.

I feel its presence squirming through my mind, see it before me. Of the women of Grace, I am the first to step forward. I put myself before Chava for what good it will do. I stand before the creature of the sea, defiance in my soul. It will not have me without a fight. My brother died helpless. I will not fall to a thing of the sea and hunger without marking my defiance before heaven. I am a Jew of Khen. This beast may have my future, but it will not have my fear.

I meet the eyes of the creature before me, witness its face of hideous and terrible beauty. And then it sings like an orchestra of whale song. It roars, sings, proclaims, thunders all at once.

"Be not afraid."

I feel it within my very soul. I have seen its like before, in dim memories of when my world was swaddling blankets and one of its like whispered into my ear before pressing a finger to my lips to lull me to silence. This is no Sheydim, no demon.

I gaze upon an angel.

A creature as old as the universe, messenger of Hashem. The holiest of creatures, responsible for the devastation of entire civilizations. The angel remains in the waters, placid as it gazes upon me. Its multitudes of eyes fill with what must be compassion.

"My name is Rivka. Have you a name?" My voice comes from my throat, hoarse and choked with tears.

It answers: "Rahab."

I know this name. It is a moniker that means "Pride." Tales speak of this angel, smote down and confined to the seas, a creature lurking in the vast oceans of the world. Bound to the waters and waves.

"Help us." I think of those still above and reach out to take its clawed hand. My fingers slip through it, soaked in saltwater. Rahab gestures to the water.

"All around you is my broken body. Before you is merely the image of a soul, confined to the seas. Insubstantial."

Chava speaks behind me, her voice trembling. "Rivka, it cannot leave the water." She comes to my side at the edge of the saltwater pool, staring at a winged and watery ghost. The angel is powerless to assist. Its true body around us, shattered and crippled.

"You summoned us to you. You must have a way. Our people are captive above. The murderers have them." Murderers. To use that word makes them human, something that can be worse than a monster. I beseech the angel not as a supplicant, but as a sister, a friend, a daughter. "Help."

Rahab gestures about itself, coral wings spreading out. I take in the chamber, realizing that we indeed stare at a ghost, a reflection. About us, encasing us, is not merely the angel's lair. This twisted, broken structure of living bone and flesh is the angel itself.

"You endure," Chava murmurs with a childish wonder. She stares at the angel before us with concern, compassion. The expression in those multitudes of eyes is a boundless love and warmth.

"There is my way. But it must be your choice." Rahab sings. "My grace is around you."

The unspoken meaning is clear: take it. We stand in the bowels of a fallen angel. These walls are not stone, but ancient flesh. I hear Rahab whisper in my mind. If the Crusaders are to die, if our people are to be saved, it must be by us.

I walk from the pool, hearing the angel's instructions like a rapturous song. An ember of hope kindles into an inferno as I listen. Rahab fell from the heavens to be bound in the sea forever, not as a being of evil. But of grace, of protection. It has seen the atrocities carried out on the Chosen, the Hebrews. It mourns for us. Monster it may be, but it promises Hashem's blessing all the same.

I probe the warm walls, feeling the great body. The cavern surface is smooth, moist with a bright fluid that stains my fingers. I take the first step. I, Rivka, no other, am first. My lips press against the walls. I consider my humanity, think of what I might lose. I think of Yakov's sweet smile, his laughter and kindness. His love of his people, those still living.

Those I may yet save.

I bite so hard that my teeth would shatter were these walls truly stone. The angel's body shudders from what might be pain, but Rahab bids me to continue.

Angel blood fills my mouth. It is like drinking mist: insubstantial, yet a sweetness beyond words. I drink more. Naomi is beside me with Chava and all the others. We find our places, breaking the most sacred of laws by taking blood within us.

Pikuach nefesh, to break the law to save lives. Preserving life is a mitzvah, a commandment from heaven. I drink more, feeling Rahab's grace fill my veins. When I can take no more, I push away with a hand that is smooth and light gray, webbed and clawed.

My talons are sharper than those of a hunting bird, pulsing with a light like Rahab's own: an anglerfish lure of the depths.

"Rivka!" Chava's voice, but as I turn to see her, I behold something new. Chava's teeth are needled, her eyes a lush coral-pink. Her hair flows about her shoulders like kelp, her body lithe and muscled, filled with spines like urchins we'd find on the beaches. I feel my face smooth and the cheekbones higher than before. All around me, the women of Khen resemble my sister now. Tall, corded with muscle and glowing with unnatural light. Pulling our clothing away, we emit Rahab's blessing.

We are monsters.

We are beautiful.

I rejoice in the flow of blood from my heart. I flex webbed fingers with claws that can gouge through stone with their sharpness. We look at one another, we women of Khen. Chava is the first to face the angel. Rahab has not liberated us, nor slain our oppressors for us. This broken angel, consigned to the waters of the earth, has granted us the most powerful gift that we might liberate ourselves.

"Thank you," my sister says, salty tears beading in her eyes. Rahab's spirit gestures only to the sea, our portal from the angel's body into the world. A chance to return home, take back what is ours.

I feel myself, flesh smooth as a scaleless serpent. I envision our oppressors in their suits of iron and my breath quickens. I picture my brother, knowing that this calls for vengeance. Justice. A returning, their lives as the price. Teshuvah.

We, the women of Khen who had the strength to change for what we love. There are no dissenters. The oppressed, the victims, do not need to be pushed into fighting back. All we need are the means.

I step into the water, leading my sister, my cousins, my neighbors, my fellow Jews. Instinct takes over. The frigid water no longer bites me. Rather it is gentle and nourishing. I sink low, submerging myself into the inky depths of the night.

The salt doesn't sting my eyes. Slits in my throat drink in the water so I may breathe it as easily as air. My webbed hands cleave through the liquid, propelling me. My body is a light, a beacon as we depart from the angel into the seas.

The ocean is *ours* now. We swim, more tightly organized than any military unit. They follow my lead into the ocean. We, who walked through the throat of an angel and drank of its blood within its very innards. We, the transformed, those gifted with grace.

The sea is mine now. The land still belongs to the beasts. My brother's bloody, sword-gnawed carcass in my mind drives me on, I swim for land, for the base of the cliff. The cavern is gone, that mouth sealed shut with Rahab's purpose fulfilled.

The sounds of revelry and laughter touch the water and my ears, offensive in their exultation in our destruction. They speak in foreign tongues, but their mockery is clear. We must be drowned or frozen by now, they doubtlessly think. Our siblings, husbands, children, parents mourn our fates as they await their own.

From the sea I come, making the land my domain. Stealthily do I creep through the night, my wrath building, kindling with each and every step. Torches burn bright and in the light I see them. Their iron helms are discarded, skins of wine in their hands. Victory has made them careless.

They are not monsters after all. Merely men. With legs of powerful muscle, I bring myself forward, into a run. My fellow women, my changed kin, follow me. We rush headlong into their camp to make it our village again. The soil becomes ours again the moment we set foot upon it.

They see us with the same human eyes of fear that too many of our people showed before the end. They shout, some trying to climb to their feet. Drunkenness makes them slow. I stop before a man of middle years. He is small before me now. So weak. He tries to lift a sword that looks more like a metallic twig before me.

I take it from his hand. Then I remove his throat from his body. My companions are sweet women, kind and gentle. So many have never thought of hurting another living soul. But for vengeance, for the survival of our own, we take life with a bloodlust and vengeance that I know has nothing to do with what Rahab has bestowed upon us. This is our wrath, the rage of the oppressed.

If we are monsters, it is only what they have made of us. We kill until our invaders are gone. The slaughter at an end, we look at one another, creatures of the sea drenched in blood. Our people look at us, seeing us as we are.

They do not look at us with fear. They behold us and see saviors. "Rivka," Chava says. "We're safe now." My sweet, gentle sister smiles with teeth drenched in blood. Perilously close to breaking our law all over again, but pikuach nefesh prevails. Naomi laughs, her eyes burning gleefully. I see in her expression she knows Chava's naivety. If we are safe now, it is only *for* now.

This was indeed a miracle. And far sweeter that it was one we made ourselves.

I should feel more trepidation about what I have become. Humanity is a forsaken horizon behind me. I cannot turn back on that path. But looking at the lives we have saved, embracing our friends, neighbors, families, there is no room in my heart for regrets. We will navigate the unknown together as women, protectors, Jews.

We are strong. We will rebuild. We will defend our own. We tell our people we will protect them as Rahab watches from the great sea, watching us put its divine blessing to use. Let more monsters come. They will find us waiting.

This is our home. It is our lair. Our Khen.

Our Grace.

Withering

By Lucy Zhang

The Sky Angels await their signal to return to the heavens, the moment they'll be welcomed back as though they'd never descended to Earth in the first place. They think they're better than us Dirt people even though we both travel the same lands by foot, one step at a time, whether in bamboo sandals or sheepskin shoes.

Abandoned is abandoned and at some point you've got to move on, which is what I tell Hao when Hao tries to guilt me into spending the night with him, claiming he'll be spirited away into the sky the next day, floating above the clouds, escaping the ground like helium. His tactic works for the most part. I live more with Hao than I do at home, more so because Sky Angels have better access to markets and healthy livestock, although I'd also feel sad if Hao suddenly vanished. I don't think he wants to return to the sky anyway, not that he'll admit anything to me.

I go home once a week to deliver baskets of silk which my parents sew into cheongsams and scarves that can sell for up to a month's living expenses. Sometimes I'll bring them dragon fruits too, a fruit particularly hard to acquire in any Dirt people stores and believed to bring prosperity and nobility. Hao provides me with silk to take home since I can't roam in Sky Angels stores alone. Technically I'm not even supposed to take the fabrics, but we're careful about when I come and go. I dress in white scarves covering my hair and neck, as though the sky gods themselves had shed their feathers to cover every sliver of my visible skin.

I leave Hao's place at night when the Sky Angels sleep, the outdoors quiet except for the sporadic owl hoot and the flickering of lights lasting until sunrise. The Sky Angels are terrified of the dark, so even while they sleep, they illuminate their streets and scare off the coyotes, drawing a path through the night that even their dreams can follow. They claim the night is when the gods are most vengeful, enough to block out the sun. Hao hates when I leave at night, so much so that he must down a bowl full of sour dates and Valerian root to stay asleep while I slip out into the cold.

My parents tried to persuade me not to venture into Sky Angels territory, but when we ran low on money or food they eventually stopped lecturing me and instead waited for my return with tense faces. They'd usher me in and I'd hand them the new offerings while they tried to stuff me full of pork and sour cabbage stew and hawthorn berries. I tell them to save it for themselves. They seem to forget that I eat better with Hao.

I return to Hao the next day. Most of the time, he looks only slightly more haggard than the previous night, but lately, he can hardly sit up until I return to help him out of bed, after which he seems to regain his energy within minutes. The Sky Angels call it the Withering, a disease pervasive and unpredictable and capable of ravaging a Sky person until their flesh shrivels into their bones and their eyeballs tumble out of their sockets as jewels.

"You can sell them for a fortune," Hao tells me of his eyeballs.

The gods built Sky Angels from precious gemstones, glued and melted together until the metals ran smooth as skin, warmed by a pulse. Their blood runs hotter than ours, composed of liquid ruby.

"I'm not an organ trafficker," I reply. "Plus you're not Withering. You look fine."

It's true. Hao reverts to his normal, healthy form after I hold his hand and support him with my shoulders so he can climb off the bed. Now he stands upright, taller and stronger than me, capable of carving stone and imbuing Essence in his handicrafts—mostly weapons or protective amulets that other Sky Angels without sufficient Essence like to wear for a sense of security. They think the amulets might stave off Withering, and Hao doesn't bother to correct anyone.

When we sleep together, Hao whispers his affections in his native tongue, a combination of gentle hisses and humming and slurred whistles. I think he forgets I can't understand because he will sometimes whisper for hours and I'll nod in response until I fall asleep. Sometimes he'll rub my calves with his toes or stroke my rib cage like he's counting on an abacus or rub the flesh over my knees like he can peel it away like boiled tomato skins that gather and fall from their fruit.

What Hao feels for me is not love though. Sky Angels possess no love for Dirt people. I learned this when I was a child and my parents warned me that the Sky Angels would wipe us out if it meant returning to the heavens. "Desperate, beautiful, dangerous creatures," they'd said.

My parents are at the age where Dirt people must relocate to the lakeside, closer to the pure spring water that might ease and prolong their remaining years before entering the earth. I tell Hao I must leave for at most a week to help my parents move. Unlike Sky Angels, Dirt people's strength deteriorates rapidly with age so I will need to carry their belongings and help them settle into a cabin by the forest edge before winter's arrival. The lakeside is much warmer than here, where I worry the cold might seep into my parents' brittle bones because they're too stubborn to wear more than two layers.

Hao throws one of his hand-crafted candle holders to the ground. It's imbued with Essence so it doesn't crack and instead clanks against the floor like thunder has struck the board. "In no agreement was that allowed," he says after a moment, staring at the toppled candle.

"It won't be more than a week," I repeat.

"People have Withered in well under a week," Hao says.

"Sky Angels, not Dirt people," I correct.

"If you want me dead, you could just say so."

Even if Sky Angels Wither, they're more gemstone than flesh. A mausoleum stands at the edge of the Sky Angels' town. It contains the remains of those who Withered, a pile of glittering amethyst and bloodstone and cinnabar and other stones I haven't identified, gathered in a basin at the center of the structure, positioned below the ceiling window that opens to the heavens so the Withered, too, may return to the sky once welcomed back. I don't consider that death.

Hao gives me the silent treatment for the rest of the day, even during the evening when he appears a bit gaunt, on the cusp of his skin losing its hold over his frame, and he needs me to hold his quaking hands steady else he'll carve off a finger rather than the misaligned edge of a jewelry box, but he's too stubborn to admit it. Hao stumbles while reaching for his chip carving knife, and I reach out to stabilize him, hands ready to grasp onto his elbows. He spins away from me, crashing onto the ground, knives clattering to the floor in a long, wrung-out cacophony, as though Hao couldn't be the only one going down and had to take his blades with him. I turn my back to him as he stands, a painfully slow process as I listen to each stumble and jingle of chisels and carving knives, afraid he might accidentally stab himself.

Most believe Withering occurs because Sky Angels have been away from the heavens for too long, their Essence weakened because the land they now occupy must be shared by Dirt people who consume life Essence from the plants and river and wildlife, hardly leaving enough for Sky Angels to thrive. Hao theorizes otherwise, although he's not so stupid to broadcast his thoughts to the rest of his people.

The Sky Angels live secluded from Dirt people, and most of us know not to approach them else risk getting caught and sacrificed on their altar. I'd heard rumors of Dirt kids who'd gone missing in Sky Angels territory, how the Sky Angels would send back sliced toes, the only body parts that remained after a ritual. The Sky Angels find toes repulsive—"critter-like appendages" that remind them of worms squirming below the earth's surface, feeding on feces.

Hao believes Dirt people possess a unique Essence enabling them to survive on land without losing structural integrity, but no other Sky person will admit a personal deficiency.

"That's their fault," Hao would shrug.

"Just because we don't dissolve into a pile of sparkling eyeballs doesn't mean we don't lose structural integrity," I argued. Dirt people grew old, time wearing down their joints, fogging their minds, and curling their spines into brittle pieces like fallen, desiccated leaves.

"That's a Dirt people problem," was Hao's rationale.

Afraid of triggering Hao's silent treatment once again, I leave without telling him. Before heading home, I hold his hand for several minutes while he sleeps, certain this amount of Dirt people Essence can stave off any Withering for at least a week. I don't even need to touch him, but Hao insists the results are better. We've come a long way since he used to flinch when our fingers grazed each other, convinced I'd contaminate his soul with Dirt.

Hao first found me while I was hiding on the outskirts of the Sky Angels' town, trying to avoid my parents' fury after I'd left the jar of rock sugar open and ants had gotten to it. A group of Sky Angels had been exiting through the gates on a scouting mission to uncover more paths to the sky, and I was crouched dangerously close to the main path. They needed only to round the corner to snatch me up and butcher me for the heavens. Hao found me first. He'd been on his way back from mining nephrite deposits, a task few Sky Angels were willing to do which only increased the value of his crafts, and I'd been shocked into stillness even as he approached from the other direction, my crouched form in plain sight.

"Are you trying to get yourself killed?" he'd asked.

I shook my head.

Hao had me sit in the basket he carried on his back, and at the time, I had been just small enough to fit if I held my knees close to my chest and ducked my head. He grimaced whenever he grazed my skin, placed a jacket over the top of the basket, and smuggled me through the gates, into his home. I spent the first few hours wondering if he'd burn me in his cavernous fireplace as a sacrifice for the gods. Instead, he ignored me, tending to his collection of colorful stones and slabs of stone.

When I asked if he looked forward to returning to the sky, Hao shrugged and glanced upward as though the clouds were an afterthought, and said, "There isn't much for me there, certainly no stones that can resist falling through clouds to the ground. It's much better here where we can dig up what we want."

In turn, I told Hao of Dirt people: my parents who threatened to whack my knuckles with spry tree branches if I spilled another jar of sugar, my daily routine of preparing the hot water for bathing and drinking and then leaving for school where we were learning to read tales of the ancient Tiger and Bear gods who'd snatched a low-flying Eagle god straight from the sky. Even then, I'd considered my routine rather boring but Hao never looked away when I spoke. Anything about the lives of Dirt people always held his attention captive.

Hao smuggled me in and out of the Sky Angels' territory while I was young, but as I grew older, unable to cram my body in the basket, I began to wear scarves to cover my dark hair and eyes, navigating by the shadows and light I could see from behind the fabric. We discovered that Hao recovered from Withering when I spent time with him, like a flower starved of sunlight and water. He grew more comfortable touching me after that.

The other Sky Angels ignore Hao's presence even though they buy his crafts discreetly. Hao is the only one they haven't seen suffer symptoms of Withering, still as beautiful and strong as he'd appeared years ago when he first carried me through the gates in the basket. We're not sure what it is specifically about Dirt people that staves off the Withering, but Hao claims the reason doesn't matter as long as I'm around.

I write Hao a note promising I'll be back next week, place it on his work desk, and weigh a corner of the paper down with one of his unpolished gems. Even if he misses the note, he'd never neglect the materials he nurtures like children, from unrefined lumps to impeccable masterpieces.

• • •

We move slowly since Mother's legs tremble with every step as the weight of her pack sways on her back. My father and I carry the bulk of the items, but Mother insists she can carry her clothing bundled tightly in a bag. The trek to the lakeside requires climbing over several boulders and rocks that resemble a castle fortress. Mother heaves, her stamina dwindling as we scramble.

"Just imagine," I say. "Over these rocks are delicacies you could never dream of. Things that only grow and live in the purest of waters." Mother was the one who told me the story of Buddha jumping over a wall to eat her famous fish maw and sea cucumber soup stewed in a clay jar. She spent days preparing the soup, soaking and boiling and soaking and boiling and simmering. If food can motivate a vegetarian monk to jump a wall, even my mother who's built from chicken feet collagen and fatty pig trotters can make it over.

"I just need some time," she pants.

She pauses between steps and I climb back to hold her steady. We continue like this for three hours until we make it through the forest of rocks.

We walk a bit further, searching for the cabins and lake maintained by the existing Dirt people. As Mother regains her energy and spirit, she lists all the things she wishes to do with such pure water, how it might reverse the wrinkles on her face, how the foods she cooks with it will taste sweeter, fresher like spring.

"You should stay with us, don't go back to the Sky Angels. They'll catch you one day," Father says as Mother walks on ahead. I remain silent.

Instead of a lake, we arrive at a flat bed of clay, encrusted with salts in clusters of white and brown and specks of sparkling gems scattered within the mud cracks. They remind me of the rows of gems Hao keeps on his shelves in neat lines, each gem jagged and uniquely formed, a collection he'd mined and refused to alter or sell. When I was twelve, I once attempted to sand one down—a particularly jagged black sapphire, thinking I'd surprise Hao with my utility, but he took one look and wrenched the stone out of my hand, the movement so sudden I stumbled and fell into a pile of dust. After inspecting the sapphire under light, wiping it clean, and positioning it on the shelf equidistant from the adjacent gems, he helped me wipe dust from my body and inspected me for bruises.

Small log cabins surround the empty basin in rows. We go door to door to find someone, but each door leads to silence. Dad opens one of the cabin doors after waiting several minutes and announcing his entrance, and we carefully place our shoes on the doormat and enter. Bamboo baskets full of winter melons hang from the walls. Jars stand stacked on the ground, and we open one to the pungent scent of fermenting fish. Several pans lay scattered on the wood stove, rusted and burnt on the exteriors. On the kitchen table, a mug sits toppled on its side, but whatever might've leaked has already dried, leaving shallow streaks on the table's boards. No one has lived here for a while. It has always been sparsely populated since those who moved often didn't stay long before passing.

"Much larger than our old home," Mother exclaims, breaking the silence. "I can fit both rice and soup on this stove, and still have room to boil water for tea."

No one mentions the emptied lake. The sink in the cabin still works so at worst, they'll be drinking the same water they had been prior to the move. It's too dangerous to venture back. I'm not sure Mother's legs would make it, especially since lately we've been waking up to frost-coated grass protruding from the dirt like tiny blades.

I stay for two weeks to ensure the water, fireplace, and stove work properly. Mother's excitement over cooking hasn't died down, and she experiments with more slow-cooked dishes, claiming she's got all the time and space in the world to let a few bits of tendon soften. Whenever she's not napping, she's in the kitchen which means the rest of us must clear out so she can focus. I spend this time trying to find evidence of where the lake water disappeared to. The depression in the earth is entirely dry, not a single sign of dampness where water might've been, the cracks so deep and long I imagine falling through if only they were wider. There's no evident water source to the lake—no river feeding into it, no convenient groundwater seepage, no trickles of streams.

"We're already here, and your mother is happy. We don't need special lake water," my father says after I come home another evening without answers, only grime under my fingers and blisters on my toes.

"But it doesn't hurt," I reply. Several days of searching means nothing compared to several years tacked onto their lives.

A day before I plan to check on Hao, I notice one of the cracks extends from the depression outward, up the sloped sides, and into the denser parts of the forest. I follow the crack, prying away branches and bushes as I attempt to keep a clear sight. Thistles nick my legs, sticking themselves into my pants and puncturing the fabric as I move. The crack widens the further I follow, and eventually, I hear water trickling.

In the clearing is a massive contraption that suctions water away from the direction of the lake, into an opaque tank feeding into pipes leading toward the Sky Angels' territory. I know they drink better and eat better than us, but I hadn't realized they'd encroached onto the land of Dirt people.

I circle the dam-like device, and at the opposite side, a steady but small stream of water enters the tank, where the flow stops completely. I place my hands on the tank exterior, like ice against my bare hands, attempting to dislocate it. I lean on my right leg, my left pushing from behind, heaving my entire body weight into the wedged tank, smearing dirt onto my shoes and ankles, and just slightly, I budge it off course—enough for a tiny path of the stream to pass, unblocked. I leave for Hao's afterward. It'll take a while until that basin fills. The initial droplets would all be absorbed on the journey there. I hope the lake will replenish in time.

•••

I sneak in through the Sky territory gates. The gates are rarely guarded since no sane Dirt person would venture in knowing they'd be dismembered and sacrificed. I enter Hao's home without knocking. He wouldn't open the door even if I knocked. "Only strangers knock on doors, and I wouldn't let any stranger in any way," he'd told me several years ago when he found me by the door, waiting hours in the cold for him to let me in. I'd fallen sick after that and ended up staying for a month, every sneeze or cough prolonging my illness even though I told Hao the coughs were due to the orchids he'd recently potted.

"I'm back," I announce quietly, shutting the door. I wipe my feet on the doormat and place my shoes on the stand. Despite an inability to clean up after himself, Hao insists on no shoes in his home. I head toward his bedroom, hands clammy despite the cold.

I can barely make out his figure within the bed, his frame blended in with the creases in the covers. I peel back the duvet. Hao's figure has Withered so much his ribs look like the cages Sky Angels use for birds they keep for prayer, as symbols of the heavens. They wrap the cages tightly with silk, guarding the birds against others' eyes until proper prayers begin.

I grasp Hao's hand, waiting for the color to return.

"I found the lake, but it was all dried up," I tell him. "So I'm not sure if my parents will be able to use it. I doubt they'll be here by next winter."

"The water is supposed to taste like honeysuckle and extend your lifespan by a decade," I continue. I don't mention the tank funneling water into the Sky Angels' town.

Hao's hand remains limp in my grip, and he blinks slowly, each blink more labored than the previous, as though his eyelids can no longer cover his bulging eyeballs, now glimmering like diamonds under the slice of sunlight that has just begun to slip through the curtain.

Offerings to an Old God
By L. P. Hernandez

A child every December. A *male* child for the cruelest month, the longest night when only the conifers appear to be living and even the howls of wolves carry the cadence of a eulogy song. The streams clogged with ice, the sun sparkling for but a moment between the harsh teeth of the mountains straddling the village, a buffer between its secrets and a world that would not understand. It is a bitter time in a harsh land. Each winter solstice, the male babies birthed that year are placed on the doorstep. One will be taken.

"It's *our* way," Papa said, with more than a small measure of pride.

The Briar is a difficult land wedged between a sea that seldom yields its treasure no matter how many hooks and nets are cast into it, and mountains that strain the neck to behold. But the short growing season is bountiful, the game plentiful. And when I was not up to my knees in muck wrangling a hog into its pen, I found it quite beautiful.

Outsiders seldom come to the village, but they do. Desperate men, always. With the rumors of unclaimed women clouding their thoughts.

They ride over perilous roads to reach us and emerge with thorn-lashed cheeks and eyes as wide and hungry as a winter-starved wolf. They are not welcomed with warmth but scrutinized by the steely gazes of unsmiling women beating the dirt out of rugs on a line.

The traveler would notice some men take many wives, and the women are attractive by any standard. Maybe it is the hostility in their eyes. Maybe it is the strange mixture of sea air and tree sap. Or something else tugging at a seldom-accessed survival instinct.

What he might forget, retracing his steps with haste, racing the long shadows of the mountain stretching away from the setting sun, is the desperation quivering behind their eyes. So weighted by sorrow they could not imagine another life for themselves. Maybe in the loose, soil-dark locks of these hopeful bachelors they are reminded of a babe trapped in time, forever crying with December air burning in his lungs.

I was nine when my brother, Einar was born. An October baby, he was such a small thing I feared he would not survive the night, whether or not he was taken. The clouds had threatened snow since November and unleashed it the day before the solstice. Mama lay on the floor inside the front door, separated from him by inches that might as well have been miles. She breathed through the small gap beneath the door as if its heat could warm him against the cold.

Einar cried for a few minutes. Then the world went silent. Papa did not even light a fire on the longest, coldest night of the year. Mama wouldn't permit it. The sound of wood popping and sap sizzling might mask the whisper of Einar's blankets shifting as he was stolen from us.

But there was no theft. And the only sounds we heard were quick sniffles from Mama on the floor and the creak of tree branches bearing the weight of snow, the breath-stealing snap of limbs succumbing. Mama did not sleep that night. I must have drifted, because at the first hint of dawn's light the door was thrown open and a still sleeping Einar retrieved.

A baby boy whose name I never learned was sacrificed. While my family celebrated, another mama opened her front door to find a bundle of empty blankets.

An *Old God*, Papa said, though if it was one of ours, he did not share. There were no altars to it, no wooden figures on the mantle. If it had a name, I only heard its corrupted form, slurred by a mourning father too deep into his cup, screamed by a mother who cared not if her wails reached its mountain lair. Papa could not tell me why our gods did not defend us from this terror. When I asked, he appeared to have never considered it.

"Why offer at all?" I asked Papa the year Einar was born. "We have swords and fire."

Papa squinted, seemingly trapped between telling me the truth and some softened version of it suitable for my ears.

"They have tried. The men of the village. There are few men for more reasons than the offering. Yes, we know what they say about us in other towns. We devised the tradition to limit competition, to hoard the women for ourselves," Papa said, breaking eye contact with me to stare at the liquid swirling in the bottom of his mug. "And every ten years or so some new father or father-to-be will rouse the men of the village to take a stand. Filling them with poisonous words of conquest and dominion. These are not the actions of a man concerned with hoarding women."

"And?" I said.

"Every ten years or so, some red-faced, shield-clanking army ascends the mountain. Five or ten men, it matters not. The war cries fade and there is silence for a while. Then the screaming begins. Here, in the valley, there are a half a dozen or more new widows, and we take care of ours in The Briar."

Maybe in the loose, soil-dark locks of the hopeful bachelors, the women saw not their lost sons but a lost husband who died on a fool's errand.

Papa emptied his mug and reached across the table to muss my hair.

"It is not our concern. This year, at least. Einar was not taken, and Mama is not with child."

I nodded and looked beyond him through the window. The mountain was there, hidden within the fog. The Old God was there, too, a many-eyed black thing according to legend.

"Papa?"

"Yes, dear?"

"What if no boys are born *this* year?"

•••

I worried Papa believed I predicted it. There were two boys born in The Briar the year after Einar, but neither survived to December. This was not unprecedented, and by Autumn Mama began to lose hair from worry. She scrutinized every woman's swollen belly, making no mystery of her intentions.

Winter came early and drove Mama inside, where she wore holes in the rugs pacing by the windows with Einar on her hip.

"We'll just leave," Mama said, smiling as if it was the first time she suggested it. "Start a new life somewhere."

Papa shook his head but did not meet her gaze. "You would prefer it be the whole village that suffers, then? You would condemn our brethren to *our* fate? It is the price we pay to live as we do, free from the count's taxes or wars. We die our own way. It is a sacrifice of our own choosing."

Those were the last words they spoke to each other that month. Mama glared at Papa as if *he* was the monster who descended the mountain to steal her child. She pushed Einar away, ripping her breast from his mouth while his belly still rumbled. I understood the feeling. It was like when the hogs I raised from a piglet grew big enough to harvest. I couldn't look at them. I had to pretend they belonged to someone else.

It was quiet that December, and I only had time to think. Papa's words repeated in my head.

A sacrifice of our own choosing.

Was there a truth in his words I did not understand? The offering was a fact of life, same as the harvest and the slaughter. It happened without thought, without question.

In one week, Einar would be wrapped in blankets, tight so that he could not wriggle free. He would be left on the doorstep, belly sloshing with a tea to help him sleep through the night. As the only male baby in The Briar, he would be taken. He would be sacrificed to an Old God who lived in the mountain. Forfeiting his life, he would enable The Briar to exist outside of the kingdom's laws and wars for another year.

Einar slept beside me. Though it was cold in the room, we

were warm together. His eyelids fluttered in the midst of a dream, soft cooing competing with the rumble from his belly.

It was easy to ignore the hogs, to pretend they belonged to someone else as Papa sharpened the blade that would open their throats. Chunks of meat in a stew could come from any animal. And, soon there would be new hogs, new piglets to fatten with treats hidden in my pockets.

There would never be another Einar even if Mama birthed another son.

Perhaps my thoughts of him pulled him most of the way out of a dream. He wriggled a hand free from his swaddle and it landed in my palm hot as a dying coal. His hands would never create. They would never grasp a sword or plant a seed. And for what?

I found Papa in his chair, a bottle tipped on its side on the small table beside him. He stared at the fire as if attempting to parse meaning from the shifting shapes within. *His* hands were rough and calloused, the nails forever black, veins like green earthworms trapped beneath the skin. *His* hands told a story.

"You will do nothing?" I asked.

He flinched, either from not realizing he was no longer alone or from the sharpness of my words.

"What can I do?" he said, sinking lower into his chair.

"Aye, what can you do?"

The question hung like smoke in the air.

"I cannot best the Old God in combat. I play-fought with swords as a lad, but I've no skill for it today. If we flee, well, others have tried. They do not get far. Briar-folk are loyal, until they aren't. And it would not just be Einar sacrificed but you, me, and yer Ma. Bound and left at the mouth of the cave as penance for missin' the offering."

This was new information. In my short life, there had never been an attempted escape. Papa's reluctance made more sense, but it changed nothing of my resolve. The idea was there, like an acorn buried in the soil waiting for the snow to melt. There was potential, an inkling.

"You would sacrifice yourself in his place. Wouldn't you?"

"Aye, I would."

"If you knew the Old God would accept it, you would offer yourself."

He nodded, eyed the tipped bottle and frowned.

"Then do it. Go to the cave and offer yourself. Bring no weapons."

Papa's rough hands knotted together, and his back bowed as if the thoughts in his mind weighed a hundred pounds each.

"It is certain death," he whispered. "And it might be for naught."

"Might, Papa. Do you wish to live the rest of your days knowing you might have saved Einar?"

Papa's eyes shimmered with tears as he lifted his face.

"You wish for me to die?"

I touched his cheek, my thumb wiping a tear, "No, Papa. I wish for you to save our Einar. If it was a bear, you would fight it with your own hands. You would die in the attempt if need be. This is just a different sort."

Papa shared nothing of the plan with Mama. They were still not talking but sliding past each other like ghosts. I shared nothing of *my* plan with Papa. He would not have endorsed it and would likely have spent the journey to the Old God's lair glancing behind instead of ahead.

There was snow on the ground, but the sky was dark and full of stars. I held Einar's scent in my lungs as I exited the front door a minute after Papa departed. His prints were half-filled with the moonlight that sparkled off the ice. I could just hear the crunch of his departing steps, and I waited, blowing into my mittens, until all was quiet. If I could hear him, he could also hear me, I reasoned.

The Old God's lair was not at the mountain's summit but somewhere in its middle, below the tree line. There was much space between the boot prints indicating Papa's haste. The air burned in my throat as I shuffled to keep close.

This felt foolish, yes. But it also felt like the only action we could take. I did not know my role in following Papa. I only knew it was my suggestion, and I owned whatever happened to him. A not-small part of me wished to punish the Old God for taking Einar before the offense even occurred. Each time the question of *how* stirred in my mind I bit my lip until the pain was as bright as the summer sun.

Crunch crunch crunch

Up the path we went. I had never climbed on that mountain, though I had many others. I did not want to stumble into the Old God's lair unknowingly. The air grew thinner and lighter in my chest as we ascended. It was painful to breathe, and I could not help but imagine my lungs floating free of my chest like a kerchief caught in a wind.

Toward the end I was on my knees, clawing at the ground for purchase so steep was the climb. Papa's prints were grouped closer together here as well.

What did he think of, I wondered. Was he cursing me? Was he afraid? I was just as likely to not survive the night and my only thoughts were of Einar safe in his warm bed.

I nearly gave myself away, stepping out from the trees, which had thinned, and colliding with Papa. I stopped just short, boots crunching and breath trapped in my lungs. He stood with his hands on his hips, a gray-blue silhouette just beyond the mouth of the cave before him. His breath issued around his head like steam from a boiling kettle.

Do you wish to turn back, Papa? Aye, you do. But you will not.

He stepped forward, hands pressing on his knees to ascend the final paces. I timed my movement with his, his noise disguising mine. His posture shifted, neck bending, knees bent and ready to run. He shielded his eyes as if it was not darkness he beheld but a bright light.

"Hello?" he called, voice cracking even at a whisper. He cleared his throat and tried again, this time loud enough to make an echo. There was nothing remarkable about this place, a cave similar to dozens I had seen. It felt stagnant. Dead, like the yellowed eyehole of a moldering skull. Was it the wrong cave? Its black mouth swallowed his form, and I realized it might be the last I saw of him.

"Are you there?"

I scurried the remaining distance, finding patches of bare soil padded with discarded pine needles. I crouched beyond the entrance to the cave, eyes straining to catch a glimpse of Papa.

"I say…" he began, then trailed off.

There was a sound from the cave. Sliding and rasping, a scraping of some unknown texture against the walls.

"I…I…am here to…"

Another sound then, like a thrum of struck metal.

Hmmmmm

Papa gasped and retreated a step, the back half of his body now glowing with moonlight.

Hmmm…where…where is your steel?

The voice sounded as if it was formed inside a throat not designed for speech. It was like boulders tumbling down the mountain. It vibrated in my chest, loosened the marrow in my bones.

"I…I have no steel."

Hmmmm…a man…and a girl with no weapons…

"A girl?" Papa said, then turned his head. He could not see me from where he stood, and I held my breath until he faced the darkness again.

"I brought no girl. Only myself."

Hmmmm…so you say. What do you want, man, if not to kill me?

Papa did not answer right away. He could not undo this action, but he still had to speak it into existence.

"My son, Einar, is the only male babe in The Briar. I have come to offer myself in his place. Take me, Old God, and spare my child," he said, then added. "Please."

Hmmm…

Your offer is accepted.

Papa took another step backwards, "It is?"

Yes.

"You will spare my son and take me in his stead?"

Yes.

Papa's back stiffened as if anticipating his end would come at that moment.

"But why, Old God?"

It is what you offered.

Papa scratched his head, "I…don't understand. I…in The Briar…the offering…"

Hmmm…these are your traditions. Not mine. I take what is offered. Your sons. Your men when they come with their steel.

Papa nodded, stepped back into darkness, "But why, Old God?"

Hmmm…I did not demand your sons. It was offered to me long ago. When your kind first came to this valley. A man and a boy with hair like fire entered my cave whispering of sleeping bears. I was in a deep slumber but roused from their racket. Their spears pointed at the darkness, but it was not a bear they found. When the man saw me…hmmmm that is a pleasant memory. His spear fell from his fingers, and he pushed his son toward me. I did not understand his words as I did not know your language then, but I understood his meaning.

"And…and they just kept…"

It is your tradition, not mine. I grow weary of this chatter, man. You have woken me from a blissful dream, and I wish to reclaim it. I accept your bargain, now step forth.

Papa's boots shuffled over the floor of the cave, "Can I ask you a question first?"

Hmmm…you may.

"Are y-you a g-god?"

Hmmm…there are no gods, man.

"Th-then w-what are you?"

I inched forward, eyes hungry for more information, but there was nothing to be seen. I did not want Papa to die even though his death would allow Einar to live. Shame burned in my cheeks when I recalled how small, how diminished he looked asking if I wished for him to die. No. I thought it was the only way.

Could I offer myself instead?

Your understanding of life is a beating heart. It is blood in your veins and air in your lungs. I have no heart. I do not breathe your air. I came to this place while dreaming, floating through the great void beyond the warmth of any sun. There are no gods in the Universe, only chaos. I am but a small part of it.

I do not survive on the flesh of your sons. There is too little to sustain me. What I take from them, you will soon know, is not their meat but something far more precious.

I do not wish to be awake any longer. Close your eyes if you do not wish to die screaming.

"Wait!" I yelled and scrambled free of my hiding place.

"Marit!" Papa cried, rushing out of the darkness and wrapping me in his arms. "You should not be here!"

I looked past him but saw only black. The idea, the acorn buried under snow, broke free of its softened shell and tasted the air.

"The offering. It is our tradition, yes?" I said.

It is.

"It could be something else?"

I am weary of these questions.

"A bigger offering! Bigger and more frequent! You will not have to descend the mountain to claim it. They will come to you," I said, then added, "Imagine how well you will sleep with a full belly. How you will dream."

Hmmm…

Papa's racing heart thudded against my ear. We stared and waited.

What do you propose, child?

The plan took shape as I voiced it. The possibilities were present within me, knowledge of the peculiar nature of our secluded village, the oft-repeated rumors of our disproportionate sexes. I listened to my own echo fade, and Papa held me tighter. Outside the cave, the wind turned the tree branches to rattles.

I wish to dream again. I accept your proposal.

"Thank you! Bless you Old God!" Papa said, shifting me to the cave floor and pulling me toward the entrance.

"Wait! One more question and then we will leave," I said.

"Marit!" Papa barked.

I stood at the border between light and dark.

"The stories in the village of those who claim to have seen you…"

Yeeesssss?

"They said you were a great black creature with many eyes. If you are not that, and you are not a god, what did they see?"

Hmmmm…

A dry scraping sound, raspy, drawing nearer to me. There were lights, faint at first, like the stars I would see only after my eyes had time to adjust. Brighter then, blades reflecting moonlight.

Not eyes. No. They saw the others, those who came before. Their brothers, some. And other kinds still, from worlds barren beneath a blackened star. They saw what they would lose, what they would become when I consumed them. Passengers, awake and static, a part of me, yes. I would drift and dream unaware of the passage of time and they would exist without living, counting every second, little lights giving structure to my form. They are with me now.

"It is like they said," the man slurred, his mug unsteady in his grasp. "The women here. So beautiful and so many."

I feign jealousy, "You said I was the most beautiful."

He abandons his mug to grasp my shoulders, "You are! I apologize, my lovely. I am just a little…overwhelmed."

His eyes trace the contours of my face and settle, as they have for the past hour, on my breasts. I do not mind. Nor would any of the women in the tavern, but he chose me.

"You can make it up to me."

His eyes flash back to mine, "How? Anything you ask."

I turn my body away before the drool spilling from the corner of his mouth dribbles onto my chest. He smells of sweat and grime. The journey to get here is not as cumbersome as it was in years past. The road is maintained but still difficult.

"There is a place, not far from here. It will require us to part, though," I say, to which he groans. "A cave. It is sacred to us Briar folk. At the back of the cave there is a waterfall. The water trickles all through the mountain but is only revealed there."

I place the empty mug in his hand.

"Fill this mug with the water. It is special. Magic. You will know it because of the glowing lights. Take no weapons, only this mug. Return it to me and I am yours. For tonight or forever if you prefer."

He glances at the mug as if it is a growth at the end of his fingers, then scans the women in the room.

He has no family, he says. None knew of his journey to The Briar. He is perfect.

"They will require the same of you. It's *our* way," I say, with more than a small measure of pride.

Her Rotten Tongue

By Vanessa Jae

When my metamorphosis was completed, dirt dripped from my lips. It was a familiar sensation, leaking uncontrollably out of me like a flood reclaiming its strength after being locked behind an embankment. It reminded me of the blood pooling in my cheeks whenever I had dared to speak. Back then, I had swallowed it all. The blood, the words, the anger, scarring my own throat to the point of being suffocated by all this raised, irritated tissue. That was before I became the fury of the forest, before people knew the sound of my voice was the end of them.

They feared my words, even when I was just young Hedwig. I had quickly understood I wasn't put into this world to question, I was born to obey. But I had never understood why no matter how small, how invisible I made myself, I couldn't escape the eyes watching my every move, the hands judging and correcting my body until my head was ruined and I was dragged into the woods, left to die alone. The village that raised me knew little girls were one of the greatest dangers to exist. That's why when they failed to tame me, they tried to get rid of me. They should have settled for scared little Hedwig asking questions until she was too worn out to argue. Instead, they beat her inhibitions out of her and created the monster they had always feared she would become.

They called me devil even after I was dealt with. I was the silent hag they warned their daughters about but weren't scared of themselves. There was no reason to. They had never heard nor seen me, yet something kept luring their daughters away, the rustle of the trees promising relief from the burdens those girls were made to carry. I had been deteriorating for decades before I was able to claim the role of the fury of the forest, lying where my father had disposed of me to become one with nature. He'd thought that meant dying, but nature knew no death. In nature, destruction meant rebirth.

Where my skull had broken, the spiders spun an indestructible web of delicate wrought iron. The trees absorbed my mind the blow had released into the wild, filtering out the polluted thoughts I had been poisoned with. The damage done to my throat was irreversible, but the river cleansed it, soothing the scars and clearing it for bigger words. I was bound to the forest, who prepared me. I became the fury of the forest to save girls like the one I had once been.

Consuming the first burden offered to me was an experience of revival, of finding a purpose for all this suffering. I had left Hedwig behind, back in the village that made her who she was, that had gnawed on her flesh until she was nothing but a brittle skeleton abiding on her knees because she was too weak to stand. They could have her body, but they couldn't have me, the creature I was meant to emerge as and who refused to let go, holding onto Hedwig's brain with barbs after her skull was shattered with a rock.

When Hedwig died, I was born.

My home was surrounded by trees, one for every little devil who hadn't made it. The river running underneath my elevated hut brought me their bones to lay them to rest where they belonged, where injustice-soaked marrow tainted the soil. Out of their maws, seedlings grew into mighty beings.

Those who came to me alive took a piece of their dead sisters. The first girl who was led to me plucked a leaf from one of the trees and placed it in the palm of her hand. I watched her release the agony her burden had scorched into her, a teardrop seeped into the leaf and she put it on the ground. I waited for her to leave, but the ritual wasn't over yet. She gasped when I emerged from my hiding spot. No one had ever looked at me after Hedwig died. I accepted her burden, picked it up, and smothered it with my tongue. I tasted the pain, I tasted the despair, I tasted it all as I closed my mouth around it and bit off the invisible string of silk attaching the burden to the girl.

She was free.

Every offering I received, I kept in my mouth. The leaves slowly rotted, turned into a thick paste of decay I revived whenever I took a sip from the river, its water of life flowing through my home. It resurged the tear that had been left and shocked my body into a new rage until every bit had trickled down my throat. It was a tiring, suffocating process, and it was hard to let it happen with no resistance at times, the feeling of being choked and the desire to spit it all out too overwhelming. But I endured it, always did. I didn't know what would happen if the ritual was interrupted, but I knew that I could handle the consequences of completing it and that I would never let the girls have to deal with someone else failing them again after reaching out for help. They put their trust into the forest and the forest had chosen me worthy to protect this trust. Knowing none of them would end up like me if I did this for them kept me enduring, willing to continue this torture that was nothing like what Hedwig had suffered.

When exhaustion overcame me, I watched the birds. I watched them land on the branches of the dead and wondered if they knew how this life was grown, if they grieved lost ones, mourned every tree cut down from beneath their talons. I wondered if they perched on these trees I grew from vengeance and felt it flow through them to the tip of their wings. If they fed on sacrifices like the deer did, the deer who began gnawing on bones once the cold arrived and the river quieted down enough for me to know it was time to rest and seal my lips for the winter. I had never seen where the deer found the bones they feasted on. All I knew was they didn't come from the river and weren't worth saving. As my eyelids became too heavy to keep open, I cupped the flame of the dimming fire in front of me with both of my hands and the forest turned dark until spring arrived.

•••

Something else arrived before spring.

My senses aroused with the realization that what I was hearing wasn't the wind pressing against the hut's walls, but the river telling me the forest's whispers had lured the wrong kind of being to me. A girl had followed them, but a man had followed the girl. The sound of their footsteps echoed through my home, shaking me to my core. They didn't know they were composing a battle hymn that awakened what had been slumbering inside of me ever since I had been taught I was a danger. I had never believed I was a danger myself, not until I felt the rot gurgling in the back of my throat, felt the metal holding my skull together start to burn. It felt like I was on fire in the deepest of winter when I should have felt peace. Winter was the rest I allowed myself after months of accepting burdens. Each girl who visited left only one leaf for me to carry on my tongue, but one leaf could feel so heavy weighted with the words a child could never say, should never be made to hold onto in the first place. No one found their way to me unless the forest led them, and the forest wouldn't lead them unless it was time to free them.

It had been weeks since I last left my hut's throne of hair, dust, and silk. I watched over my realm within. My limbs slowly came back to life, my left knee dragging a numb foot through fallen leaves. I was breathing hard enough for my nose to start running. It was all releasing now. It would be hard to hold back, was the last conscious thought I formed, the last thought that held a sliver of young Hedwig, before I stepped outside and faced the girl whose burden I was thirsting to devour. Behind her, the burden itself.

"Get out," I spat the first time the fury of the forest spoke.

I had never heard my true voice, had never felt its essence before it was running down my chin as burning black venom formed by the blood of all the burdens I had ever consumed. I had been starving my entire life. The hunger for those leaving offerings for me was eating pieces of my guts, craving the blood promised by the whispers of the woods.

The girl ran, the burden stayed.

I trembled in wrath as eyes dared to look at me the way they hadn't since Hedwig's death. The forest wasn't a place for the wrong kind of eyes, it was to be perceived through the guidance of its spirit. As all the burdens I had swallowed crept their way back up my gullet, the paste scratched the scars the river had once soothed, re-flaring them. With all the rot oozing out between my teeth, my stomach had been emptied. It was time to feast.

A man weighed more than a leaf. But a man was empty of unspoken words, empty of the grief anger turned into when left leashed. He was empty of the burdens he imposed onto those around him. A man was a meal I shared with the woods who delivered him to me. His bones were returned to the earth. The birds got his organs, the deer his flesh, and I kept chopped pieces of his skin to chew on during coming winters to keep the fire inside of me burning. These powers the forest had bestowed on me—ripping apart the burdens themselves instead of letting them tear me apart—required me to keep the flame fed, eternally.

When spring arrived, I opened my eyes to sunlight performing a shadow play on the walls of my home. I watched the spectacle in anticipation of what would await me outside. I sighed at the prospect of young trees sprouting, remembering my deal with the deer. I had provided them with the rare treat of human meat and in return for this nutritious delicacy, they would let roots prosper. The more breaths I took, the more apparent the lack of struggle became. I couldn't remember my throat ever being this clear. First, my own repressed words, then the rotting burdens had always clung to my trachea, no matter how much I drank from the river. The ritual required for the leaves to fully decompose on their own or it would be of no help for the girls. I realized, rather than taking the burden from the girl who visited me in winter, her burden had relieved me from mine for a brief period of time. My hunger sated, I wondered what had become of her.

I left my hut to look at the life all this death had fed. A doe walked up to me and bowed. I put my nose between its ears, thanked it for the trees and asked about the girl. The doe raised its head and left a wet kiss on my forehead, whose trail of blood running by the corners of my eyes told me everything I needed to know. I needn't worry. The girl who arrived in winter was chosen by the forest to be beside me. She would come back and provide me with the sacrifices I needed, we would be the liberators of girls the world failed to silence.

Exuviae

By D. Matthew Urban

My big sisters look exactly alike. Two of them stand by my bedside, their mouthparts moving in flawless synchrony. "Grandmother wants to see you," they say.

The long sleep has numbed my limbs. I stumble down the upstairs hallway, a sister supporting me on either side. Half-open doors slide past, offering glimpses of the shadowy nurseries where my nieces lie swaddled in their uncles.

At the end of the hallway, my sisters shove me into Grandmother's room and shut the door behind me. The cavernous space is lit only by a floor lamp with a green shawl draped over its shade. Grandmother stands in the far corner, her eyes glistening in the dimness, the air thick with her cold, heavy breath.

Grandmother's joints creak and pop as she approaches me. Her stinger drags along the floor. My legs tremble, and I lean against the wall for support. Its pulpy surface moistens my hands.

Grandmother's eyes are the biggest I've ever seen. She looks me up and down. "You're close to term, child," she says, her voice a buzzing rasp.

"A few days, my sisters say."

"That means an empty bed. Who'll fill that bed, I wonder?"

I know what's expected of me. I lift my chin and swallow the fear coiled in my throat. "I'll find you a new granddaughter, ma'am."

She raises a thin foreleg, runs a claw gently down my cheek. In the green dimness, her gaze shimmers almost like love.

• • •

Downstairs, the living room is full of family. Big sisters crowd around the table, a swarm of aunts on the ceiling, a rotting heap of half-eaten uncles in the corner. Another little sister, the newest, stands trembling against the wall, her arms wrapped nervously around her stomach. She must have wandered from her bedroom. The light of the bare, dangling bulb gleams on her shaved head, on the black wells of her eyes.

Pity floods me, drowning the thought of my errand. The girl seems so lost, so ill at ease in her new home. In the first days after my induction, I must have looked the same way.

I sidle up next to her and force what I hope is a comforting smile. "How are you feeling, little sister?"

"I feel okay, little sister. Thank you." Her voice is shaky and quiet, almost a whisper. Her gaze is fixed on the table and the spindly forms gathered there.

"Don't worry," I say. "They're not paying attention to us."

"How do you know? What are they doing?"

"They're praying."

The girl's senses haven't sharpened enough to hear those high, chirping voices that scrape at my ears like crushed glass. Somewhere beneath perception, though, their prayer reaches her. She shudders, turns her head away. At the top of her neck, the induction mark glistens, red and swollen.

I raise a hand to my own nape. My hair's grown long again, but the mark is easy to find, a rough, puckered mouth among the curls.

Feeling the scar brings my errand back to mind, along with a fresh stab of compassion for the girl. How terrified she must be, how lonely, how confused. When I was new to the house, I would have given anything for a kind word, a human glance.

"Little sister," I say. She turns back toward me, tears shining on her cheeks. "I'm going out. Do you want to come with me?"

She darts an anxious glance toward the chittering, jointed things around the table. "Will they…"

"It's fine. They know I'm running an errand."

When she realizes what that means, her mouth falls open and her eyes widen, but she quickly masters her revulsion. She gives me a small, determined smile, a smile that says she'd do anything at all rather than have me leave her in this house with our big sisters, our aunts and uncles, Grandmother.

I take her trembling hand. "Let's go."

The moment I open the front door, the room behind us fills with screeching. The girl yanks her hand from mine, whirls around with a terrified gasp. I turn and touch her shoulder, hoping to calm her.

Above our big sisters' bowed, angular heads, our aunts howl on the ceiling, fluttering their hindwings and flailing their antennae. Their eyes glare and swivel, almost as big as Grandmother's.

"It's okay," I whisper into the girl's ear. "They're not angry at us. They're just hungry."

A dirt road runs between fields of coarse grass that were green and sweet-smelling when I was brought to the house, slumped in the passenger seat of a rusted-out station wagon while a little sister drove. Now I drive that same car through a gray, withered expanse under a gray sky, the girl sitting ramrod-straight beside me with her hands folded in her lap.

Did I know how to drive before I came to the house, or did I learn while I slept, my niece whispering instructions in my ear from the inside? I can't remember.

After so long in the house, the world horrifies me with its breadth and brightness. Every jolt of the wheels on the pitted dirt sends a wave of panic through me, as if the station wagon is about to fly off into an infinite distance. Soon, I'm longing for the house's closed-in world, its endless, whispering twilight behind plywood-covered windows. I want to talk to the girl, if only to distract myself from the vastness all around, but my head is full of chirping, buzzing, screeching, a swarm of noise choking all human words.

When the girl finally speaks, her voice stills the clatter in my brain. "What's your name?" she says.

"It's…" A shadowy syllable wavers at the bottom of my mind, but it fades before my tongue can grasp it. "It's little sister. I had another one, but I lost it in my sleep."

"You sleep a lot. You've been sleeping since they brought me."

"Sleep ripens the sisterhood. It takes a long time. I woke up every day or two at first, but after a while I stayed asleep."

"I don't like sleeping in that house." Her voice quavers, panic-tinged, but when I glance away from the road her face is calm. "My dreams make me forget things."

"That's the ripening." I tap a finger against the back of my neck, the hidden scar. "The niece goes in and makes you a sister. While you sleep, she's eating up the old parts of you, making you new. You have to forget the old way before you can learn the new way."

"I don't want to forget. I want to stay me. My name is Clara. I want to keep it."

My heart breaks for her. Before the long sleep, I felt the same way, seeing only the terrible side of the transformation. Now, I've begun to feel the wonder, the miracle of it. "It's not so bad to change," I say. "When the old parts of you go away, the fear goes away, too. I used to be as scared as you are, Clara. I'm still scared now, but only a little. Mostly, I'm happy, because I'm part of a real family where everyone belongs and we all have a place." As I say it, I find myself believing it more and more. I smile. "In a few more days, I won't be scared at all. I'll be completely ripe. I'll be a big sister."

We sit in the lee of the little house, watching columns of dust swirl as the wind sweeps across the neighboring field. The road that runs in front of the house is completely empty. The station wagon parked on the roadside is a rust-colored speck in the distance. Nothing else in sight but dust and wind and dead grass and darkening sky.

My little sister's been silent since we arrived. Is she frozen with terror, lost in thought, waiting for something? I can't tell. She can't be listening to the sounds from inside the house, the father and daughter talking as they move from room to room. Her ears aren't keen enough yet.

At last, she breaks her silence. "Is this how they got you?" she whispers.

"Yes," I whisper back. The memories surge up out of swirling darkness—waking up in my old bed, my old room, the stars through the open window. The little sister's head silhouetted against the stars. The little sister's hand covering my mouth, the poison of her changed skin overwhelming me.

Waking up again in the station wagon. Being dragged across the yard into the house. That awful first glimpse of the big sisters' jointed limbs and bulging eyes. The aunts' famished hissing. The uncle's lips pressed against my neck as the niece that had hatched in his guts squirmed out of his mouth, her tiny teeth rasping my flesh. The aunts' shrieks of delight as they feasted on the spent, moaning uncle, tearing gobbets out of him with their mandibles.

I squeeze my eyes shut and wait for the memories to subside. Those things happened to someone else, I tell myself, someone whose name you can't even remember. Just think of what you've gained at the price of a little fear, a little pain. Think of your wonderful new family.

Are those really my thoughts, or is it just my niece whispering lies as she chews up the last bits of me?

It doesn't matter. The family is what matters. My niece in my head is me. The big sister I'll be in a few days is me. When the big sister's shiny carapace cracks, the aunt that squirms out will be me, and the egg the aunt lays in an uncle's flesh will be me. When the aunt's work is done and Grandmother bites her head off, it will be my own jaws rending my own body, my own stinger quivering in my own guts.

The sun has set behind the clouds. The lights in the little house have gone out. "It's time," I murmur. "Do you want to come get her with me?"

My little sister trembles with cold, or fear, or memory. "No," she whispers.

I rise in the darkness and creep along the side of the house to the daughter's bedroom window. Through the glass, I can hear her steady breathing. The window slides open as quietly as I'd hoped, and I make no noise as I slip through.

The room is pitch-dark, but with my sharpened eyes I see the daughter lying on her side, her legs tucked against her chest and the blanket tight around her chin. As I approach the bed, she stirs in her sleep, the blanket rippling like an uncle's belly with a wriggling niece inside, but she doesn't wake.

Gently, lovingly, I reach for my new sister.

A storm of noise shatters the silence. Fists pounding on the door of the little house, a ragged voice shrieking from outside. Clara's voice. "Wake up! Wake up! She's coming to get you!"

The daughter's eyes snap open. Her scream mingles with Clara's keening howls. I clamp my fingers over her mouth, but there's no time to put her to sleep that way. I need a faster, stronger poison. My fingers worm between her lips, and once I've pried her jaws open, I lean down and spit into her mouth. She gags and splutters, but my changed juices are already working on her, numbing her tissues. After a moment, she's sleeping more soundly than ever.

A crash thunders behind me as the bedroom door slams against the wall. I whirl to see the father rush into the room, a metal bat clutched in his hand. "Get away from her!" he shouts, running at me. Behind him, I glimpse another dark room, another open door, the empty night beyond. Clara stands on the threshold, her face slack, paralyzed with horror.

I leap toward the open window, but the father swings furiously and the bat clangs against my skull. Something in my head cracks, and I fall to the floor with a wail of shock and pain. The father swings the bat again, hits me in the hip. Another crack. With a writhing lunge, I get my fingers around his ankles. He totters but doesn't fall. I'm still wailing, my voice rising and rising, higher than any human can hear.

Another lunge forward, and I sink my teeth through the thin fabric of his pajamas and into his calf. He roars with pain and swings again, again. My arm splinters, not the bone but the arm, the hard shell that's grown inside the skin. I feel my niece squirming inside my broken head, straining to bring me to ripeness before my life drains out. The father's blood is hot in my mouth. I shove my tongue into the wound I've opened, slathering the bite with venom.

The metal bat rings against the floor. The father crumples and falls.

I'm too shattered to stand. With my unbroken arm, I drag myself across the father's convulsing body toward the window. Stretching up as far as I can, I curl my fingers on the edge of the sill, but I'm too weak to lift myself. I slump against the wall, my head lolling.

Feet shuffle outside the room. I lift my eyes. Clara trembles in the doorway, her cheeks slimy with tears.

I do my best to smile. "It's all right," I mumble. "I forgive you, little sister."

A tide of sleep rises around me, darker than the darkness. The last thing I hear before oblivion swallows me is my little sister's footsteps running through the house, out into the night.

Something hard and sharp presses against my temple. Hard yet gentle, sharp yet delicate. As it moves across my face, my skin sloughs off, but there's no pain. I feel unbound, as if I've spent my whole life wrapped in damp paper. I'm emerging from myself.

When the sharp thing moves over my eyes, cutting the lids away, I can see again. A big sister's face looms close to mine, her eyes twitching with concern. I'm still slumped against the wall of the daughter's bedroom. Across the room, another big sister watches as the first's sharp-clawed forelegs strip off my husk.

My new face comes free of its soft, wet prison. I stretch my mouth, roll the great globes of my eyes. Even at the very end, I'd feared this ripening, this final departure from human flesh.

Now that I've changed, I know there was never anything to fear. There is no final departure, only a chain of transformations leading onward through form after form.

"How did you find me, sisters?" I say. My new voice comes easily, its chirps and trills flowing sweetly from my mouthparts.

"You called out for us," the two of them say in unison. "We do not abandon our own."

I try to stand, but my legs only twitch. I look down at my new body and see a battered, twisted thing, my limbs cracked and thrown out of joint by the father's brutal assault.

"Lie still," my sisters say. "Let us help you."

They lift me carefully in their strong, hard arms. As we leave the bedroom, I see that a sheet of plywood covers the window, nailed to the wall with crude spikes.

My sisters carry me out into the front room of the little house. Here, too, the windows have been covered, and all the lamps are burning. Against one wall, the man who attacked me lies naked and unconscious on a leather couch. The leg I bit has been cut off at mid-thigh, the wound sealed with brownish-gray pulp. Blood trickles from a fresh incision just below his navel.

On the ceiling above the couch, an aunt clutches the man's severed leg in her foreclaws. Scraps of flesh drop from her nibbling jaws. The sound she's making is pure pleasure, almost a purr. Her ovipositor trembles behind her, its spear-tip red from the new uncle's guts.

"You did well," my sisters said. The pride in their voices fills me with joy.

"And the daughter?" I say.

They carry me to the open door of another room. Inside, the daughter lies on a wide, high bed with her legs curled against her chest, just as I first saw her. Next to her, on her back with her arms straight at her sides, lies Clara.

"Little sister!" I say, my voice shrill with relief. "Where did you find her?"

"She didn't get far," the big sisters say with satisfaction. "We do not abandon our own."

Something occurs to me, a sour note amid my happiness. I click my mouth in confusion. "But why are we still in this house, and not at Grandmother's?"

In the pause before they answer, I feel their compassion like a vibration in the air. "Because you cannot go there, sister. Your injuries are too great. You must remain here."

At first, I simply don't grasp what they're saying. The words seem as broken as my body, their meaning draining out like blood. When I finally understand, I feel a door slam shut in my mind. My house, my family, my life, all torn away. An endless, unbearable amputation. I twitch and flail, twisting feebly in my sisters' arms. A shriek wrenches itself from my chattering mouthparts.

"Hush, hush," they croon. "Be still, be still." They carry me to the daughter's bedroom, lay me down in the tangled sheets.

I'm ashamed of my outburst. That's not how a big sister should behave. I force myself to lie quiet. "I don't want to stay here by myself," I whisper.

"Must we say it again?" my sisters say. "We do not abandon our own."

"But…"

"Listen. The family has conferred, decided what must be done. Surely you can guess the decision?"

I shake my head.

"Just think of what you've seen already," my sisters say. "The family has sent an aunt to this house, and she's set a niece to hatch inside the uncle you found. Once the niece is ready, we have a vessel to put her in. We have a little sister sleeping the long sleep. And a pair of big sisters, too."

"And me," I say, still resisting the ultimate, incredible conclusion.

"And you. Just think of all you've done! You've fought boldly, suffered bravely for the sake of the family. And you've found this house. Not as big as the other house, true, but just as fine a hiding place. Who'll ever stop along that road? Who'll ever find us here? It's a perfect nest."

"But a nest needs…"

Their eyes tremble with excitement. "Exactly."

We sit quietly together for a while, saying prayers to the infinite nest that embraces us all. Afterward, I sleep to regain my strength. When I wake, a bowl made of pulp sits by my bedside. The thick, pale jelly in the bowl tastes bitter, but I drink it eagerly. The jelly makes me sleepy. I wake again to find another bowl. I drink again, sleep again, wake, drink, sleep. My legs become longer, my eyes larger, my stinger thick and sharp. My breath grows cold and heavy, filling the room, moistening the walls. My heart swells to bursting with love and hunger.

I know I'll make a wonderful Grandmother.

Dead East

By Andrew Leon Hudson

Nearing the end of a quiet day. Main Street was almost empty of folk. From his chair on the boardwalk, Sheriff Royce thought about taking a drink in the saloon, before business picked up and it felt like fraternizing.

His eye was caught by two specks wrestling in the dust of the boardwalk: tiny wasps engaged in jerking, jittery battle. Gradually one gained the upper hand, and the head of the other was clipped from its body. Dead—yet the body struggled on, even while the silver-black wings were separated from it, one by one, and the still struggling body was dragged into the air by the victor and flown away.

Mrs. Mitle clumped home on the boards across the street. Royce tipped his hat, but as she raised a hand to wave she faltered mid-step, and Royce turned to look.

His first thought was that the stranger would drop dead the moment he stopped walking. It was a figure like out of one of the preacher's more outlandish tales, wasted down to the skin in an outfit that looked as though it had been worried by dogs, yellow-gray with dust from head to toe. His feet dragged and a satchel trailed behind them from its strap, bumping belatedly over the ruts of the street, kicking off his heel.

The Jeffers boy was staring from the doorway of Royce's office, broom in hand from sweeping out the empty cells. Royce stepped off the boards to the dry earth. "Go on down to Doc's shop," he said, "and if he's not there run fetch him from home. Then get yourself out to the church and bring the preacher too."

The boy got moving as the sheriff hitched his belt and settled the weight of the revolver on his thigh—just in case—before making after the staggering stranger.

It was care not prayer the stranger needed, but Reverend Mack kept handy just in case, taking advantage of the fact that Doc Sutton's first diagnosis was that under no circumstances should the sun-blasted man be given strong liquor as fortification.

"A drink'll kill him faster than a bullet," Sutton said, peeling back clothes caked with dust and sand. The skin had cooked like pork rind where exposed, but was revealed ghostly white where it had been protected beneath tattered cloth.

So sheriff and preacher sipped a shot or two apiece, while the stranger got no more than a periodic dribble of water between the cracked brickwork that was his lips, and most of that he coughed out again. The doctor smeared the burns with some oily remedy of his own patent, the stranger moaning and twitching with every contact. He'd not yet said a word, and Royce was far from sure he would.

Eventually the stranger fell unconscious, so fearfully silent and with such shallow breaths as to seem dead after all. The three men left him in the back room and retired to the shop out front, Sutton sagging into his own barber's chair.

"Miracle he's living," Sutton opined, before tossing back a drink. "Worst case of exposure I've ever seen."

"Where did he come from, I wonder," said Mack, topping them all up.

"Well—" Royce sniffed thoughtfully "—there's nowhere close enough on the east road. And Hogan's stagecoach came that way just three days gone. They'd have passed him, or at least passed his horse if he'd had one die on him."

"What then?" Mack said.

The sheriff watched his glass fill. "He didn't even know he was back in civilization—he'd have staggered on, straight as an arrow. Maybe it's coincidence he hit the road at all. Maybe he was just out there in the desert, heading west."

Doc Sutton grunted. "What would a man be doing, off in nowhere alone, without a horse, without water or food, without anything at all?"

"He did have something," Royce said.

The sheriff opened the satchel the stranger had dragged mindlessly through the dust and they pored over its contents.

It was stuffed with loose sheets of paper, crushed carelessly together. Each page was decorated front and back by the spartan shapes of the badlands, an unforgiving terrain. Some were fine with detail, some barely a sketch: a horizon line, perhaps broken by a distant mesa, a skeletal tree. One page had been spoiled as if by rain.

"Was a storm to the east, last week," Mack said. "All through Sunday."

They passed the sheets between them. It was Mack who noted that half the pictures showed a sunrise. It was Sutton who noted they could be sunsets instead, with a pointed glance to the darkening street outside.

Royce sent both men to their beds. He tipped back the barber's chair, getting settled, his view of the stranger's makeshift bed unobstructed, and once more studied the drawings. All had at least the memory of skill to them, though many wavered as though the hand guiding the pencil lacked the strength even for that. Royce ordered them from strongest to weakest.

A hill with the sunrise or sunset behind it. Ten more like it, and one destroyed by rain. Could they be a map? *Find the place that shares this final view by finding all the other scenes that followed it?* As strategies go it wasn't very reliable. East might be an easy find at dawn, but a man walking through desert for days without food, water, or shelter might wander in circles at noon and not have the slightest idea.

As dawn tinted the air, the artist moaned and the sheriff stirred from an uncomfortable doze to feed water to a face broken like old leather. If the artist had ridden through town a week ago Royce doubted he could have recognized him, even if he'd spent a night in the cells.

"Tell me your name yet, Mister?" Royce asked, but a series of convulsing coughs forced Royce to hold his shoulder to prevent him toppling to the floor.

"Easy now," he said, "easy," the artist suppressing dry barks until his breath came cleanly. At last he held out a hand to the sheriff—pointing weakly at the illustrations Royce had left by the basin where he'd filled the jug.

"These pictures," Royce said, "they show some kind of trail, correct?"

The artist nodded, and the sheriff flicked through the sheets to the most perfect, in which the sun was obscured by an arcing rise in the ground with what seemed an opening in its face.

"That's the place, right? This hill, with the cave," Royce tried, but at this the artist only let out a long, shuddering sigh, head swaying. "If you don't know, how did you even get there yourself?" he muttered, then bit his tongue.

He studied the best picture again, but had no point of comparison by which to judge its size. Was that black opening a gaping cave mouth beneath a high hillside, or an opening a grown man would need to squeeze through, like crawling down into a heathen's smoke pit?

"*Not a hill.*" The voice was a ruin croaked, the word a twig cracked from an old branch destined for the fire.

Royce jerked in surprise. "What's that you say?"

"*Met a man. Told me...'bout a place. Gave...instructions. Got to...go see.*"

"This place?" Royce poked the picture. "What was there?" He waited for more, but the artist's expression, already made mask-like by the sun's rough work, seemed still more withdrawn—the eyes unfocused, seeing something distant and past.

Royce shook his head. "What in the Lord's name happened to you, son?" he muttered, not expecting a response.

The artist's gaze sharpened for a moment, flicked to meet his own, then flicked away. *"Don't rememer,"* the artist mumbled, but the sheriff wondered if he was being lied to.

The artist slept again, or feigned it, and Royce took the sheaf of pictures and headed for breakfast at the saloon. On the earth beside the boardwalk twin trails of ants passed, one laden down beneath tiny burdens. They made skittery progress across the mighty hills and crevasses of the baked, rutted ground, heedless of what seemed an endless journey ahead of them.

Had the artist been as single-minded?

His mind kept returning to the image of the hill—*not a hill*—and its black entrance. Something about it itched in his head, an old but familiar path trying to reawaken in his mind. Abruptly a word arose: *Barrow.* He hummed under his breath. His grandfather used to talk about such things: legends of Vikings from back in old England, buried with their treasures under man-made hills. Haunted by barrow-ghosts… or something like that. Tales to excite a child, to give him dreams of swords and dragons and battles and adventure. Or maybe just of green fields instead of desert scrub.

Not much more than scrub in the pictures, either. Still, there were a few landmarks. A plateau, first viewed from a distance. That could be a place to start looking.

A couple of years back, a private surveyor had come through and hired a room in back of Smith's General Store as a small office, sent by a corporation back in New York that was most unhappy to learn oil did not flow from the ground here. The maps he had drawn up and then abandoned were years out of date now, but not so much that a mesa would have escaped their creation.

On the spur Royce changed his mind. Breakfast could wait.

It was only a short walk, but for the trail of ants beside him it was surely akin to the great western spread. He saw larger movement: a squat black beetle, lumbering across the path of the ants like a lone buffalo. The ant line was interrupted, milling and circling while Royce followed those ants already safely beyond—their path led them under the General Store, he couldn't help but notice.

Royce got the key and set to work. No ants crawled through the back room at least. After about an hour he found his prize—*perhaps*—at the far extreme of the surveyor's ranging: a line of elevated land dismissed as of no potential, beyond which he had not ventured. Due east from town. The artist had walked with one on his right for all those days. *Would make those images sunrises*, Royce mused, as he returned the keys and headed back.

The columns of ants were no longer trooping under Smith's property as he left. Their route had changed: instead of their relentless east-west wagon train, they veered off at right angles and disappeared under the boardwalk. Right where the beetle had crossed their path. Distracting them, or leading them astray? The artist was the more determined after all. Whatever had driven him from however far beyond that mesa he had come, nothing had broken his focus. Even if it almost walked him to death.

"I have an idea where you came from," Royce said as he reentered the barber's shop—but the artist wasn't on the bed-made-operating table any more. He sat in the tilting chair, Doc Sutton's best straight razor in one hand.

"*Go back*," he said, and carved his own throat right to the bone.

Blood washed down him, painted his shirt in two shades, dark red and bright. His burned face paled to the color of sand, the cracks in his skin like those of a dried up riverbed, his eyes just two gray stones left behind by a long forgotten flow.

The papers fell from Royce's numbed fingers, but that flat gaze never wavered from his face, even when the killing hand hung slack, the square-tipped blade unmarked by all the blood it had set loose. It pointed to where the earthen mound lay, the sunrise behind it, the dark opening at its center, and now a lake of crimson forming at its edge.

• • •

When the grave was dug and a marker erected, the preacher spoke brief words. Only Royce and Doc Sutton attended—plus the Jeffers boy, who'd get a few pennies for the digging.

The marker read *An Artist, His Name Unknown,* and the year, no more.

Reverend Mack raised a toast to the poor soul who, being a suicide, lay beside ground reserved for those destined for His grace instead of under it. Sutton's customers returned and he did a roaring trade, retelling the story from start to finish. All were thrilled to sit in The Very Chair, and Sutton was quick to extol the wisdom of entrusting a blade only to trustworthy hands.

Royce returned to more ordinary duties, but as the evenings drew in his mind returned to the artist, whose sole possessions of significance had not been buried with him. As the blood lay cooling, Royce had saved the pictures from ruin, stained rusty brown along the paper's edge…something out of his grandfather's stories, crossing an ocean and a thousand years, waiting to be discovered again.

Royce felt sure the artist's mesa and the surveyor's were the same. He had their east and west. The approach of the mesa. A dead tree beside a pool, with the mesa's high wall to the north beneath a darkly cross-hatched sky.

How many miles could a sun-racked man walk? How long for a hale man on horseback to travel the same? What could be so important for a man to so laboriously record the route back to it? And what would cause the same man to take his own life instead of the journey?

The pictures showed the way, a way which could be followed.

If a person were so inclined.

Royce provisioned himself and his horse for eight days of scant eating and some water, trusting that the pool by the dead tree would provide a place to replenish. He set off at dawn, riding into the sun, with Doc Sutton expecting his return in a week.

Late on the first day he saw a cactus bearing a similarity to a forked scrawl on one of the uncertain pages, compared each side with the lay of the land, and was encouraged. On the second day he passed a low butte, whose ghost he now recognized in the same image, a disturbance of the level horizon which he had ascribed to the artist's fatigue. Soon after he saw the mesa, far ahead.

For hours a line of greenery ran almost parallel to his path, hinting at a source of accessible water, if not on the surface then at least close enough that roots could reach it. As the sun descended, with the mesa finally looming, he spotted what amounted to an oasis nestled at its foot.

He found a spring-fed pool, freshened his flasks and made camp. His horse drank its fill, but Royce was troubled in the night. It was hard to imagine the artist had missed this place. What compulsion could drive a person so relentlessly as to ignore water in the desert?

Near the end of the third day—spent entirely alongside the high flank of the mesa—Royce saw the dead tree ahead and the ghostly shadow of the pool at its foot. The water here was stale after the freshness of the oasis, but his horse was willing to drink. By his best guess, he had covered in three days what had taken the artist seven or eight. Only four pictures charted the journey from the barrow to the withered tree now at Royce's back.

He bedded down feeling confident. Plenty of food still, and full flasks once more. He mused on what awaited, childish dreams of gold twinkled as sleep descended. Maybe he should cache some food here to make room in his saddlebags for treasure…

He stirred: *no.* Whatever the spoils, he wasn't so foolish as to sacrifice survival to them.

Next day, the mesa dwindled behind in an emptying landscape, the world flat and barren in every direction—just as the pictures showed. The hours drew out long, and he spared the horse hard-riding in the heat, halted on open ground as darkness came, and slept under turning stars in the chill.

But with sunrise, he woke to find a long finger of shadow pointing towards him from out of the dawn-sharp distance. He didn't need to raise the pictures to recognize its source.

The shadow shrank as he rode towards it, the finger beckoning him on.

The barrow was nothing like the grand structures his grandfather had described. It was ten feet at its rounded peak, roughly circular and weathered smooth, the same dense-packed earth he rode. He dismounted, hobbled his horse, and approached the last on foot, free hand close to the holster on his thigh, the artist's life's work grasped in the other.

The entrance showed only thick shadow within, its floor sunken and obscured, layered with detritus which his sun-strained eyes could not make out.

Barrow-ghosts, said an echo of his grandfather's voice.

Royce drew his pistol, ducked his head, and entered. But as his eyes adjusted to the gloom, the word which came to his mind was not *barrow* after all, but *burrow.*

The sheriff awoke in utter darkness. He got to his feet, one hand instinctively raised overhead to press the low ceiling of a tunnel which he didn't recall entering.

An amber shadow drifted in his vision. The tunnel mouth, waiting steeply above.

Something made him turn, to look deeper into the throat of the earth, but he saw nothing in the absolute blackness that lay below.

He began to climb, hanging heels communicating the sharp angle of ascent, knees bent with each step, hand brushing the silken smoothness of the tunnel's surface. As the tunnel mouth drew closer it slowly revealed the inside of the mound, cast dimly in sunlight through the opening to the world outside. At last his head emerged from the slanting threshold, and he stopped…and looked back.

He found no sucking depth. The absolute blackness of the tunnel had risen behind him to this cusp, its throbbing pressure like sheenless oil somehow not bursting from its well. He had the sensation of a gaze upon him, the closeness of a face staring long and shamelessly into his own—but he saw no rustling, chittering thing filling the tunnel, no maw agape with needle teeth that clung without piercing, that drew in whatever they touched, manipulated it, presented it for scrutiny by too many eyes.

Some vital aspect of mentality collapsed in that moment. Or perhaps all that was gone already, and he was only the illusion of a man, still standing after taking a mortal wound, not recognizing death had already occurred.

The word *Royce* would have no meaning were it spoken to him.

Sunlight pooled hot-yellow before the white arc of the hole. At his feet the artist's pages were scattered, only the freshest leaves of a long fall. There were maps, both precise and rough-drawn; carefully kept diaries; long texts that had the mad, rambling look of confessions; detailed charts of distance, time and direction—but far more beneath them, older, drier sheets, crumbling and illegible. There was a tattered tanned skin, scraped smooth, the ghosts of its painted lines fading into non-existence.

All marked paths to this place in their different ways. A powerful new idea was born and took hold of him: *he must do the same.*

He stooped to leave the mound and found the sun halfway to the horizon. His horse waited stupidly in the glare, head lowered into the shadow of its own body for lack of any other shelter. The sheriff frowned. Why had he come here? Some person in need, some crime? Not something one lawman could handle alone, though. He would need more men.

A wash of relief took him. Yes, to bring others here, that was what he must do.

He snatched the horse's bridle when it shied from him as it never had before. No paper in his saddlebags, no pen—he could only tell them the way. Carry the information.

"East out of town," he said, freeing its legs.

He heaved himself into the saddle, muttering under his breath as he yanked the beast into submission, ignoring its rolling eyes.

"East, past the butte and the oasis. To the mesa. Always east."

He knew, somehow, that his return wasn't needed, and that the need wasn't his. But if he couldn't give a map to those who must follow, he could *be* the map that brought them.

"Alongside the mesa, past the dead tree and the pool."

Carry the way with words, as a trail of ants carry food back to the nest.

"East, always east."

He kicked his heels, pointing the horse toward the sunset, the deep orange blazing in his unblinking eyes, cutting tears from them.

"Dead east," the sheriff said, "dead east." And kept saying, riding west.

Sister to the Sea
By Jordan Hirsch

The sand slid past my feet as the water receded. I'd finally arrived.

The ocean had always been three weeks' journey away, but now it spread out before me in a way I'd only seen sand do. The rolling waves and constant motion were like a storm, mesmerizing in their steady rhythm. A different blue from that of the sky, but nearly as big.

Cold and smelling of salt, the water was all that was with me, no one else in sight, no structures up or down the coast. Every village I knew depended on water and clung to it like a heart's beat.

I headed north to the trees. Trees aren't so different from us, needing fresh water to live.

From the mouth of the river then inland, I came upon a village, bustling and mostly alive but not right on the coast like I'd imagined. The breeze off the sea is often too cold, I was told. And the Saronai. It was more so the latter, the quiver in the villagers' voices giving them away when I'd asked.

The Saronai. The sea ghosts.

Our winds in the desert don't only carry sand; we have plenty of ghosts, but none of the kind I was looking for. The sea ghosts could only be found in the water. And I needed to find them. I needed their help.

I introduced myself to the village healer as Naoba, a desert-dweller, then quickly got to the crux of my journey. "How do I find the Saronai?" I asked.

The healer's face blanched. "You can't find them," she said leaning closer. "They find you."

That wasn't helpful. "But how?"

"A young girl like you should stay on the far side of town, away from the water."

"But what if I want to be found?"

The healer sucked in her lower lip and went about her business.

I staked my tent on the outskirts of town, the crashing of waves barely reaching my ears. Despite the anticipation, weeks of travel and the rhythmic sound lulled me to sleep, like the voice of my sister, Kasara, steady and soothing after I'd awakened from a nightmare.

"Well, have you ever tried to count them?" she'd asked.

"Why would I? It's not possible to number the stars." My voice was hushed like hers, our hands gripped tight together.

"It's not possible because you haven't tried."

She couldn't have seen me roll my eyes in the dark, but I'd suspected she'd felt it.

"Give it a go." I'd known what she was doing, even at the time. It was her trick to help me calm down from bad dreams.

"Fine. There's Chisa. Hordus. Iayia. Tarjan." I'd named a few more, but impending sleep had made it harder to think.

"What about the stars in Estayya the Hunter? What are her stars?"

I'd named what I could till I'd drifted off, sleeping next to Kasara till morning woke both of us.

I started awake in my tent, pulse beating in my ears. I was alone, the half-moon's glow illuminating my solitude.

Opening the flap, wiping sleep from my eyes, I tiptoed all the way to the shore. It was as silent as the desert; the waves settled in for a night's rest as well, gently lapping at the shore, the water almost inviting. In the dark, though, the sound of water drifted my mind back to that day, back to the sound of splashing that would echo inside me forever.

The gentle landing of waves on the sand rose and rose to a crash, and the pit of my stomach rose with them. Face sweaty and hot, I threw up in the bushes.

I lifted my head back up, wiping my mouth on my sleeve. I was no longer alone. Someone stood in front of me, moonlight drifting through a veil of a face.

"You search for us." Their voice was a screeching felt in the roots of my teeth.

It took me a moment to find my own voice, gorge rising again. "I do," I finally managed.

"We have killed for less." The screech was nearly unbearable, but I winced and held my ground, refusing to wipe the blood that trickled from my ears.

"Then kill me if you must."

I don't know where my audacity came from, but having lost my sister Kasara, losing myself didn't seem so bad.

"I'm looking for my sister," I said after they didn't respond. I saw no recognition in the black voids that must have been their eyes. "Kasara Nooun. Do you know her?"

The Saronai hacked and spit, but nothing hit the bushes. "Do you have no ghosts in your desert to bother?" Their screeching caused less pain this time.

"We do. I asked them." Again nothing, and my adrenaline and patience both waned. "They haven't seen her."

"And you think we have?"

Nodding, a feeling like a knife in my chest staggered my breath. "She died by water. Drowned. I thought the Saronai might be able to help me."

Something in their face flickered like a cold flame, chilling me in a way the midnight breeze never could. "Come with me."

"Where?" I wondered for a moment if they were going to kill me.

"Mother Earth is mostly water, just like her children."

I followed behind, gazing straight through their being. We reached the sand of the shore, so different from the sand I knew. Ocean sand was less abundant and more sacred. The door between two worlds.

They walked into the water without a word. Hesitating only for a moment, I followed.

The waves caressed my legs then hips then stomach as we descended. Despite the cool coastal air, sweat dotted my hairline and my palms, and I kept my eyes on the sea ghost, their vaporous form beginning to glow as it submerged.

My toes worked hard to grip the sea floor as my chest slipped below the surface. When I was up to my neck, the water like a claw around my throat, the Saronai guide disappeared, the wisping top of their head drifting under. Panic flooded through me, and I gasped for air, realizing what they were asking me to do, where they were asking me to go. I couldn't force my foot to take another step.

I glanced back to the shore, looking at how far I'd come. "Kasara," I whispered, plunging under before I could change my mind.

I forced my eyes open; the Saronai was inches from my face. I fought the scream back down into my chest, mouth clamped shut against the water.

Turning, they continued their descent, and I followed for a few steps, but my chest already burned for lack of air. Looking up, the surface of the water hovered a foot above me, and I kicked off the seabed, rising toward the air and toward life.

Something grasped my arm and pulled me back down. I flailed, legs kicking; my vision telescoped down to a point.

The Saronai placed one hand on my chest, grabbing my tunic. The fingers of the other hand, somehow much more solid underwater, pressed against my throat.

They pushed.

My mouth filled with water; I couldn't help it. Water cascaded down my windpipe, and I saw my sister, blue-lipped and lifeless, on the shore.

"Kasara!" I screamed.

But I was still breathing. I was not dead. I had not drowned.

What in hell had they done to me?

They turned, continuing their descent into the darkness, their glow lighting my way.

And I kept breathing, or whatever I was doing.

We walked, wading through the water at a snail's pace, and I lost track of time, mind and eyes focused on each next step in front of me. It might've been minutes. It might've been hours. Down there in the stillness, time didn't feel the same. The sea swam by me in rivers of current, but despite the dark, I saw fish and seaweed and many creatures I didn't have names for. The road to the home of the sea-dead teemed with life that couldn't have been found amid my hot, arid sand.

Following the Saronai closely, I didn't let myself think about where I was. From the moment I'd lost Kasara, I'd known what I'd needed to do.

Older than me by only a year, we'd both been born during the rainy season. Mama had said that was why Kasara loved water, even though I didn't. She'd learned to swim early, passing afternoons at the oasis whenever she could.

She'd been bold and wild and full of life.

Until she wasn't.

My Saronai guide and I topped a seabed ridge, and what looked like a village spread out before us. Dilapidated boats, makeshift huts, and mounds of debris dotted the valley floor, ghosts moving slowly between.

My guide turned, gesturing for me to follow them down.

As we entered the town, if I could call it that, glowing, mist-like faces slowly swiveled towards us. I kept my head down, hair drifting in and out of my view, peeking out from time to time to see the other Saronai around me.

There were so many; how devastating, all these souls whose bodies had died by water. My heart ached deeper for Kasara. Was she there?

I hoped so. I hoped not.

A glow approached me with the slightest displacement of water, and my eyes met a cold, blank stare. We held gazes for a few steps, and they opened their hollow mouth. The screech pierced me straight to the core. My bones shook with brittleness as the sound resonated in me, and the pit of my stomach swirled with eddies.

I sped up my steps, nearly crashing into the back of my guide.

More Saronai came near, and each time my eyes fell on their translucent faces, they screamed with the voids of their mouths. Closer and closer they came, forcing my guide to slow. Before us, behind us, on both sides of us.

Is this it? I wondered. *Was I brought here to die?*

The screams. Rusted hinges, bark stripped from trees, the cry of a desert cat hot with anger.

The sea ghosts pressed in around us and grabbed at me with their moonlit hands, nails long and black. The weight of their touch surprised me; the ghosts had substance in the sea.

As panic gripped my chest, I remembered a different hand on my back. A touch light and gentle guided me out of my dreams and into the sunlight dappling through our tent. "Time to get up," Kasara had said, hand rubbing between my shoulder blades. "I know it's early, but we have to face today."

I'd kept my eyes closed, pretending I was still sleeping.

She spoke again. "Naoba, he's going to leave whether you're there to say goodbye or not."

She'd been right, and I'd known it. And her hand on my back had been so comforting in the too-early morning, so fortifying in my father's leaving.

"You'll regret not seeing him off," she'd said. "We may not see him again." I'd held my breath at this. "But even if we don't, we'll not be alone. We'll have each other, Nae." And she'd rubbed my back till I'd given in, dressing and stumbling from my tent to hug my father goodbye.

Will Kasara have substance if she's here, too?

They scratched, they screeched, they clawed, and then they went silent. Before us, the Saronai split, making a path for me to continue on. But no—it was not for me. Someone drifted toward us.

Kasara! Sister!

No.

It wasn't.

Their hair was smothered coal, their eyes a starless night, and the grin on their face—crooked and sharp—made my knees buckle.

I turned to run, but the other ghosts held me with iron grips.

A screech sounded behind me, soft and melodic down here in the water, and somehow I understood it.

"Naoba," they said, and I turned at my name. "You come to us with purpose."

They knew my name, and I suspected they knew my purpose, too, but I had to respond. I knew I would die if I didn't. "I seek my sister, Kasara."

Something struck the back of my neck, pushing me to my knees in the silt of the seabed.

"You will address me as Saron," they said.

"Yes. Of course, Saron. Forgive me, please." Ignorance was not equated with innocence in this kingdom of the dead.

"Most on your shores hide from our faces, but not you. You've sought out the Saronai and have met our gaze boldly." There was a rustling silence—an impatience. "What do you seek?" they asked in their bird-of-prey voice.

"Saron, I seek Kasara, my sister."

"You think she is among us."

My tongue felt twice its normal size. That day had been beautiful. Hot and breezy, with the sun pushing us toward the water. We'd swum all day, shirking chores and letting the oasis's small waves plug our ears to the sounds of our mother's future scoldings. I had wanted to go home, but Kasara decided to take one more turn around the pool. I stood on the shore, letting the sun bake me dry, and she dove under the water in the middle, where it was deepest.

She didn't come up.

I waited and waited, and finally, I rushed into the water, planning to swim out to her and dive as deep as I'd needed to save her, but I was afraid of the depths.

I'd looked out to the last place Kasara had been before sprinting off in the direction of our village. It was already still as a grave.

"Yes, Saron," I said. "I do think she is among you."

They cocked their head to one side, black hair drifting around their face. "Why do you seek her?"

"Saron, I miss her." Their stare was blank and uncomprehending. "I was hoping to find her," I continued, "I was hoping to see her. To be with her again." The ache in my chest deepened, tapping into parts of me I hadn't known could hurt. "Without her," I said, "a part of me is missing."

Saron's eyes flashed, and they grabbed me by the neck, lifting. "You would try to take one of our own from us?"

"No," I choked, toes clutching for the sand below me. "I wanted"—each word was a struggle—"to see her one last time."

"You lie!"

"To say"—I tried to shake my head, but they held it in place, a vice—"goodbye."

Their grip tightened further, my sight fading with it. "You come here uninvited to steal from our number."

"No…"

"You disrupt those who have passed on for your own purposes. As if the living hold more value than the dead."

They were right. I had disrupted them, had sought them out down here in their seabed home. But if they thought I valued the living more than the dead, they did not know my love for Kasara.

I'd arrived back at the oasis with two older boys from the village, the first people I'd found that I thought could help.

I'd thrown up then. I did so every day for weeks, crying too hard to keep down any food my mother forced into me.

And then I'd made up my mind. Kasara had said we'd always be together. It wasn't her fault she'd not been able to keep that promise. So I'd trekked three weeks through the desert to find the Saronai. If Kasara was with them, I could at least live on the shore, near her.

Never had I valued anyone more than my Kasara, living or dead. But I couldn't say this.

"Kasara," I forced her name through my constricting throat.

A twisted grin split the Saron's ember face, their eyes ablaze.

I hit the seabed, sucking water like wind; they'd dropped me.

Over the rush of consciousness coming back, I heard Saron speak, and I wished they'd kept their grip until they were finished. "You are not welcome among us."

The Saronai dispersed as quickly as they'd gathered. Rubbing my neck, tender and already bruised, I rose to my knees.

She's not here? Where else could she be?

She was not with the sand-ghosts of the dunes. She'd died by water.

A pressure on my shoulder—my guide beckoned me to follow.

Retracing our steps, my eyes stayed glued to their feet as my tears mixed with the salt of the sea. We crossed the hills and valleys we'd come through, working our way back toward the shore. My guide never turned back to look at me, and the water around me was heavy and still as night.

Until suddenly, it wasn't.

A flurry of motion came toward me from behind, and the shallow surface above me became waves.

Something caught my hand, pulling me back.

I turned.

And there she was.

Kasara.

My lips parted in a sob, and her black eyes were deep pools of sorrow as she pulled me to her. I hugged my sister for the first time in months, the substance of her like freezing mist, her breath on my face like the fog in the morning, even in this underwater hell.

But I didn't care.

Kasara. My Kasara.

She'd escaped to let me know she was here, despite what I'd been told. To be together again as she'd promised.

Her face was hollow and disfigured, no eyes where amber used to shine, no mouth where her reassuring smile used to be.

I had too many words to say. I clutched at her hands, her wrists, her shoulders. I touched her face, now bony and sharp, and she flinched at first, then she reached for mine, too. I never would have forgotten how my sister looked, the curve of her nose, her butterfly lips, but now I memorized every line with new desperation.

We embraced again, and then she pulled away, eyes on my guide, something knowing and urgent passing between them. "You must go," Kasara said, her screeching voice nothing like her living voice. "Before the light hits the water."

I followed their eyes above us, and just barely, the sky through the water was lightening.

Kasara pushed me then, and I stumbled to stay on my feet. She clasped my arm in a bone grip, helping me balance but leading me toward the shore. She and my guide moved more quickly then, and I did the same, wondering why we were rushing. We rose and rose, and the sky lightened and lightened, and Kasara dragged me on, never dropping my hand till we reached the shore.

Her dark brows furrowed as she looked at me one more time, stroking my cheek. Then she hugged me, hand rubbing between my shoulder blades, and when she let me go, she gestured to the water line.

It was time for me to go back to the land of the living.

Ascending the last few steps toward the shore, my head broke the surface. The crisp and clean air filled my lungs, making them ache, making me cough. It smelled of the sea but not like before. Never again would it smell as it had. In the east, a sliver of sun peeked over the horizon, and I wondered how long I'd been down there. How was it already morning? How was it only daybreak?

Coming the rest of the way up the shore, peeling my hair from my forehead, I looked to my left. A boy stood in the sand, his fishing nets ready to be cast, his eyes as wide as they'd go.

I'd scared him.

"Hello," I said. "Sorry to startle you. I'm Naoba."

The boy fell to his knees, clutching the sides of his head, and I stepped toward him, reaching out a hand.

I pulled it back; it was translucent as the fog coming off the sea after a storm. My other hand, too, was barely there, merely mist in the dawn.

"What's wrong with me?" I said.

The little boy groaned in pain as his ears began to bleed.

"Moonshine"

אוֹר הַיָּרֵחַ

By Emily Ruth Verona

Benny told me to hide in the barrel. And when your brother tells you to do something, you do it. So, I crawled inside without complaint. Benny told me not to make a sound, because he's not supposed to have me here while he's getting the cases ready. So, I crouched down quiet—pinching my nose 'cause the barrel smells like whiskey and damp.

Footsteps—I can hear 'em—big heavy boots. *Thump thump thump.* The boots ask Benny how the shipment is coming and Benny tells 'em it's going good. Real good. Goes on and on about a whole lotta nothing. Just shooting the breeze. Saying how he likes working these quiet nights all by himself. Believes they're good for right, proper, heavy thinking. That's Benny. He knows how to weave words together in appealing ways. They aren't necessarily fine words, but they sound honest. He has that way about him—an approachable quality you don't always find in big brothers.

I give up on holding my nose, breathe in the whiskied air. The boots offer Benny a smoke. Benny ain't supposed to smoke. Momma tells him not to, but he won't listen to her and he won't listen to me when I talk like her. *Little girls don't have to be just like their mommas,* he says—never minding the fact that he's exactly like our momma. He's got her brown hair dark like burnt firewood and green eyes; her grim moods and a laugh so loud it almost sets your ears ringing. Sometimes when we walk home at night after shul, under the moonlight, I don't recognize him. Just like I don't recognize her. Benny says it will happen to me too, when I'm older, and that I won't mind it. He says eventually it's all the same. Looking and not looking. Feeling and not feeling.

Hiss. The striking of something, likely a match. A sharp, crisp sound set against the emptiness of the barn. Benny must have accepted the smoke. No surprise. He never says no to a Lucky. But he's told me plenty of times not to mention the smoking to Momma. Says it will worry her and she don't need more worry in her life and even though he's right I know it's not why he wants me to keep his secrets. It would make Momma angry to know Benny collects spare Lucky Strikes from the fellas at the still; how he keeps them in our father's old cigarette tin under the loosest floorboard by the dresser. Benny doesn't like upsetting Momma—or, even if he does sometimes, he doesn't want to do it all the time. No. He's afraid of her just a little bit. More than a little, most days. It makes my stomach sour when he's afraid—because it takes a lot to make his hands tremble and his head stoop—the green of his eyes sinking like something disappearing deep down in the sea. Gone forever. Lost. So, I haven't said nothing yet. And I won't either, no matter what Momma asks or how she asks it. Because I love Benny and I don't know what she'd do to him if she caught him in a lie.

"Wallace wants you driving five extra cases out tonight, that gonna be a problem?" ask the boots. I can picture Benny shaking his head the way he does, bangs swinging side to side. They aren't too even, I know, because I'm the one who made them uneven. 'Cause there was no one else around to do it and Benny doesn't trust Momma with a blade. I even kept a little cut of hair for myself, tucked it into the small wooden box Momma gave me for my birthday last year. Sometimes, when the moon is teetering high in the late-night sky, I go and check on that lock of hair. Because I want to see how the colors move under the shine of the moon. It never looks to be any different than it always does, but that hasn't stopped me from checking all the same. That hair is a part of him, which makes it part of Momma and part of me. But it don't feel like me. It don't feel like anything. It's just hair. And hair has no heartbeat.

I'm trying to breathe real low now—real quiet but every breath feels like a rush of wind booming all around. Mighty. Fierce. Monstrous. I want to clap my hands over my ears, but I know that won't stop me from breathing loud, so I press a palm tight across my lips—letting air in and out only through my nose. The smell is terrible but it helps, I think. Hope. It's impossible to tell. Everything sounds louder in this barrel. A deep dark everywhere and nowhere all at once. I want to get out, but I can't. Benny will get in trouble with the boots. And we can't have that. No, sir.

Benny ain't even supposed to be working for Wallace no more—Momma warned Benny he'd get himself pinched driving hooch all over town the way he does. But Benny told Momma she wouldn't be able to get a decent drink if fellas like him didn't drive the hooch. And Momma always needs herself a drink. So, she can't say nothing to that. You'd think Benny would be fond of the liquor he risks his life for but I've never seen him touch a drop of it—not even when he manages to make it to shul on the Sabbath, even though Rabbi Shimshon has special permission from the government to use real wine. Not moonshine. Real or not makes no difference to Benny. He says drinking too much of any of that stuff makes you ugly, like Momma. Swears if I start on it then it'll make me ugly too.

I shift my weight. The hand across my mouth smells like earth and grass. I want to escape. I want to sit under the moonlight, stare up into the starry sky that stretches from one side of forever to the other. I can feel those stars glowing—that moon humming—even if it's dark in here. I can feel it in the way the hairs stand on the back of my sweaty neck—in how my toes press deep, deep into the wood of the barrel, desperate for the soft tickle of grass. It's hard enough to breathe as it is and so I let my hand drop, fingers all knotting together. I want to move. I'm itching for it.

My brother tells the boots five extra cases are no problem. No problem at all. He says it in his usual, amiable way. Benny knows it's better to be amiable, even when you don't want to be. That's how it is sometimes or—when you're young—all the time. Benny says I have to be amiable with Momma, even when I'm mad. That she can taste my anger when it hangs too long in the air between us. And when you're mad at Momma she goes ahead and gets mad right back.

The smell of tobacco's sinking into the barrel now—I can taste it in my mouth—but I don't move. Not an inch. It's what Benny said to do. And when your brother tells you to do something, you listen.

The boots ask if Benny knows why he'll need the extra cases. Benny says he don't—which must be the truth. Benny only ever lies to Momma. Never anyone else. Never me. Momma says he lies to me all the time, but she's the one whose lying. Besides, I'd know—I'd be able to tell—if Benny was being false with me. Sisters can always tell that sort of thing.

"The feds stormed Lou's place," the boots explain. "Shut the whole enterprise down."

"That right?" Benny asks.

"We think someone tipped 'em off…"

"Really now?"

"It's the only way they could have known."

"Not the only way."

"Maybe," agree the boots. "But it's more than likely all the same."

A *click* like ice fissuring beneath your feet. I hear it clearly, one of those little sounds that comes out big in the quiet of the night. The cocking of a pistol. Momma made sure Benny and I both learned to recognize that sound as soon as we were old enough to know that sounds could mean something. Because sometimes, if you're real lucky, whoever's preparing to shoot won't aim true straight to the heart and it can give you a chance to get away. *Don't count on that though,* she's told us time and time again. *Hunters aren't the kind who miss.*

Momma knows more about all that than me and my brother put together. She was there when our father died—me just a babe in her belly. Benny a scared little boy clinging to her skirts. Benny remembers that day—I'm sure of it—but he won't talk about it. No with me. Not with Momma. He can't even think about it without that look crawling into his eyes—something hateful and soft and wounded. Like an animal bleeding out all alone with nowhere to go.

"We think it was you, Ben," say the boots.

My brother laughs. He's always laughing too much. Even when things aren't funny. Even when it'll get him into trouble with the fellas at work. With girls. With Momma. I could live out the rest of my life in this very barrel, not hearing another soul for years and years, and I'd still remember the way Benny laughs. High and loose. Not quite a cackle but almost as sharp. "Me? You're saying—you believe I went to the feds?"

"Unless we've got two of you on the payroll."

"You might," Benny replies, probably giving one of those easy shrugs of his that are never as easy as they look. "You'd be surprised."

Benny's being cheeky now. He shouldn't be doing that. He knows better than to be doing that. It only ever gets him into trouble. My knees ache from crouching and my feet are starting to cramp and I want to leap out of this thing—grab Benny by the arm and make him apologize. Before he says something he can't take back. *We live with our mistakes until they won't live with us anymore.* Momma says that all the time.

"Sorry, Ben," say the boots.

"For what?"

"What has to happen now."

"It don't have to."

"But it does," the boots continue. "And you knew that when you went running your mouth, too. You knew it Ben and goddamn it, you did it anyway."

"Wasn't me."

"No one believes you."

"What's believing got to do with it?"

A shot. A bolt of sound in the dark. *Bang!*

My skin jumps off the bone, but I don't move. No. Benny said to stay in the barrel.

Something like a *thump* follows, Benny don't carry a gun which means he's the *thump* not the *bang*. I listen, ear pressed to the wood. I want to look—more than anything I want to look—

The next sound I hear is a scramble, my brother—I'm sure of it. He's pulling himself to his feet. Not a hunter's shot, then. A hunter's shot would have gone through my brother's heart. Left him dead on the ground. The boots start moving just as quickly, I can't tell in which direction, then stop again. "*Jesus Christ…*" the boots mutter.

"I told you," Benny croaks. The words are garbled. The bullet must have hit him in the throat. "It wasn't me."

The boots say nothing. Because there's nothing to say.

"Guess it's my turn to apologize," Benny adds, spitting what I'm sure is the bullet out into the dirt.

I know what comes next—I've heard it plenty of times. When the moon is full and Momma tells me to stay in bed and the wolves howl all over, from every which way. So, I cover my ears. Hum the mourner's kaddish to myself. The one we say every year on the anniversary of Daddy's death. The prayer for the dead. *Yit-gadal v'yit-kadash sh'may raba…*

When the boots start screaming, I stay put. *B'alma dee-v'ra che-ru-tay, ve'yam-lich mal-chutay.* Even as those screams turn to shrill, sharp shrieks. *B'chai-yay-chon uv'yo-may-chon uv-cha-yay d'chol beit Yisrael.* And then wet, bloody, helpless sounds. *Ba-agala u'vitze-man ka-riv.* I don't move an inch. Not one. *Ve'imru, amen.*

Even when it's all gone quiet and that red metal smell floods the barrel, I stay put. Because it's what Benny said to do. And when your brother tells you to do something, you do it.

Karakondzhul in Love

By Koji A. Dae

The Earth closes like a wound, and I claw into it, searching for some flap to peel open. Nothing heals that quickly.

But no. The rooster has crowed, and I am left alone.

I sink my teeth into the roots at the base of the tree. It's harder above the surface, and the sap tastes too sweet. Still, I drink.

The fluid carries thoughts. Memories of the surface. Plants. Animals. Humanity as more than prey.

I spend months clinging to the Ironwood's roots. Its wide canopy shades me, but the watery daylight burns my eyes and makes my pale skin blister. Breezes rush at me, as I have rushed upon so many souls. I do not fall, but my inadequate flesh puckers tight enough to split. I learn that pain ranges from dull aches to sharp stabs, and I envy the humans and their quick deaths.

Again and again, I try to burrow into the Earth, but my horns crack and my claws bleed. Below, my cousins hissed and murmur, "The tree must die. Chaos must reign." When I was with them, we attacked the tree together and grew fat on its blood. On the surface, the howling wind drowns out my lonely voice until I forget our mantra and the fury it bred in me.

A new voice whispers in the quiet. Stories flow into my mouth. Myths invade my mind. The tree tells me of man and religion and destiny. It calls me Kara.

I hate it. I spit out the sap and leave the tree.

I take one step away from it. My cloven hooves crack. I take another step into the sunshine, and my skin sizzles. I hiss and step back into the tree's shade to wait for night. I'm determined not to suckle the tree, but my jaws ache to gnaw.

The moon takes too long to rise, and I cannot resist. I let the tree fill me with lies.

My horns don't grow back. By spring, my skin has toughened enough that I am able to wander during the day. I can walk nearly an hour away from the tree before my jaw tingles, and I can get to the edge of the nearby village before it seizes. I try to trick it with other trees, but my teeth snap their branches and my claws, even weak and brittle, tear out their roots. I always return to the Ironwood, but not until blood runs down my chin from my teeth clenching so hard.

When I return, green things have budded. I gnaw them off, refusing to let the tree grow.

My gardener, the tree laughs.

I seethe but gnaw and suck and learn of the humans. I learn of the other animals, too, but the tree is obsessed with humanity.

The first time I see you, I'm not quite sure what you are. A human, yes. I've killed enough of those to recognize one. But the way you lean back on a rock, your bare feet dangling in the icy stream, confuses me. You're like those shiny objects the humans set out to distract us. We get pulled in by their glitter, then are tied to counting each of their perforations until half the night is wasted. Your playful voice is the shiniest of things, though. If the men set out their daughters, we'd be so distracted by their charm that there wouldn't be a single human death during the dark days.

My skin's blistering, and I should return to my tree's thick canopy. But I lean closer until my weight pulls me forward and I stumble heavily toward the rock.

Your song is cut short with a gasp. You gather your apron and socks to your chest, scramble from the rock and flee.

I run, too—I run through the patch of forest, up the hill, and back to my tree. I set to work on the newest leaves, even though there are far too many for me to tame.

The tree laughs.

I take down an entire branch, but it doesn't dull the tree's amusement.

My pounding heart slows to the rhythm of grind, grind, suck, breathe. Like a baby, I allow the tree to lull me to sleep.

The next day I return to the rock, but you're not there. I circle the rock, sniffing, but all I find is a sock. I pull the soggy bit of wool from the water. It pricks my skin, but I hold it close to my chest.

By midsummer, I've scouted the outskirts of your village, and I know you lay your laundry near the southern wall in the morning but take your afternoon walks towards the apple orchard. While I've watched you, I've gathered boots left out at night, a white shirt with red and black symbols sewn around the collar and sleeves from the washing line of an old woman, and pants from your laundry basket. None of these things are comfortable, but when I put them on, I look enough like a human that you won't scream.

The only problem is my teeth. It's impossible to hide the three rows of sharp, cutting things unless I keep my mouth shut. But if I concentrate on walking upright and don't talk, I can pass for a man.

On midsummer, I step boldly onto the path near the apple orchard and wait for you.

The day is long and hot, and I almost turn back to the cool respite of the Ironwood, but if I lose my nerve today, I may never meet you properly.

We bump into each other, and you laugh. It's a tinkling sound, and I'm counting the holes in it until it stops abruptly.

You wait, and I can tell you want me to say something. I smile, just a bit.

You back away, frowning, then murmur some excuse and return to the village.

I'm particularly vicious with the tree on my return. I want to pull it from the ground and reach my cousins. I do not want to be stuck on the surface, fascinated by a mere human.

The next morning, I set myself on that path again. This time you stay longer, filling in the blanks I can't explain. I must be unable to speak. You've heard of that before. It must be a lonely existence.

I nod encouragement at your speculations, but they die off after one or two sentences. My mind wanders. I wonder if I've ever killed one of your cousins. Maybe your grandfather.

Again there's that frown and a flash across your face like maybe you recognize me for what I am. Then you're gone. Back to the village.

We meet like that for a dozen mornings. We draw close, like two wild animals getting used to the scent of each other.

You explain how you know everyone in the village, but haven't seen me before. I must be new. Visiting or passing through. Perhaps I am staying in the cabin just over the next hill.

You point beyond the Ironwood, and I nod eagerly.

Your smile is like sunshine and wind all at once, but this time it doesn't hurt. I shiver and realize that just like pain, pleasure comes in variants and degrees.

I step closer to your warmth.

You don't back away. You turn, but not toward the village. Instead, you continue on, and you allow me to follow.

I can't talk to you, so I begin talking to the tree.

"She's wonderful!" I say while sawing off branches. I lick my lips. I've come to like the sweetness of the tree. "She knows so many things, and she talks so freely." I snip off a flower. "I could listen forever."

You won't have forever, the tree reminds me.

I grumble and set to work on a larger branch, closer to the heart of the tree.

You have a destiny, Kara. You'll tend to me, you'll fall in love, and you'll die.

"And if I refuse?"

The tree says nothing. I curl myself up near the trunk and claw idly at the Earth. I no longer try to get into the nest of roots that was my home for so long. It seems like a lifetime since I fed on mania and mantra beneath the surface.

Before long, my belly aches for more sap. I climb the tree and begin pruning. The damned thing's gardener.

Every day, we meet at the orchard, and I think you're as eager as I am even though I give nothing to our conversations. You talk about the weather and the village. Who does what. Which crops you help sow and how much you love embroidery. Within weeks, it seems natural to tuck your hand in my elbow and lead you to your favorite rock. I sit beside you, and you dangle your feet in the water.

You insist I should take off my boots as well, but I know they cover cloven hooves as out of place as the teeth that silence me.

At first you're playful in your request. You splash and tease me.

But two days later, I've still not given in, and you cross your arms. You insist.

You threaten to leave.

Maybe you don't know how much that terrifies me.

Maybe you do.

I bend over and slowly take off one boot.

You're barely looking, and I plunge my hoof into the icy water.

I take the other boot off quickly, and I think your gaze finds my hoof, but you say nothing, only smile smugly as I sigh with relief.

Being barefoot is as refreshing as the water.

The sun turns the sky to fire. I don't want to leave you, but the tree calls me. I need to return. Who knows how much it's grown since I left? New branches everywhere, threatening to take over the planet and shroud us in darkness.

I walk you back to the road and bow. You giggle—another cascade of sound that leaves me counting—and kiss my cheek.

Fall turns the surrounding hills gold. I hold your damp hand as I take you to the Ironwood. You admire it in a human way, commenting on the knotted branches and saying the leaves reach up to heaven. I ache for you to make the connection: the roots stretch down in that same curling unpattern. But you do not see the umbilical cord feeding from the Earth's core.

I return you to your village, never stepping into it during the day.

You think I'm a strange man, and you tell me the people in your village whisper about me. They say I'm a devil. Maybe even a karakondzhul. I bite my lips to keep from laughing and hope you don't notice the blood running from the corner of my mouth.

The people don't really think I'm a karakondzhul. I'm nothing but a myth. My tree is old, but not magical. You warn me before they come with their gas-powered chainsaws, expecting to rip through the branches in the name of growth. I hide nearby, in the always sickly undergrowth, and laugh at their attempts. The tree bends their metals and exhausts the strongest of men. The bits of dust they manage to scrape off float into the world to sow fortune, and the tree continues to grow how it will. A bit like you.

You tell me about the village, the way your father demands your obedience and your mother wants you to find a husband. You hold me with your words later each evening, but every night I sleep with the tree. As the days grow darker, I feel the vibrations of my cousins hacking at its roots. On the full moon, I bare my teeth and gnaw at the Ironwood. The exquisite bark sends shivers down my spine, and the sap runs like blood in my throat. I drink to keep it from covering our world. I eat and stop it from growing up to heaven.

I prune and wait for the dirty days. More darkness. You seldom leave the village, and I pass the cold hours alone. I wish I was wrapped around you instead of this tree. But I can feel my cousins stirring. They're anxious. Excited.

I gnaw off one of the lowest, strongest branches. This time, the tree gives itself willingly. The usually hard wood melts between my teeth and doesn't solidify until I have fashioned a sharp and unbreakable sword.

"The holidays are coming," you tell me. You pick at the threads on my shirt, then scoot closer to me. I'm not sure if you're cold or you're offering me your warmth. Either way, I wrap my arms around you.

You grow quiet, giving me more space to speak. I say nothing but kiss your cheek, far back by your ear so you can't see my teeth.

"I'd like you to meet my father."

I squeeze you tight.

"I dreamed you were called Kara."

Another squeeze, softer this time. Listen to the tree, girl.

When the dirty days begin, you are inside, celebrating with your family. The drunken revelry floats down the road we've walked so often. I inch nearer until I can feel the warmth of your fireplace. The warmth of your smile. Your arms.

I hesitate at the door, my arm raised. There, near the straw mat, a shining colander draws my attention.

I bend down and run a finger over it. You put it out here to protect your family from creatures like me.

It's difficult to turn from its shining metal and black holes and even more difficult to turn from the warmth of your family, but I must.

I trudge to the coldness of my tree and wait with my sword. The canopy shuts out the moon, and there is complete darkness.

My eyes are useless, and unlike my cousins, I've come to depend on them.

They scurry by me, running to cause mischief.

I wait. Let them have their fun. Your home is protected, and you believe the stories enough to not step outside until the sun comes up.

When they have left, the tree begins healing its roots. It drinks deep of the Earth. I feel it turning plump. But I also feel the slithering beneath it. The wet ground shifts as the serpent wakes and makes its way to the surface.

The serpent's scales reek of an evil I once bathed in. Its breath is sulfur. I shake in its steam as it emerges. I am not strong enough. My sword is not good enough. This is a god, and I am a mere monster. But I think of you, waiting for me to say something, and I take a fighting stance. This is the only way I can say I love you.

The fight is brutal. I slice bits of it. Dodge its claws and sharp teeth. Scramble away from its poison breath. It heals and attacks again, hungry to join my cousins in their revelries. But where they create mischief that might end individual lives, the serpent knows no restraint. I fight exhaustion as much as the god. Please, let dawn rise.

The watery sun comes up and the serpent slithers underground. My cousins skitter around me, wrapping into the roots. They will rest for the day.

I should, too, but I need to see you.

You tend my wounds and, for once, do not ask questions.

"I should boil water. Or make a fire to keep you warm. I still don't know where you live."

I point towards the tree.

"Ah, yes, the cabin on the other side of the dell. I could take you there. Make up a fire, boil tea."

Your kindness makes me smile so much I reveal a single sharp tooth. You back away.

"No, of course. You like your privacy."

I want to say thank you for being so kind to me. But there's only one way to do that, and I'm not sure if I'm strong enough to do this for twelve days.

• • •

By the final night, I'm more blood than skin. I won't make it. I was never meant to. But the impossible happens, as it does every year. Dawn comes, and the serpent returns to sleep for another twelve months. My cousins, too.

I catch the slowest one and hold desperately to its ankle while the first rooster crows. It turns to me with anger. How could I betray it so? How could I condemn it to my fate?

I lock eyes with it, twisted and pale from underground life, gnashing its teeth. The Ironwood will harden it. The sun will bronze it. It will be fascinated by a girl or a fox or maybe just the way the sun glints on the mountain stream. Next year, the only way you will be able to tell it is not a human is if it smiles. Or speaks.

To Guard a Garden

By Kevin M. Casin

Jeffrey was a flower once. It's how he knew George enjoyed the fragrance of hyacinths. But Jeffrey had never been a hyacinth, so he brought gardenias, a flower he had been, and hoped George would love them too.

"They remind me of buttercream," said George, clicking the stand-mixer into place and commanding the paddle to whip air into two flaccid sticks of butter. He wiped the residual sugar from his brown hands and gently cradled the plastic bouquet. "Mmm but they smell…"

Jeffrey watched the fleshy chest expand, the broad nose flare and vanish in the bleached petals, and the man groaned, and Jeffrey smiled—George made that sound because of Jeffrey and he knew he was on the right track. Anutenda would be most pleased with his progress.

"They're beautiful, Jeff. You're coming back later, right?" He asked, plucking a kiss from Jeffrey's white lips.

Jeffrey nodded. "Dinner's at eight. I'll come by at seven to pick you up. Anu is so excited to meet you."

With a slender pair of silver shears, George maimed the gardenias' roots before slipping the stems into a vase by the register. Flowers weren't meant to be kept in a porcelain jar, Jeffrey wanted to say, they belonged in the ground, with roots intact and worms to keep them warm. But Jeffrey kept quiet. Abominable behavior by humans that Jeffrey had to ignore for the sake of saving his home.

George wrapped his arms around Jeffrey and scooped up his lips. For a long while he held them. Jeffrey liked kissing George, the softness of flesh pressed on flesh, of the rhythm one fell into after a moment, of the tingling urge to push further, to feel more, explore more.

"Oh," he said when he bumped into the register and the chime of the drawer opening made him tear away. "Mmm let's leave all that for dessert."

It had been eighteen months since Jeffrey had "bumped into" George in the fields just outside the city. He was hoping to build himself a house among the wild hyacinths and gardenias the area was so famous for, he had said. George seemed kind. He never snapped a bud or bloom with his boots. Jeffrey trusted George would tend to his family with care, but it was Jeffrey's home to protect. It was his duty to never let anyone take it. Not even someone as beautiful as George.

George ran his hand through Jeffrey's curls and planted another eager kiss before Jeffrey headed for the door.

"Oh, do you want me to bring anything?" George asked.

Jeffrey paused and turned around. There was one thing he could bring, one crucial piece of the plot.

"A vase."

There was little to say on the ride to Anu's cottage. Jeffrey was too nervous anyway. Everything had to go right, if the plan was going to work, and it had to work. George had only said one thing that evening and it was as he slipped into the passenger's seat.

"I closed on the land today," he said, closing the black door behind him, the darkness hiding Jeffrey's frown. "I want you to move in with me. Would you be into that?"

Jeffrey was ready to explode. He had no answer. He let the question linger as he watched the silver towers of the city grow small in his rearview mirror, as frail white pines that guarded fragrant fields devoured the human world. He caught the For Sale sign bordering the spring fields, *his* fields, and the neon red letters that said "SOLD!" sparked a quiet rage. How did humans deal with such emotions? His senses told him to twist the leather on the steering wheel and block out the anger swelling inside himself. That land belonged to Jeffrey. Who was this human to ask *him* if *he* could live on *his land?!* Jeffrey sealed an unkind response behind his lips. If he snapped now, George would insist on stopping to talk about it. There was no time for that. Anu was waiting.

Her cottage sat far beyond the reach of humans. Once Jeffrey left the highway, he made for the lonely, gravel roads where the weeds bloomed. The bog musk was strong, but as he grew closer to the cottage, the stench softened with the warm air of the pine trees and the fragrance of gardenia hedges. And he saw the brownstone walls. They peeked out from under a straw-thatched roof consumed with ivy and a single coffee-framed window barely seen from behind overgrown ferns and grass. These were all but wonderful fractions of Anu's haven for wayward flowers.

"We're home," he said, yanking the key from the ignition with so much enthusiasm he nearly tore it out of the machine.

He threw open the car door, slammed it shut and got all the way to the porch before he realized that George wasn't behind him. He did the "what's up" gesture, but could hardly see what was happening through the glare of the moonlight on the windshield. So, he shuffled over to the passenger door, set his shadow on the glass, and peeked in.

George, whose hands were nestled tight between his legs, seemed ready to melt.

"What's wrong? Come on," Jeffrey shouted. His voice echoed off the brown manor, but he was sure Anu was likely still sleeping anyway. A few loud noises weren't going to wake her up.

"George," said Jeffrey, opening the door. "What's up?"

George's eyes were fixed on the dashboard. His fingers squished the seams of his jeans. Jeffrey knew this behavior well. He had to speed the discussion along. He had waited long enough for this night. No one was going to keep him from it.

George huffed and said, "It's okay if you don't want to move in. I'm not trying to guilt you or pressure you. I shouldn't have said anything. I know it was too soon. I'm sorry. I didn't mean to mess anything up."

"Everything is fine. No problem here." Jeffrey said, reaching into the car and taking the man's hand. "I'll move in with you, whatever."

George snapped his head and glared. "Whatever?" He unclicked his seatbelt. To Jeffrey's relief, George slipped out of the car, but to his horror, he was storming off in the wrong direction.

"Come back!" Jeffrey shouted.

"I'm going home," said George, shoving his hands into his pockets. Jeffrey hated these tantrums.

Still, Jeffrey ran after him and blocked the way with open hands, gently placing them on George's cheeks. He wanted to smush them, to purse George's pink lips into a perfect blossom. Jeffrey often wondered if George had been a flower once too.

"I'm sorry. I didn't mean that. I just wanted to get you inside."

George's small nostrils flared. He swatted away the hands and roared, "Whatever is what you say to a trick who just asked if you were dating other people. Whatever isn't what you say when your boyfriend of a year and a half asks you to move in!" He took a breath. His body softened as if love dropped from his bones. "I bought that place for us."

It was Jeffrey's turn to tense up. It was *HIS* place. The human couldn't have bought *HIS* field for them both. He was stealing it. Plain and simple. But he took a breath. The end of this plan was so close. He just had to get George in the house.

Jeffrey set his hands back on the plush cheeks. He could pretend the field wasn't his for a little while longer.

"Thank you, babe," he said. "I love that you did that. I really will move in with you. I'm sure the field…land is beautiful."

George broke into a beaming smile. He threw his arms around Jeffrey.

"Thank you," George whispered into his neck. It carried a gentle warmth, like the sun resting on petals.

"Come on. I'm starving," said George as he pulled away and slipped his arm down to Jeffrey's waist.

"Oh, almost forgot." George reached into the car. "The hyacinth I bought. For your mother. I hope she likes them."

It was strange. Jeffrey hadn't noticed the soft gray vase George had tucked under his legs as they drove was filled with soil and a green sprout quivering in the center. It was a baby.

"She could plant it in the garden," George added. "You told me about her famous gardenias. I'm the hyacinth. It can be us."

It was as if he knew what Jeffrey had been, but how? He would never have said anything about his flowerhood. That would have ruined the plan. Some humans had talked about the mysteries of love. Perhaps this was one. Maybe Jeffrey loved him too. But the plan. He needed his field back.

Jeffrey approached the oak-crafted door and unlocked it to welcome George into the lonely halls. He offered George a tour and took him around the lower floors where he could set down the vase. As they went up stairs, George gasped at the sight of the chandelier, and they paused for a kiss in the bedroom Jeffrey pretended was the one from his childhood—he had to sell it. If the human wasn't stealing his field, maybe he could love him instead of leading him to the end of the hallway, to the den of Anu.

"This room is beautiful!" George said, breathy, marveled at the glass-domed sun room saturated with exotic plants. "What are those?"

He strolled down the riverstone path, each finger caressing a different plant, as Jeffrey offered their names. He honored each tall and wide and velvet and fenestrated leaf of the voluptuous aroids hanging and bulging and unfurling with a name. It was a shrine. One held sacred to all who were given flesh by Anu. She slept still. A little further.

"Oh this would be a great place for it," said George, who promptly, gently took the vase from Jeffrey and set it by the gray stone, in a nook the other plants had prepared. It was perfect. The light streamed in just enough, the earth was loose, and Jeffrey sensed the others would welcome it.

"We just need to get her some fertilizer. These hyacinth'll make the most beautiful flowers that way." George looked back with a smile. He seemed…to care. Maybe the land would be okay with him. No, the land belonged to Jeffrey.

"Leave the vase on the plot," said Jeffrey. "The plants will take care of it."

Jeffrey had expected the man to react. It wasn't usual for plants to tend to themselves, but George only smiled, trust in his eyes. "Come on. I want to show you something." George slipped his hand into Jeffrey's, locked as if nothing on Earth could tear them apart.

Jeffrey led him to the center of the conservatory, to gardenias bathed in moonlight pouring a crystal eye at the zenith. He paused at the edge of the bed. These were Anu's brothers and sisters, born from the same gentle soil he longed to rest in once again. This would be a nice place too. He watched George take in the rich white bed, like the buttercream he loved to make; the streams of silver light raining down; the crystal above keeping the mound alive.

"Selenite," George said, "up there. It's a high-energy crystal. Didn't know they got that big. What is this place?"

"A sacred place. Anutenda, we call it. A haven for all plants in need. Come on. Mother would love to meet you." Without question, strangely, George came with Jeffrey as he stepped into the center of the mound. "Don't be scared. She'll love you."

"I'm not. I'm good with you."

He did something Jeffrey didn't expect. Jeffrey closed his eyes, poured his will into the moonlight, imagined his energy slithering down through his feet into the gardenias, tickling their roots, and asking them to wake their mother. It was a simple process, but one that didn't involve a kiss. As if awakened suddenly, Jeffrey inhaled, taking George's lips with him. Two wills burrowed into the garden.

"Whoa," said George, breaking their kiss, "they're glowing."

But Jeffrey didn't care. He wanted more. Something in his chest felt tight, like a hole had been carved and George had to fill it. He reached out for George, gently set his hands on the man's chest and nuzzled his cheek. George was distracted, but his lips found Jeffrey's ear, "Later," he said, "look."

Jeffrey had seen Anu wake before. Though, he had never shared the moment with a human. The gardenias were aflame with light striking each pigment, brightening them into a flood of white light. The plants of the conservatory looked to the mound and bowed. Anu had come, she rose once again for her children.

"You know," said George as roots slipped from the soil under their feet. The gray vase appeared beside them and rose between them, "I'd heard stories about this place. Rumors mostly. Everyone in town was afraid of the house in the woods. I was scared of it. Never in my wildest dreams did I think I would come here or, hell, buy land in the middle of nowhere for some guy I'd just met. But I'm not scared anymore. I don't get scared with you." He looked down at his feet, at tendrils coiling around his ankles, slithering up his jeans. "I'm not scared."

Jeffrey felt the tug at his feet, Anu calling him home. But he wanted his garden. This wasn't his home. He had fought so hard to save it. But if George had bought it, maybe it was safe, maybe Anu could send them there if he asked. This isn't the way Jeffrey had thought his journey home would be like. He had envisioned leaving George in the vase, assuming his life with the magic of Anu, and returning to the garden as a human protectorate until Anu's blessing was gone. Plans could change, he supposed. He could go home with George.

The roots crept up Jeffrey's chest, reaching his neck, and he took George's arms, already covered. And George welcomed his lips. The lovers smiled as the roots covered them completely, never breaking their bond, and Anu guided them under the earth, carefully, painlessly breaking their bones, melding their skin, unraveling their blood, fastening their roots.

Jeffrey had never been a hyacinth. He would never return to his field of wild hyacinths and gardenias. But he found a new home to protect and a new hyacinth to love.

The Last Guardian

By Fatima Abdullahi

You slipped through the opening because it was your last resort. Your quest to prove everyone wrong led you to dangerous paths, and perhaps in another life, you would have known the wisdom in staying away. But alas.

The rough splinters of the narrow doorway snagged on your ragged clothes as you walked through the vastness of *Jangare*[1] and commenced the study of The Boundless.

You had never been a particularly dutiful student. You had talent, but no fortitude. You did not come out of a craving for knowledge, or a desire to improve the world. You came only for yourself.

You thought it would be easy. You had always managed to scrape through whatever life had thrown at you, after all. You thought it would be so this time as well. You were wrong of course, but you did not understand that yet.

When the *Aljan*[2] led you to the room with the single platform suspended amidst nothingness, then you understood. When he left you in the darkness, a single lusterless lamp to light your world, then you understood. When the door dissolved after him, leaving nothing but smooth, pale marble in its place, then you understood.

Fear found you first. And there *was* so much to fear. The constant shadows that moved on the walls. The skittering on the edges of the platform from beasts you could hear but could not see. The wispy figures in the corners of your eyes that

---

1. *Jangare* is the mythical city of the *Isoki* in Hausa folklore.
2. *Aljan* is the Hausa word for Djinn.

vanished when you turned your head. You dreaded waking up, and you dreaded going to sleep.

Misery followed, fueled by the hunger that followed you like a faithful hound. You were fed only once a day from bowls you never saw appear, and while you may have been the black sheep of your family, prior to arriving at this place you had never been denied food. And then there was the cold. It seeped into your very marrows until you all but forgot the memory of warmth.

You abandoned hope soon after. Curled up in the middle of the raised dais so you did not accidentally roll of the edge, apathy descended on you, until you spent weeks or maybe months in a haze that would not lift; a fog that clouded your mind and sunk so deep you felt like you were turning to mush.

When anger finally arrived, it was with a sudden rage that had you screaming at the walls and tearing at your skin. You had never angered easily, so perhaps it was without surprise that your anger quickly burnt itself into resentment. That was also an old friend. With your diminutive height and skittish disposition, you had always been a ready target for bullies and the bitterness they caused. And here you learned to nurture it.

Towards your father, who had never had time for you. Towards your mother, who had never loved you enough. Towards your siblings, who had always overshadowed you. Towards your few friends, who only hung out with you when they had to, and who never noticed your loneliness. Towards the one you had been fool enough to give your heart, who had chosen another. And finally towards yourself, for not being worthy of them all. And for being stupid enough to come to *Jangare* seeking The Boundless. You'd thought it would give you something to live for. Something to take you away from the ocean of regret that was your life. Something that would make those who scorned you finally see you as worthy of their esteem. Instead you had been trapped into this interminable prison, with your dreams of glory shrunken about your neck.

But finally, after all your emotions had been wrung out of you, you settled yourself, breathed in and out, and began.

How far does knowledge go?
As far as the mind goes.

You had wondered why you did not see this fabled Guardian of The Boundless as you were led in. Most of you still thought it was all nothing but a story told to frighten children, even if you *had* passed through the opening.

The story went that the Last Guardian—who was also *Baleri and Duna and Barade*[3] all at once—was the custodian of all knowledge, bound into what was called "The Boundless," and all who sought the two out and had the nerve to learn, would attain that knowledge for themselves. The catch—because there was always a catch—was that the Guardian had to be defeated before the student would be allowed to leave. No one who went seeking The Boundless had ever returned. They came anyway.

The platform shuddered as you steeled yourself and addressed the nothingness, *Where do I start?*

A great tome appeared out of the dark, landing in front of you with a thud. You reached forward slowly. The pages were infinite, so that no matter how many you turned, more just appeared. And then you realized, *this* was The Boundless.

You searched for the selfish things first. *How do I get endless power? How do I become the richest in the world? How do I hurt those who have hurt me?* And the answers were given, but none of these things mattered if you could not escape your confinement. So you questioned, *How can I leave this place?* And the answer, *Defeat the Last Guardian.*

How do I do that?

You cannot. It is impossible.

You wanted to weep with this knowledge. You wanted to wail. You curled into a ball on your suspended floor, and gave into despair.

---

3. *Baleri, Duna,* and *Barade* are all powerful spirits in Hausa folklore.

The stars turned. The tide rode the sea. The moon fell and rose in the sky. Morning came and went, night on its heels. Or so you assumed. You could not, after all, see anything beyond the darkness of this room. But finally, finally, you picked yourself up, and decided to try again.

You turned to the tome and searched for the simple things. You sought the tricks to better illuminate your abode, and your weary eyes thanked you for it. Then you sought the spells to create food, and you were rewarded. You had to retrain your body to accept your new meals, but it was worth it in the end.

When you dredged up the great knowledge of the entire universe in a bid to shorten your stay, you almost went blind. The runes flashed before your eyes in flame and shadow and your head rang fit to burst. You bled from your eyes and your ears and your gums, and you soon slipped into unconsciousness, defeated by that which you could not comprehend.

When you woke, you finally sat and really thought. You spent an entire day on your knees, your meals left untouched. You sat and contemplated and considered, and then you stood up once more. Everyone who came here came with a plan. A list of all they wanted and sought to accomplish, but you now knew how foolish that was.

So, after you uncovered the knowledge to protect yourself against harm, you looked into The Boundless and requested, *Teach me everything I need to know.*

And you were taught.

And taught.

And taught.

You did not know at the time how invaluable it was—seeking what you needed, instead of what you wanted. You did not know how great a leap you had just made, by humbling yourself to what was greater than you.

You were taught the knowledge of the seas and the land they partnered. You were taught of the beasts of the earth and the people they hunted. You were taught how to summon the mystics and how to chain the lesser spirits, and how to uncover the secrets hidden beneath the very bowels of humanity.

You learned to wield fire and snow and ash, and learned how to make them do your bidding. You were taught the power of illusion and the power of *knowing* the names of things. You were taught how to acquire strength and how to diminish it. You were taught of ancient languages and cultures and texts, and of curses and charms and light magic. You were taught courage and bravery, and guts and valor. You were taught all that you needed to know.

When you finally stopped to rest you realized you did not know how long had passed. Your hair had grown to the middle of your back, and your hands now had wrinkles. You were thinner and older and it scared you; the possibility that if you ever left this place, there might no longer be anyone alive who remembered you.

It was then that you realized, you had to find a way out.

How far does knowledge go?

As far as the mind goes.

So you tried again to gain information on the Last Guardian. Other names you did not already know, powers, strengths and weaknesses, but no matter what you sought, the pages of The Boundless remained blank.

So you inquired about those that came before you, hoping to be gifted some hidden morsel of intelligence that had escaped them. Their lifeless forms fell around you in heaps, burying and choking you with the stench of rot and decay, until weeping and crawling, you raised your hand in desperation and chanted the spell of banishment, and they disappeared. That would be you one day, you understood, if you did not get out.

Once, you would have been too scared to continue, but those days had passed.

You circumvented the knowledge regarding those that came before you, and instead sought mastery over what had been used to build this place. Lines and lines of text appeared before you and you rejoiced. You learned them and memorized them and repeated them again and again, until your voice became hoarse and you could speak no more.

You spent months honing your physical body to match the strength of your mind, and sought the art of healing to compensate for any injury you could not prevent. Afterwards, you spent an entire day just looking at your room, and all that had happened to you here, and knew you were ready.

You closed the great tome in front of you, looked into the nothingness, and called to the Last Guardian of The Boundless to come and face you.

How far does knowledge go?
As far as the mind goes.

What was thrown at you was nothing you had ever known or experienced. You were torn and shredded, beaten and burnt and drained. When you called for all the knowledge you had gained they did not fail you, but they were battered aside so easily you wondered if they had been worth it after all.

You had never known a being of such power. You fought demons and wights and shadows that had been summoned from Beyond, and they almost consumed you. Your energy was gone, your will turned to dust. You were wrung out and twisted, and your soul was hollowed. Bound between the boundaries of air and water, between light and shadow, the manacles of your failure lay cold against your skin.

At last, at the end of all your strength and your wits, for a space of time that lasted no more than the moment between the rising of a foot and its falling, you were there on the threshold of escape, and then you found yourself again on the platform, in the room without end, and you knew then it had only been an illusion.

You swore and prayed and raged, until you thought all the world must now know the color of your voice.

You pleaded for mercy and relief and made promises, until your lips cracked and your tongue bled and your tears turned to sand.

You cajoled and threatened and bribed until you had offered all that you had, with nothing left to bargain with.

Finally you sat on your unmoving platform, and leaned your head in your hands, weary and defeated.

And then you raised your head and looked at me and asked me to let you go.

And because you were the first person who had ever thought to simply ask, I did.

Your Ballad from within His Gourd

By Ai Jiang

I sat, back turned to the windows, a blindfold over my eyes. If I shook even slightly, the thin fabric might flutter off. I remained still, fearing the taboo might cause bad luck to find me again. I'd already lost both my parents, and soon, Liyue too.

Maybe what I needed to do to change my fortune was taboo. I itched toward the blindfold with my fingers, but before I could tug it off, it was whisked from my face. In front of me stood Liyue, a secret held at the tip of her tongue. She waved the blindfold above her like a flag and gestured past my shoulder.

The warmth of her breath tickled the exposed base of my collarbone. Liyue flitted out of Aunt Yeyu's hut. I followed, the faint scent of lilies from Liyue's robes guiding me.

The villagers surrounded us in a semi-circle and in front of them was my nineteenth birthday feast: overflowing bowls of frog legs, meat of rabbits, tusks of a wild boar decorating its own severed body, and wooden cups filled with sap. Everything was set on uprooted stumps, tree leaves, baskets woven from vines and sturdy, thick twigs. The celebration was the same for all the children coming of age in the village. The only thing that differed were our titles and who we would become. Often, our professions followed that of our family—what they had taught us growing up, and if it was more than one thing, we had a choice.

Choice was rare.

For demon hunter families, it was nonexistent. There were already so few remaining.

Aunt Yeyu's small frame wavered. She clutched at the sealing cork at the mouth of Father's gourd, the smooth tea-stained yellow body almost shrouded her face, but it reached only chest height for me. I knew it was as light as air, even given its heavy-set appearance and the knowledge that it held thousands of demons captured across generations. I hadn't seen the gourd since it was hidden away after Mother and Father's disappearance. I reached for the stone charm engraved in the shape of a peach around my neck, given to me by Father when I was ten.

Aunt Yeyu's voice was cautious. "Your father wanted to craft a new one for you. But I thought perhaps you might prefer to inherit your father's instead."

Because he's dead. Keep this as a memory, a token, a reminder. She didn't say these words, but I imagined that was what she thought.

"Thank you," I said, accepting the gourd.

The sun rose. The first rays pierced my eyes, and a hush washed over the celebration. I felt no different, but some of the villagers looked at me as though I were a god. I searched for Liyue. But when I found her among the crowd, she looked troubled.

When the feast concluded, Aunt Yeyu avoided looking at my face even as she pulled me back into the hut. Everything within was cast in shadow by a single standing candle.

"I had hoped you'd be only like your father and nothing like your mother," she said.

I was surprised at Aunt Yeyu's harsh tone.

With her eyes focused on something past my head, she said, "Multiple families told me that their daughters have begun asking, pleading for you to wed them."

I immediately thought of Liyue. None of the girls in the village had paid me any mind prior to this day. The only reason I could think of was that I was now a full demon hunter, though it came with great honor, few wanted to be betrothed to one given that high risks of the role.

"Why?" I asked.

Her eyes fixed on the gourd I placed next to my bed. "Your mother's blood." She paused to swallow. "She isn't who you think she is."

Why don't you let me tell him…sister. A harsh whisper came from behind us.

Mother.

I turned to the gourd, mouth hanging open. Aunt Yeyu's lips pressed so tight I could barely see them.

"M-Mother?" I called.

The voice was unmistakable, dipped in honey, like a flutist's fluid melody. But there was a roughness, an edge I didn't recall being present in Mother's lullaby voice.

Erzi.

Mother's voice turned jagged with each word and tone.

Did you miss me?

I thought I had, but her voice called my loyalty into question. It sounded more like…a demon.

Aunt Yeyu saw the question in my expression, but her response only dried my tongue. "It's your mother."

"But how?" I asked.

"Jiuweihu," she uttered the specific demon's name, the nine-tailed fox, after a moment, then left the hut, leaving me with the flickering candle, threatening to extinguish at any second.

Before the door swung closed, I saw the watching eyes of the village's maidens transfixed on me. Liyue was not among them. Perhaps once I would have desired such lustful gazes, but they only unsettled me now.

"Mother?" I called, wanting her to speak, to hear her voice, but also worried about what she might say.

You are a half demon, erzi.

I leaned away from the gourd, even though I knew she couldn't see or touch me. "I'm a demon hunter."

Laughter rattled the gourd. *A half demon that hunts other demons? Surely you know how that would be received.*

"I am my father's son." My voice trembled.

You are also my erzi.

The allure, the love Father had for Mother that bordered on obsession now made sense. And my love for her growing up as well—none of it was real. It was all simply a part of her demonic charm. But Father was a careful man, he would have never allowed himself to be charmed by a demon, a jiuweihu.

"Where is Father?" I said, pounding my fist against the table.

Is that how you speak to your mother after we've been separated for so long? It's been years since he first sealed me in this gourd. I haven't seen him since. How he grieved when he did so.

"Why would Father grieve after having to seal a demon?" Even as I spat the words, I desired nothing more than to return to my youth, settled within Mother's arms through autumn's chilled breezes and winter's snow.

He loved me, just like you. You still do, don't you?

I didn't admit it, but I knew I still did. But her reference to Father as though he were dead caused a boil within me. I picked up the gourd and brought it to the garden out back. I didn't want to hear her voice any longer, even though the familiarity brought me momentary joy, her words only brought me pain.

I was to be a demon hunter, not the demons I would hunt.

Mother remained silent through the night, but my thoughts warred at the choice to free her or keep her imprisoned. But releasing her meant releasing all the other demons Father had trapped in the gourd throughout the years, along with those Grandmother had caught before him.

Before night left, I pulled out aged paper from Father's desk. With a small hunting knife, I sliced my finger, allowing the blood to bead then pour into the ink holding. I dipped the rabbit-hair ink brush, still tinged with pink from previous use, bristles stiff until it met the blood of a hunter. I painted the sealing enchantments onto the five demon talismans, waited for them to dry, before folding and packing them into a small sack secured to my waist. There was another peach charm dangling by the opening of the sack.

I wondered what Father had given me these charms to be protected against—Mother or myself.

When the sun returned, I would go on my first hunt—a rite of passage for demon hunters when we turned nineteen. The knowledge of being half demon would not sway me from the path I dreamt about since I began training at the age of eight.

The monk who taught me was expecting me to report back with my first sealed demon. Most hunters returned within days—the fastest was within hours.

Tomorrow was also Liyue's birthday. I would find her before heading to the mountains.

In the morning, I hoisted the gourd onto my back, securing a red braided rope across my body. Over my shoulder I secured a bow half the size of Father's next to the gourd, but it worked with Father's needle-like arrows, pooled in a quiver I fastened to my waist.

On my way to my usual meeting spot with Liyue, the gourd quivered against my spine. I imagined Mother's fists pounding within its hollow. The walls quaked with each blow. I couldn't feel its full force, but the thought of Mother's violence through my robe, against my naked skin, caused my back to arch in attempts to detach myself from the gourd.

Mother, no doubt feeling my resistance, pounded harder. Never before had I felt the will of a demon so strong. Those I have practiced hunting under the guidance of my mentor were demons far lesser—small mountain creatures of little concern. The other demons trapped within the gourd were silenced by Mother's presence alone.

Enough, I wanted to say, but held my tongue out of respect.

Release me, she said, her breaths audible—deep and low.

I checked the sun; I had to hurry before Liyue would wait no longer.

Mother laughed. *Free me, foolish erzi.*

"No, " I said. "It's his duty and also mine," I rationalized, speaking more to myself than to Mother. "To find and seal evil, and to keep it imprisoned." Perhaps that might mean one day sealing myself, though as long as I posed no danger to others, I would set out to carry forth what Father would have desired for me.

Tongren, there is evil inside us all, just as there is good.

I flinched at how strange my name sounded coming from someone who should be familiar. As I recalled my study of demons, and in particular, jiuweihu, I said:

"…But you tricked Father into marrying you, didn't you?"

She didn't deny this. *Not trick. Begged. But he only agreed because he truly loved me. And I had to escape.*

"Escape what? Escape who?" I asked.

Dong yao.

I'd heard there were dong yao up in the mountains, nestled deep in their caves, coming out only at sunset or in the dark of night, but I had not seen them in person. I wondered if they were as giant as the legends suggested, as monstrous, as cannibalistic to both humans and demons. If demons were an enemy to humans, dong yao was an enemy to all.

I imagined Mother's panicked state, sprinting on all fours away from her own kind, the wars humans fought, the seeming inability for us to live in peace for long, and I felt pity for her, for a demon, for the first time.

I met Liyue at our usual meeting point: a curling eldon tree growing where the edge of the village met the mountains.

She looked deep in thought, hanging upside down. Her face remained unflushed, as though she had no blood at all. To me, she always had a beauty too perfect to be human, but today she appeared even more ethereal.

"Liyue—"

"I thought you'd never come," she said, swinging upright, smiling. Her initial brightness waned as soon as she spoke her next words. "I'm leaving. Now."

"But Liyue, this is your home," I said. "Our home," I dared, but looked away as soon as her intense stare met mine. "I—" I cleared my throat. "I want you to stay."

"I'm just like you," she said, dismissing my words as though I hadn't spoken them. It should have stung, but I was more surprised by her own words.

A demon.

"I wanted to know what it was like to be human, to not have to always hide in the mountains, running from the dong yao. To have a home that wasn't always moving." Liyue dropped from the tree and stepped toward me. I wanted to step back, but I stood my ground. "I wanted to know why humans despised demons so much."

Looking at Liyue now, I wondered the same. The girl was harmless, unlike other demons I had encountered, like Mother yet also completely different. It became difficult to understand if what I felt for her now was love or pity.

"They're afraid," she said.

"Of course they're afraid," I said.

Liyue looked thoughtful. "What they're afraid of is not being in control—of their own evils, desires, temptations. And somehow, our existence reminds them of this." She sighed. "Not all of us use our abilities for evil, but the thought of losing emotional control for humans is terrifying." Her eyes flicked to my gourd.

Liyue made me question whether having demon blood was truly such a curse. Why had I shunned demons when they were much like humans—some blameless like her while others vicious and cunning. The crash of guilt whisked the air from my lungs, cooled my blood, dried the sweat beading across my forehead.

"I fell in love with the village and its people." She gazed at the mountains, and I wondered if that was where her blood family remained. "But after today, they look at me differently now. They know. A slip up with a rowdy traveler passing through. I had no choice, but the others thought me the villain."

My hands twitched with the conflicting urge to both protect the girl I'd loved but also to hunt her into the mountains. Jiuweihu, in their human form, I had been told, were equally charming, equally vicious. But Liyue seemed simply human, and that was the most dangerous of all.

"I wanted to thank you," Liyue said as she turned for the mountains. "For showing me that humans can be kind."

And in a white gold flurry of tails and fox limbs, she was gone.

What a lovely girl you found, Mother said, as soon as I set off for my first demon hunt, after watching the spot where Liyue had disappeared for an hour. *You love her, don't you?*

I thought I did. But maybe it was her demonic charm all along. The same one Mother used against Father. Or maybe what drew me to Liyue was the unconscious understanding that we were similar, that we had shared blood running through our veins.

"Can I," I thought of the nine tails, the glistening fur, the striking eyes so unlike Liyue's human ones, "shift as well?"

Mother hummed. *Unlikely.*

Though Mother's words reassured me, I wondered if, like Liyue, other demons could sense my true nature.

As I made my way towards the mountain, my mind tugged in two directions: complete my demon hunter rite and to track Liyue, following her instead of returning to the village. But halfway up the mountain, there was a piercing cry that sounded half beast-half child.

When I was younger, Father had brought me on a hunt when I first began my training. There was a small river monster sighting. It was supposed to be an easy hunt, but the demons brought their family. Even with fifty demons gathered, it was still nothing for Father, but to have me as a liability made everything more difficult. He'd lost an arm, I'd almost lost an eye, and Mother almost lost her heart in fright when we returned.

I hurried toward the sound. Mother quaked against my back.

"Tongren!"

It was Liyue.

And it was the dong yao.

I had seen Father trap demons before, but never ones so closely resembling humans. The images of the dong yao in the painted scrolls of my teacher's temple depicted demons' features as far more warped, their limbs muscled but gnarly. Dong yao were supposed to be grotesque, but this demon resembled an abnormally tall and strong man; this demon resembled a stronger, wilder Father.

The dong yao's large hands gripped several of Liyue's tails.

I hurried to nock an arrow, my hands unsteady as I drew back the string, the sweat on my fingers threatening to release too early. I couldn't aim at any vital points without hurting Liyue, so I shot at the dong yao's leg.

It howled and released Liyue.

But just as she hid behind a tree, the dong yao staggered the few steps it took to reach me, and for a moment I was paralyzed by its looming height. I was never great at close combat. By the time I thought to run, to attack with the hand knife hidden in my boot, it was too late. The dong yao's hand made contact with the side of my head, its nails grazing my shoulder, down my arm. I flew to the side, into the tree Liyue hid behind.

"Tongren!"

Tongren!

Both Mother and Liyue's cries echoed around me. Pounding blood rushed to my head, dizzying my thoughts, mixed the two voices together into a demonic garble.

My ears rang, and blood dripped down the side of my face. The gashing wound along my arm soaked my robes.

The dong yao returned for a second swing, and I had just enough time to pull and jab an arrow into his uninjured foot. As I rolled from the dong yao's striking zone, he roared, removing the arrow and breaking it in half.

At half my height, with fur as luscious as silk, Liyue darted forth, her tails whipping toward the giant. The shrill cry of a newborn child left her lips as the giant, with astonishing speed for its height and stocky stature, grabbed her, lifting her into the air.

Before I could free myself from the shock of Liyue's attack, I noticed that this had been her plan all along. Liyue's tail lengthened, gripping the giant's limbs like thick ropes, tightening. The giant thrashed to no avail, only his lips remained free. He grunted, his body vibrating along with Liyue's.

"Hurry!" she cried.

I scrambled for the demon talismans, cursing as I dropped two which were quickly stolen by the wind. The remaining three were stuck together in a clump, the mass flicking back and forth in the strong, churning breeze. My freshly spilled blood had soaked through the words, making them almost illegible. But I had no time to fret and ran forth. I jumped, slapping the talisman onto the middle of the giant's head, whispering the activation words in the tongue of ancient hunters in hopes the talisman would work.

The demon stilled. Liyue kept her cautious hold.

The talisman, rather than holding, flew off. The demon thrashed once more. A humorless laugh escaped me. The same blood I'd used to create the talisman was what also rendered it useless, smudging the characters that had been carefully painted on.

"I'll keep him still." Liyue's eyes met mine.

Though her gaze was firm, resolute, I couldn't help but see the fear within them. She would be locked in the same prison as the giant, the same cage as Mother. Someone as innocent as her didn't deserve it, even if she was a demon.

At that moment, I wanted the fur of the jiuweihu to sprout over my body, the claws to replace my trimmed down nails, the nine tails to push from my back—even if it was just one, it might have been enough. But my rage, my desire, my wish was futile. I was only human with the blood of a demon. I was still charming, but my half ability was useless against other demons.

For the first time, I wanted to be a true demon.

"Quickly!" Liyue yelled.

That was when I realized Father had not trapped Mother because she was a demon.

My grip tightened around the strap that held the gourd to my back as I swung it forth, the cork still firmly screwed tight.

"I'm sorry," I whispered before muttering the words that would loosen the cork, and I fought back the urge to sob.

Liyue mouthed "No," but she looked as though she wanted to take back her words, let loose the giant, and save herself.

She doesn't.

Instead, she said, "As they say, keep your friends close, and your enemies closer. But I suppose we're both, and that makes things a little more complicated, doesn't it?"

I almost wanted to laugh, but the breath that carried the sound choked on its way up my throat, dying before it reached my tongue, before it grazed my teeth.

Like a wormhole, or a pit of quicksand, the gourd drew the two tangled demons toward it.

I wanted to break the gourd before it could take her—my friend, my enemy, my love. But I knew I couldn't, and that thought alone, the chosen inaction, frustrated me more than discovering Mother's secret, my demonic blood.

"Don't worry, Tongren. We will meet again," Liyue said, her smile already melting as the gourd dragged her into its stomach, consuming her, disintegrating her, until she was nothing but specks of kaleidoscopic sand.

"See you again," I whispered, not knowing whether it was a lie or the truth.

I made it to the demon hunter's temple at sundown, and my teacher, the Elder Monk, was waiting by the entry arches.

"Well done," were the only words he said, as he placed two demon coins in my hand. As stoic a man as he was, his face held great pride.

All my life I had trained for this moment, but rather than victory, I felt a wrenching loss. I had learned the same lesson Father no doubt had. We had to be firm in our path and continue to do what we had been born and raised and trained to—to both protect and to seal evil, but sometimes that meant letting go of what and who we loved most.

When I climbed back down the mountain, the moon cast the village in a cool shadow. At the entrance, a few waiting villagers darted back toward their huts upon my arrival, while others came to meet me, including Aunt Yeyu.

Hushed whispers brushed across those who gathered.

My eyes roamed the faces of the villagers, wondering if there were any demons among the familiar. But it didn't matter before, and it shouldn't matter. We were all family.

"I'm leaving," I said.

No one seemed surprised. Aunt Yeyu offered a single nod.

I wasn't sure where Father had gone, or if he was truly dead like Mother believed, but I wanted to follow in his footsteps and hopefully cross paths with him again. Though I knew it meant that I would not only be trapping demons, but also saving them. Even if I didn't end up finding him on this journey, maybe I would finally find myself.

And as I turned, I said in a low voice, "Thank you," but I knew it was loud enough for everyone to hear in the held silence.

Carried on my back were the gentle whispering voices of Mother and Liyue, their reassuring words, along with the now-audible howling, the incomprehensible anger, the violence, the pain of the other demons battling to be heard, clawing to be free. Though I was outside the gourd, it felt as though I was trapped within.

I left the village, but I knew I would return again, even if it didn't seem as familiar as before, even if it had whispered more lies to me than the truth. This was the only home I knew.

A Journal of Strange Creatures and Beasts from Africa

By Damilola Oyedotun

In memory of my Grandfather, Maki Lebongo; hunter, healer, explorer, and hero.

Translated to English with the help of Dr. Scoffield Brixton.
An heirloom for generations yet unborn.
Toutei Lebongo, 1922.

Zaâde

Grandfather woke me in the middle of a soothing sleep. I jolted out of bed without him tapping me a second time. He is the kind of tigerish man you do not want to irk. It was time to leave. As we sat on the wobbly canoe, I asked him where we were headed. "You will see yourself soon when we arrive," he said, maintaining his perfunctory demeanor.

We arrived ashore. Men with grizzled hair awaited our arrival. Clutched to my bag was a leather satchel, inside it were seme blade, holy water, dry roots trussed inside a bottle, cowries and shells, and a pungent powder of a different mixture. Their village was under a spiritual attack, this I later came to learn. Little kids were the common victims. They were placed on lappas, separate from each other. Their limp bodies and sallow eyes remained motionless. Stench of vomit still lingered in the air. The plaque emanated from a child who was the carrier. Grandfather's friend, Dr. Brixton thinks it's malaria, prevalent in Africa. Grandfather thinks it's worse than that.

The child who was supposedly the carrier narrated how he was drawn to the fireflies when the moon lit from its horizon. He caught a few fireflies basking in the threat of the zephyr marinating under the wings of the sky, put them inside a bottle.

The next morning, the bottle had broken. Innards of three cows were splattered on the red sand. Someone must have broken the bottle. But why kill the cows in a gruesome style? Grandfather had a clue. Only a Zaâde could do this.

"Some natives of Badagry have mentioned seeing a hybrid taking the form of a firefly and a human. They say it scouts its areas of hunting for weeks, foraging for where there are many children," Grandfather said. "It doesn't like to be caged for long. It changes into its human form, eating the organs of anything it finds."

Nine children already lost their lives before we arrived. Four were convulsing, ejecting foam, and a brown liquid which I think is a concoction. This creature can only be killed by catching it when it has shifted to a firefly. I was the bait set to catch it. The Zaâde never strikes a spot twice. We traveled thirty kilometers to where it might attack next. Grandfather was right—fireflies filed out in mass, dotting their bioluminescent light to attract kids. Scared, I caught one, quickly placed it inside a bottle.

That midnight we anticipated it breaking the bottle, biting more kids, and infecting them. Right before my eyes, the harmless fly broke free from its restraint, changed into a naked bony monster with fangs. Grandfather darted a mixture of garlic soaked in holy water and granules of lead on the monster. It shrank, shrieked, melted into liquid. The sick children were recovering before we left.

Dr. Brixton says Zaâde are vampire descendants.

Nkikii

Hunters are like trees. When one of its parts is severed, the whole body feels the pain. Monsters are real, undoubtedly. But when you hear of one whose description leaves you in awe, you are agog to see it, even if it's the last thing you set your gaze upon.

Fishermen who fended for their livelihood in the Tujering River reported to the village head about a dragon-like creature.

They said its scaly body is akin to a crocodile's, head like a black stallion with horns like gazelle, elongated like a giraffe—forty to fifty feet long. After we heard of this tale from the fishermen, Grandfather didn't utter a word. He was processing the information. Dr. Brixton thought the men had been drinking too much palm wine. Grandfather sat under a mango tree, flipping through his journal to confirm if he had encountered the beast before.

"Eureka!" he blurted. His Greek was getting better.

It turned out the fishermen were not demented. The creature is a Nkikii. An ancient beast feeding on fishes, and animals who swim in the rivers at the appearance of the crescent. When it gets tired of a conventional meal, it goes for a bigger diet—humans.

The fishermen offered to help us after we requested the service of three fishermen. Their knowledge was luciferous. Grandfather and Dr. Brixton went close to the river. The fishermen were aloof, having pointed to the spot the Nkikii routed. Grandfather clasped his assegai, wore his cowrie amulets and anklets on both arms for protection. Fear was far from the sacs under his eyes. Mother says he has appeased the water goddess, hence, he is invulnerable to the danger that lay therein.

Surreptitiously, tucked in between leaves, grass blades itching on our skin, we waited for the beast. The water rippled, stems wavered haphazardly. The head of the Nkikii sprang out of the water with a heavy splash, quivering the canoes with an ebullient push of the water. The fishermen cowered in fear. Grandfather stood his ground, feet rooted in the sand, pointing the assegai at the creature. He muttered incantations, moving closer as his voice pierced the chilly wind. The Nkikii tilted its head, gnarled, lowering its body. Like a tamed animal, it came down to Grandfather's level, less violent, and fell back into the water.

Delighted, Grandfather was about to leave when the Nkikii stretched its tail to him, yanking him into the waters. The rest of us came out of hiding, hurling stones into water. It pulled Grandfather inside the deep. All we saw were bubbles and ripples. I called out his name. I shouted, hoping he would return to us alive. Grandfather bobbed out of the water, and back inside.

This happened for a while until he stayed afloat. We pulled him out. A scale of the beast was plunged into his thigh.

"It's nothing serious," Grandfather said, muffling his groan.

"Where did it go?" a fisherman asked.

"It won't be coming back," Grandfather assured us. "That's all that matters."

Mbaba Ape

The joy of every parent is to give their daughter's hand in marriage. There is a saying from where I originate: a child who is dead is better than a child who is missing. Grandfather was fast ameliorating from our last mission. Yesterday at cockcrow, we received two male chiefs and a female adorned in *shuka* and coral beads from Zomba. Their story was that some young ladies set to get married were missing. They had vanished without a trace, leaving the families in fear of the unknown.

Grandfather retorted, saying the ladies might have absconded, perhaps, eloped with another lover. Anyways, we took the job, thinking this wouldn't be a tedious task.

Faces of the men whose fiancées were missing didn't shroud the disappointment. Parents of the missing girls had a garland of melancholy around them. Our investigation started at the place the last missing girl was last seen.

"She went to the stream to fetch water," a bereaved mother said.

Ladies who had been missing were last seen on their way to the stream.

"Why didn't you declare the stream unsafe after the first two incidents?" Grandfather scolded the village authorities.

He scoured the area close to the stream, looking for something that might give a clue. Too many footsteps had etched the sand, tampering with the evidence. Finally, Grandfather found something when he used the magnifying glass given to him by Dr. Brixton. A tuft of gray hair hung loosely on one of the jutting rocks west of the path.

"It is an ape," Grandfather said.

Remember how apes take a penchant for a young dame? They are convinced that the ladies will be better taken care of by them, rather than the human partner who will fall sick and die eventually. The Mbaba Ape is drawn to females who are voluptuous, sing mellifluously, trudging towards the stream. It waits for the coast to be clear, then kidnaps them. Its coral eyes have enchanting power, once it stares at its victims, they are locked in its charm, dropping their water barrel to follow it. You can call it a forceful elopement.

"I will lead you to the creature. But I have to warn you, your lovers might not be the same again," Grandfather said.

It wasn't hard finding the Mbaba ape. It resided in the caves, feeding its victims with fruits, catching deers for them to make a meal. He was the polygamous ape with many wives. We trailed it from the tufts of hair strewing on the rocks. The irked men shot arrows at the Mbaba ape, wounding it as it scampered for refuge. They followed the trail of blood, finishing what they started.

The ladies returned to their fiancés. Grandfather was right. The ladies cried, clamoring for the Mbaba ape. The magical aura of this creature would wear out of its victims if they did not see the sun for three days.

I penned down the words Stockholm Syndrome when Dr. Brixton says that's what the ladies suffered from.

Pepo Mwendawazimu

One-eyed beasts are not easily found on the shores of Africa. These are the words of Dr. Brixton. Zanzibar, 1966. A vicious demon camouflaging its identity by day, and shifting to a one-eyed bat by night had been tormenting the indigenes. I remember Dr. Brixton using the word PTSD after examining one of the patients who came in contact with the bat. The victim, a twenty-something-year-old man, couldn't break words when he was asked about his experience. Instead lineament on his face carved out hysteria. Grandfather showed sketched pictures of bats, asking him to point at one which supposedly attacked him. Sweat sprang out of his face. His chest pumped and raced with fear.

The next day we combed caves where most bats resided. Grandfather didn't want to jump into conclusions. The victim was stable for now. Identifying which of the bats attacked him was our challenge.

"These are normal bats," Dr. Brixton said when our gape was set to the frolicking bats.

In truth, the bats posed no dangers of any sort. The only way to know what we were dealing with was to allow the demon bat another strike. And so it happened again. This time the creature had carnal knowledge with a boy. What kind of a beast attacked its victims, and then defiled them.

Settling in our lodge, thinking of a means to end this madness we heard the shout of Dr. Brixton. I have known him to be a brave-hearted man. But by the time we got to him he was seated on one side of the bed, cringing in fear, knees up to his chest, body quaking as though he had seen the unthinkable.

"What is the problem?" Grandfather asked.

Dr. Brixton was already infected because he had examined the original victim. The majority of the villagers suffered the same fate. The Pepo Mwendawazimu had successfully caused a scourge of hallucination. Its victims communicated the disease to those they came in contact with. If only we saw what the creature looked like, perhaps the curse would be broken. Our stay there was precarious. We could fall victims, too.

The shaman intervened. The victims were locked inside a room. Their cries permeated the walls, making my legs unsteady. Out in the open, we brought out cows and sheep from their hovels. The few who were not infected tied the animals to a tree. The victims were released, facing the leashed animals. High-spirited incantations jumped out of the mouth of the shaman, spraying water with leaves from his earthen pot on the victims. No one stayed close to the animals. A bout of loud shrills ensued. One after the other, the possessed victims fell. The animals became crazed, unsettled as they struggled to break free. The infected were set free eventually, loosed of their hysteric hold. We cut the rope binding the animals, watching them go to a destination unbeknownst to us. The shaman says they are going to meet their master.

No one knew the whereabouts of the demon-bat. My best guess, it had migrated to haunt another village.

Egbere

Those who know about the Egbere picture it as a malicious creature akin to a wood gnome. It has the frame of a child, but the stout body of a baba over a hundred-years old. Donned on the Egbere is an outfit of raffia, slung over its shoulder is a raffia mat guarded jealously. An old lantern with dancing flames is carried in its right hand. Grandfather reiterated this tale is common to the Yorubas.

The progenitors of the tribe speak of the creator, a man who traversed between worlds to find a place to begin a new world. In one of his quests, he handed all of his possessions into the care of a man he trusted with his life. By the time he returned home, this trusted servant had absconded with the magical mat which granted humans their wish for anything. For fear of having the mat stolen by insatiable people, the Egbere now takes refuge in the deep woody bushes, skulking under large canopy trees. It has become allies with a few bush spirits, feeding them from his mat. In turn these sentient bush creatures create a façade by making an atrium to confuse hunters.

"Give me back my mat. It doesn't belong to you," Grandfather said, mimicking the Egbere. "These are the crying words of this spirit if you steal its mat."

Grandfather spoke of his friend whom he wanted me to visit. This friend, a hunter who roamed the forest in search of animals, had an encounter with the Egbere. Let me reiterate that at this point this was my first solo mission. I lucubrated, and with sleep deluging my eyes, I turned the pages of Grandfather's scribblings on this creature I was about to encounter.

On arrival at Ile-Ife that night the hunter's wife craned her neck, asking for Grandfather. I did not blame her. Who would send an apprentice to solve a mysterious case like this? The hunter, a man strong enough to hew a wood in one strike. His eyes were red from insomnia. He didn't look possessed. But perturbed by a spirit only he could see.

"Give me back my mat. It doesn't belong to you. These are the words we hear every night when we prepare to sleep," the hunter's wife said.

"Ma'am you need to ask your husband where he kept a stolen item that doesn't belong to him," I said, shifting my gaze back to the hunter.

It wasn't a big house, still finding the mat belonging to the Egbere felt like an impossible mission. That night while I lay in bed, waiting for the Egbere to come wail about his stolen property, I thought about why humans invoked curses upon themselves.

"It's here," the hunter's wife ran into my room, quickening my feet to shamble after her.

The hunter covered his ears, the eerie cry of the Egbere infiltrated the atmosphere, slithering in the crevices of the house. The children cowered in fear, holding each other for comfort. The hunter's wife pleaded for her husband to return the mat. But the obstinate man stood his ground, refusing to give it up.

When morning arrived and licked away every footprint of night, the hunter was nowhere to be found. The longer you endure the ululations of the Egbere, it will eventually capitulate, allowing you to possess its mat. There has been no account of any person surviving the umpteen cries of the creature. They die of emotional torture.

Grandfather shrugged when I relayed the happenings at his friend's. The hunter knew what he was getting himself into when he stole the mat. This was all Grandfather said.

Omiran

Famous for being behemothic, the Omiran do not cohabit in human settlements because of their avaricious desire for food. Their diets are raw meats, basically fresh kills: fishes, buffaloes, wild dogs.

In 1823, Portuguese explorer, Joaquin Roan, came across an anomaly floating in agitated waters in one of his expeditions. The mouth of a whale was ripped apart, the upper jaw missing. He was skeptical about the legendary tales of mythical creatures lounging in the deep of the silvery waters. But this gory sight gave him a rethink. He and his men trailed the blood stains and large footprints etched on dry earth like a meteoroid forming a gorge in the ground.

After weeks of searching for this unknown creature, they found it near a butte with a large deposit of chernozem and clay. It was dead by the time the men saw it. Perhaps, it had fed on poisonous meat. Joaquin ordered the tall house of the Omiran to be ransacked. Amidst the search, muffles from a dark room shook the invaders. They were the Omiran's children, giant babies the height of a mare, big teeth like chisels, callused hands and feet, hunched backs. The last anyone knew of the babies was that they were stolen from their homes, researched upon by scientists hired by Joaquin. No one knew their whereabouts until today.

What was supposed to be a vacation in Weldiya turned into a case of me pleading for the life of a girl. I sighted her mother along the central market doused in a state of Weltschmerz. I had earlier been warned about witches cloaking themselves in the form of helpless women, so I tended to my business of sight-seeing. A few inches to where she was, she gripped my arms, begging me to save her little girl.

"She only caught fish like every other person," the woman's voice soaked in tears coaxed me to give her an audience.

The girl was charged for killing a whale. Upon sighting the child, she was nothing but a twelve-year-old frightened child held in bounds. No way would that child be an Omiran. The only way they could transform to their true form was in the sight of danger. Omiran have an uncovered pot of seething rage waiting to erupt.

I watched the nescient villagers chanting for the girl to be stoned to death. All attempts to speak to the village chief proved abortive. He granted one last request to the child. The girl's mother carried raw eggs in a basket. We watched her break each one of them, pouring them into her daughter's mouth. *What was she doing,* I thought. Consumption of raw eggs is poisonous to Omiran. The woman hadn't moved ten feet away from her child when the girl began to convulse, dropping dead in seconds.

Silence wafted all about until it broke at the increased size of hands and legs and body of the dead girl. She grew bigger and bigger, towering at the same height as the iroko trees. Marveled at her presence, I supposed the raw eggs didn't kill her, but rather forced awake the sleeping giant in her. The Omiran growled, gripping people in her wide palm, slamming them and squeezing them like paper. Everyone ran for safety. From where I watched, she genuflected in front of her mother, carrying her in her palm, leaping away from the village.

Evidence of animals missing vital parts were seen in bushes. The Omiran now lives deep in thorny bushes. It built a home for itself called Onilegogoro.

Dulundu

The Zulus greatly revere witch doctors. They are of the belief that he is an intercessor between them and the gods. For this reason his importance in the village cannot be sidelined. When the night swathes the day in its arms, and gelidity clambers down from the sky, evidence of a bird the size of an adult human is seen.

Night is not for humans, the villagers have been warned umpteen times. Some people peeped from their windows after the harsh cry of the Dulundu pierced the misty fog of the unholy night. They say the flap of its long wings can quench a fire from a distance. The presence of this bird invites thunder and lightning as its sentries. Upon command by the witch doctor, the Dulundu attacks its enemy, draining them of their blood. All of these were of no concern to us until the witch doctor died.

Our host, a nonagenarian man accompanied by men not much younger than him, narrated the recent happenings after the passing of the witch doctor.

"It's a case of an unleashed pet running amok after its owner dies," our host said.

Grandfather cogitated on his yarns for a while, drinking from a calabash filled with undiluted palm wine.

"If the pet owner is dead, why doesn't another person put the pet on a leash," Grandfather replied, drinking some more.

The men gazed at each other, a veil of dreadful look flapped on their faces. The Dulundu is no parrot or finch you cage in your house. It can only be controlled by men chosen by the gods. The village had a problem, else we would not be here. They told us of the bird perching on the roof of houses, crying—a frightening voice that shook the mind of the house owner. Its cries are esoteric. One could tell it was mourning its master, or something of value was glommed from it.

Grandfather was engrossed in questioning eyewitnesses while I did a tour of the village, asking questions about the creature. A little boy scampered by, teased by his contemporaries who pursued him with chickens in their hands. I thought it was one of the ways children played until the scared child burst into tears. Obviously, he had a phobia for chickens. I scolded the boys, telling them to leave him be. The child offered me something in return. Funny. I shook my head in disapproval. But his insistence sent a signal that I better check out what he was offering.

Twilight abounded. Remnants of the sun's vestige hued the sky. Grandfather would be expecting my return by now. I met the boy's mother whose welcoming voice was oleaginous. She and her son conversed in their native tongue. Her voice overpowered his own. Perhaps, the gift I was here to receive was the bone of contention.

"Sorry mister," the boy's mother pleaded. "My boy is senseless. Forget what he must have told you."

I was about to leave when the boy came running over with an immaculate cloth in his hand, housing some round items. Gingerly, he placed the items on the ground. They were three big eggs the size of coconut, speckled with brown on a background of a cream color. They belonged to the Dulundu.

"My husband is sick," the woman said.

I later realized the eggs of this bird have medicinal powers that can heal all kinds of diseases. As expected, Grandfather was furious at my disappearance. We trailed the bird to its next settlement. I have never seen a bird so fierce in all of my expeditions with Grandfather. Its talons were curved, sharp enough to clasp an adult in its grip. The beaks were as a rapier, out of its mouth came vibrating shrills. I placed its eggs where it could see them. We watched it grab its eggs in its talons, flying away from our sight.

"I am sure we won't be seeing killer birds in our village any-more," an elder said.

Grandfather nodded. We were ready to leave. My alter ego questioned me. *What if the bird returns? Would you say you sacrificed the entire village just to save one family?* I locked such a question in the farthest of the secret chamber in my mind. One of the Dulundu's eggs was given to the boy who earlier had it in his possession. The life of his father depended on the yoke of that egg.

Who the Sun Gets to Eat

By Oleander Dudek

The day of my wedding dawned cold. My father claimed it was good luck, for a cold wind meant a warm home, and a warm home meant many children. He set me to laying the fire so some of my good luck would stay behind for my sister's sake. I did the work slowly.

Neither my mother nor my father had met my groom, but my uncle had, as he dealt often with the giants. My uncle claimed he was a good man. My father claimed I would be safe.

My mother braided promises into my hair. When I turned my head, their weight swung into my face and she worried I would get cut, so we tied a kerchief around them. Such braids were only ever done for deaths. This was her only chance to do them for me. They were more extravagant than my brother's, who'd fallen from a tree. They'd had to lay a cloth across his forehead, to cover the wound.

"Keep them in," my mother kissed into my brow. "For as long as you can."

I felt where each bit of the copper pressed against my skull. When I took the kerchief away, perhaps my hair would drip blood.

We had all woken early to wait for who my husband would send to collect me. Winter kept the world dark, though my mother had told the hour by the chickens and claimed it was time. We went outside, for it was cruel to ask a giant to stoop.

I wore my father's best furs for warmth. I did not want to take them with me, but he had insisted, afraid I would catch a chill before I'd ever lain in a marriage bed. They still smelled of sweat and smoke from where they'd hung above the fire to dry. They always shifted in the rising heat, and I always thought them still alive, only lying in wait, hiding their teeth. If I'd asked, if I'd disturbed their slumber, they would spring to life and eat me.

The wagon came over the horizon faster than a blink, for giants had the grandest horses that had ever seen the sun. In a single step it covered the same as ten for a man, and it never needed rest. The horse only stopped because it was forced, head rearing as the driver pulled the reins.

The driver was twice the height of my father, who was tall among men, and when they shook hands the driver's enveloped my father's like a flood.

My sister watched the giant.

I watched the horse.

It was taller than the giant. Its hooves were like claws, tearing up the earth as it waited. Slobber bubbled around the bit, and I thought it bloodstained, for the coat of the horse was gold and copper speckled with dried dark brown. Flies buzzed around its flanks now that it had been halted, and I wondered if they had come all the way from the giants' homeland, or if these were flies I knew, just as curious. The horse's tail kept swatting at them. It kept trying to twist and bite at the largest patches, but the reins kept it from reaching. It was never still.

There was little talk between my father and the driver. He did not acknowledge my mother or my sister. Only gestured for me to come close enough that he could place me among the wagon's load. My sister mourned me before I picked myself out of her hold, but she let me go.

I could bring nothing but myself, packed amid the rough spun bags. My mother came to the wagon, but the distance was too grand to reach between. She rested a hand on a wheel. Her palm did not cross it.

"Be who he needs," she whispered. "Stay strong."

I nodded.

She touched the lock of my hair twisted into her necklace. It had been taken from me when I was an infant. It would be my responsibility to make one for whatever children I had. I was to die with it held close. She was to intertwine mine and my brother's once I was gone.

The driver gave my father a letter. It was thick, folded much to suit a man's hand. Then he was upon the bench of the wagon, and the horse began to run.

Frost crunched under my boots when I was placed down before my husband's house. I was thankful for the furs.

I had to squint to look up and see the house. It was a large structure, larger than I had ever known buildings could be, even for a giant.

We were above the clouds. It was so blue. I could not see the roof. If the wind hit the house too strong, I worried it would crumble, boulders and tree trunks collapsing from its weight. It would not care what it buried.

The door was made of much wood nailed together. Even if I stretched, I would not reach the handles.

The driver fussed with the horse, but it did not want to move, so he tied it in place. He had me wait while he sought my husband. He left the door partly open, and I could see it was dark inside. I did not think giants could see in the dark.

The horse huffed behind me, and I turned to look.

When it saw me staring, it curled back its upper lip to show off its teeth. They were a mess of sharp, each one broken, like shards of pottery had been shoved into the gums. But each was still fatter than two of my fingers. If I put my hand within its reach, it would bite through bone with ease.

I could fit fully within its stomach. It would not have needed to chew, though I had no doubt that it would.

It would be warm inside of there.

I thought of asking for the horse's name. I wondered if the horse knew it.

My husband pushed the door the rest of the way open with such a thrust that it hit the wall, and I flinched back, worried it would split.

With his mass of dark beard hiding all other features, I thought him a storm cloud, the twists of gray the lightning. On seeing him over the horizon my mother would pray for a quick death, and my father would bolt the doors and windows. I thought my sister would have cried. I could not reach to see my husband's gaze.

I did not know my husband's name.

He did not offer it.

"Are you prepared?" he asked. His voice was thunder, and he kept it low. If he wanted to, he could shake the world, spawning earthquakes in afterthought.

I swallowed. "Yes, Husband."

My husband led the way to the kitchen, and the driver trailed us at a far distance to be the witness, but I kept worrying about the driver stepping on me. I doubted he would even notice.

My husband had to shoulder the doors with much force to make them open.

The stove, pressed against a wall, was hulking. I might have climbed inside and sat comfortably. It had been kept at a low heat.

Beside it were prepared wood and coal. My husband added the coal, strengthening the heat. The wood I placed was only a sliver. It burned up, crackling. The wedding went quick.

My husband had to carry me up the stairs. Each of the steps rose higher than my thighs, but they seemed no trouble for my husband. Like he might have taken three in an easy step.

He placed me on the end of the bed and did the courtesy of backing up so I did not need to strain my neck, though I still could not tell much through his mess of beard.

"Your furs," he said.

"I would like to keep them."

He nodded. When I passed off the cloud-damp furs, he laid them next to the fireplace. I had never thought a bear pelt would seem small.

He turned away to undress, as if modest. I could not tell what he thought when he turned back to look at me. I did not know of many giants who had taken a human for a wife, though I was not the first to be carried off by one of their giant horses to keep a giant house. I hoped my family had been paid well for my taking.

I was layered in gooseflesh when I had reached only my shift.

I crawled to the headboard to wait for my husband. It was far. My head was heavy with the braids, and they kept swinging into my vision, gleaming amid the dark. My husband had said nothing upon seeing them.

They dug into my spine when I sat back.

My husband sat on the bed beside me. He splayed his hand, studying the bed's furs between his fingers rather than me. They might have been a river splitting a wheat field.

"Lay down, Wife."

I did. The furs cushioned the braids.

The ceiling was so far above. There might have been stars.

My husband stroked my hair. His hands were too rough to be cut.

My teeth ached when I woke, deep in my jaw. I ran my tongue around them and tasted the furry strangeness of so long without water.

I was alone in the grand bed. It was cold without my husband.

It was dark. I fumbled my way off the bed, worsening all of the bruises, and towards the fireplace. A rough bundle of fabric had been left, which I thought was a dress when I unfolded it and felt around the hems and seams. The candle it wrapped around was thick wax, too wide for even both of my hands to wrap around.

I must have scattered the flint and steel when I'd unwrapped the dress, for they lay a bit to the side. They were unwieldy, and I took time to get a proper grip. The light of the candle was a relief. I knelt before it just to warm my hands, for the wick was fat and the burning strong.

The dress looked crudely made, for it cannot have been easy for giant hands to sew something so small. The fabric was thick, which I appreciated for the warmth, but it made the dress heavy. I felt I had been dropped into a lake.

There was no sign of my father's furs. I hoped my husband had taken them somewhere to dry.

Holding the candle carefully so it could not tip, I slipped through the small gap the open door had left. It was just big enough for me.

The staircase was difficult, as to descend each one I needed to fall, and then turn and reach to take the candle down without losing the flame or dripping wax on myself.

In the kitchen, the stove no longer burned. The logs collected beside it were of a size for my husband to lift, but I pushed them over to find shards and sticks that I could stack.

I knew how to lay a fire. I knew how to do the work slowly. I hoped my sister had watched me carefully.

I needed to roll over a log to even be able to reach the water pump, and then it took the entirety of my body weight to shift.

There was nothing to catch the water, so I scooped from the puddle with my palms.

The door to the larder was closed tight. I could not see onto the counters. I felt a mouse, unwanted and lost.

With no cloths, I used my dress to wash myself of the marriage bed, though I worried how it would make the fabric stiff. My thighs stuck together.

I smoothed down the stray mess of my braids, and cut myself on one of the copper gifts. Hungry, I sucked the wound clean.

None of the doors opened. I could not hear anything through them. My husband might have only been a room away and I never would have known. The windows were shuttered, my only light the candle. I did not know where chickens were kept to tell the time. I did not know if there were chickens at all.

I had not been given shoes, and giant feet were tough, so the wood of the floor had been left to splinter. I left a trail of bloody feet behind me in my husband's house. I would need to ask him where cloths were. Where I might find soap.

I went looking for it.

I went looking for the thing that crashed, again and again and again. Like waves, or a tree in a storm, or my mother weeping over her son's broken body.

The door I found bowed around the force. It had a shard missing at the bottom.

The horse flung itself against the door again, but the wood did not break. The hooves clattered as it rebounded and prepared for another hit.

Laying the candle beside me, I crouched to look through the crack, but could not get close for the smell. The room was sour with hay. With wet hair. With horse shit left long to rot.

I pulled my dress up to cover my nose and mouth. It made breathing easier.

The horse, as if it had heard my shock, stopped ramming the door. It lowered its head to look through the crack. I wondered if it could smell me.

It breathed heavily, its exhale hotter than the stove. It could have lit a fire, had it wanted.

It whinnied for me. Saliva dripped as the horse parted its lips, and I could see its teeth, and I could see the blood coating the gums. Its lips were scattered with cuts, and its great tongue licked them.

My husband brought a few root vegetables for me to eat for dinner. They were pale and weak. I asked after salt. He said he would find some.

The meat my husband had hunted for himself was not a bird.

We sat at opposite ends of a long table. I was too small to sit on the chair and still reach, so I sat on the table itself, on the edge of my large plate. I burned my fingers with the heat of the roasted vegetables. My husband had not cooked his dinner, only carved off the bits that were not good for eating.

The meat my husband had hunted for himself was not a cow.

"How was your day?" I asked my husband.

He grunted in the affirmative. He licked his fingers clean of gleaming red.

The meat my husband had hunted for himself was not a goat.

"I need scraps of fabric and soap to clean," I said. "And a bucket, for the water."

He nodded.

"Where are my furs?"

He did not answer. He broke open each of the bones to suck the marrow clean. The shards clattered when he tossed them aside.

When we finished eating, my husband left to dispose of the scraps of meat he had declared unfit. He had already forgotten the rest of the mess. I found all the bone shards he'd scattered in the corners, and I collected them.

I licked each before I put them in the bag I made of my skirts. Some blood had been left over. It was sweet.

I brought the bones to the horse, and the blood stained water I had used to clean up my bloody footprints. At the smell, it slammed itself against the door again, so I did not duck down. Only got close enough that I could toss the bones through the crack.

I worried the horse's teeth would break on the bones, but it eagerly took each new piece I tossed, cracking them with a starved glee. When I tipped over the bucket I'd dragged through the house, it lapped at the stream. I tried not to pour too quickly, so I did not drown the stable. It smelled worse than the day before.

There was a bit of light in the stable, golden, and I thought it meant sunset. My eyes had adjusted to the dark that day. I did not bother with the candle.

I could see the horse's mane as it ducked its head to drink. The braids were old and caught with straw and burs. Stuck with clumps of mud it had kicked up when running. There was a long rock, its end as sharp as a horse's tooth, and it kept hitting the horse's eye.

The meat my husband had hunted for himself was not a sheep.

It had arms. He'd left them attached this time, dangling over the table edge.

"Do you hunt with the driver who escorted me here?" I asked, picking apart the steaming vegetables. I had been sure to burn them so there was the flavor of char. My eyes ached, and I rubbed them when my husband wasn't looking.

My husband nodded. His beard was caught with chunks of bloody meat.

"What of the horse?" I asked.

"It's too loud. It eats whatever we kill. Always so fucking hungry."

My husband pried off a rogue fingernail before eating the hand down to the wrist.

I asked after my father's furs, and my husband told me to keep quiet.

My husband was less careful with his cleaning, for I'd promised it was my responsibility as his wife, and so I could bring one of the chunks still soaked with blood to the horse. When the horse smelled it, it pushed.

The hinges shook with the force, and I thought about cutting off some fat to render, to help oil the hinges. I did not know the door was locked, but the horse knew, so it kept its focus on the center, where it could break.

The door creaked. It splintered. I stepped back, out of its reach.

The horse used its hooves. It reared back and pushed again, laying all of its weight where the wood was already weak after so many days, so many years, of this same attempt. The door bent.

The door burst. I covered my face against the shards of wood. They still sliced my skin like claws. I heard some bounce off my braids.

The horse clattered forward in the aftermath, but it did not trample me. Only came to lick my wounds, to wash them clean of blood. The saliva stung like tears.

I lowered my arms slowly, and the horse's neck followed them, bending even lower. I could finally see the entirety of its body, unbound by a wagon, and my gaze lingered.

Its spine was like a terrible mountain range, filled with hollows and dips like valleys. Even I, whose family could not afford to keep a horse, knew how to tell when one was far too thin. Giant horses were stocky and well muscled. They could outlast any storm. They needed to be, in order to handle a giant's weight.

The horse could not have been ridden without snapping.

The blood I had seen on its flank in that first meeting had come from a large cut. The wound had reopened in the struggle with the door, and beaded fresh blood. More flies buzzed around it, and the horse swatted its tail with a tired effort.

I gave the horse my name as it ate my blood, and in return it gave me its own, and I knew it was not a name my husband had given it.

He would not have named it after something as beautiful as the sun.

Once there was no more blood to lick, the horse let me pick some of the mess from its mane. It dipped lower so I could reach. I tried not to pull or cause pain to it. It kept hitting its head against my side as lightly as it could, to make my braids chime.

The horse trailed me back to the kitchen for fresh water, and I cleaned its wounds, finding others hidden beneath mud and knots. The horse nickered with pleasure when I caught some of the dripping blood and water in my cupped palms, and drank.

The horse had to lay down so I could climb over it and straddle the shoulders, dabbing at a wound there that looked like the sharp strikes of a whip. It bit at the flies I sent scattering.

When cleaned, the horse's coat shone. I rubbed some of the hairs between my fingers and thought it might have been woven of true gold.

I brought the rest of the scraps for the horse to eat, but it only nosed bits towards me until I took up a piece and brought it close to my mouth. It only ate after I took the first small bite, for my teeth were weak and could only manage some of the meat. But I was hungry, and when I realized why the horse was waiting, I ate eagerly.

Even once I'd started, the horse would not eat any until it was certain I had gotten all I could. Then, it ate from my palms until its teeth nicked me, for they were sharp and hard to always watch. The horse hurried to wash the wound, and then refused to take any more of the meat from my hands. It did not want to injure me more. It did not want to eat what I did not wish to give.

The time when my husband returned home was dark. It was late. Though he never thought to tell me, he always worked late tending his flocks and hunting something suitable for dinner. The stables had a small window near the roof and when I stretched, I could watch the sunset over the mountains.

My husband looked for me, first, in the kitchen, for that was all he thought I knew to find. The stove was burned out, and he cursed how foolish I'd been. I should have known better than to wander from the stove.

He searched the house for me. He called only for "Wife," and left doors open in his wake so I could hear all of his grand footsteps shaking the boulders and trunks and nails, long rusted stuck.

I had been careful to wash my footprints so he did not even have a trail of blood to follow. I did not know if he would have thought to look.

"Wife," he called, checking each of the corners, for that was all I could reach to hide in.

"Wife," he growled, checking under the furs he had never given back.

"Wife," he roared, going for his horse, determined I had somehow gotten outside. What door did he think I had opened?

There was no way we might have repaired the stable door, so it gaped, splintered and broken and scattered on the floor. My husband had to duck to fit through.

"Wife," he asked, confused.

We smiled with sharp, sharp teeth.

My husband was not quick enough to outrun us.

In Pursuit of The Black Chuck Wagon
By Michael Boulerice

The Circle E. B. Ranch was a swollen blister of affluence on the desolate Pecos River valley. The aging proprietor strode from the porch of his immense home to greet The Hatchetman at the main gate as he tethered his horse.

"Merrick String. The veritable Hatchetman of Apache Pass, as I live and breathe. Had I known we were expecting a bona fide war hero, I'd have had a feast ready!"

The rancher known as E. B. Günther locked eyes with The Hatchetman and vigorously shook his hand.

"Your efforts to cure the New Mexico territory of the native threat precede you."

The Hatchetman broke eye contact. Only for a heartbeat.

"I got a block of ice that goes real well with a bottle of rye," Günther said. "Come on in."

The two sat in a garishly appointed den. Taxidermied hunting trophies, leather-bound volumes with unbroken spines, and polished rifles festooned the walls. It was the refuge of a man who came from nothing and had no idea how to make it appear natural once he found himself with entirely too much.

"Now what can I help you with, Mr. String?"

The Hatchetman splayed his worn leather-bound diary on one thigh, pencil nub hovering just above it.

"I'm searching for a chuck wagon cookie. I've heard tell you once employed him."

Günther took an exaggerated draw off his glass of rye, and rummaged through a small cedar box for a cigarillo.

"I've employed thousands at the Circle E. B. Ranch. Hell, I first raised these timbers at the age of seventeen. Nary a cock whisker on me! You'll have to forgive me if I don't remember every single hand. Can you be more specific?"

"I reckon this was about thirty-five years ago or so. Corpulent man. Wore a bowler hat."

"Thirty-five years ago?" The rancher quipped. "You can't expect me to—"

"Boiled his own fucking head in a Dutch oven."

Günther shot up from his chair. "You son of a bitch. Almost made it to the finish line without that business coming back to haunt me."

The Hatchetman let the rancher breathe, allowing time for whatever resistance was left to drain away.

Finally, Günther took his seat.

"His name was Ephraim Tibbets. I needed a dough puncher for longer runs. Colorado, Louisiana, and such. Held a hiring drive at the local watering hole. That fat whoreson Tibbets was in line, greasy hat in hand, offering up his services. Figured a man that stout had to be a good cook. Plus, he already had his own chuck wagon, which saved me the cost of building one."

The Hatchetman's pencil nub danced across the diary page in practiced shorthand, absorbing every detail.

"We put him up in the bunkhouse with the rest of the cowpokes. Ended up having to build him an entirely separate shack, on account of him being so godforsaken smelly. Man had a strong aversion to soap. His chuck wagon was a whole 'nother story. Must've been thirty coats of black lacquer on it. Looked like a god damned shadow, even at high noon. Downright odd. Still, he cooked like you wouldn't believe. I had my own house cook by then, and I was still sneaking out at sunup for Ephraim's biscuits."

Günther refilled his glass with a shaky, liver-speckled hand. The Hatchetman got the sense he was fortifying himself against something.

"Time went by. My business grew. I had more cattle. More employees. More complaints about Ephraim. His demeanor had always been rough, that wasn't new. It was the other stuff. The shit he'd say in his sleep, the books he'd buy from unsavory folks along the way. My boys couldn't read, but they peeked at them while Ephraim was serving up beans, or heeding nature's call. Disturbing drawings, they said. Lost a couple cowboys in the middle of a thousand-head cattle drive from Colorado because of them."

The Hatchetman rested his pencil nub in the fold between two pages, and massaged his aching hand.

"I'm surprised your men didn't just run Tibbets off."

"Almost came to that," Günther said. "The two boys who quit came back here to collect their belongings. I told them I'd fire Ephraim when everyone got back, but I still had a thousand head of cattle in transit, which meant I needed happy cowboys, which meant I needed a cook feeding them, even if he was going bat-shit. I doubled those two boy's pay to stay on, and told the rest of my men I'd double their pay if they stayed on until the end."

"And that worked?" The Hatchetman asked.

"It did, until it didn't."

The Hatchetman picked up his nub.

"By the time those two boys got back to the drive, Ephraim had gotten considerably worse. Holding full-on conversations with vultures. Screaming gibberish about how he ain't got no place in the livin' world into the night sky. Still, he cooked, and his chow was outstanding. Those damned biscuits. That and my extra money kept them driving those cattle home.

"One night, Ephraim lit out to jaw with some Pueblo medicine man by them cliff dwellings around Puye. Cowboys said they were relieved to be rid of him for a few hours. They passed a bottle, sang some songs, and went to bed feeling good for the first time since they first hit the trail."

Günther filled his glass to overflowing. Sweat darkened his shirt. He occasionally pulled a curtain back to peer outside, as if mentioning Tibbets might conjure his presence back to the ranch.

"The screaming woke them up. It was barely sunrise; coals were still red in the campfires. It came from behind the chuck wagon. That's where they found him. His big Dutch oven was hanging on a hook over his cook fire, and he was…"

The Hatchetman nodded, signaling the old rancher to take as much time as he needed.

"Tibbets must've been at it for hours; dunking his head in that boiling water, surfacing for air, doing it again. Skin and meat sloughing off his skull like a stew chicken. The raw hollows of his eye sockets. His stained teeth, no longer hidden behind his sooty beard and chapped lips, moved up and down, as if he was trying to say something."

"And then what happened?"

"My people got on their horses and left Tibbets in their dust. Supposed to be a two-day trip, but they managed it in one. Cattle were exhausted and dehydrated. Some had to be put down. I was furious about it until I'd heard what happened. All those work-hardened men talking at once, like frightened kiddies telling their pappy about a dog getting run over. I grabbed the men who still had balls left in them, and rode out. I was just starting out, and broke as all get-out. They'd left equipment behind I couldn't afford to replace."

"Did you find the camp?"

"I did. Tibbets was gone, but everything was still there. Bedrolls, saddles, even that God-forsaken chuck wagon. Made you nauseous just looking at it. The boys packed up, and I went ahead and opened its back gate, figuring I'd salvage pots and knives for the next cookie I hired."

Without warning, Günther pulled a spittoon from a corner, and vomited into it. When he'd finished, he looked at The Hatchetman with watery eyes.

"And…I saw it. That burlap bag, bottom dark with stale blood. Reckoned it was full of soup bones or some such. Something inside me told me not to look, but it was like I was watching myself reach for it, undoing the twine holding it closed, my mind screaming for me to stop."

The Hatchetman leaned forward in anticipation of whatever came next.

"Those shoes. Hundreds of little leather children's shoes, with their little beads and buckles. Some with little feet still stuffed in them. That's when I knew. The desert sun hitting that black lacquer turned the inside of that chuck wagon into a veritable oven. That's how he rendered the fat out of those little bodies. Sweet merciful Christ. I'd eaten hundreds of those biscuits…"

Günther grabbed the sloshing spittoon and let loose another volley.

"Children…" The Hatchetman let it float in the air between them like a grotesque balloon.

"Books and supplies weren't all Ephraim was procuring on his little expeditions. Was going to put a bounty on him, but decided against it. Didn't want the law sniffing around my livelihood. Besides, ain't no way he'd survived what he done to himself."

"What did you do with the chuck wagon, and Tibbets's things?" The Hatchetman asked, no longer writing.

"Tried burning it. Wouldn't catch on account of whatever retardant he'd mixed up in all that lacquer. Was like trying to burn stone. I buried the shoes, gave those kids whatever dignity I could, and left that abominable wagon where it stood. Figured nature would reclaim it. As for his belongings, there's an armful of his books down in my root cellar. Everything else was tossed in a bonfire, including that smelly old shack of his."

The old man, chest heaving and chin glistening, had exhausted himself recounting the tale; a confession that drained the soul instead of setting it free. The Hatchetman asked for directions to the medicine man Tibbets visited. Günther obliged, but not before demanding The Hatchetman take Tibbets's books with him.

"You hate it," Günther said as The Hatchetman strode for the door.

"Hate what?"

Günther reached for an antique blunderbuss mounted on the wall and absently polished it with a handkerchief. "Hate what you done. Apache Pass. I saw your face when I brought it up. You want my advice? Leave this Tibbets business alone. It won't bring back none of them Indians you hacked up."

The Hatchetman paused, hand hovering over the doorknob.

"I imagine it's similar to knowing you're responsible for employing someone who killed countless children and fed their fat to unsuspecting folks. Guess we just have to live with our sins. That, or we do something about them."

Günther winced. "I suppose those are the two available options, yes."

The Hatchetman put Tibbets's books in his saddlebag, and rode from the Circle E. B. Ranch in the direction of Carlsbad. The cooling evening air was sweet with wild lavender.

He was several hundred yards away when the muted bark of a blunderbuss discharging perked the ears of his horse.

The setting sun was a bloody coin in the sky.

Nestled by a small fire, The Hatchetman's body spasmed with the sudden onset of sleep. Flames guttered in a light breeze as he slipped deeper and deeper into a dream seasoned by the revelations of the day.

A young Merrick building a cabin in the unyielding heat. His smiling wife Etta coming to greet him with a cool jar of lemonade. The smell of her hair as she embraced him, despite his being caked in sweat and sawdust. Both of them washing in the stream that evening. Making love on a nearby picnic blanket as the sun dips behind canyon walls. Melting into each other like—

—Glistening fat seeping from a small boy's corpse as it bakes inside the black chuck wagon. Thick, yellow fluid draining from precise slits, collecting in an iron bucket below—

—A frazzled Etta holds their infant daughter Mildred, pacing around the cabin to ease her crying. Merrick pulling his boots on, another long day of pounding iron at the smithy ahead. "Just leave already, like you always do." She tells him, tears cascading down flushed cheeks. Not knowing what else to do, he—

—Lumbers over to several children playing on the edge of town. He offers them peppermints. They take them greedily. "You ain't allowed in," a ruddy-faced girl with a pronounced limp tells him. "On account of everyone having the fever. Us kids who ain't sick get to play here, though." Excited breath whistles through his nose. His heart thrums against his gravy-spackled shirt, and the ether-soaked pocket square tucked inside one suspender strap, as he grabs for—

—Etta as she fights against him. Flies swarm unwashed cookware in the sink. Their hungry daughter screams as her parents tussle. "Why haven't you fed the baby? What's happening to you?" Etta howls and struggles against the protective bear hug he's put her in, not wanting her to hurt herself, or to hurt Mildred. He—

—Cracks open a book resting on a bucket in his shack. He strains to make out words, silently working his mouth as a grimy fingernail passes under terms like "manducation" and "autosarcophagy." A torn page is pasted next to his cot; an illustration of a snake eating its own tail with the word "ouroboros" printed underneath it. He reaches into a pocket, produces a golden, flaky biscuit from it, and—

—Asks the doctor if Etta's behavior is normal. She is sitting in a rocking chair facing the wall, her head resting on her left shoulder, giving her the affectation of a curious puppy. "Lethargy is a common side effect of laudanum. Just make sure she takes it until her nerves are settled." The doctor exits, leaving Merrick to feed Mildred a dinner of breadcrumbs soaked in cow's milk. He lifts her out of her crib, cooing, removes her lavender bonnet, and—

—Kneads a ball of dough with his meaty fists. Hungry cowboys are yawning in their bedrolls. His yellow-brown smile is—

—Drooping. He holds a bouquet of wildflowers he picks on his walk home to discover the front door wide open. He announces his arrival to an empty house. No Mildred in the crib. No Etta in her chair. He looks out the window and spies a corner of their picnic blanket peeking from behind a tuft of sweetgrass on the stream bank. He smiles. That's when he notices the empty bottle of laudanum. And that the cleaver he made her is missing from its hook. And a torn page from the unused diary he'd bought her that reads "I'm sorry." He sprints out the door, toward—

—A pair of vultures pecking at a prairie dog carcass. He approaches slowly. The carrion birds break from their meal, and appraise the corpulent man with a cool, almost royal indifference. "I seen you over here eatin'. My-my name is Ephraim. I'd like a job." He quickly swipes his hat off to prove his deference. "I got books. One of 'em says to approach y'all when I'm ready, or some such." The vultures' polished coal eyes assess the groveling human. And then, after a long pause, one of them scratches at the sand with a clawed foot. It is all the confirmation Tibbets needs. He—

—Frantically stumbles to the stream. Etta bobs face-down in the gentle current, legs anchored to bank mud. Her forearms play host to desperate crosshatches of slashwork. The cleaver is missing. Probably in the stream, slowly being covered by silt. A wad of blood-spattered linen lays crumpled on the picnic blanket. There is something buried inside the linen, something small, and still. Merrick drops to his knees, screaming. It's not so much an act of lamentation as it is his heart attempting to escape his horror-stricken body. He doesn't know how long he's been kneeling there, or when his neighbor Bode Straub arrives. "Oh, oh god damn. It was them God damn Apache, wasn't it? God damn it, Merrick. Get your guns. You can mourn later. Let's get them bastards while they're still close." What can he say? That his wife butchered their baby before taking her own life? The truth is too awful to admit to himself, let alone a near stranger like Bode. No, it's easier to just agree it was Apache, the catch-all boogeymen of the west. It was Indians. It was Indians who did it. Of course, it was Indians. He'd hunt for the Indians. After that, he would bury his—

—Pain in the sand his fists clutch on both sides of the cook fire as he submerges his head in the boiling cauldron. Flashes of color flicker before his eyes as they rupture, floating out of their sockets like steamed jellyfish. Bellows of anguish escape his blistering mouth in the form of air bubbles, which quietly burst on the surface of the steaming vat of human broth. "Soon," he thought crazily. "Soon I will meet the"—

—"Bastards who did this to my family," Merrick repeats like a desperate mantra as he stalks through the Dragoon Mountains. Tanned Chiricahua Apache warriors ride bareback, defending against the might of the California Column at the Battle of Apache Pass. A war club pings off the back of his skull, sending him sprawling forward, rifle skittering into the hardscrabble. A Chiricahua warrior whoops as he dismounts from his horse, brandishing a knife. Merrick rights himself and produces a steel hatchet from his belt; the last thing he forged in his smithy before he sold it to Bode and joined the Union Army. Merrick whirls around the warrior's stabbing lunge, and buries the hatchet into his back. After that, there's nothing but chopping. And blood. And pleading in a language Merrick cares not to understand in his senseless rage. And screaming. And his wife's pale corpse begging him to stop. And his baby's broken body wriggling in bloody linens. And chopping. And chopping. And—

The Hatchetman bolted upright from a bed roll dark with sweat. His chest heaved with the effort of recollecting air he'd screamed out in his sleep. A turkey vulture rested on a petrified log not twenty feet from where he lay. It gazed at him placidly with its shiny black eyes buried in its scalded red face.

The details of the dream ebbed as he packed, but flickerings of horror and shame lingered long into the ride to Puye.

The Hatchetman reached the Pueblo ghost city the following evening. An azure-cyan sky swelled behind the sheer cliff faces of the mesa, still gilded by the dwindling rays of the day.

He trotted around debris along the crumbling wall's edge, examining endless rows of black holes carved high into the red rock face. None showed signs of occupation, save for the handful which had become shit-speckled bird roosts.

When sundown yielded to a night sky choked with pinprick stars, The Hatchetman went about gathering kindling. He fed his horse the last crabapple from his saddlebag and rested on a wind-blunted stone with some dried beef for himself.

As he chewed, The Hatchetman soaked in the loneliness of the desert cliffs; the jarring lack of presence. The medicine man may have moved on, or simply died in the years since Tibbets spoke with him. He would be old, too old for scrambling up rickety ladders, or long horseback treks for provisions.

Just as he decided he'd backtrack to the nearest town at sunup, The Hatchetman caught a glimpse of something in the cliff wall. He smothered the fire with a few kicks of sand, and waited for his eyes to readjust.

A steady orange glow illuminated a cave opening at the far end of the mesa wall, maybe two-hundred feet high. He remounted his weary horse and rode over to investigate.

When he reached the wall, a rope ladder hung from the cave opening. The Hatchetman tested its strength with a foot on one rung, then ascended at an awkward, twisting pace.

Lantern light danced on smooth carved walls, revealing recessed shelving holding all manner of pottery, herbs, tools, and books. The low ceiling was black with soot of ten thousand fires.

Sitting on the floor, draped in a banded woolen blanket, rested a wizened man with a brown, heavily wrinkled face.

"Do you speak English?" The Hatchetman inquired.

The medicine man pointed to his ear and nodded in the affirmative, but then pointed to his mouth, and shook no.

"My name is Merrick String. I was hoping to speak with you about someone I'm looking for."

The Pueblo man grinned with far too many teeth for someone of age. He scurried to a corner of the dwelling, and produced a slab of slate and a stick of chalk.

He motioned for The Hatchetman to sit by a small fire, over which a kettle steamed. The Hatchetman obliged, and was handed a tin mug of greenthread tea.

The old man used his chalk to write.

My name is Okawae. Who are you looking for?

"This was thirty-five years ago. I believe you met with a cattle drive cookie named Ephraim Tibbets. A big white man."

Okawae quickly erased the first words, making room for more.

Don't know him.

The Hatchetman spun the mug in his hands, revealing a stamped circle with two letters inside it. *E. B.* A quick glance at the kettle on the fire showed a similar Circle E. B. Ranch stamp.

The Hatchetman reached into his satchel and produced one of Tibbets's strange books, titled *A Treatise on the Gibbering Saints.* He handed it to his host.

Okawae's eyes grew large.

How?

"A man named E. B. Günther gave it to me. He employed Ephraim Tibbets."

The elder didn't respond. He flipped through pages, enraptured by the unnerving figures and illustrations within.

"I have more in my saddlebag. Those can also be yours, provided you tell me what I need to know."

Okawae finally pried himself from the book, and put chalk to slate.

I will tell you what I told him.

It was morning by the time The Hatchetman departed the cave. Creosote bushes on the desolate trail gave way to the Chihuahuan Desert. Sandy soil made for labored walking. The splintered peaks of the Organ Mountains loomed like the petrified remains of felled gods.

He stopped his horse in a clearing that offered a view of brushy desert expanse, and laid out his bedroll, as well as the handful of provisions he'd secured from Okawae alongside his instructions.

The first step required to gain an audience with the white man's hell requires capturing their attention. You do something that gets you seen.

The Hatchetman collected kindling as he thought about the desiccated children's feet Günther discovered inside the black chuck wagon; Tibbets's greasy signal fire for the denizens of the underworld. It was a step The Hatchetman knew he needn't dwell on. His actions at Apache Pass were sufficient.

The second step involves an act of self-sacrifice to prove yourself worthy of palaver.

A fire was lit, and a skillet full of Okawae's cooking lard rested atop strategically placed stones to keep it flat as flames licked heat into it. The pinks and oranges of sunset yielded to bruised blues and purples.

The Hatchetman retrieved the bitter slice of ceremonial cactus Okawae had given him, and chewed it as he watched the lard deliquesce into three inches of boiling fat.

Some committed cherished belongings to fire. Others slaughtered loved ones. Not enough. Ephraim understood this. To become a servant of hell, he desecrated the very flesh the white man's god gave him.

A tingling warmth spread through his body, quickly spread to his mind, and softened his vision. He discarded his duster, and rolled his left shirt sleeve up to his elbow. Emerging stars twinkled their horrified objections as he approached the cook fire.

Only an unnatural commitment to self-violation will prove one's worthiness.

A searing white light flooded The Hatchetman's eyes as he submerged his left hand into the skillet. Molten lard roiled around his wrist, sending needles of scalding spatter up his forearm. His body convulsed in an agony not previously thought possible, and he employed his right hand to keep the left from escaping too quickly. Each second was a torturous, floating eternity.

One must contemplate the ouroboros. The snake consuming itself is a sigil of eternity, as well as the act of recreation through destruction.

The Hatchetman lifted his hand from the skillet. His skin slid into the fire, where it sputtered and sizzled. His gorge rose as he appraised the curled gray mass of dead, steaming fingers. The aroma of fried meat faintly reminded him of the pork chops Etta sometimes served for supper.

You must commit to this second act with mindfulness and intent.

The Hatchetman slowly raised the ruin of his hand until it was level with his sweating face. Günther's description of Tibbets's self-immolation suddenly made itself present in the chill of the night air. "His stained teeth, no longer hidden behind his sooty beard and chapped lips, moved up and down, as if he was trying to say something."

A joyless laugh coughed out of The Hatchetman as he brought his hand ever closer to his bone-dry mouth. Tibbets wasn't trying to say something.

He was chewing.

The twittering shriek of a vulture shook The Hatchetman from unconsciousness. His eyes fluttered open to a deep blue pre-dawn glow.

He took in the skeletal remains of his hand, swaddled in Okawae's bandages. There was no Ephraim Tibbets before him. No black chuck wagon. The medicine man's instructions hadn't worked. There was nothing but pain, and the promise of a slow death by infection. There was–

His bleary eyes landed on something in the sun-hazed distance. Its darkness stood out against the landscape surrounding it.

With great effort, he shuffled to his horse, which he untethered from its tack, freeing it to live out its days on the plains. The horse wandered off to graze but didn't stray far.

The Hatchetman stumbled toward the object, with only lightning strikes of pain from his hand keeping him conscious and upright for hours.

And hours.

And hours.

And—

There. Parked amongst the mesquite and tarbushes. Impossibly. The black chuck wagon loomed before The Hatchetman like a tumor on reality itself. Its midnight black lacquer radiated heat. He dropped to his knees and sobbed.

And there, perched atop the driver's bench, was the repulsive bulk of Ephraim Tibbets.

A filthy bowler hat topped his mummified skull at an absurd angle. His considerable girth was clad in grime-caked pants and a sleeveless shirt that bore the drippings of a thousand meals.

At the head of the blighted wagon, a horrifying eight-legged amalgamation of children's shoes and living tendons was lashed to the driver's reins. It noticed The Hatchetman, and playfully pawed at the sandy desert floor with a leathery hoof the size of an anvil.

Tibbets's swollen, sightless head regarded The Hatchetman, drinking in the dying man's exhaustion and agony like brandy.

Finally, he patted the creaking driver's bench. And there he was. The Hatchetman couldn't recall crawling to the wagon, or scrambling up its sides. He'd somehow lost time. He was on his knees in the sand. And then he was sitting next to the gargantuan child butcher, whose ravaged mouth issued gurgling squelches.

Perhaps it was by some brand of hell magic that The Hatchetman, whose eyelids drooped with the strain of staying awake, was able to convert the muffled mastication into words.

State

Your

Business

With

Hell

With his good hand, The Hatchetman reached into his pocket, and produced the lavender baby bonnet he'd carried with him since he was a young man.

"I want to know if my wife and child are there. If they are, I wish to exchange my soul for theirs."

A sound like tree branches throttling a clogged abattoir drain issued from Tibbets. Try as he might, The Hatchetman couldn't make sense of it as he did before. The sloshing, rhythmic gasps grew louder, jiggling the great man's gelatinous chest with the effort.

It was laughter.

When it finally subsided, he answered.

> *We*
>
> *Don't*
>
> *Have*
>
> *Them*

The Hatchetman's eyes bulged. Tears melted into the sweat moistening his pale cheeks. His tongue struggled, thickened by dehydration and blood loss.

"But suicide. Baby not yet baptized."

Again, Tibbets's meat grinder of a laugh turned The Hatchetman's stomach, and thrummed through the lacquered bench like an approaching storm.

> *You*
> *Believe*
> *Your*
> *God*
> *To*
> *Be*
> *An*
> *Infant*
> *Torturer*

The Hatchetman jaw slackened as an inherent truth buried under withering effort and self-deception steamed up from his core. Of course, they were safe. It had all been for nothing. Decades of self-torture and contrition in pursuit of the black chuck wagon, wasted.

Tibbets raised a flabby hand in objection, as if he were reading The Hatchetman's mind.

Not

Wasted

And just like that, he knew. The chase was never about saving his family from an eternal suffering they'd never earned. That was a lie he fed himself to keep from swallowing a gun. He'd spent the remainder of his miserable life seeking worthy punishment for the lives he'd taken in a fit of delusion and grief that awful day. And he'd finally found it. It was as if a millstone had been lifted from his tired heart.

It

Is

Time

With that, Merrick String climbed down from the driver's bench, and spent his last remaining strength crawling to the rear of the conveyance, where the gaping maw of the cook box awaited him. As he pulled himself inside, the darkness and searing heat embraced him like a relieved wife greeting a husband returning from war.

He grinned as he shut the heavy hatch behind him.

Moloch's Children

By Rajiv Moté

Sunlight, white as bleached bone, streams through the window when we awaken drenched in our own blood—again. The only color in this world is red: on our bodies, our clothes, the sheets, splattered across the walls. Everything else is black, white, or gray. My arm is still entwined with Bryanna's. So is Javi's. There's no romance here. She was only thirteen when she came here and she's still the least broken of us, so we're protective. Not that we were much older. Not that we can protect anybody. The Pale Man killed us together, passing noiselessly through the unbroken glass of our seventh-floor motel window, so we resurrect together. We've all met and traveled with other kids, but we never see them again if we die separately. Javi, Bryanna, and I go everywhere together now. The Pale Man can appear anytime, anywhere. Better to die together than to resurrect alone.

"I've got first," Javi says. He's the oldest, sixteen. Usually he lets Bryanna and me use the bathroom first, but he's edgy now, touching invisible wounds like he can still feel them. Dying takes a toll. We take turns using the bathroom, washing the blood as best we can from our clothes and skin. We have no wounds. Only the memory of pain, but that's bad enough. Our modesty long dead, we leave the bathroom door open, just in case. Plumbing works, sometimes electricity, even without adults to pay the bills. Just us kids wandering a colorless city, waiting to be killed again and again.

"I want breakfast," Javi says.

Bryanna shrugs and gestures at her bloodstains. "I want new clothes."

I want to be done. I think I'm here because I tried to be done. But Javi and Bryanna always keep going, and they keep me from giving up even though we're all so tired. We can't be "done" here anyway—Javi and I have both tried. It went badly.

Javi insists we're in Hell. Bryanna is Catholic and thinks this is Purgatory: the prayers of the living will save us. I'm not a believer, and I have no name for what this is. My memory about how I got here darts away like a floater at the edge of my vision. If this is Hell, maybe I deserve it. But I've gotten to know Bryanna and Javi. They don't. The question that gnaws at me isn't *what* this is, but *why*. If this is punishment, what for?

I shut the door to the blood-splattered room, and everything but our clothes is gray again. The number on the door is 512. *Wait, wasn't it…* No, it doesn't matter. Things change without reason. It irritates me. There ought to be a reason. "I just want to understand," I wish out loud, not for the first time. Bryanna and Javi don't even glance my way. Bryanna has her faith, and Javi wants payback. Neither of them need reasons.

The elevator worked last night but doesn't now, so we take the stairwell. The concrete is pitted. The lights flicker and cast shadows. Shadows are dangerous. We hold hands as we climb down. The Pale Man usually lets us live a day or two before killing us again, but not always.

The lobby has the same tired look as everything else, cracks in the paint, edges worn dull. There's a spinner rack of tourist brochures in a corner, all the same. On the front, a cartoon Minotaur beckons to a stage with velvet curtains, held open a crack with braided rope. "Tommy Moloch's Theatre of Pain." It's almost colorless, but the wedge of space between the curtains is alarmingly red. Bryanna said she recognized "Moloch" from Bible study. A pagan god whose worship was forbidden. I've seen these advertisements before. I take the brochure and fold it into my pocket.

"I'm famished," Javi says. He looks it. Every time we die, we come back a little thinner, harder. Strangely, food is never a problem. There's a diner on the ground floor of the hotel. It's empty, but the door is unlocked.

"I hope they have pancakes," I say. Bryanna and Javi throw me a look that I ignore. On the cracked Formica counter is a plate with a tall stack of flapjacks, with packets of butter and syrup on the side. We've learned that inconsequential wishes are sometimes granted. There are three place settings at the counter, paper placemats and silverware rolled into napkins.

"I choose next," Bryanna says, but she helps herself to two flapjacks and tears into them like Javi and me. There's only a hint of flavor, like the memory of pancakes and syrup seeping into an absence, but the texture is right. It feels filling, but we never fill out.

"Should we drive today?" Javi asks, between bites. I notice he's bitten his tongue. A tiny trickle of red appears at the corner of his mouth. I pass my tongue over my own teeth, testing.

"Clothes first," Bryanna says.

"Might as well," I say. "Maybe we'll meet some others. Tell them what we know. Maybe they'll know something."

Javi nods. He wants to grow our ranks. Fight back. With enough kids…

Bryanna is satisfied as long as we get to swap our blood-stained clothes for clean, better fitting outfits. She believes salvation will come from without, and all we can do is wait. People can get used to anything. Even a world where kids are murdered endlessly and our blood is the only reality. There must be answers. I have an idea where to look.

The sky is lead-gray. A department store is across the boulevard from the diner. On the median between the empty lanes is a row of stone garden pots, filled with dust instead of flowers. Runts crawl all over them, chittering. Javi is already crossing the street, his shoulders set, his bony fingers curled like claws. We call them Runts because they look like the Pale Man, but small. Barely as tall as our waists. They're gaunt, naked things, maggot-white, eyeless, their heads mostly mouth, their mouths mostly needle teeth, like those weird fish that only live in oceans so deep the light doesn't reach them.

Unlike the Pale Man, they can die.

"Javi, wait," Bryanna calls, but without urgency. Runts' teeth and claws break easily, even against bare skin, and Javi never misses an opportunity to rain carnage on them. He leaps onto the curb, snatches a Runt by its neck. He squeezes, and its head pops off. Head and body dissolve into white dust. He aims a savage kick at another, disintegrating it. He holds one by the leg and swings it, bashing its head against the edge of a flower pot until it explodes into powder. He shouts, cusses, tears into them until they're gone or dust. They leave no blood, no color but ash white. We don't know if Runts are the Pale Man's children, but Javi has decided so, and goes out of his way to deliver "payback."

I don't know. I've never seen adolescent versions of Runts, and I'm certain the Pale Man who kills us is the same every time. I feel his joyful malice radiating like heat and stink. The Runts never attack us, and they die with ease. If they actually die. For all I know, they resurrect like we do. I've killed a few Runts myself, and I was rattled by how much satisfaction I got. Javi might be right that killing Runts protects us from future enemies, but I trust there's something else to this place. Some purpose I haven't understood. And I've never wanted to hurt anyone except…my mind shies away from that black chasm.

"Let's go shopping." Bryanna makes as close to a smile as any of us can manage.

The department store is dingy, its aisles haphazard and shabby. The girls' section is on a different floor than the boys', but we don't split up. Bryanna shops like she's still alive, considering and discarding outfits. She even takes her short-list to the dressing room. She doesn't close the curtain, and Javi and I stay in arm's reach. The Pale Man has crawled out of mirrors before. Bryanna strips to her underwear and considers herself in the mirror before trying anything on. We're long past averting our eyes. Fear crowds out other feelings.

"If I get any paler," she mutters, "I could pass for white."

She's right. She's pale and thin. We all are. I glance down at my hand and wonder if my fingers have always been so bony.

Finding clothes is faster for me, and Javi is quickest of all. He pulls off his bloodstained sweatshirt and leaves it in the aisle, a splash of red on white tiles. He grabs another sweatshirt that almost fits, and puts it on before stripping off and replacing his jeans.

"We done?" Bryanna says, impatient despite having taken the longest time.

"I wonder if they have a sporting goods department," Javi mutters. "Maybe we can get ourselves a g—"

A wave of panic seizes me. I want to plug my ears, or scream. For all three of us, that word is an abyss.

"A g—" Even Javi is choking on the word.

"Shut up, Javi!" The word is filth to Bryanna. She won't have it in our mouths.

He struggles for a horrifying moment, trying to say it out of sheer, cussed stubbornness. But after nearly choking himself, he gives up.

"Let's just go," he finally says, and the panic passes. We've tried other weapons against the Pale Man, actual and improvised. Nothing works. We've stabbed, slashed, bludgeoned, and strangled him, to no effect at all. No reason a…another weapon would do any better. I'd go mad if I even saw one.

Javi, Bryanna, and I have talked about how we died the first time. Javi was walking home through the park. Bryanna was at church. They remember other people. Terror and chaos. I was in my bedroom, alone. The news was on TV downstairs. Birds chirped outside my window. I remember an invisible, lead weight crushing my chest and throat for so long, and a hope for relief that was no hope at all. My body moved mechanically while my *self* was far away. My mind won't go beyond that. There's a black hole in all three of our memories that could suck us in if we got too close.

"I hope someone left their car keys on the sun visor," Javi says. The boulevard is empty of traffic, but not of cars, pulled up to the curb and empty as though its occupants parked just before the city was raptured. The first car he checks has keys.

Javi drives. He had a license, before. He's competent. He weaves between abandoned cars and accelerates down the boulevard. Sometimes he swerves to run over Runts, but he's not reckless.

We can't kill ourselves here, but we can break bones, hurt ourselves. I threw myself from a twenty story balcony once, to lie shattered on the pavement for three days until finally the Pale Man came and gobbled me up. I could feel every chew until he finally swallowed my head. I woke up lying on the pavement, unbroken in the gray dawn. I could tell from Javi's reaction to that story that he had stories of his own. Bryanna just scolded me. "You shouldn't have done that."

Javi doesn't ask for a destination because there's no real plan. The city isn't familiar, except in bits, and it changes. Javi had the idea to find someplace defensible, and to find allies to make a stand. But every time we found a likely place it became something else when we went out to forage and recruit other kids. This isn't a world we could claim and shape into a place of safety. We can only be hunted. We keep moving.

The buildings of the city grow sparser, and soon we're on an open, empty highway, with gray, dead fields and vast plains sliding outside the window. The radio has only static, and none of us wish for music. It would probably be like the pancakes: a memory of a tune, a faded echo of something we loved. A reminder of loss. Silence is better. Every few miles, I see billboards for the Theatre of Pain, with its cartoon Minotaur and glimpse of red between the curtains. I reach for the brochure just as I remember that I left it in the pocket of my discarded jeans. But somehow there it is, in my back pocket. I unfold it, and there are words, but the letters seem to dance and swap places, dissolving into gibberish. It makes my head hurt. I stuff it back into my pocket.

We pass a gas station, abandoned like everything else, and only looking back do we see there are kids standing there, jumping and waving at us frantically.

"Should we?" Bryanna asks tentatively.

Javi slams on the breaks and reverses the car.

There are two young boys falling over themselves to climb into the car.

"You've gotta help us!" says one.

"There's a monster after us!"

Red puncture wounds dot their t-shirts.

Bryanna is soothing them and Javi throws me a look. It's not worry, or pity. We can't help them. We can't even help ourselves. They can travel with us for a while, but we all have the same fate ahead. At best, we can stick together. Build our ever-dying army.

"You have to drive as fast as you can," says the boy named Eddie. "He's coming back!" His companion, Josh, nods vigorously. They're so new.

"If you want to stay together, you've got to stick close," Bryanna explains to them. "When you see the Pale Man, hold hands, link arms. With each other, and me. Don't let go no matter what."

"But how will we get away like that," Eddie asks.

"There's no getting away," Javi says.

The boys start to cry, and I can't bring myself to scold Javi, or comfort Eddie and Josh. They'll learn.

The gray sky deepens into black. There are never stars. The road ahead is a different shade of black, with white stripes passing below that gleam in the headlights. An illuminated billboard punctures the blackness periodically; otherwise, the whole world constricts to the road ahead.

Eddie and Josh are asleep in the back seat, with Bryanna stroking their hair. I know better than to ask the question, why bother? I've lost something Bryanna held onto. Compassion. If that's what faith does, maybe it's worth having. She could have become a great mom, I think, just as the bitter injustice puts my throat in a vice. Maybe we all had potential. Even me.

The blackness slides by in silence.

"We should go to the Theatre of Pain," I tell Javi after another billboard. "Exit 303."

"Haven't you had enough pain already?"

How much worse could it be? It's the only direction we've had. "We'll find answers there."

"Answers to what?" There's no heat in Javi's question. No place is worse than another. This is just conversation. "It all seems pretty obvious."

"You don't want to know why?"

"There is no why. It just—*Ay puto!*"

A tall, skeletal figure stands in the middle of the road, pale in the headlights.

"Bryanna," I call back.

"I wish I had a gu—a gu—" Javi says. "But I'm going to kill him anyway." He floors it.

"Oh God, wake up, boys! Hold onto each other! Hold on to me!" Bryanna reaches between the front seats and grabs both of our arms. I hear the anguish in her voice. "Wake up!"

Eddie and Jacob have each other in a death grip, screaming, "It's him!"

Javi yells in wordless rage. I grab his arm. The Pale Man rushes to meet us.

"Die!" I scream as the car connects. The Pale Man passes through the windshield like it's water, teeth first. Everything is the white of his claws, the red of our blood, and agony. One of his thin, arm-long fingers pierces the roof of my mouth, enters my brain, and the last thing I feel is the lead weight of crushing guilt.

Bryanna, Javi, and I awaken in the car, stopped in the middle of the long, empty road. Blood is everywhere. Eddie and Josh are gone.

"They didn't hold on to me," Bryanna says, without emotion. "I hope they're still together." She's paler than ever, but it's nothing compared to Javi. He's almost as ashen and wasted away as the Pale Man himself. Everything in his sunken features is cold fury.

"I'm so goddamn tired of this," he says, his voice preternaturally calm.

"It's not in our hands," Bryanna says, her voice dead.

"Let's go to the Theatre of Pain," I say. Among the shifting letters on the brochure, I clearly see Exit 303. It hasn't changed.

Exit 303 leads directly into a vast, empty parking lot in front of a ruin of what looks like a Gothic castle. Oddly, spotlights swing back and forth over the massive double doors. Iron letters arch over the doorway: TOMMY MOLOCH'S THEATRE OF PAIN.

"We're just walking in?" Bryanna says dubiously.

"What's the worst that can happen?" I say. The worst happens almost every day.

The doors open to a lobby of moldering carpets and draperies. A chandelier hangs alarmingly askew from a ceiling of impossible height. Another pair of double doors beckons ahead, but stairs curve on either side to upper balconies. Behind the doors is loud chittering. Javi motions to the left, and we silently agree. Whatever awaits us in the theater besides a hoard of Runts, we can get a look from a safer vantage.

The lighting is dim, and we hold hands. The Pale Man could be around any turn, but I surprise myself—my first thought is that we'll just wake up on the steps and continue our climb. I want to see what's on the stage.

We stop at an arbitrary landing and we push through velvet curtains to box seats. The balcony has a view of the main floor, which is packed with Runts crawling over each other. But only a few are bold enough to venture onto the stage.

The stage is dominated by a huge clay dome with an opening at the bottom. It's a furnace with bright, angry flames within, vivid orange and yellow—full, dazzling color. Even at this distance, heat blasts my face. Atop the furnace, like a chimney, rises an idol, its muscular back to us, its arms outstretched, entreating the darkness backstage. Horns curve from the idol's head, like a bull's.

Slots riddle the idol's torso. Holes. Through them I see all the color of the living world shining in. The slots are windows onto men in suits, pounding their fists on podiums. Judges in robes, banging their gavels. Police. Crowds of protesters. Men in camouflage. Teenagers swaggering on blighted street corners. Little kids hiding behind their classroom desks. A bearded man with a gravelly voice shouting into a microphone. So many American flags. Ceaselessly, the slots fill with small, writhing figures. They start to blacken in the furnace's heat.

"Are those…kids?" Bryanna whispers. The whites of her eyes show all around.

She's right. As if in response to the scenes beyond, children materialize in the slots and begin to burn. Tirelessly, the Pale Man pulls out the charred, squirming figures one after the other. He *rips,* and blood drenches the idol, crimson and bright. The children disintegrate into ash that floats away into the darkness of the theater.

I know that somewhere in this colorless Hell, more children are awakening, to be murdered again and again.

Bryanna's eyes close. *"You shall not give any of your children to devote them by fire to Moloch, and so profane the name of your God,"* she recites.

As the Pale Man takes child after child, bolder Runts scuttle up the idol and climb into the emptied holes. They're incinerated instantly, but their ash wafts into the world beyond, unnoticed by the politicians, judges, policemen, protesters, militia men, and terrified kids. The sight of anything from this hateful world crossing over fills me with inexpressible dread.

My long, skinny fingers ball into fists. "They did this to us."

In the world beyond, the politicians shout about freedom. The protesters shout and go home. The bearded man shouts that the dead children never even existed. And children keep filling the slots to die and die and die.

"Why?" Bryanna whispers. She sounds betrayed. We were all betrayed. Maybe there are people out there praying for our souls, but all we can see are the ones sacrificing us, by what they do, and what they don't.

I realize that Runts don't die here either. Nothing dies here but hope and goodness. And when all that's left in them is horror…

Javi watches, and there's a hunger in his pale, gaunt features. "That's our way home."

Bryanna and I look at him. He couldn't possibly—

"I should have gotten us *guns.* To clear the way."

Javi is so far gone. That word is horror. It's memory. It's the taste of metal I shove into my mouth before the world explodes. It's the sin that earned me this punishment. But I'm different from Javi and Bryanna: I did it to myself. This Hell was done *to* them.

"What are you talking about," I say, swallowing all the unlocked horror, pushing it down into a lead ball in my gut.

"The other side," Javi growls. "That's where we get payback." He turns and dives through the curtains behind us. Bryanna and I freeze. We've been in arm's reach of each other for so long, having Javi *leave* us is like losing a limb.

"Javi!" Bryanna calls, too late.

He's on the main level faster than should be possible. He carves a swath through the Runts straight up the aisle. He hurls them out of the way, pummels them to dust, lashes out, but always pushing forward, to the stage.

The Runts fight back. They're more effective in these numbers, slashing at Javi with teeth and talons. His clothes fall off in shreds. So does his flesh, but he keeps pushing forward. A small trail of red follows him, but it's not much, as though he's run out of blood. When Javi climbs the stage, he's more like one of them, a bone-white, impossibly thin figure.

The Pale Man pays him no mind. For a fraction of a second I feel a surge of hope, but the bottom drops out. Javi dives into a slot and for a moment hangs suspended within, as the furnace burns away the last scraps of his humanity. Then what's left of him is blasted to white ash that floats out into the world of the living.

Bryanna is sobbing, but her eyes are dry.

We're both so dry.

"I wished for this," I say. The words are white ash in my mouth. "I wanted to know why."

Bryanna looks at me without expression. "Does it help?"

I pass my tongue over my sharpening teeth and taste iron. "No."

The Pale Man continues to pull children into Hell, and the little monsters we all become continue to crawl back into the living world. I don't know what the people on the other side are buying with our sacrifice to their machines of death, but the only thing they receive is the dust of fear, despair, and violence. They'll choke on it. On us.

I wanted to be done, but now I understand. I can only try to break the cycle. I can only try to keep my humanity enough to never, ever cross. Even if I failed the first time, when I was human and alive.

Patch Job

By Kaitlin Caul

Momma was always a strong believer in the power of a patch job. She looked over my nightly laundry like a hunter searching for prey in the tall grass. Any stretch, any thread out of place, any pinprick hole, and her eyes lit up with a hunger that'd make a starving wolf wary. She'd disappear with the offending piece of clothing, and I wouldn't see it again for a full day or two. Then one day, sitting at the top of my laundry pile, gift-wrapped in its own perfectly folded lines, would be the missing article. I would search and pick at the place where the blemish used to be, but Momma was good. She'd patch that hole so well you'd think she'd just gone out and bought a new one. One with faded colors and a few stains that refused to come clean, but whole and strong like it had threads of steel.

Momma had a talent with other tools too. Rusted knife? Shiny new the next day. Bent rake? Snapped back into shape like a saluting soldier. Squeaky floorboard, cracked paint, ripped toy, nothing escaped her notice. Throwing something out was sacrilege in Momma's house. The garbage bin was for food waste and tissue, she used to say.

Me and my sister never picked up on Momma's repair habit. Bessy May had it worse, throwing things away when she was done with them, then receiving Momma's wrath before the end of the day. I had a knack for machines, but I didn't know how to fix them like how Momma did, making problems disappear. Pa tended to his trucks and his tractors, but left the house alone to Momma. The most I ever saw him do was bring in lumber when she had a big project in mind. Otherwise, we all steered clear of Momma's "work room." We treated that room with more sanctity than the church.

Growing up in a small town, wearing the same patched clothing for years on end, never bothered me much. Saved money for the family, and the fabric was worn in so well it felt like my own skin. Even when me or Bessy May outgrew something, we'd see it again a few days later reworked into a new piece of clothing or part of a new blanket. Nothing went to waste in Momma's house. Nothing with so much as a scrap of usefulness left in it went to the curb.

Remembering all that now makes the headlines even funnier, if you ask me. They said not a scrap of the truck remained after it went over the cliff. Nothing but an oil stain on the rocks below.

Cousin Frankie, that arrogant piece of shit, he'd been daring me to take the truck up the hillside. I knew it was too slippery that day, rains having washed out all traction that morning, but he just wouldn't shut up. I told him he'd have to drive it alone up first. Maybe a good scare would knock the piss out of him. He kept pressing. Kept goading. Said I wasn't man enough to do it myself. So I got in.

He jumped out of the driver's side just before the truck went over. I jumped too. Just not fast enough.

When I woke from the coma, the doctors said I'd never walk again. They said my brain got scrambled and my organs would need a whole lot of surgeries to function proper, if I could even survive long enough to get to the point of surgeries. I wanted to cry. I wanted to scream and rage and hit anything within reach. Instead, I just hung in those stirrups like a goddamn plant strung up from the ceiling.

Momma came to see me every day. She wept for me and she screamed for me, and when Aunt Martha and Cousin Frankie came by days later, she near took their heads off for me.

When the doctors discharged me months later, Momma didn't let anyone take control of my wheelchair but her. We got to the house and I saw a ramp where the stairs used to be. Inside, the house looked as clean as the day we moved in. No half-finished projects on the floor. No discarded shoes lying about the entryway. Bessy May said she'd done what she could to fix up my room. I looked up at her and tried to say thank you. Drool pooled on my shirt collar.

Momma wheeled me into the house and straight down the hallway. Past my room. Bessy May started to protest, but Momma just shushed her with a scoff and took me into the work room. I heard the lock on the door click shut while staring at a wall of sewing supplies. Needles, threads, fabrics, yarn, patches, all the pieces that had held my childhood together. All of them neatly slotted into shelves across the far wall like a shrine to hard work waiting to be done. The other walls held boxes of nails and screws; tins of cleaner, degreaser, oil, and glue; tonics and tinctures and all other manner of remedies for a house showing its age. Momma had a whole arsenal in this one small, closet-sized room, and it was the most beautiful thing I'd ever seen.

Momma knelt in front of my wheelchair, her knuckles white as she held the arm rests. Momma had strong hands. Proven hands. Momma closed her eyes as she passed her hands up my arms and over my shoulders. Her fingertips pressed into my collarbone, against my neck, my throat. They pressed and prodded and searched. And when Momma's hands reached my face, she opened her eyes and stared at me. She stared right through me. Momma molded her hands to my head, fingers pressing to my temples, palms shaped to my jawline, and she drew herself close to me. Then she smiled, and deep in her green eyes I saw the hunger again.

"My boy," Momma whispered in my ear. "You were my precious, perfect boy. Bessy May, she's got too much of her father in her, but you're mine. Don't you fret about a thing. I'm gonna fix this. You'll never even know what was broken when I'm done."

The first thing Momma did was move my bed into her work room. She set it up right under the shelf of her sewing supplies and fixed a lamp to the headboard. She sent Pa out for fresh needles and scissors and a scalpel. Pa looked real confused as he brought the brown bag from the corner store into the room, but he didn't say a thing. He just kissed Momma on the head, nodded to me, then backed his way out of the room, reverent as a worshiper.

Momma lay me on the bed and told me I wouldn't be moving much. Not that I could to begin with. She rolled me onto my stomach and her fingers began their penetrating search again, up and down my spine, pricking at the skin and chasing the contours of bones. I used to have muscles there. The shoulders of an ox, Momma used to say. Judging by how Momma lifted me like a sack of flour, I don't think I had much muscle left anymore.

I don't know what Momma found back there but after a minute, she seemed satisfied. The heat of Momma's touch withdrew, and the door shut behind her.

Cousin Frankie came by later that evening. I heard his voice in the hall and felt the rage close over my head like a tidal wave. When I heard the thunk and the silence that followed, the rage ebbed away.

I don't know what happened to him, but I remember Momma humming a lullaby to me as little pinpricks of fire danced up and down my back. She told me he wouldn't be playing any tricks on me ever again. Then she gathered up the bloodied sheets and told me to get some sleep.

The next day, I felt the itchy fabric of the wool blanket beneath my fingertips. I smiled and tried to tell her how wonderful it felt. She answered my hooting with a smile while she worked on her cross stitch in the corner.

Pa got upset that night. I couldn't hear all of what they said as they shouted at each other, but I caught bits and pieces. Momma was a monster. Aunt Martha was gonna be livid when she found out. How was he supposed to tell his sister what happened? Well, Momma made sure Pa didn't have to worry about that.

Late in the night, I saw the glow of a bonfire turn the window curtains blood red. I heard the fire crackling, and wondered if it was just the sheets Momma burned, or the scraps.

The next day, I sat up for the first time and ate a whole bowl of soup without throwing it up. Momma was so proud of me. She said my scars were healing up real good. No one would even notice the stitch lines in a couple months. We worked on my letters all day. I wanted to show off to Bessy May how much

I'd improved, but Momma said she wouldn't come out of her room. All she did was cry.

That night, Bessy May screamed. I started to feel bad when the screaming went on and on. I tried to tell Momma to stop. I could improve the slow way like the doctors wanted. Momma told me the doctors didn't have her gift, and that this was the best thing for everyone. Bessy May was hurting, and Momma was going to make it better.

Bessy May had powerful lungs. Strong and healthy. When I breathed in deep for the first time since the accident, I was real grateful for all that singing she used to do.

The next to go was Aunt Martha. She came snooping around the house early one morning. I didn't regret what happened to her. I helped. Kept her distracted while Momma did her work. Momma said there wasn't much of use to shriveled old Aunt Martha, but there were scraps. I helped Momma clean up after, and that night I joined her at the bonfire.

For the next week, Momma didn't start any new projects. She cleaned the house and cooked us meals and took care of the animals, but whenever I brought up her work room, she just shook her head and looked sad. At the end of the week, Momma said she wanted to watch the sunset with me.

We sat on the porch together, the hot summer air sticking to our skin. Already the sun was nothing more than a red jewel on the horizon. The farmlands all around were drenched in the ink of oncoming twilight. Insects hummed and buzzed in the brittle grass of the lawn, and the whole world seemed to be winding down for the day. I closed my eyes and drank in the coming evening.

"There's one more thing you need, my boy," Momma said after a sip of her lemonade. She stared straight ahead, stared through the sunset like she could see into the Heavens beyond. "You're very nearly fixed. All's you need is a heart. Problem is, there's no one in the world with a heart as big as yours. Well, almost no one." She turned and smiled at me, but the edges of her mouth refused to stay up. "You make me so proud, my heart wants to burst every time I look at you."

"Momma, no," I said. I reached across the table between us and gripped her hand. The hard calluses of her fingertips scratched against my knuckles.

"Don't you worry, my boy. I said I'd fix you and I mean it. This way, I'm always going to be with you. Now the problem is I won't be able to do the final stitch. It's time you learn the trade."

"I don't got your gift," I protested.

"Nonsense. You're my boy. You've had the same sparkle in your eye your Gramma did, and her Gramma before her. Bessy May never had that light, but I see it in you when you go looking at those old junkers of your father's. You got the need to break things down, understand them, so you can build something new. What we are is saviors, my boy. Most people just see a patch job, but you and I see a thing that needs to be made whole. Now finish your juice. We've got work to do."

So we did. Day in and day out, Momma taught me her trade. She taught me how to look beyond the frayed edges or broken ends and identify the heart of the problem. She taught me how to decide what was lacking, so we could meld it in and make a thing whole again. I learned to sew and darn and scrape and sharpen. I learned to glue and shape and cut and burn. I learned what made rust and what unmade it; what made a motor tick and what made it stop. Momma was right. I took better to the machines than she did, but she could make a needle dance across a piece of fabric when I only made it follow a straight line.

As summer gave way to fall, Momma announced that she'd taught me all she could. The final test would be in the biggest project of her life. Her Magnum Opus, she called it.

Momma lay in my bed that night. Her suntanned skin didn't look as healthy beneath the harsh white light of the reading lamp.

I'm not perfect. I know there are parts that still need fixing. My last stitch wasn't as neat as Momma's would have been. I'm going to get better though. Now that I got Momma with me always, I know I got enough love to last me a lifetime. Several lifetimes. All I need is some more practice.

To Meld Flesh with Gown and Gown to Flesh

By Marie Croke

Janie showed back up at my front stoop three nights after she'd disappeared from the loft where all my girls slept. Her flesh sewn into a gaudy dress, ruffled and taffeta-puffy with fake diamonds decorating the bodice while blood seeped against the fabric in spreading pinprick dots. I sent the younger girls straight up to bed and ordered Lea to get me my embroidery scissors. My new ones. The ones I kept sharp as tacks with its little curved tip easy to slip under the sort of tight stitches that Lea tended to. She came racing back, black shoes tapping against the floor, her hair a wild mane about her head, and her eyes like torches in the candlelight, swallowing up the folds and dips and curves of Janie's glorious gown of gold and turquoise like she could devour it into herself.

"Now to bed," I said, more sharply than I'd intended to. Lea's face fell and that flickering desire in her eyes banked itself like an ember needing a good breath of fresh air. A good breath I had no intention of ever letting her have. "These gowns aren't as gorgeous as they seem. They're…" I was wasting my breath. I sighed and made a shooing motion and lessened my sharpness with a smile to show I appreciated Lea's fetching of my scissors.

As she crept toward the kitchen where the loft staircase was, I swore I could see her twirling in her mind, her hand holding onto imaginary silk draping as she danced her thoughts to bed.

Then I turned, armed and ready for the blood that would flow tonight. And began to cut stitches off Janie's dimpled flesh to release the gown from her body.

• • •

The first woman to go missing had been a hawker in the emporium. She'd set up on the outskirt of her parent's stall with a tray of tiny pinches of cinnamon bread. One day she'd laid that tray down on the table and disappeared without so much as a word. Reappeared a few days later on the wharf, dragging herself along the boards, her gown of silver so shimmery that those working that night had thought her to be moonlight coming to rest on the earth.

Yet, moonlight don't leave ripped silk off every exposed nail. Moonlight don't bleed from a million stitches.

Moonlight don't come knocking on my door in the dark and scream like I'm cutting out a piece of her soul as I remove that dress from her skin.

Janie breathed hard and fast and shallow as she lay half-collapsed against my sewing table. She didn't scream like the first women who had lain here. I'd given her a good dose of whiskey and a hefty handful of fabric scraps to grip as I cut away the dress, leaving behind raw holes in tight, beautiful lines that were endlessly marred where her blood smeared.

"Who did this to you, girl?" I asked as I worked, tapering off my emotion so I might concentrate. She was one of mine. Been working in my shop since she could scarce hold a needle. I was methodical, moving quickly, efficiently, tugging out the threads as straight and short as I could to reduce any pain Janie might be feeling. Which, if I went by her taut shoulders and twisted expression was quite a lot, despite the stitches being generally shallow, just deep enough to reach blood through her layers of dermis.

It was like I was cutting off a piece of her heart along with those stitches.

She shrugged, messing up my pace with the movement. "She said she could give me a deal. Put me in a gown fit for a goddess. Let me walk on sunshine itself."

"And did it?" That was a cruel question and I knew it, but I asked anyway and doubled down. "Did you get to walk on sunshine?"

A tremulous smile flickered against the edges of Janie's lips. "Oh, did I. I could feel the glow from my skin, Miss Cass. I could taste the wind. I could fly through the sky and set down anywhere the sunshine touched. I danced with people on all the ends of the world, always keeping ahead of the dark." She sagged and shuddered, her eyes drooping closed. Then added, in a whisper, "Then it caught up to me."

I wanted to believe her drug-addled. That she'd fallen from a chemical high, crash-landed after a stolen trip into a lady's deep closet. But I knew better. Had heard too many stories of the same ilk.

There'd been an older woman on my table a few short months prior. She'd been a windy gray cloud before collapsing at my doorstep one early morning. Her hair pinned. Her chewed fingernails painted in a glorious black. She'd been a weakened doll against my ministrations as I slowly cut apart her gown, her hands limp and her gaze a waning storm.

"I lived in a castle up there," she murmured. "Danced on a rain cloud and felt it spill beneath my feet. Fell in love with a woman made of sleet and kissed another made of air."

"Who did this to you?" I peeled off a sticky thread caught between my fingers and wiped red against a towel.

"She is the mistress…who sews us into our best lives."

But she'd say no more, that waning storm in her gaze disappearing completely.

I settled Janie's dress against a headless mannequin. Stepped back from it to study its gold and turquoise folds and its sparkling bodice. Only a lady would wear such a gown, and then only to a ball, something my girls would never see in the flesh. No, I might design something of this ilk once in a far off blue moon if a lady deemed my shop the right one to set foot in, but she'd have to foot the bill for the fabric in advance for I certainly didn't keep such dreaminess in stock. My patrons were working, needing good thick trousers with extra padding on the knees, skirts that wouldn't rip when they tread over cobbled or rocky paths, hidden pockets or fat loops against their waist to hold their tools. I had no reason to design something this glorious.

I caught myself stroking the gown and yanked my hand away. That thing was fire. Eats up who was sewn in it, surely. And the seamstress behind it was a witch, a wretched evil goddess…or something far, far worse.

Behind me, Janie slept curled on misshapen cushions sewn by girl hands learning the art. Her body picketed with scabs. Fences where she would scar just enough to remind her of her sunshine days and this dangerous night when the dress had betrayed her, flung her back to the ground.

From upstairs came the soft harmony of girlish snores and whimpers. There'd be no convincing them of the dangers after this. They'd hear Janie's stories of sunshine and would walk around with living dreams I would not be able to contain.

Some of the women I helped insisted on keeping the gowns. Some threw them in the bay. Others set them afire. None of them thanked me. They would whisper about the life they'd touched that had been stolen back from them. Like they were still dreaming of it.

One of them, a girl who had belonged to a brothel since her birth and had known nothing but that her body was never solely her own—she begged me to sew it back on. As if she thought I had the same power as the one who'd designed her sea-foam draping that allowed her to run across the top of the ocean, far from hands that might hold her down. She sobbed in my arms, bleeding from a million tiny needle holes.

While all the while, I thought of how evil one must be to hand hope to those desperate for it, knowing it would dissipate like sunshine and clouds and the gentle sparkling of light on dawn water.

The tools of my trade were sharp and piercing, better to get the job done. Scissors as dangerous as a butcher's knife, when wielded correctly. I tucked my new ones, small and curved, into the deep pocket of my skirt and left a note in the quiet wee hours of the morning alerting the girls they'd have to open shop without me. Lea would take charge, I knew. She was a quick study, that one, with a deft hand for all she touched. She'd make sure Janie was fed and that the youngest girls were set to the less particular tasks where the stitches wouldn't need to be as straight, as tight, as clean.

Then I took to the streets with the lamplighters.

Six days ago a woman had shown up at my stoop dressed in a tangerine glow, her gown more drapery than puff, more sheen than sparkle. She had been standing tall, the pins in her hair fixed up, though she couldn't do much about the red over-taking the whites of her eyes or the thousands of brown pinprick stains of drying blood against the orange of her dress.

"I need you to remove this dress." She'd spoken in a slow, deliberate fashion, her chin raised proudly. She had no tears when I set to work, nor after as I offered her the removed gown. She sat, naked and straight-backed, on my bench, one palm closed over the other on her lap. Had a stoicism none of the other girls or women had possessed, even as Janie averted her gaze in embarrassment as she brought in some black tea.

So when I asked, "Who did this to you?" that woman did not whisper about a dream or sob over broken promises. She merely answered, "The new mistress seamstress in Locked Land Alley. She has many hands to help her."

While I internalized this information the next few days, worried over it like a knot needing picking, I didn't realize Janie had been turning it over too.

The streets held the dampness of an early morning fog rolling in off the water. The humidity curled the hairs at the nape of my neck and sat heavy in my lungs as I went uptown to the market streets. This early, the bars were quiet and cold. The shadows were black and blue on the stones of the houses. Vendors strode slow as they set up, their steps dogged with sleep they hadn't yet shook off.

I found Locked Land Alley between a fancy hatter shop with the heads from mannequins displayed in their glass windows and a restaurant that spilled tables and chairs into the street. I wove between the tables, eyeless faces staring at me all the while, and found the rusted street sign for the alley hanging limply off the stone wall, lichen eating its way across the letters.

The alley was a long one. Long and quiet and windowless. I resisted the urge to hug myself. And then resisted the desire to turn and run back to my own shop where my girls would sing as they worked, their giggles and murmurs filling my hours. My girls kept me rooted. Images of Lea and all the others bearing the million stitches Janie wore—and the bleed in her heart that might never scab over—giving me the courage I needed to continue deeper.

The stones smelled brackish, like the saltwater in the sewer had backed up and seeped through the mortar holding the walls together. They were cold to the touch, the night still clinging to them even as the world beyond the alley began to pick up speed.

Janie had walked this alley. Had likely tucked her shawl tighter about herself, reset her hair behind her ears in a nervous habit.

I paused when I found the door and wondered how many girls, how many women had been welcomed by the same sight. Gorgeous fabric, untouched by dust or dirt or life, lay draped from sign to ground like an enticement to enter. The door had been painted with ripples and I wouldn't have been surprised had it shivered and pulled aside like a curtain.

The sign above the doorway was in an odd shape: a fat middle, almost like a giant spool of thread that tapered at one end, with many, many thick threads that extended outward from it in curls and bends. It read "Mistress Seamstress."

Inside the shop, formal dresses and ball gowns hung from the ceiling, not a mannequin in sight. They were somehow tied up in delicate poses, this one standing with one sleeve bent up as if the invisible lady wearing it reached for her coiffure, that one bowing slightly at the waist with sleeves outstretched, another caught mid-spin so that the dress twisted about her. The lighting in the shop was dim, hiding the corners and crags, the dust and mites and occasional scraps that might gather in corners where the broom struggled to reach.

"Hello?" I called. "Is the seamstress in?" It was the same call I'd heard time and time again in my own shop after the bell on the door tinkled. I'd hear Lea or Janie or one of my older girls murmur an answer and then they'd poke their head into the workroom for me.

There was none of that here. No apprentices came scrambling at the call of an early-morn customer while shoving stray strands of hair into bonnets. The shop was thick with silence and dancing gowns held up with silken lines, but little else.

I hunted through the maze of silks and cashmere and linens, ducking under sleeves and stepping around trains left to droop against the creaky hardwood floor. The fabrics were soft against my shoulder, lace tickling my cheek when I strode too close.

"Hello, the shop?" I called again. I spun slowly, seeing nothing but ball gowns in lipstick red and lavender fields. The door to the shop was swallowed by layers and layers of arrayed fabric.

There came the high squeal of a hinge. The ponderous groan of a thick door swinging open at the back of the shop. Close. Very close now.

I breathed as shallowly as Janie had during the night, caught as I was between invisible dancers. The next time I called, my voice was hushed and broken: "Mistress Seamstress?"

Where the shop was dim, dresses shimmering in their glorious maze, the open entrance to the workroom in the back was darkened shadows. I heard no giggling of apprentice girls, no tapping of their feet, or the shushing sound of fabric shifting through tiny hands.

From the shadows came a shuffle of noise, then the shifting sound of a roll of fabric being unwound. Creaks against the wood, heavier than my own tread on the flooring.

"Mistress Seamstress," I said once more, attempting to keep my voice stern, of the like I'd use with my girls when they were fooling about. "My apologies for interrupting, but I've a need to speak with you before your day begins."

More creaks from the back of the room, higher this time, and my chin rose unconsciously, my eyes struggling to find the loft where she might have still been abed. I stepped back, abruptly aware that I might have invaded during moments of undress, but stopped at the rasp of a throat clearing.

"You've come for a dress." The voice held a decrepit quality, like the words hurt to speak. An older seamstress, I reasoned, one who'd been in the business for long, yet perhaps not in my city.

But the voice, despite its decrepit quality, or perhaps on account of it, bolstered my confidence. I stepped forward, into the workroom, remaining in the beam of dim light so my shadow stretched long against the floor. "No. I've come to request—" I cut off, then straightened my shoulders. "To tell you to leave the city. What you're doing to the girls here…it's wrong."

"Granting beauty is never wrong."

"They're already beautiful," I snapped, an anger, sewn together one stitch I cut from flesh at a time, overtook my politeness and professional respect. "What you're doing goes beyond our purpose. I don't know how you do it or what possesses you to, but it stops." I paused. "Now."

"Would you like to know?"

The loft cracked and groaned under a weight and the darkness revealed movement to me finally as a body descended.

"I've not come to learn your cheap tricks."

That movement continued, a weight that grew wider, longer, until it overtook the entirety of the back wall. A trick of the light, or of the dark, I reasoned. My own shadow long. Hers a presence that felt larger simply because I could not put fine details to her, see the wrinkles that must come with her voice or the hunched back from bending over her dresses, or the curling fingers from gripping needles for endless decades.

"Cheap?" The voice seemed stronger, but rather than sound affronted, the Mistress Seamstress sounded bemused. "Nothing I grant is…cheap. Now, tell me, what do you feel is missing in your world? Do you wish to fly with the birds? Speak with the stars? Dance down rainbows or curl in a buttercup's embrace? I can give you peace of mind or the excitement you crave. My gowns can sink into your very soul."

Janie had likely heard this same spiel. Had likely pressed her fingers to her lower lip as she was wont to do when considering, before she whispered about sunshine rays. About light and happiness.

The thought infuriated me further, a boiling under my skin. "Your gowns, Mistress Seamstress,"—I spat her name like a curse—"sink into their flesh."

The seamstress hesitated then. I could feel her breathing, a raspy sound in the slowly easing darkness. "It can be both. I cannot have one without the other. You are a woman who understands the cost. Understands that beauty is…ephemeral. My gowns…they are eternal."

Then she shimmied forward, causing me to swallow down a surprised cry. She was a presence that extended up and up, out to either side, her arms stretching ominously toward me against the floor, her back legs curled about the low rafters. Her eyes glittered. Her bulbous stomach settled against the end of the lighted path cast through the doorway, just above the shadow of my head.

My breath came shallow, my skin breaking out in a cold, damp sweat. I licked against the backs of my teeth, twisting my tongue until I found words. "…Eternal? Your gowns…they aren't…"

The Mistress Seamstress stepped forward on all eight limbs, movement flickering at the end of the closest drawing my gaze. She was not quite a spider, I saw in a slowly creeping dread, for the ends of every one of her legs morphed from blackened and furry to humanistic and…many. Split, each leg did, into many, many hands. Brown ones and white. Soft ones and callused. A few with painted nails. Others with scars. Some flat against the ground, other gripping the wooden rafters. But all of them, every last one, was tiny and deft, like a little girl's, who had come knocking one evening, asking after a job, explaining how she might cut up fabric or sweep the workroom, yes, learn the art at the seamstress's feet.

Her many feet that were now many, many hands.

"What gown for you?" Mistress Seamstress asked in her decrepit awful voice. The sound of it swarmed against my ears, kiting into my mind like scratching fingernails desperate to claw their way into the thick of my thoughts.

I backed up toward the doorway, finding my legs sticky and hard to move, like I waded in the sea wearing a dampened heavy ball gown. As if the silken threads that had held the dresses posed in the shop were now looping about my limbs, holding me tightly so I might be as frozen.

"Ah, I will sew one on you. Free of charge," she whispered, her body gloating above mine as I struggled to reach the door frame, my arm sluggish, my body twitching against her silken webbing. She bent to murmur in my ear, promises of a gorgeous piece, as her many, many fingers curled and sifted through my hair, my clothes, gripping my ankles, sliding up my calves. "Let us discover the world you truly wish, shall we?"

So I relaxed, slipping my fingers down, into my pocket to palm my scissors, their little curved tip digging into my flesh. Allowing the tension of her webbing to tighten.

She worked in the darkness. The fabrics a blur of shadows, though she would whisper to herself as her many hands worked. "A fine, fine green lace pattern for your back, I think." Or "A lovely cinching of the gold at your waist."

I jerked at the prick of her needle. Felt her silken threads tighten about me in admonishment. Slowly, I breathed, hearing the snip of multiple pairs of scissors cutting fabric and the clatter of spools of thread, until I could close my eyes, allow the pain to sweep me up and away.

Until I no longer startled at the sharp piercing of her needle. Until the layers of fabric, cut and folded, hemmed and cinched, seeping into my flesh. Until the Mistress Seamstress, content as she set the finishing touches to the gown, to my flesh, loosened the hold she kept on my limbs.

Until I could slide my little embroidery scissors around in my palm, their curved point exposed, and stab them through the faceted eye of the seamstress.

Leaving the stitches against my stomach unfinished, my body shivering with pain, covered with ichor, and the dreams she had promised seeping from each and every stitch.

Lea found me, her small gasp pulling me into alertness. She stared at the Mistress Seamstress. At her bulbous body, her thick legs. Her many hands.

At the scissors still embedded in her eye.

An anger flickered over Lea's face as she approached, quickly replaced by something unreadable. Then her small, deft hands quested about the gown partially stitched to my body, lifting layers, smoothing folds. Her fingers felt along the stitch lines on my flesh. Bump, bump, bump down the paths tracing the pattern, memorizing its form.

"Lea…the scissors," I murmured. Maybe my voice wasn't strong enough. Maybe she couldn't hear me. For she did not respond and did not fetch the scissors. "Lea…"

Instead, she leaned close, her breath hot and humid on my gown-clinging skin. She moved her lips, like she were counting something out, taking a measure. Her fingers stretched against all the stitches keeping the dress entwined with my flesh. But then she tugged me up against her, bade me lean against her shoulder. "Come Miss Cass. I'll get you home."

I existed, curled in the corner of my sewing room—Lea's sewing room now—the stitches holding the gown to my flesh constantly examined, studied…yet never removed.

Watched with glazed eyes as she brought in a young woman in a brown frock, and promised her a dream of silks and beauty.

Watched as arms began to expand from Lea's back, her body misshapen, hunching, graying, skittering. The workroom turning to shadows as the light ceased being needed.

And when the first of my littler girls came begging for Lea to help them too, give them a gown of starlight or rainbows, I watched as Lea told the girl that she had other plans for her. Better plans.

Because Lea just didn't have enough hands for all she desired to accomplish.

Said the Spider to the Fly

By V. F. Thompson

They step out of their cars, perhaps casting a furtive glance over their shoulders, and then look up at the building. It is a squat gray box, betraying nothing of the red neon heart beating inside. The only indicator of her sinful nature is the battered pink sign that hangs in the parking lot: *Fantasies Unbound*. Hands slip into pockets, fingering black cards with slender silver lettering, and some of them think about their wives or husbands at home. Some of them have no wives or husbands, and that is why they are here to begin with.

Their palms rest against the greasy door handle, potentiality tensing in their wrists.

It is past the world's bedtime, the light pollution above smothering the stars so that the only illumination comes from the fast food joints across the street.

Some of them climb back into their cars, not looking back, just driving until they return to their safe places, where they climb back into bed and stare up at the ceiling, wondering.

The rest of them, the ones whose curiosity is too strong to resist, push open the tinted glass and step inside, bell jangling.

Whoever is working the counter looks up from their *Alien vs. Predator* comic or their Angela Carter paperback, one of the rotating cast of tattooed miscreants who keep the engine fed and firing. They're all pierced and they're all trans or gay or some other flavor of social ill, and here they find solace, here they find, if not a safe space, then a familiar one, one from which they can suckle solidarity and no one cares that they dropped out of college and that they smoke weed on break and that sometimes they date more than one person at a time.

They smile, and sometimes the guest smiles back, but more often they bite their lip, avert their eyes, itch for a cigarette even if they haven't smoked in a decade.

"Let me know if I can help you find anything," the employees say. "Or if you have any other questions. Porn's in the back corner, if that's what you're here for."

Then the guest will pretend to browse, because he doesn't know how to ask for what he's really there for. They'll look at the dildos shaped like fists and they'll look at the blind bags with their promised *$20 WORTH OF FUN INSIDE* and they'll look at the fuzzy handcuffs that come in pink and green and purple and blue.

Every so often the doorbell will jingle again, and someone will come in: a regular, they will laugh with the desk person, split a few cracks, and then the employee will lead them to the black door near the silicone asses, will unlock it, will hold it open as they step inside.

The fresh meat will watch as they disappear into that dark and hungry maw, will catch the glimpse of flashing lights and music and moaning that spills out before the door is firmly closed.

Sometimes, then, they will buy something, and they will leave, and they will drive home.

Usually, though, when they've come this far, they'll follow through.

They step up to the counter, clear their throat.

The employee smiles, already knowing what they will ask, relishing the anticipation, stretching out the moment. "Yes?"

"I, uh," they will say, mouths dry. "I'm here for this."

The card will slip out of their pocket, slide across the glass case with the bongs inside, and the employee will pick it up, consider it.

The Criss-Cross Club, reads the shining font. *Where fantasies are fulfilled.*

"Follow me," the employee says, and together they walk to the black door.

I hear all of this, of course; I feel the vibrations, even through the music, tip-tapping across the tile. I hear everything, I feel everything. How could I not? This is my little world on a string. This is my home, the chapel of my hunger, the epicenter of my love, and now, for tonight, it is their home too.

The employee will explain the rules. *No touching without consent. Condoms are not required but are encouraged. For God's sake, clean up after yourself.*

"There are private rooms, at the back," they say. "Club is free. Those aren't."

"How much?" the guests always ask. Almost always, those rooms are the reason why they are here. They heard a story from a buddy at work, or on the putting green, or twisted their ankle on some other grapevine, and fell into this new world. Whatever they have heard, it has smoldered in the back of their mind, driving them just a little bit crazy, until they followed the white rabbit.

"That's up to the ones they belong to," the employee replies.

"I have cash," they say.

"Maybe that will be enough," the employee will grin. "Maybe it won't." And then the door will open, the flashing lights and pulsing house music will beckon, and the door will close behind them.

They find themselves in a lounge, pornography blown up on enormous screens. Nipples are flicked with the tips of tongues, bodies are bent and penetrated and punished, toes are sucked as loud, guttural whimpers cut through the electric beat. People are draped over black leather couches, sipping drinks and fondling themselves and their partners, ties undone and pants unzipped.

They stand and watch for a moment, and some of them even consider leaving.

Instead they head deeper, sometimes stopping at the bar for a gin and tonic or a glass of bourbon, sometimes letting the sights and sounds and smells be lubrication enough. They walk through black velvet curtains and down a short hallway, into a wide-open space, and here there is real friction, the treachery of images abandoned for the vitality of flesh. There are glory holes cut into curving plyboard shapes, bodies on either side of the partition. There is a man leaning back in a swing as another man crouches between his legs, and there are St. Andrew's crosses and a pool table where a woman in a leather dog mask is being flogged.

They sit on a violet velvet settee, next to an oak end table laden with disinfectant wipes, and the ones who are married will think about their spouses, and the ones who came here alone will wonder how they ended up this alone.

They sit there, cocooned by music, psychedelic colors shimmering even behind their closed eyes, knuckles pressed against their foreheads.

And then, when they have made their peace, they will head to the back, for the private rooms.

There are three of them, three red doors stark against their black frames.

The center door, my door, is painted further: a cobweb, concentric strands echoing out from the sign at the door's center, delicate black lines cutting across bleeding crimson.

Sometimes, it reads *OCCUPIED*, and they will knock on one of the other doors. I will hear them through the music, hear them slip off to spend the night with one of my sisters-in-arms, and as I continue my work I will wonder how that lost prey would have tasted—but only for a moment. I never like to lose on what is in favor of what might have been, and quickly I will return to spinning screams, spinning dreams.

Other times, though, the sign will read *OPEN*, and when that is the case, without knowing why, it is always my door they will come to and knock upon.

And when they knock, I am waiting.

"Come in," echoes my voice, curling through the music like smoke, and the door opens.

My room is lit with taper candles, scattered across the floor and trickling down jutting geometry. The music disappears as the door shuts behind them, and they look around for the source of the inviting voice.

"Welcome," I say, the flickering flames throwing my shadow into scuttling relief as I descend from the ceiling, as his mouth opens to scream, as nothing comes out but air, each of my legs settling onto the floor.

Sometimes they back up as I advance. I never advance too quickly. I always give them a chance to run.

They never do.

Instead, they find themselves on their backs, my body looming over them, admiring the angles of my limbs, the curve of my abdomen, the red heart of my lips. They find their own lips parting as mine press against theirs, as I taste their liquefied fears and their liquefied love and drink them both down.

"Am I beautiful?" I ask, my mandibles tickling their neck, and they nod, they mumble assent, their hands in my hair, limbs trembling.

I draw them up, into my waiting web, where they are bound with silken cords, stripped of their clothing, bared to the candlelight. It dances across their chests, over breasts and through curling hair, and I stroke them gently, tease them, make sure they know they are safe here, that it is a safe place to be afraid.

I will be gentle with their fears. I will take their fears and cradle them softly, will eat of them tenderly, will hold them in the darkness of my tight belly and spin them into something wonderful.

We kiss, and we touch each other, and I touch them in ways they did not know they could be touched. I draw screams to their lips, screams that do not escape my chamber but echo in the silence, ecstatic keening delight that is like rich red wine upon my tongue.

It is pleasure, pure in purpose, and as I feed their hearts beat faster and faster, growing as loud as the music outside.

I will not tell you everything that we do there, dancing in the dark. If you want to find out, you must come to me, must find out for yourself.

Suffice to say I make them scream, and I make them cum again and again, their cocks and their cunts twitching and trembling and aching. I make them face their nightmares and buck with pleasure in response. I make them choke on their own voices as they beg for more, as they thank me, as they worship me, this goddess whose name they do not know.

I break them, I rebuild them, and when they are spent, when I have drank as much as they have to give, we will lay there together, their body cradled in my tangle of legs, pressed against my chest.

To love the other is often a hollowing, hallowing experience, and though I am firm, I am not cruel. They have tasted bliss, and I have no desire to discard them without letting them process, letting them recover.

I use them, but do not abuse them.

When their breathing has slowed, when they are ready, I lower them to the floor.

"How much do I owe you?" they ask as they dress.

"You have already paid," I say.

"Can I see you again?" they will ask.

"If you come back," I say, reaching into a drawer and fetching one of the black cards, "I will not let you go." The card transfers from my slender fingers to theirs. "But send another."

And so they leave, cutting back through the music, stepping back into the night.

They blink, trying to understand what it is they have seen, have felt, have loved, and then they climb into their cars and drive back to their lives.

I return to my hungry darkness, my little hidey-hole where I sit and spin and dream, and to fill the time I sing, dark, perfumed words that toll like bells in the candlelit air.

I sit, I sing, and I wait for my next patron.

Some of them do come back, despite my promise.

"I had to see you again," they say, closing the door, undressing.

I do not pounce right away. I give them once more chance, hovering in the shadows, out of the candlelight.

They always stay.

They are my best customers, and I love them most of all.

I make sure it never hurts, make sure it is nothing but rapture as I wrap them tightly and drink more than their fears. "Kiss me like you mean goodbye," I whisper in their ears, their bodies writhing beneath me, their own fluids salty on my lips.

And they do, they always do, even though now, we will always be together.

The Hunter, the Monster, and the Things That Could Have Been

By Leah Ning

You find the dying woman-thing in an alley, breathing her final wet, rasping breaths in a heap of white trash bags that seems more like a throne.

Everything tells you to run: twenty-four years of instinct, the government monster information pamphlets, the hard, practical voice at the back of your head that sounds a lot like your monster hunter girlfriend.

And then the woman-thing looks up. Her dark, scaled cheek drags on the distended belly of plastic that makes her pillow. Her chapped lips part and she says, in a voice like acid and smoke: "Eiko."

That should make you run, too. Things that know your name and shouldn't are firmly in "get the hell out and don't look back" territory. But something in her voice hooks into the bottom of your soul and tugs.

You walk into the alley and she reaches for you. Her fingers are too long, dusky and scaled like her face. You shiver when they rasp over your cheek, your hair. Your heart pounds. You should run. You should run now.

That tug in your soul, a deep ache like kinship, won't let you.

Something passes from her rough palm into you: a jolt, warm and slimy and slipped between your skin and the muscle beneath. Your body goes soft, like puking and collapsing and passing out all at once, only you can't do any of those, something won't let you, and you have to shiver and listen to the last of the woman-thing's clotted, choking breaths as she dies half-buried in trash.

You are left with a sour breeze, a hollow where that ache hooked into your soul, and the sudden, desperate certainty that you need Mia right fucking now.

She opens her apartment door for you in loose sweatpants and that white ribbed tank top you like. You don't want to tell her—you know what it'll do to her, and you're so scared—but what else are you going to do? You don't know what you're doing. Mia hunts things like you saw in the alley for a living. If anyone can fix this, it's her.

So you sit her down on her scruffy couch. There's a catch in her breath when you say it, so small you wouldn't have noticed if you weren't looking for it.

But you are not a thing to kill. You are a thing that can be saved. When you reach for her hand, she leans into you, presses a kiss to your hairline.

"We can still save it," she says. "It's all right, girl, I got you. You stay with me until I get this fixed."

There's a hard burst of relief in your chest. "But I have to work—"

"Call out sick." She squeezes your hands. "You can't go in like this. We'll get it fixed up and then you go back in and it won't matter. Two days, okay? Tops."

Or you won't get it fixed up, and then you won't go back in, and it still won't matter. You try to shiver and can't. The feeling sits in an unsteady pocket at your core.

Mia sits at her desk, one knee up, blond curls edged in blue laptop glow and books laid out across each other. You try not to pace and you pace anyway and you apologize at least once an hour.

"You do what you need," Mia says, and slips an absent arm around your waist.

Your fingers ache to do *something*, so you peel away from her. You make coffee and set a mug on the edge of her desk, then flinch when she flips a few pages because someone's replaced your nerves with razors.

"Thanks, love," she murmurs, but you're already halfway down the hall.

That feeling of cold-but-can't-shiver trembles beneath your skin. You roll your shoulders as you pad into Mia's room and it doesn't help.

You pull the blanket from her bed: an aged blue quilt, faded but soft. You wrap it tight around yourself and it helps. Not all the way, but it helps.

You turn to go back out to Mia. Hesitate.

Too open, you think, and have no idea what you mean except that it rings true in that hollow place the dying woman-thing left in your soul.

You drop the quilt in the corner. You grab the pillows. Toss those in the corner.

You take a step toward it.

Hesitate. Some buried animal part of you sending up an inexorable negative. A pull toward the closet.

You go. More blankets there, towels. An extra pillow. You yank them out and it stills the wrongness in your chest.

Into the corner with the rest. A soft, warm pile, inviting, smelling of Mia's fresh laundry detergent. Clean cotton.

You crawl in and wrap yourself up. And it's good. So good. That shivering feeling fades back until it's almost gone.

"Baby, I found—oh. Gods."

Your head snaps up. Mia frozen in the doorway, her expression strained, yellow hallway light tracing the point of her jaw.

"Found what?" you say. Your voice rasps in your throat.

Her hand leaves the door frame, then braces there again. "You're nesting."

"Nesting." You look down and suppose you could call it that. "What did you find?"

"This is bad," Mia says softly. "The…nesting. It's so fast—"

"Then we should start…whatever it is…soon. Right?" you ask. The whole thing feels like watching paper bounce off Plexiglass. Your mouth feels like cold spitballs. "What did you *find?*"

She steps toward you. Stops. "I don't…know if you're dangerous."

"Does it matter? If we—"

"Rot."

"Hmm?"

"Rot. You found a dying rot goddess. She turned you."

You press your back into the wall. "Why does it matter?"

"Because I don't think I can stop it."

Something falls out of the bottom of your stomach. It doesn't feel like Mia looking at you anymore. It looks like a little girl with a silver knife backed into a corner.

"But you said we could," you say.

"That was before I knew it was a goddess."

That shivery feeling starts to come back to you. This place isn't safe.

"Then what do I do?" you ask.

Mia's mouth works. "I—stay here. Just stay here, and I'll—I don't know. If you're not dangerous, I can just—but your work will—fuck, Eiko, I don't know."

She wants to keep you here. She wants to hold you here.

This place isn't safe.

"Okay," you say.

"I have to go," she says. You realize she's dressed up in her hunting gear, all black and packed with blades and herbs and guns.

"What are you hunting?" you ask quietly. "A goddess?"

She flinches.

"No," she says. "A werewolf."

So she'll be a mess when she gets back.

She was starting to watch movies with you instead. She was starting to fall asleep on the couch with you. Starting to let you make her pancakes and coffee for breakfast instead of cramming down half an energy bar and a couple beers.

You wonder if she'll ever touch you again as she locks you in behind her.

• • •

In a perfect world, you could've trusted her. You could've curled up in your nest until she came back in the morning, and she might've crept in to curl up with you.

You wouldn't have thought to use one of her bobby pins to work on the lock until it sprang open with a satisfying *snap*. You wouldn't have scanned her desk, heart skipping, for the books she used, and then decided to take all the open ones.

You could've read them together when Mia got back. Scoured them for something she missed, any hint of how to stop it, any whiff of whether you'd be dangerous.

You wouldn't have had to fear that she'd be there when you slipped out the door. You wouldn't have had to slip out at all.

You start to run home and can't.

Every time you put a foot down, your skin *slips*—just a little—toward your heel, and every time you pick a foot up, your skin springs back into place. You trip over the first few running steps you take and almost eat tar, so you walk.

Quickly.

You still almost fall a few times, but you make it, and you lock yourself inside.

First things first: that shiver is back in your bones.

You don't want to *nest*, because that is apparently bad news, but you can't concentrate when it feels like your skin is trying to crawl off your body. You yank the duvet from your bed, the pillows, then all the soft stuff you can find, and throw it into a corner.

You hesitate. It isn't quite right. But it'll do for now. If you can prove you won't be dangerous, maybe Mia will come back around. Maybe she won't be so scared of you. Your body feels funny, but your mind feels fine. Mostly. Except that you need what amounts to a den instead of a bed now.

It doesn't matter. A den doesn't mean you're *dangerous*.

You settle into your corner to read.

In a perfect world, the books would have told you more than half of what you could do. The goddess in the alley would have died curled in a home she dug with her own two hands, surrounded by candles and incense and attended by you.

You would have known that her name was Isabel. The sound of your own name on her tongue would have been comfort, not fear.

She would have taught you, as her days wound to a close, what would happen to your skin, how to care for your new scales, how to dig your own home, how that space would give you safety. Give you power.

You would have known what you could do. You would have learned how to rot, to feed dead things back to the world that needs them in that form as much as its living one.

You would have learned, too, that you could preserve. Keep a bouquet fresh, stop a wound from festering, hold wet, decaying wood together long enough to be replaced before it collapsed on whatever soul had the misfortune to be beneath it.

You could have done good. In a world that loved you, you could have done so much good.

But this is a world that will see your scales, your unearthed ribs, your skin sloughing from your face to slop onto the carpet and recoil. This is a world where creatures like you are called monsters, and hope doesn't enter the equation.

This is a world where no one thinks to donate blood to vampires, hire doppelgangers as stunt doubles, lock werewolves away until the moon wanes.

This is a world where if a woman turns into a werewolf, there's a silver knife in the house, and the only thing her ten-year-old daughter would know to do is use it.

And sixteen years later, as you listen to the deadbolt at your front door clunk back and watch that little girl walk in, still in her hunting garb, you prepare to run.

But, gods, you still want to *hope*.

There are two brief points in which things still might be good for you, for Mia.

In this point, she is standing in the doorway to your apartment, watching you shed your skin in one smooth shrug.

In this point, she doesn't recoil from the glint of bone in the pale post-dawn light through the window.

She is reaching for you, palms upturned, face gentle, hair mussed and sleeves torn.

She doesn't reach for anything sharp, anything loud or hurting. Just you.

She says, "Love, it's okay."

She says, "I found a way to stop it."

It might be okay still. If she trusts you. If you trust her.

You go to her.

You shouldn't have.

In the perfect world you'll never find, Mia meant every word she said.

She didn't pull a knife wound with bramble from the sheath at her back.

She didn't whip it around her side so fast you might not have seen it if you were still human.

You did not, in your fear and your ignorance of your own power, put your arm up so fast that it tore hers off.

• • •

You didn't mean to hurt her. You didn't. But here she is bleeding into what used to be your carpet, gasping, making thin noises in the back of her throat with every breath.

You didn't mean to hurt her.

You begin to back away. Stop. Start forward, scaled hands held up. Stop.

"I'm sorry," you whisper. But that won't stop her bleeding. You have to stop the bleeding.

Mia sits down, hard, like she can't do anything else. So heavy. Out of her own control. It catches at your heart and you go to her.

"Don't," she says, and scrambles, weakly, for the knife. You kick it aside. "Don't—"

You lift her up. One arm under her back, the other under her knees.

"We can save it," you say in your new voice, like acid and smoke. "I got you."

You begin to run, and now, with your skin gone, you don't trip. You don't even come close.

In a perfect world, even though Mia couldn't keep that promise, you could.

The slowing of the blood from her arm would've meant that her bleeding was stanched and not that her blood was simply running out.

The way she looked up at you, the fact that she could say, "You're trying to save me," would've meant that she was gaining her legs again, not that she was on the last they had left.

You would've been fast enough.

You wouldn't have showed up at the hospital with a body in your arms.

You would've realized that laying the corpse of a hunter at the door of a hospital didn't look like sorrow, like regret.

You would've realized that it looked like a challenge.

• • •

The first of them finds you at sunset the next day.

He must've tracked you by Mia's blood, because you didn't go to her apartment, and you didn't go to yours. You ran until you found woods, somewhere outside the city, and you dug down into the dirt with your new scaled hands until you didn't feel like collapsing-shivering-fainting anymore.

You don't want to kill this hunter. You don't want to kill anyone. But he's trying to kill you, and it doesn't matter what you say, he won't stop, and eventually you do kill him.

He came to your home with a knife wrapped in bramble. What else were you supposed to do?

You don't let the rot touch his body, thinking someone might like to bury him. The hunter that comes after him breathes something about unnatural bullshit and tries to kill you, too.

Your legend grows teeth, grows legs and starts to walk: many go to the goddess's lair. None return. This will be the way until there is someone brave enough, strong enough, fast enough to put her down.

You leave their unrotted bodies among the trees. At first you hope someone will come for them, bury them, mourn them instead of trying to avenge them. When this doesn't happen, you keep it up, hoping it will scare the rest away.

When this doesn't happen, it's so much a habit that you keep it up anyway, your silent standing army of the dead with their throats rent and their chests crushed and their guts swaying against their thighs.

At the final point where things might have been okay, there is a woman. She carries a lush bouquet, picking her way through your carefully preserved crop of enemies. You eye her from the dark beneath the dirt.

"You don't let them rot," the woman calls, casting her free hand at those who came before. "You could do something good with that magic. Couldn't you?"

She's not telling you anything you don't know. Your home is lined with ageless flowers now, everlasting grass braids hanging from the ceiling.

The woman holds out her bouquet, velvety yellows and rich greens shot through with sunlight. "Will you do that for me?"

Oh, but you know this trick. You know all about gentle lies you wish like hell you could believe. About knives in cleverly hidden sheaths.

So you call to her. Invite her in.

And she comes to you.

She shouldn't have.

Goodbye Gutleech

By J. W. Allen

Mira had never seen a Gutleech, but she was freezing her ass off hunting one. Other hunters called this place "the Forest of Memories." More like the forest of fuck-all, Mira thought, tripping over another root hidden by snow. She staggered to her feet and collapsed into the hollow of a nearby tree. It was cold, but at least it was out of the wind.

Her stomach groaned and Mira knew she had to find food soon. Either that, or become forest food. Or Gutleech food. She shivered at the thought, looking around, her eye catching on a dark hole at the base of the hollow. Removing a mitt, she placed one hand over, excited to feel warmer air. An animal might be burrowed from the cold.

Mira carefully reached into the hole until her fingers brushed against something long and coiled that wasn't bark. A family of sleeping snakes. Not ideal. Better than dying though.

She grabbed a serpent and chewed the head off, ignoring the thrashing tail. Fighting for life in sleep. Admirable. Mira retched as she gulped down the blood and noticed something else sticking out beneath her feet, half hidden by dead leaves and ice.

Bones. Littered neatly about, each one licked clean, the surfaces smooth and shiny, all marrow sucked out. Too many and too big for a snake to eat. From the size and shape of each, ugh. Two people. She had stumbled into another grave. Half angry, half scared, and definitely all cold, Mira lurched out and threw the dead snake in a rage of inspired swearing and death threats.

The Gutleech had found dinner.

Spitting, Mira glared at the frozen trees, trying to determine which way the monster had gone. Snow had long since covered any tracks the Gutleech may have left. Mira stood up and kicked the bones before remembering they used to be people like her family. She took several deep breaths and closed her eyes. Allow a moment's grief, before calmly imagining how to gut the Gutleech when she found it.

Reining in her temper, Mira trudged through the snow. Her breath puffed like clouds as she moved. She sang to distract herself from the cold and the hunger.

"Gutleech, Gutleech, Hiding in the snow,
Kill-er, Kill-er, Hunted far and low,
Gutleech, Gutleech, Catching friend and foe,
Hunt it, Hunt it, Give the crowds a show."

Wind and snowfall turned the sky a murky blue, and a thin plume of smoke rose above the tree canopy ahead. Despite her cracked lips and a groaning ache in her legs, Mira's heart thumped wetly.

Shelter. Maybe even some warm food she could eat. Would they ask for money? She didn't have any. Fuck it. She could always offer them part of the Gutleech bounty. Anything to keep her going.

Keep her hunting.

Mira stumbled towards the cabin, tripping twice before banging on the door. Someone called something above the wind as the door opened. Mira almost fell across the threshold. The cabin was small, but blissfully warm. Mira surveyed the room quickly; two women. A small wooden table with three chairs and some musty blankets piled high in the far corner. Heat came from a merry little blaze burning within a squat fireplace.

"C-c-cold outside," Mira muttered, annoyed with her chattering teeth.

The taller woman pointed a long finger to a wooden chair near the fireplace.

Mira did as she was told, her body too stiff to object.

"Who have we here then?" the shorter woman rumbled from a seat opposite.

"Mira," Mira sniffed.

The shorter woman examined her, dark eyes glaring deep from within hollow sockets. "What are you doing out here?"

"Building a snowman. You?"

After a shared glance, the taller moved to rest a hand on her shorter companion's shoulder.

Mira sighed. "I'm a hunter and I'm out hunting."

No one said anything.

"I know what you're thinking," she smiled, holding up her hands, "'Mad! Hunting in winter? In a forest? In the middle of a blizzard?' And you're right, but I go where the work is."

"And you think there's work for a hunter out here?" the taller said, ignoring her companion's attempts to shrug her hand off. "The few hunters who come out this far are usually looking for trouble."

"Or running from it," the shorter murmured.

"I don't run from anything. But if I were looking for trouble, I wouldn't waste my time chatting."

The shorter woman scratched her chin with one hand.

"Fair point."

Mira wrinkled her nose, noticing a pot hanging above the fire. Again, her stomach rumbled, the bitter tang of snake's blood still on her tongue.

"I don't suppose you have anything hot to eat that isn't a dead snake?"

The tall woman called herself Yash. Her shorter partner was Oti. No more was said until after dinner. The meat in the stew was stringy, but at least it was warm. Better than snake's blood. Mira chewed through the silence, grateful for it. Small talk wasn't really her thing anyway.

After their bowls were empty, Yash cleared them, then stoked the fire. When the flames were high enough, she sat beside Oti, placing an arm around the shorter woman. Wind and snow pattered the thin window pane by the door, and Mira saw that night had truly fallen.

How far ahead was the Gutleech? Had it found shelter? If it was anything like her, it would not enjoy the cold. Not for the first time, Mira wondered what it looked like close up. All she had was an artist's impression and vague accounts from the families who'd hired her.

"Hunters rarely come this far out," Yash murmured, interrupting Mira's thoughts.

Mira coughed before wiping her brow with one sleeve. "Yeah, you said that. The thing I'm looking for seems to know I'm on its tail…if it has a tail. I'm not entirely sure."

"So, this creature is intelligent then?"

"If by 'intelligent' you mean 'able to sniff out the vulnerable and attack folks that can't defend themselves', then it's a genius."

"Huh," Oti grunted. "How can you judge something you haven't even seen?"

Mira studied the shorter woman whose dark gaze was lost somewhere within the crackling fireplace. Oti had no idea. No idea at all. Still, they had offered her shelter, so best to ignore that remark.

"Fortunately for everyone, I'm told my monster is one of the last of its kind. Now if I can just find the fucker, I'll…"

"Kill it?" Oti growled. "Hang its head above your mantelpiece and brag about the hunt to friends and family."

"No family to brag to," Mira mumbled. "Not anymore."

She bowed her head, feeling a sting at the corners of her eyes. For a moment, no one but the fire spoke. The pops and crackles did a fair job of filling the void between Mira and these women.

"We're sorry to hear that," Yash whispered. Mira looked up and saw her glaring at Oti. "Aren't we?"

"Tragic," Oti said, looking more interested in the fire than in Mira's story.

"It's fine. Once this monster is dead, you'll be safe. And I'll be paid."

Mira's stomach growled again. That stew was a temporary salve at best. She needed more food if she was to catch up with the Gutleech. Behind her, she thought she heard a ruffle and turned quickly to check. Nothing. Firelight made shadows dance across a small mound of blankets in the corner, but there was nothing else in the room.

"Safe," Oti repeated, as Mira turned back. "From what exactly?"

"Well, from things that will kill you before you even know they're there. Things that gut you from the inside out before licking your bones clean. Safe from monsters that can butcher your wife and your children," she paused, swallowing hard, "children that never get a chance to grow up."

Mira heard her voice crack, and was furious. Talking with these women had somehow lowered her guard. She didn't want witnesses to her pain. Furiously she rubbed her face, refusing to close her eyes. Closing her eyes left her alone with nightmares and blurred memories. Neither were of use to her.

All that mattered was the hunt…and money enough to give her family the burial they deserved. Small comfort. But incentive enough to keep trying. She just had to find the Gutleech.

"She should stay the night." Yash's soft voice brought Mira back to the room.

"What?!" growled Oti, rising from her chair, but Yash held up a hand until Oti slumped back, defeated. But then Oti leaned forward, her glare half demonic in the firelight.

"You're lucky she likes you."

Mira's stomach bubbled like a cauldron as Yash explained how she and Oti had fled the central continents. Left to live in the southern wilds, safe in this "Forest of Memory."

"People in our village were getting paranoid. Rumors of shadows and strange growls from the dark. It got worse when the Mayor's children disappeared. Suspicions cast on anyone even slightly different to the status quo. Our own neighbors," Yash paused, shaking her head, "our friends. They started looking at us in a way that made us feel like we were somehow guilty."

"Local authorities sent in hunters like you," Oti snarled. "Didn't help though, especially when they began disappearing too. We heard of hunters attacking villages. And if they couldn't find what they were looking for, they'd fight each other. We got out whilst we could."

"Oh, we don't blame hunters," Yash added quickly, seeing the look on Mira's face. "You're just doing your job."

Oti snorted, but was silenced with a sharp look from Yash. "But, we're prudent when it comes to safety and we've seen how terribly fear can affect even the most rational of people. So, we came as far as we dared and found this old cabin. Abandoned but sturdy. And here we are."

Mira nodded, her hands shaking despite the fire. She had heard of couples like Yash and Oti. Oddities that were guarded around hunters. Eccentrics.

Yash collected a blanket from the large pile in the corner and threw it across Mira's shoulders. It smelled nice too. There was a faint aroma of something delicious that Mira couldn't quite place.

"Where do you find your meat?" she asked, drawing the blanket tighter.

"There's a lake a few hours' hike from here. Frozen, but fish still live underneath. And Oti found a colony of rabbits last year."

"Hard to get the snares not to freeze, but we manage," Oti grumbled.

That explained the stringiness of the stew, and her continued hunger, Mira thought. She prayed the Gutleech was as miserable as she felt. Somehow, she doubted it.

Yash angled her head slightly to one side, staring at Mira. "You don't look well."

"I'll be fine. Just tired."

She hoped that wasn't a lie and raked her eyes over Yash and Oti, wondering if either was capable or willing to try anything against a hunter. Probably not.

"I need some more food if you have it and I'll be out of your way," she coughed. "I promise I'll come back and give you a percentage of the bounty as payment for your help."

"You'll have to wait till morning," Oti yawned. "Stew's all gone, and we won't be able to check the snares until sunrise."

"Oh. Probably best I leave now," Mira said, standing and nearly tripping over the long blanket around her.

"Why?"

"Because…" Mira racked her brain, trying to think of a polite excuse. "…If I stay, I'll just steal the whiskey I spied above the fireplace. I tend to piss people off, so it's best I go. Besides, I can't let that Gutleech get too far ahead."

Not even the fire popping in the grate could deafen the silence that followed. Mira cursed herself for allowing the word to slip out. She saw something bloom in the eyes of the two women. Noticed the way the shadows didn't quite hide a flinch from Yash. The last thing she needed was to frighten these people.

"'Gutleech?'" Oti repeated, dark eyes narrowing, one hand reaching out to steady her partner. "That's what you're after?"

Mira's pulse punched her in the ears as Oti stared. And then the short woman did something unexpected. She laughed.

"Do you hear that?" Oti giggled, elbowing Yash in the ribs. "This hunter is after a Gutleech."

Yash smiled politely and turned back to the fire, bending low to prod it even as Oti continued to laugh.

"Careful now, Yash. Stoke that too high and a Gutleech might see. We wouldn't want it paying us a visit now would we? The things it might do, wooowee…doesn't bear thinking about."

"Laugh all you like," Mira said, trying not to clench her jaw.

"I will, hunter, I will."

"You won't be laughing if you meet it. By the time you realize, your insides will be on the outside."

Oti's bottom lip wobbled and another chuckle spluttered out. "Oh, this hunter, Yash. This hunter is exactly what I thought she was."

"And what is that?" Mira snapped.

Oti took a breath before staring seriously at Mira. "Clown! There are no more Gutleech. Hunters killed them all nearly two hundred years ago."

The bitterness in her voice returned.

"Slaughtered every last one. No mercy. No quarter. Destroyed the lot, until all that remained were vague memories of what happened. Remind me, because I'm very old and feeble minded, but you haven't even caught a glimpse of your monster, right?"

When Mira didn't answer, Oti nodded and leaned back.

"Gutleech is just a name given to anything people are frightened of. Oh, it's true there was a species called Gutleech. Bit like us actually. They even lived similar, eating, sleeping, making a life where they could. Nice folk. And they did their best to counter the stories. Horror stories to be precise. Told by one idiot to another until you go several generations where what we once called 'a neighbor' has become 'a monster.'

"Gutleech didn't even call themselves Gutleech. Their original name was 'Gutlich'. 'Gutleech' was something hunters called them, presumably to frighten everyone. Rumor goes they even turned Gutlich against Gutlich as their numbers dwindled. The monster in the tale became real, in a way."

"Creative story," Mira said. "Absolute crap, but creative crap I'll grant you that."

Oti snorted again.

"Hunters! What do you know? Most of us just want to live in peace. The people who pay you," Oti paused, piety dripping off every syllable, "are just small minded pricks scared of their own shadow. They wouldn't know an intelligent species if one came up and debated philosophy with them."

"They know enough to pay people like me to protect people like you."

"People like us never asked for your protection. We don't need it."

Mira shrugged in the blanket.

"Well, you got it anyway, even if I think you're fools for being out here."

Oti slowly shook her head before turning to Yash.

"You see? Doesn't even know what happened."

"What we think happened," Yash interjected softly. "No one really knows for sure."

Oti waved a dismissive hand at her partner.

"Come on Yash, you saw our village before we left. We were lucky to get out. Those hunters would have killed us if we'd stayed. They were looking for a fight, and they didn't care against who."

"Maybe they were," Mira said. "But that was them, and this is me. I can be ruthless, I'll give you that—it is part of my job after all—but you don't know me," she continued hearing the pulse rise in her ears. "You don't know anything about what I do to help people. Even people who mock my profession."

"Really? Well, tell me this, hunter. What happens when you can't find your monster?"

"Oti," Yash tried to interrupt. But Oti appeared in no mood to stop.

"I'll tell you then. Same thing that happened in our village. You'll look for other things. Other creatures. Other people. And your employers will call them all 'Gutleech.'"

Yash stood up sharply, turning to place a soothing hand on Oti. "That's enough. She's our guest."

Mira swallowed. Oti was definitely one of *those* people who didn't believe the Gutleech was real until it was too late. Mira actually felt sorry for her. For both of them. The Gutleech would take advantage of nature-loving do-gooders that didn't know any better. They even believed children's stories about hunters.

Living so far from civilization had dulled their minds. There was one bright side to Oti's fairytale: it had convinced Mira that it was definitely time to go. She threw off the blanket and approached the door.

"You'll freeze out there," Yash called out.

"It's better I leave now before the Gutleech gets too far ahead."

"Ah, let her go," Oti growled. "She's just like the other hunters. Conditioned to kill. Never to think."

Mira turned to face the women, determined to thank them for their hospitality and say goodbye politely. To prove to them that hunters were not just killers. She saw the way Oti's hand was clasped firmly around Yash's. Mira managed a curt nod to both before opening the door to a blast of wind and snow.

"I'll catch the Gutleech. And when I do, you can both go on living and cursing hunters till you're blue in the face."

"You'll catch your death before you catch any monsters out here," Oti called out above the noise. "But if it makes you feel better, you go on hunting, hunter. We'll be here long after the snow's buried you."

Even as the words left her mouth, Mira knew Oti thought she was mad. Yet, there was something above the anger and disgust in the stubborn woman's voice. Something that Mira knew quite well.

Fear.

Yash offered a sad smile before closing the door behind her. Slowly, Mira turned to brace herself against the snow and the wind and stomped away from the cabin. Stupid women! Stupid snow! Stupid Gut—

She stopped.

The blanket. That smell.

That smell.

Looking back over her shoulder, Mira studied the cabin through the blizzard, smoke from its chimney wrestling with the cold. A tense feeling gathered in the pit of her stomach. Could they see her? Doubtful in this weather. Nevertheless, Mira walked on a bit further before taking a sharp right behind some trees. Gradually, she circled back, careful to keep the trees between her and the cabin until the last possible moment.

Mira darted from behind a tree and up to the rear of the cabin, flattening against the wood. She inched around until she spotted light escaping a knothole in the wood. Heart pumping, Mira bent down and peered inside.

Oti and Yash were fussing over something by the fire. Its hair was long and bushy, sticking out in all directions around a frightened little face. Two skinny arms ended in five bony digits. It wore a set of rags that might once have been clothes held together by an odd amount of stitching.

It looked nothing like the artist's impressions Mira's employers had given her. For one thing it was a lot frailer. No blazing red eyes. No razor-sharp hooks on its skin like the ones that had torn Mira's own family to pieces. And it stood upright. It didn't crawl on its belly. It looked more like some kind of feral child, and yet…

The smell from the blanket brought her senses alive. That… whatever it was, held the scent of prey.

Stomach growling, Mira returned through thick snow to the front of the cabin. She raised a hand to knock on the door, but paused. Yash and Oti would no doubt hide the child-thing again before they answered. Better not to give them that chance.

Mira kicked the door open in one go.

Oti made a grab for the thing's arm, trying to pull it back, but the creature darted out of reach of the two women.

"Don't," the thing said. "She'll leave you alone once I'm gone."

Gutleech were supposed to be mute animals. Gutleech were said to be slimy naked things, their skin covered with flesh ripping barbs.

"You found me, hunter," the thing said, swallowing hard and moving to stand in front of the two women.

Gutleech were not supposed to look like…well, people. And it appeared nowhere near capable of being able to rip a twig apart, let alone a person. The thing shook as it took a step towards her, whether from the cold or its own fear, Mira did not know. Her stomach raged inside, and she could feel sounds and voices colliding and fighting in her mind.

"I'll go with you, just please leave them alone. They…they've been very kind."

Mira took a step back, pressing herself against the door as she tried to reason with something primal in her mind. Something was urging her not to trust this thing. Gutleech were monsters. Everyone knew it. They tricked. They stole. They lied. They killed innocent people. Children.

Mira's vision clouded. Deep in the pit of her stomach, her hunger was rising into a groan.

"Oh my God!" a voice said. Was it Yash? "She's one of those… *things* from the village!"

Mira's pulse surged. She doubled over, clutching her belly, then screamed when she saw her arms. Her skin…what was wrong with her skin? It appeared slimy and barbed under the firelight.

"Please, don't hurt her," Yash shouted from somewhere far away. "We can help you. I know we can help you if you let us, but try to think. Try to…"

"You should run," the thing interrupted from somewhere far away.

Mira tried to tell the child that a hunter doesn't ever run. A hunter stands her ground. A hunter doesn't stop until she has her prey and collects her bounty. She only realized the thing wasn't talking to her when she saw Yash dragging Oti toward the back of the cabin.

Mira tried to tell them not to worry. That there had obviously been some sort of mistake. That she would just take the…whatever it was back with her, leave them be and let the authorities figure it all out. Instead, all Mira heard was a long rising moan that curdled into an unnatural screech. At first she thought it came from the child-thing; the Gutleech? But then she saw the way the thing just stood there looking at her, trembling in fear. Mira fell forward onto her belly. From the corner of her vision, the child dashed for the door, and the scent of prey overpowered everything.

Mira couldn't recall how she had found shelter from the storm. The cabin she'd woken up in had done a fair job of protecting her from the worst of the blizzard. She smiled, grateful that her hunter's survival instincts could still operate even if she couldn't remember every detail. Hunger will do that to you. This hunt was becoming more blurred and endless by the day. Yawning, Mira stretched in her tattered clothes, then sniffed the air and shivered.

The inside of the cabin was cold and smelled like death. Her shoulders slumped as she looked to her left and saw the bones. Small piles lay at the center of the cabin. Three people. From the looks of it, two adults and one smaller set that looked more decalcified. Every bone was smooth, the marrow sucked clean. Mira bowed her head and felt the familiar sting in the corner of her eyes.

Much like the bones she'd found in the tree hollow yesterday.

Much like her own family.

Three more piles to add to the collection the Gutleech had left in its bloody wake.

She allowed the dead a moment's grief before standing up, pausing only to grab a blanket from a musty pile in the corner. Mira wrapped it over her coat and went outside, closing the door gently behind her. The slippery monster couldn't have gotten far. Snow had covered the Gutleech's tracks, but Mira would find it.

It was only a matter of time.

Old Bogg Bones

By Gretchen Tessmer

Old Bogg Bones squats in his swampy quagmire, crouching on fallen birchwood, digging at the spongier spots of black-striped bark with long, claw-like fingernails. His knuckles are covered in coarse white fur, as is the rest of him, shaggy patches springing up all over his hunched and twisted back. The white mixes with nut-brown curls that reach his bent and knobby knees, his beard tangled with mud, twigs, leaves, and thorns.

Everything around him stinks of decay.

His keen eyes watch the oily mud of his bog like a fisherman watching water, and soon he reaches down, swirling his meaty paws around, picking out a blanched bone—*too long, too tall,* he mutters—casting it aside, then another. As the larger bones slowly sink back into mire, he hugs the smallest ones to his chest for safe-keeping.

"Come! We have to hurry!"

Little Amka leads the man over muddy swamp and moldy tundra, all damp grass and pockmarked puddles. The ground is crusted with the brittle remnants of winter's ice but it's soft-bellied beneath, with crawling beetles and wolf spiders and shoots of sedge pushing out of brown earth, showing white roots and black mulch.

A mist hangs in the air, like the earth's lungs are breathing in deep and exhaling. The temperature is cold and humid both, stuck between seasons. Winter is being staved off unnaturally, and spring is being forced upon the land too soon.

The air hums and buzzes with warfaring magic—too many new spells for the clouds to absorb, too many old ones melting from ancient ice—and it's starting to spill into the land.

The weather looks violently changeable. Sparks of lightning ring the black-plum horizon, but there's no thunder. Not a growl or grumble in the distance. The breeze is hushed, timid under angry skies. The animals are in hiding, too afraid of the silence, eerie signs in the sky and blood-stained waters. Those little streams and creeks that flow from the shrubby woodland behind them trickle pink.

A red fox darts between lichen-licked rocks. Or was that just a shadow?

It begins to rain. The man's moody and miserable. His skin is soaked, the rags he wears are soon sopping wet and sticking to him. His nut-brown hair is matted against his scalp, wet strands falling into dark eyes. He's not made for open country and he should seek cover now, before hypothermia sets in. But where would he go?

Ahead of him, Little Amka darts in and out of the scrub like she was born to it. And she was, amongst the briars and snowmelt dotting the biome. She's one of the tundra-children. Her kind sprung up from the thaw above the permafrost many years ago, born in spring muck with cat eyes seeking pale sunlight, green vines in their hair and leaf litter crushed into their amphibious skin.

They think this land is theirs. But doesn't everyone? They all stake their claims and mark their borders—the woods for the knights, the marshlands for the tundra-children. They murder trespassers and burn down the huts and cabins that straddle the line. The territory is too wild and too big for anyone to control all of it, but that hasn't stopped them from trying.

He's sick to death of it. And he's sick to death of running.

But he keeps going, even as he grows winded and weary, a stitch burning at his side, his feet numb and his steps clumsy. He scrambles to keep up with Amka, stumbling on uneven ground, as her pace has quickened since they left the woods.

She's smaller than him, only half his size, with bones like birds. She's much faster. Her skin sheds the water and her webbed feet offer a better grip on the lowlands than his ragged boots, showing holes and caked with mud. He keeps slipping, cutting up his hands on shale.

He wants to go home.

But he doesn't have a home. He hasn't had a home in a long time. And it makes his heart grow cold to think on the word, as cold as the icy rain that continues to pelt down on them. His expression flashes hard and bitter as he wipes the rainwater from his brow. He wants to scream at the sky but thinks his lungs might give out if he tries.

He stops on a grassy knoll, forces another breath, before following Little Amka.

Where does the monster live? Old Bogg Bones demands of his guests, the wanderers and wayfarers who come by his lair, some on purpose, most by mistake.

The scent of damp soil, worms, and dead things warns off many long before they reach the borders of the swamp, but there are always some who persevere past the stones, the toads, piles of old bones, to reach a lagoon of black mud and the creature who has lived at the center of it for a thousand years.

They stutter their reply to his riddle.

"He—Here?" comes the halting answer, a quaver in their voices. They've been told that Bogg Bones values fear and respect above everything else. They bow, they flatter him, they beg for their lives, "Please, my lord…"

Old Bogg Bones smiles patiently at their manner—if that snarl of lips can be called a smile—and speaks in a voice that resonates deep in the marrow, not the ears, *Why are you afraid? The answer is in your own head.*

• • •

He slips in his haste, banging his knee on the roots of a dwarf willow, so bent it seems to be growing downward. "Curse it all!" he cries and means every bit of it, while his hand stretches out to find a solid hold. The heel of his hand sinks into a puddle of moss and pink water.

The water's always pink these days, traveling ahead of them, heralding news of the skirmish in the woods this morning. It was a bloody business. It always is. Those knights in their fine armor are still back there, standing over three of Little Amka's kind, all slain, all dead on the ground.

The knights' greatswords are dripping red.

A foreign priest in black robes is with them, and a moon witch too, wearing a face that isn't her own. They hover over the dead tundra-children. They kneel on brown leaves that are slick with blood and icy dew. There's a ceremonial knife in the priest's hand, blessed by holy water, but the moon witch forgoes metal, using her strong fingernails to pierce flesh instead, intent on carving out the hearts and organs before they go cold.

The moon witch takes a bite of the warm heart for herself, tempted by the pulsing magic still beating within. The honorable knights glare at her, receiving a blood-stained smirk in reply. Generous, she holds the flesh out for them to taste but they look away in disgust.

And in shame.

"We aren't monsters," they say to the hag, but she needs no convincing. She doesn't care either way. She just shrugs and takes another bite.

The knights say nothing more. They don't stop her feast, even if it makes their stomachs turn watching it. They look uneasy. They're used to bloodshed but not like this.

Of course, they aren't the ones giving orders here. They have been forced into alliances that they'll not be able to take back. Not until this fight is over.

So have the tundra-children, making friends with outcasts and broken men, to fight off the steel of their invaders, to keep the woods from encroaching into their marshlands. It's a desperate and dangerous thing, to put so much trust in those with cold, cold hearts.

Like *him.*

But he helped Little Amka escape the slaughter this morning, having known they were coming and warning her to take cover just in time. He's so often in the right place at the right time. He wonders if Amka or any of her kin ever notice.

No, he thinks not.

They are no wiser than the knights, whose minds are as dense and dull as their worn armor, dented as their lost chivalry. With the information he fed those men in the forest, they'd gained a toehold at the edge of their borders but they'll lose two dozen of their numbers tonight, as soon as he sows his usual seeds of chaos and hate among the grieving tundra-children.

It was supposed to be four slain in the woods this morning, but he expects three will suffice. Saving Amka wasn't the plan, and he's not sure why he did it. A moment of charity, or something like regret? He's not sure how that would be possible. His heart is so cold it burns sometimes. Unlike the rest of him, which feels like it's freezing over.

Little Amka urges him forward, calling back in the old tongue, "Hurry!"

There are others who come to the swamp. Ones who seek out Old Bogg Bones on purpose, knowing he has ancient debts to fulfill. They come under moonlight, wearing faces that belonged to their great-great-grans, always asking after bones.

They aren't picky. Bogg gives them the long ones, rotten ones, the mangled ones with mummified skin still attached, the ones he wrinkles his furry snout at. But not the little ones.

Never the ones that look like little bird bones.

• • •

They are far from the woods now. Open steppe surrounds them, low hills, dead trees and hidden bogs. The knights will have given up their chase miles back, hesitant to go so far from the cover of the woods. The open country is still the tundra-children's domain. For now, at least.

When they reach her kin, Little Amka disappears behind mossy stone, a tall slab of granite caught in the marshland like a loose tooth. Her glance back at him is an odd one, he thinks. Just before she ducks out of sight, her expression goes stern enough that he slows his steps.

He wasn't supposed to see that look.

Have they reached their destination? He's breathing heavily. With a guilty conscience, his nerves begin to fray a little. But only because he's ever worried he'll be found out. He looks around, unfamiliar with the place the tundra-child has brought him.

That slab of stone is one of many. He's in a grove of stone pillars, set up unnaturally like grave markers or door frames to other worlds. He's almost loath to walk between any of them, worried he might tumble down somewhere he's not supposed to be. Lost to the known universe, trapped in the netherworld, too far away for anyone to hear his screams.

And that look on her face…

Do they know? Do they suspect something foul?

He's been so careful. He's never given himself away. Not to either side. His cold heart has served him well in this. He has a mind that can't be easily read by those who might try. Hate fills up all the empty places, churning up a thick, black mud that congeals and coats all other thoughts, making it nearly impossible to dig through.

Besides, there's nothing in what happened back in the woods that might be traced back to him.

But what is this place? None of Amka's kind have ever brought him here before.

He lays his hand on the first pillar, cautiously, feeling the soft fur of damp growth underneath mint-colored lichen. It's warm, as if soaking up the heat of magma pools far beneath the surface. Half a dozen tundra-children are huddled together nearby, with Little Amka soon crouching down to join their secret whispers.

They look at the marshy, black bog at the center of their stones. They look at him.

They have a rope.

Old Bogg Bones never really knew love. And what little he remembers, he's forgotten.

They burned his house, he remembers that. His family too. Fire, blood, screams and charred ashes. Not even the bones were left when the flames burned out.

Was it one of the tundra-children setting fires? Or one of the knight's torches, pitched onto his thatched roof? For those living on the border, there was no way of knowing.

He supposes it doesn't matter anymore. They were all monsters back then. And now they're all gone. Except him.

They strip him of his clothes and pull off his boots, tossing them in a pile. Where they touch his stomach, his arms, his wrists, patches of white fur begin to appear. This unnerves him. He shies away from their touch and their wide green eyes. But they seem pleased by how the fur grows and spreads, the spell already taking root.

"You're a monster," they say to him. "And now you'll look like one too."

He tries to get away. But he can't. Not with their rope binding his hands. It's charmed with something stronger than sealskin. It scratches deep, rubbing against his wrist bones, making him weak and helpless. He struggles against them as they drag him towards the bog, but his feet slip in mud, his eyes widening in the horror of what they intend to do.

"I'm sorry! They made me do it!" he insists, falsely, before they gag him, wanting to hear no more of his lies.

They must know. They must have found out somehow. That red fox on the tundra, that dwarf willow on the trail? The eyes of the tundra see too much and meddle too often.

And now he will pay for his treachery. He'll pay a thousand times over.

Little Amka rises from the huddle of her kin and approaches him slowly, her expression stern as the stones around them. She feels betrayed, burned by it, mourning her sisters and brothers in the woods, mourning a friendship that she thought was forever.

She shakes her head at him, hot, angry tears in her eyes, "How could you?"

When she pushes both her webbed hands against his chest, it's with surprising strength.

He falls backwards. He cries out, his screams muffled by the wad of moss in his mouth, his bound fingers grasping and reaching for something, anything, but he's already off balance and falling, with nothing to hold onto. When he hits the bog, he feels a burning heat and then a scalding cold.

He feels loathing in his soul, for everyone and everything.

And then, he feels nothing at all.

He misses the tundra-children sometimes. Despite what they did to him, despite what they turned him into. They couldn't know how it would go after they pushed him down into the bog, how the knights would finally leave their woods at the behest of the mystics, how they would grimly finish a war they no longer believed in, how the moon witch would raise him up from the mud and charge him forevermore with gathering up bones.

There were so many to gather in the end, as the knights were tricked too. Trapped in those stone doorways, left behind by the moon witch and the priest with black robes.

Little Amka came out from her hiding spot after the slaughter was done, after the wily tricksters had gone, crawling to the side of the bog, wounded beyond mending. She lay down beside the miry pit, her mud-and-blood-spattered little cheek pressed against the damp moss ringing the swamp. Her breathing was so shallow. She murmured something about how she was sorry. To the knights? To him? To her brothers and sisters? To no one at all?

Me too. He told her, speaking for all of them. He repeats, *Me too, Little Amka.*

He gathered her up by strong paws, noting her scant weight—just like a little bird—holding her against the white fur at his chest and shoulder.

But too soon, she was just bones.

God Stalker

By Wailana Kalama

Our hunting party tracks God to the Ruins on the bank of the lagoon, where mangroves dip their gnarled toes into the water. Three days had passed since our old seeress had jabbed a bony finger into sundown, three days of stealing across the jungle with spears and bows, all the while already knowing where our destination lay.

Gods love Ruins, you see. I don't know if it's the mildewy scent of black moss on stone that draws them here, or the cacophony of years that collect in the mudpools, so many centuries cradled in a single cursed place. Perhaps all Gods can sniff out Time, wrap it in their teeth, yank on it and savor it with all the slow pleasure of an ageless dominance.

Or perhaps, like myself, they are drawn by curiosity. For when I bend my ear to the fluttering grass, I swear I can hear something leaching from the soil.

And how it excites me.

The Ruins speak with their own voice. Liver-colored steeples, crumbling steps, half-eaten archways, chipped stone smothered in hair weed, how they all seem to resonate with secrets, secrets that strain against soil, stirring against unseen tethers. If only I understood it. What endless wonders lie beyond the realm of mortals?

I wonder, when you become a God, do you learn? Can you finally hear those mysteries that seep up from the porous earth? Do all those secrets that Time jealously guards in its grasp uncoil themselves before you, embrace you like the arms of a long-lost lover?

I have sworn to find out.

• • •

Kaloso, who always bested me at bone-toss when we were children, caught a God three years ago. His hunt numbered thirteen. But before the day was over, their headless, limbless bodies scattered the ruined yard. Kaloso buried his face in God's cheek, and when he drew away, I saw its teeth.

The Hunt, five of us this time, slink past the broken bulwarks into the Ruins. The scent of God is a strong, shimmering warmth—warm, but not like the coziness of a tent-mate, nor a straddling bonfire. But rather like the fresh warmth of a beleaguered breath, like an unquenchable sigh, laced on the edges with Life teeming, multiplying—an open, dripping maw.

I can smell Infinity in that scent, and the vastness makes us shiver in our catskins. We drag bitter turmeric over our brows to dull the pull, because if you're not careful, when the time comes you won't be able to stand the stink of God.

The yard is littered in mossy boulders and fragmented pathways. Rain trees sweep our vision in their tresses, and for a moment all is black and gray and green and faded pink. We need the morning drizzle to cease, because that's when the God will be at its most pungent. So we hunker among the slender snake-like boughs, and wait.

We're hungry, so hungry you could feel it in the sharpness of our limbs, the tautness of our muscles, the way our necks snap with every creak of a branch. We haven't eaten since we left the village. On the split stump where I rest my aching back, a yellow gecko unfurls its tail. It stabs the air with its delicate toe-pads. I make a single swift move to catch it—but it vanishes without so much as a croak.

I see hands grip on spears and tighten over arrows, and, in spite of the fear, the trembling, their faces clench with resolution.

Faces of children. Dula, who stands taller and older than them all, is just sixteen. She casts black looks at me because the seeress didn't bless me with her kiss of tar. I waited until the blessings were done, caught up with the hunting party the day after. They didn't welcome me, but they didn't drive me away either. But Luk caressed his shark-toothed blade while locking eyes with me over the campfire, and Baruja kicked me awake in the mornings. Dula called me a Curse. Perhaps, like the rest of the tribe, unbridled Age frightens them.

They think themselves warriors, but their untested calves, arms, shoulders say otherwise. Like all juveniles, they wear weapons like they do catskins, as if they're borrowed. Their youth, which burns bright in their bodies, makes them fruitful, hopeful.

Makes them dead.

Then there's Anay, so-young Anay, who used to catch chameleons in the copse of ficus behind my hut. Who sometimes shared their little bodies with me. The two of us would sit by the fire while they roasted. The tails he'd save for last, rub so the charcoaled scales came off in his palms.

Now he's wiping those trembling hands free of sweat. He plugs one finger into his left ear, stirs it around, yanks it out. All so quickly you might not have noticed, if you weren't looking.

But I was looking, and when he sees me see him, his face flushes. It's the sweetest sight I've seen in a long while: a blushing boy who does not know he's meat slowly rotting.

"The gecko?" I ask.

A few winters ago, Anay confided to me that, at times, he heard a low thrum whenever he twisted his head to the left. But over time, it grew. Louder, and more frequent. *It never ceases*, he told me last week over my campfire, stealing glances over his shoulder because he shouldn't be seen with me.

It crept into his dreams, stole sleep from him. It was always lurking.

And because it resembled the chirp of a gecko, he called it the same.

"It's been getting worse," he whispers.

I glance to the others, but they haven't heard; they're restless in their corner of the yard, their stares fixed to the Ruins like that's enough to kill a God.

"Louder," Anay says. "A bit more insistent. Stronger with each passing day. *Tsuk, tsuk, tsuk! Tsuk, tsuk, tsuk!*"

He tries to stifle his panic in the low of a folded voice, but it runs off to Dula, who snaps at us to be quiet.

"They say geckos are messengers of Gods," I whisper back when she turns away. "What do they say to you?"

He shakes his head. "Nothing! It's not words, Kalli-e, it's a curse. It's poison, it's a nightmare!"

And he bores his eyes into mine, as if thirsty, as if sucking at the moisture there. We don't notice the rain has slowed to a gentle patter on molave leaves.

"Kalli-e, it scares me. It scares me more than anything else. More than Death. More than God."

And as if summoned, somewhere in the depths of those hallowed halls and maze-like chambers, an awful bellow surges forth, strikes the walls from every direction, like the inexorable crescendo of a stampede.

When Kaloso first assembled his hunt of thirteen, the tribes-folk told me I was too old to join. Too many aches in the knee, they muttered into their palms. Too many flecks in the waters of my eye.

I live on the edge of the village, alone in my hut. I scrounge up roots with an old spearhead, check my traps for an unlucky shrew, and each morning I grasp at my heart, wondering if today will be the day it fails.

Unnatural, the seeress spat when I begged. She struck the earth with her bone-staff where my rotting tent-mate slept. As if saying, *Look look! Here lies one honest man, here stands one woman abnormal!*

Deathless one! Deathless one! The children taunted, those brave enough. All except poor cursed Anay.

Death comes to those who wait. So I waited, and waited, but it did not come, and when I tracked Kaloso's hunting party all the way to the Ruins and saw what he became, I knew it never would.

. . .

It is a scraping of toenails against rock. It is a hurried thudding of weight on packed earth. It is a thousand furious, visceral howls reverberating through the halls, voices trawled out of pure furor, a great need to be unfettered, to be freed. We feel its vibration dig into our lungs, it's raking at our throats, threatening to rip our own gullets out with a scream. Luk's hand flies to his mouth to stifle the shrieking.

We steal into the Ruin's endless corridors, using the great shadows and towering halls to our advantage. Spears and bows at the ready. Wait for each corner to be the one where we come face to face with God. It knows we're here, because of course, it has been waiting. Perhaps it can hear the beat of our heels against the soil, the blood running through our veins. Perhaps it can see how we have come into this world, and how each of us will die.

I can almost believe it, because it comes swiftly, far swifter than I would imagine. Baruja trails behind, the last of us. And the first. The worst is that we do not see it. We do not smell it, we do not taste it. And what we hear is no scream. It is bone, it is muscle and sinew, it is finality and collapse.

We find her slumped in the corner of a dark room, chest on a bed of soft grass. Her mottled bow lies still in her palm, snapped in two. Her legs and the dark tattoos ornamenting them all ravaged into tatters by a dozen hungry jaws. One missing foot. Deep gashes in her belly, shredded into meaty strips and fleeing intestines where God touched her. A gush of red runs from her nostrils and mouth like she's been blessed.

Of course, she didn't want it enough. If she did, she would've been quicker. Sleeker. Fiercer. To really catch a God, you have to be close to Death. You have to feel it scrambling up your lumbar and gnawing at your creaking knees, its deep and eager pulse beating in your veins.

We fling our backs to the wall, senses and weapons flaring. As if we can brace against the vibrations. The walls shake, the ground-stone trembles, and the heady stink of Infinity is everywhere.

· · ·

Our tribe has always killed Gods. It was clever Kaloso who discovered you can become one. He knew then, what I know now—what I suspect the first white-tongued seeress knew all along, when she bade our ancestors to slaughter the first God— that immortality is contagious.

In the cold light of dawn, over the slaughtered corpses of a huntsband, Kaloso changed everything. And from my hiding place behind the knotted fingers of a banyan tree, I watched. I saw what he did. I saw what he became. And I kept the secret knot-tight, in that soft crevice between teeth and tongue.

Dula's face is a mask of tight control. She motions us to huddle beside a shallow pool in the corner of a damp chamber. The only light spills in green from a square-cut window. I can see my reflection in the pool: all the wrinkles, the lines, the days cut into my skin. I can hear what these children can't: the insistent clamor of Age, pricking at my joints. Gnawing at me little by little, so that each day is an exercise in wasting away. As hungry as the rest of us. No, more so. Much, much more.

Anay is staring into the pool too. I think at first it's our bloodied tribeswoman he's remembering, but he is studying the pool itself. I take a step back to see that it curves out in the shape of a lizard. His gecko haunts him even in this place. He lifts his head and I see terror.

And though I can't hear what he hears, I read it in the frantic twitch of his left eye.

Rapid spasms, and then again, and again.

Tsuk, tsuk, tsuk!

"We must trap it," Dula says solemnly, crouching low. "When the last hunt slew their God, they must have trapped it."

"Or so their footprints made us think," Luk mutters. "We don't know for sure. None survived to tell the tale."

"There wasn't even a Godscorpse," I say.

"Don't doubt it!" Dula hisses. "They slew it. If not, it would've sundered our tribe within days."

Dula sets me to watch one entrance to the chamber, and Luk the other, swinging his shark-toothed blade. In the middle, Anay stands with feet planted firm into the cracks of the floor. His face is blank and pale, the face of one who finally grasps that above all he is meat, he is *bait*.

I grip my hatchet and wait, and like we all know it will, it comes.

It is pruned gristle and fermenting sweat. It is one hundred moaning and weeping and laughing faces of our dead kin.

No, not dead. Terribly alive.

In the span of a few heart beats, the God sweeps from the far end of the hallway to the prick of Luk's blade. And the faces, how they twist and turn toward us. Some dribble out words in a forgotten language. Some vomit, some yawn, some giggle, some cry out with harrowed eye sockets as if seeing the moment of their death again and again.

The very image of Humankind.

Just more. Much, much more.

Fingers and toes and calves and half-eaten biceps and flayed scapula and half-white, unfocused eyes and somewhere in the midst of it all I spy a brown foot with a black leather ring circled around one toe just like Baruja's.

And the foot kicks into the air, like a fish gasping for water.

The endless, endless mouths lurch toward Luk and his blade slices one face clean away, lips and tissue tumble onto his wrist and then the God is upon him, devouring. Gnashing teeth obliterate him into a spray of red and bile, and the deepest of all his mortal secrets are free and loose and squirming on the grass.

Dula cries out in fury and fear, and Anay stands still gripping his spear as if in a moon trance. Dula rushes forward and her mighty pike gores the God, but only one head wails in pain; the others make quick meat of her with deep, penetrating fingers, they pierce her skin and peel her apart in lumps like she were a ripe jackfruit.

Anay watches it all, a stone cast out from the pool.

And then: his left eye twitches once more, and it's what saves him.

He snaps into action, and staggers to me, we run together down the cool darkness of the corridors, as if the spores percolating the air were a coat that could conceal us and it's not until we're both out of breath beneath the cold shadow of a pink bell-less steeple that we stop.

"Anay?"

He is a shadow. He has retreated somewhere deep within himself. His eyes pucker out; I'm not sure where he's gone. It's deeper than I thought youth could reach and I don't think he can see his way out.

But I can hear the insistent, rhythmic beat of his tongue against teeth. Like a gecko was tapping on the insides of his cheeks, trying to get out.

Tsuk, tsuk, tsuk!

The God will come again. And whether Anay wakes by that time, I have no way of knowing. We crouch together in the circular chamber beneath the steeple the height of five tribesfolk. The sporous air we breathe is eager, escaping through two slits far above our heads. But there is only one egress, one severe cut into the stone, where we entered. Only one way out.

"Anay!"

I want him to understand. To explain to him what I'd planned. What I'd been planning since the moment this small boy crept up to my fire and told me his terrible secret.

But he's locked deep into a darkness I can't reach.

And I don't want him to be alone. So I bend down close to his ear, because he is giving me the sweetest gift and I owe him mine.

"You know that sound you dread? That you probably hear, even now?"

His tongue clicks as if in answer, and I have the sudden, wild feeling I'm speaking to the sound more than to the boy. My tongue slips ever so slightly on this doubt, muddles what I have to say:

"You don't have to fear it any longer. I will free you from it. It won't haunt you in your sleep. I promise. This I can give you."

His unfixed stare takes nothing from my words. But it's all I have, and time is running out.

I pull a rope from my waist-sack and bind his wrists. I turn him gently so his side is cradled in damp grass. His tongue clicks ferociously as if possessed, but I can't bear to stuff his mouth, to mute him in these, his final moments.

I tell myself: he wants this.

He *needs* this.

The roar of a furious and cackling and crying God splits all thoughts and I turn to see it squeezing past the chamber entry. It tilts its humongous and inevitable mass and its hundred gaping mouths toward Anay, bends his sweet face in its many jaws.

"Kaloso!" I cry, and that one shrewd face, those thick eyebrows and pointed lips, they all swivel to me. Here is the one mind that keeps working, that keeps thinking, the one mind not mindless, the one who can still speak the human tongue and call himself a God.

I saw Kaloso sacrifice his kinsmen to the God. I saw him bind them in place while the mouths swallowed them. I saw him find the one face that was lucid and strike it, slice it down to its shoulders, all the blood spilling out, soaking moss. Kaloso yanked the face up to his and chewed it to flakes and slivers. And the divine multitude quivered and shook with violent tremors, defenseless; he dipped his head into the hungry meat of that headless, pregnable ribcage and let it chew away everything he was, mortal and then some. His useless body collapsed, bounced off the squirm of that shrieking mass. And the God's many arms ripped away flesh and bone from its own dappled tissue, pasted it all together back into a single expression of victory and rapture. Kaloso's face.

He tilted his ear to the earth, like it was speaking to him. Like he finally understood all those deep and rhythmic pulses running beneath his feet.

He closed his eyes as if he were hearing the sweetest music in the world, and howled like a newborn.

He howls now, furious at recognition. But he's too slow, and I *do* want this enough.

I hack off his face with a few true blows of my hatchet, and yank away his eyes, his nose. The orbs pop like shucked oysters; the cartilage is tough and squirms in my mouth. I can feel the great, hulking barrage of bodies shiver against my thighs, my breasts, press forward with their ageless, fleshy lips. All of them hungry in the same insatiable way. Their weight pins me to the ground, and the last sight I see are the ravaged muscles spurting from Anay's headless torso—then it is warmth, it is eager, sweaty lust, it is the throbbing pulse of countless heartbeats.

And then I am one surging face among many.

I am hands, toes, knees, shoulder blades, globules of fat, and pendent triceps.

I am in dark, stinking halls and my new faces yawn, my new fingers unfurl, my new knees uncoil and the wheezes and murmurs and moans of stitched heads compress my skull.

They are my brothers and sisters, they are me, we are all, we are God.

Undying. Beyond Death.

And yet…

I creak softly in the cradle of that pink steeple, bend our collective ear down toward the soil.

The earth seems strangely silent.

Much quieter, too, than before.

Nothing creeps in the dirt. The stones say nothing. And if ever there were whispers of secrets, of timeless mysteries, I can't hear them. They're muffled.

Drowned out by one awful sound that crawls right up to our ears.

Swift and surreptitious, the sound latches onto each dangling earlobe, shuddering louder with each second and burrowing down into our canals—and so all of us convulse with the same new, incessant pain. I drive every working finger I have into every suffering ear, stir them around, yank them free in a hollow effort to quench that awful noise, but the sound worms its greedy way down through our cartilage and cavities, thrusts into our hundred deathless hearts and taunts again, and again, and again, and again:

Tsuk, tsuk, tsuk!

Paladin
By Abhijeet Sathe

Despite the ruinous battle at the outer wall, the holy host of Chikara breaks through the Enemy's defenses. We are within spitting distance of victory.

A final wall of moss-flecked boulders separates us from the enemy's stronghold. An ancient temple-mount looms beyond, jet-black against the twilight. From the desecrated sanctum of that ancient and arcane temple, the Enemy spreads its eldritch tentacles, ensnaring the minds of men across the world.

No more. At dawn's red light, we will breach the final wall to scour these ruins of the evil reborn into them. Trevan, the Great Enemy, trickster-god of the heathens, will fall again. Light will prevail. All we need is to survive the night.

You could join us instead, my brother.

I clap my ears shut in a futile reflex.

You know it is right.

Join us.

The Enemy's voice grows more potent near the heart of its virulent empire. Its whispered promises, a faint itch in the depths of every living soul, sneak into unguarded moments.

A warmth pulses into me through my tether to the lord. Chikara wishes me to succeed.

Goaded by Chikara's intervention, the Enemy redoubles its assault.

Ma serves your evening meal: watermush and a little lump of jaggery to help it go down. You watch as she places a fourth plate for nobody. It has been years since Charu Mama left, but she sets a spare plate every meal.

The villagers never understood Charu Mama's decision, did they? Why do you think he did it? Why do you think he joined me? Your uncle is happy now, Mohan.

Don't you want that?

Shaking myself free of the reverie, I head for the alchemist's tent to relieve Jagdish. Inside, blasphemy and rot hang thick in the air. Men strapped into their beds rant and rave against Chikara, spitting at the ceiling and trying to tear off their tether to him. Jagdish hands me the dripping mercy-blade and leaves the tent without a word.

A soldier with one eye gouged out smiles at me from his restraints. The rips in his cheek splay open, revealing teeth yellowed by campfire brews. "Brother Mohan!" His smile gushes blood and spittle with glee. "Brother Mohan, take my hand. Join Trevan's embrace!"

Take his hand, brother.

Even through the blood-haze and battle-weariness, I feel a twinge of shame. I don't even know this man's name. His fingers twitch under the leather straps as they scrabble to reach my throat. "Lord Trevan will pull back the curtain, and you will see the way of the world."

Take his hand.

Men taken by the Enemy seldom return from the brink whole. Usually, we are lucky, and they simply disappear. Sometimes, we are unlucky, and the men return with evil hiding in their hearts. Last time the Enemy appeared, we heard evil tidings for decades after his fall: stories of men who came back only to snap in the dark of night, drowning their children and slitting their wives' throats, setting fire to their villages.

You lead a charge, banner a tongue of flame. A lancer blocks your path, his skeletal steed rearing in defiance. The lancer rips off his scarf, revealing a broken nose and a bushy beard. You and Jagdish lock hands and turn to face the horde. Chikara's holy host falls before your steel. You scythe a path through the zealots before rising slick and red into the heavens. You are crowned with bones. You are glorious. You are righteous, for once.

"Mohan, you don't have to do this!" The soldier strapped to the table whines. "Heed Lord Trevan! Talk back! If you let Him in, He will show you the truth."

I press the mercy-blade through the soft flesh of his eye.

He screams. They always do.

This is what the Enemy's reincarnations bring: agony.

Mercy without steel only prolongs it.

A purple glow appears around the soldier's head as his tether to Chikara becomes visible. The braid of light reaches heavenward from the soldier's mangled face before disappearing into the tent's oilskin ceiling. It pulses in time with the soldier's heart.

I press the blade deeper, and the braid splits into a million strands.

My hand quivers, but I press on. One final jiggle of my wrist, and he is gone.

The light dissipates as his soul flees into Chikara's bosom.

Swallowing bile rising in my throat, I move to the next bed. This work is a necessity. If the Enemy tears past my defenses, I will welcome a mercy-blade to the eye. I know this, yet knowing provides no succor. I keep seeing these thralls as they once were: men with families and futures and dreams.

These are the Enemy's thoughts in my head, weakening my resolve.

It is the harvest festival, but the rains have failed. You are playing marbles with Jagdish under the village banyan when a sharp shriek pierces the sky. You run towards your father's hut to find three men standing over your parents. Your parents, once so tall before you, cringe on the mud floor of their hovel. The largest of the men calmly chews a betel leaf as the other two pummel your father with sticks.

You run towards them with murder in your heart. You have taken almost no steps when Jagdish holds you back. You curse and fight and spit, but he is bigger and stronger and older. He drags you away as the men extinguish the lives of your parents in the name of their false justice.

You know the fiend that did this.

Chikara.

I jerk awake to the stench of burnt flesh. The Enemy makes my belly rumble, nauseating me with the idea. Jagdish is waking up next to me, slumped against the tent's wall with a distant smile under his beard. My hand slides surreptitiously to the hilt of my axe.

As he opens his eyes, his familiar frown settles in. I take my hand off the hilt, releasing a breath I didn't know I was holding. He turns to me and asks, "What did it show you?"

"The harvest festival."

"It's lying." He begins pulling on his bracers.

"Of course." I shrug on my mail coverlet. "Come now, dawn approaches."

As the first rosy-red beam falls on the charnel ground before us, the raucous bellow of a war horn tears the morning stillness. At this signal, a seam appears in the wall and an artfully hidden gate groans open. We watch with mounting dread as the gate swings wider and wider, revealing the extent of the horde arrayed against us.

Hunched-over men and women with open sores and emaciated frames leer at us across the narrow field between the walls. Scurvy and swollen bellies adorn their front line. Their clothes are tattered, their hair matted with dirt. We are out-manned ten-to-one, perhaps worse. I like those odds.

We fall into line as the horde lurches forward. Their unholy yowls clamor against the moss-laden walls, deafening us as they close the distance between our lines. Chikara's blessings flow into me through my heavenly braid, lending me strength.

My blood runs cold, then heats again as the frenzy of righteous battle purges all doubt.

The war-priests ride into Kohragaon, wearing the turbans and swords of their clan. You ride behind, squiring for the head priest. They raze the village and salt the earth. My flame is extinguished in Kohragaon that day, alongside the lives of those that had seen its truth. That evening, as you hunch over a pail of vomit, the head priest reminds you, "Think of what the Enemy would have done with them." What more could I have done, Mohan?

My armor clags to me, heavy with jungle sweat and the buzzing stickiness of battle. Our foes lie broken behind us as we march through the gate. Behind it, the temple-mount rises from the top of a crumbling ziggurat. We clamber up the stairs, thighs burning with exhaustion, buoyed by the flush of victory.

Inside the temple, the air is clammy despite the summery swelter of these ruins. The cavernous roof of the temple-mountain disappears into the gloom above. A single window gleams at its apex like a silver leaf floating on a pool of ink.

Gargantuan statues watch us from between granite pillars, their eyes veiled in shadow. Rusted bronze chandeliers hang in thick ropes from the ceiling, relics of the heathen tabernacle that existed here long before the Enemy was birthed into it. Many generations ago, a constellation of wicks lit this cavern. Now, eldritch red orbs float in the air, casting their dancing shadows on us.

Against the far wall of the temple, where a king might hold court, a statue of the original godling lies shattered at the foot of a granite throne.

In its place sits an elephantine mass teeming with feelers, dark in color but limned with an oily-red light. Tentacles reach outward from it in a snake's tangle of undulant flesh, clambering the pillars in all directions.

At the heart of the dark mass, an obsidian-like face watches our approach with empty, porcelain-white eye sockets. It is the face of a high-boned woman with a soft sneer upturning her lips. As we near, the face is replaced by a bulb-nosed man. Then it is replaced by a child with a cat-lip. Faces slip in and out of being, always a polished black, always with those porcelain-white eye sockets.

The great Enemy itself, in the flesh before us.

Come closer, brother. I will show you the truth.

Anticipating a trap yet powerless to resist, we step forward.

The head priest bids you to step out of the frigid stream. As you fall to his feet on legs made useless by the cold, he anoints you and reveals the bond between you and Chikara. A braid of purple light ascends from your gooseflesh skin into the heavens, where the lord of light blesses you into his fold.

"This tether is your power," the priest says. *"Chikara's blessing is the most potent truth in this world. In exchange, all he wishes is what one would do regardless. You must defend Chikara's world from the enemies of light, who are the enemies of mankind."*

This is what he said, wasn't it?

They lied to you, Mohan.

"They hid it from us?" Jagdish mumbles by my side.

The Enemy's mass writhes in excitement, and I know what comes next as if it were written across my eyes in pitch and embers. Perhaps even before he does, I know Jagdish's future. My hand drifts towards my axe, hoping he gives me a reason not to draw it.

Jagdish spins toward me, sword in one hand and dagger in the other. A few of the others follow suit. While parrying, I recall Jagdish from the harvest festival, saving me from the landlord's men. Then I remember Jagdish from last night, sharing the mercy-row with me. Finally, I see Jagdish's snarling visage as he swings his broadsword down onto my head.

Hands heavy, I parry his blow and fall back, waiting to gain an advantage.

And then, as easily as it began—

Blood for the mill! Approach, brother. I shall curse you with the truth.

Four of us faithful remain after this last assault. We inch closer to the fell god, not meeting each other's eyes. Jagdish's blood drips from my axe, staining the silty floor underfoot. I clench my hands tight to stop their trembling. I'd known Jagdish's family. I'd known the dreams rattling in his head. I'd even seen the plot of land the priests promised him.

The great Enemy watches us through the empty eyes of its rotating cast of faces. If there is a trap coming, we do not see it. As we reach within spear-throw of the Enemy, it reveals its last defense. Before I can react, a gash appears in one of the tentacles sprawled on the floor. Strange ichor sprays frothily from the tear, and a man punches his way out of it.

He looks whole but thinner than I remember. His weathered frame and roguish smile transport me to the last age of Trevan, when my mother's brother walked away into the night, never to return.

Uncle Charu's voice is unchanged. "How have you been, Mohan?"

"Step aside, wraith. I am a sworn brother of the Lord of Light."

"That's nice." The illusion steps around the tentacle and approaches me. "How are Sumitra and Jayan? Still paying off the fat bastard?"

"Step aside."

"I see." Uncle Charu cocks his head as though listening to something at his side. "I'm so sorry, Mohan. The Lord just told me they were killed by Chikara's men."

"They were killed by the landlord's men!" I snap. Charu raises a curious eyebrow and taps his chin. I glance to my side and see my brothers similarly occupied in conversation with their own illusory revenants. The priests had warned me of such sorceries. I turn back to the creature that calls itself Uncle Charu. "Your wiles will not work on me, trickster."

"I can see that." Charu smiles. "You're happy where you are, aren't you?"

"Step aside," I repeat, readying my axe. "Or I will hew you down."

"We're happy in Trevan's world, you know." Charu's words worm their way into my ears. "I till my fields and feed my neighbor. He tends to a henhouse and gives me eggs. Nobody beats anybody to death because the rain didn't fall. No cleansing. Orphans don't get sent to die in service of a demon."

"Shut your blaspheming mouth." I ram the butt of my axe into Charu's stomach, sending him folding to the floor.

His laugh is wheezy as he catches his breath. "I paint in my spare time." Couched in Charu's voice, the trickster's words worm deeper into my ears. Behind him, Trevan changes faces at a feverish pace. "Do you even know what painting is, Mohan? Do you know what spare time is? Do you know any music that isn't hymns?"

"Quiet!" I bark, indulging myself in one well-aimed jab.

Charu spits real-looking blood onto the floor and continues in a tender voice, "Have you ever kissed a woman?" Seeing the answer in my eyes, he shakes his head in dismay. "At least see what Lord Trevan offers."

"Lord Chikara's blessings are all I need, demon." I hold the axe against the illusion's chest. A red line forms as I press it forward. The trickster winces and steps back. It feels pain. That is good. "You cannot tempt me from the righteous path."

"What did this path get you, Mohan? What kind of life is this?" The creature shrugs. "You've never lived, only survived. *You* killed the last person you knew, Mohan. *You* did that. For the sake of your demon!"

Chikara's blessing trickles down into me from above. The renewed bout of energy reveals how close I was to breaking. "The Enemy killed Jagdish, not me. You will not sway me, trickster. The Lord watches over me."

"That old thing?" Uncle Charu looks directly at the braid tethering me to the lord.

"You can see it?" I asked, shocked.

"You think that leads to your god?"

Trevan stirs in his throne.

A jungle obscured in low-slung mists. A tiger bellows in the distance. You flee, sweat cooling on your bare skin. As you return to the tribe's camp, the trees burst apart into stalks of wheat. Scythes lop off their heads, which run a rusty red that drowns the world. The blood drains to reveal the sanctum. Dangling candelabras blaze with light and heat. Heads of wheat, tall as a man, sway in place amidst the temple's columns. A reaper swings one by one, setting the chaff alight. The temple burns. The temple-mountain erupts with volcanic fury, shivering the rocks into rubble. Black silence descends, hanging from the finest of breaths. Banging metal and the hissing fire impinge on this hollow silence, growing muffled as creepers and moss scrabble forth on the temple's walls. They ebb and flow across the floor and back up to the walls until the cultists of Trevan finally beat them away. The world stirs in place. The materials of history flow into your heart and soul.

Something odd flickers in the corner of my eye.

A new braid of purple light extends from the steel head of my axe.

It reaches a few dozen feet before disappearing in the gloom around me. I look around and notice more braids stretching from me. Hundreds! No, thousands! Some are attached to my fingers, some to my arms, to my tunic, my bracers, my chest, my quiver… Every part sprouts a braid stretching toward thousands of unseen points.

Each one is indistinguishable from my divine tether to Chikara.

"What is this trickery?" Rolling back up to my feet, I fall into an attacking stance.

"No tricks." Charu mimes a swing at one of the braids. "Try it. Cut one."

Even if it were possible to cut the braid tying me to the lord, it would be unconscionable. Instead, I test one of the false braids revealed by the trickster. As I wave my axe foolishly through the braid extending from my left palm, the edge glows golden, and the braid snaps with a twang.

Exhilaration rattles my body as an incomparable joy fills it to the brim. It feels like a great and historic weight has rolled off my shoulders. Experimentally, I snap another braid. The breezy elation wafts through me again. Charu watches as I spin about, hacking away at his illusions, feeling the rush as each one snaps. To my side, I can see my brothers swinging their weapons at something unseen and smiling in manic bursts.

"Great, isn't it?" The creature pretending to be Uncle Charu smirks knowingly.

Disgust burgeons in me at his leering smile, compounding further as the braid on my left palm reappears. Its painful weight drags me down again. Another tether reappears, passing through my heart like a flung spear. "What are you doing, trickster?"

"That is the Chikara's great lie, Mohan." Charu answers a question I hadn't thought to ask. "Your strength doesn't come from the one strand that demon's acolytes allow you to see. That tether is merely one facet of a brilliant and endless truth. Your strength, your very being, comes from this web of obligation that ties together all of humanity."

"You're lying!" I cry out. I look up to meet Trevan's eyes. "Make it stop!"

Come to me, boy. I will show you the truth.

The braids weigh me down as I step toward the throne. Clearly, Trevan has attached them to me using Charu's corpse as a vehicle. There is but one way to escape this. "My Lord. Allow me to approach you." I plead. "I understand now."

You lie.

"What can my feeble mind hide from you, Lord?" I fold my hands in supplication. "You see plainly in my mind that there is much for me to unlearn, but allow me to fall at your feet, Lord Trevan. Allow me to learn."

The otherworldly deity regards me in oppressive silence. The weight of Trevan's silence is making me jittery. My brothers are still locked in animated conversations with the apparitions conjured for them. If he decides to end me, I will have no help from them.

Thankfully, he relents.

Approach.

A glowing red tear appears under the ebony face—a narrow-eyed, eagle-nosed man—and spreads like a grotesque mouth. As I watch, the tear rips open, widening into an arch that glows the same eerie red as the floating orbs above.

Enter. And be free.

I stumble forward in genuine awe, pushing Uncle Charu aside.

At the foot of the throne, I step closer to the portal. Beyond it, as if through a veil of red gossamer, I see a meadow. Huts are lined along it in rows. Small farms and fat cows dot the countryside. Through Trevan's magic, they all appear faintly red. The feeling of driving my axe through my Jagdish's skull returns to scour my heart.

Stifling the bile rising in my gorge, I lunge ahead.

What are you—

A well-placed swing of my axe dislodges one of the granite throne's legs. Stone crunches as another leg snaps under the sudden strain. Uncle Charu cries out in tandem with my howls of pain. The throne tilts sideways and slides into the nearest pillar.

Fool!

With a catastrophic crash, the pillars holding up the temple-mountain topple under the throne's weight. In the infinitesimal sliver of time between the throne's toppling and the columns collapsing, Trevan exacts his revenge.

You grow up in the crook of black soil where the Amothi enters the plains... You inherit father's farm after your wedding. You grow runner beans. You are blessed with two children. A plague sweeps the land just as the little one has learned to walk...

You grew up the third son of a greengrocer. Father and mother are slain before you by the raiders. Mina is sold to the slave markets. You survive, maimed and alone, begging in the city. Your dying moments are tainted with unavenged bitterness...

You grew up in Kolaran, far from the provincials. Your debut is attended by hundreds. You marry a minor nobleman. After three girl children, he discards you. You die of consumption in the open street...

You are a child of mongrel descent...

I live a thousand lives and die a thousand deaths. Misery upon misery lashes my soul, worrying at its bones until what remains is unrecognizable. As I begin to fear for my sanity, Trevan's spell breaks, the better part of the granite temple-mountain thundering down on it.

Released from its hold, I bolt for the entrance as the rest of the ancient ruin crumbles. We who survived reach outside, choking on dust and sweat as the ruins collapse behind us. Under the rosy-red sky, there is no sign of Uncle Charu or any of the other facsimiles.

Despite its defeat, some of the Enemy's illusions remain. A web of purple braids still reaches out from me with translucent tentacles, faint against the half-light of dusk. I pass my axe experimentally through one of the braids extending from my hand. Same as it had in the temple, the braid disappears in a burst of light before reappearing again.

Perhaps the trickster's lies have been burned into my soul. I look up and see my tether to Chikara disappearing into the sky overhead. At least that one is real. Before I can dwell on this matter any further, one of my surviving brothers raises his voice in a ragged cheer. Flush with victory, we all join in. We won! Still cheering, we limp down the stairs, eager to return home and to the service of Chikara, the only true god of mankind.

To Gut a Fish, First Gather its Bones
By Lyndsey Croal

Aggie had survived more than a lifetime of worries and woes when she heard the dreaded song of the Marool across the sea and knew that her last remaining grandchild had been taken from her. There was an inevitability in the song of the great fish—for many years, it had haunted her, as her husband, sons, daughters, and grandchildren had set out to sail and one by one, failed to return. For a long time she'd been deemed too frail to sail upon the water, her bones too weak for the journey. Now, she'd been left behind on the slowly withering island with only the memories of her stolen family as company.

The old tales had always warned of what lay in the depths—of the dangers of sailing further and further from shore, to cast off nets and bring in more treasures or riches from the deep. But it took too long for the islanders to listen. Too many boats scuttled, crews drowned, and too many bones of the dead drifting up on shore.

Every time a tragedy befell a ship, the islanders saw taming what lay in the sea beyond the horizon as a challenge, so they built the next boat bigger, stronger, more seaworthy, and made offerings to the Sea Mither for a safe passage. But the sea, as with seasons and time, cannot be tamed, even by the fearlessness of youth.

As the sea stilled on the night that Aggie heard the Marool's fateful song, two days since the last ship had sailed out with her grandson on board, she looked out over the water to see the distant glow of the great fish's lure drifting upon the horizon. It was a soft blue light casting across the waves.

Before her grandson had left, she'd implored him to stay behind—asked him at least not to be foolish, not to join a hunt if one was begun. For the islanders had woven nets large enough to catch a whale, and stone-tipped spears sharp enough to fight it. Aggie knew that it wouldn't work. The Marool was too cunning for wood and rope.

When the boat didn't return, Aggie knew weather nor the stormy seas were to blame, but the great fish himself. And there and then she vowed she would get her revenge.

None left on the island had seen the Marool, though Aggie had always believed the old tales. How else could so much be told of a fabled creature if none had witnessed it in the first place? Perhaps the Marool was malevolent once, roaming the seas, his crest of flames a soft glow to aid travelers as they cross dangerous waters. Perhaps the island folks had angered him, and now he sought vengeance. There was nothing in the old tales about the reason he had become such a monster. As is the nature of such tales. They're old. They miss important details. But in the stories told to warn youngsters from swimming too far from the coast, the Marool was a hideous beast, a fish the size of a whale with razor-sharp teeth and a stare as dark as night. He was said to have a shining lure that hung between his myriad eyes making his gaping maw look like it glittered with treasure. Then, if any were swimming deep enough under the waves, they might see the lure and swim unwittingly into his jaws, eaten alive merely for the curiosity of youth. All that would remain would be the discarded bones that washed up on the island's shores.

Every morning, Aggie limped along the eastern beach, her walking stick in hand, collecting washed-up bones. The remains were clean of skin and sinew and barely distinct from driftwood, not even in shape. Indeed, most islanders told themselves that's what they were—hollow and pale white wood, made smooth by the sea. Though none would touch them, nor look closely enough to be proven wrong. When they saw Aggie gather the pieces each morning after the tides receded, she may as well have been invisible for all the attention they offered. They muttered under their breaths about her then went on their way. It didn't stop Aggie, though. If anything, it added to her resolve.

Aggie had long gathered the bones together in a sea cave near that eastward shore. She had tried, at first, to reconstruct their many parts so she could lay them to rest. But in death, bones are too similar to distinguish a pattern of belonging. Sometimes, she thought about turning them into something beautiful as a way to respect them—she had been a carpenter before arthritis withered her fingers and left her knees stiff and weak. But, as she looked at them laid out every day, the whisper of the sea nearby a reminder of what had taken them, she could not decide a purpose. So, the bones lay in indistinct piles, a shrine to the sea and the danger within. The piles grew and grew, until soon every crevice of the cave was filled with the remains of the dead.

Weeks after hearing the Marool's song, Aggie wondered if she would recognize her grandson if he washed up on the shore. She would be combing the beach and a hand would reach up from sodden sand, skeletal fingers, broken and half missing. Maybe she would recognize the one that was broken as a child, that still held the scars of injury. And she would collect them nonetheless and await the rest of the body.

In reality, when the latest bones washed up, she could not distinguish any feature that set them apart nor tell whether they had come from her grandson's boat or one from months before.

The wreck of his ship did, however, eventually wash up amidst the flotsam and jetsam. An array of splintered wood, the whole structure gutted and destroyed by the great fish. Everything discarded, broken, except for those who had lived aboard it. Their souls belonged to the Marool.

The islanders gathered the wood from the coast and built a ceremonial bonfire to remember the dead and pray to the great Sea Mither. There was a song the island folks sang for lost souls at sea, and Aggie imagined it as a counter to the Marool's own tune. Though, she imagined the great fish hearing their mournful ballad and not feeling fear, nor worry, but instead believing them weak. The islanders sung of great tragedy yet never learned from their past mistakes—every time, they sailed right into the jaws of the Marool, unprepared and foolhardy. Aggie was not so naive. Not after losing all she had to live for. Besides, the Sea Mither must have left these shores a long time ago. There was no one left for the islanders to pray to.

After, an island meeting was held, a gathering of all who remained, and Aggie sat quietly at the back. Again, the options for the next sailings were discussed, and it was the same as it always was. A hunting party, a bigger ship, more supplies. But Aggie believed that the bigger the ship, the bigger the target.

She raised her hand slowly and when the island leader called upon her, she said as unwavering as she could, "You cannot continue like this. We must try something else."

The islanders turned their heads but didn't give her much heed. After a quiet pause, the conversation continued again with plans for new weapons and nets. Losing patience, Aggie stood up, walking stick in hand and found her way to the front. She cleared her throat, and eventually they gave way to let her speak.

"We must find a way to trap the Marool, trick him, blind him, cut off his lure so he can no longer see," she said. "And we can't do that with the ships we're using right now. They're too large, he will see them coming from a mile away."

"So your plan to defeat the monster is to use less force?" the island leader said, humoring her, at least.

"Yes. We must be strategic, precise. A smaller crew on a smaller boat. And it must be made of something stronger. Something that can withhold a fight with the Marool and not be crushed in his jaws."

"What alternative do you have in mind?" the leader asked, with a frown. "There is naught more on this island but wood, sand, and stone, and I'm *sure* you're not suggesting we throw stones at the creature?" There was a murmur of laughter, but Aggie didn't rise to the provocation.

She stood her ground. "If we are to defeat the monster, we must think smarter than it. Fight not to defeat his brute force, but to counter with something different. It is the only way."

The island leader shrugged and looked around. "An alternative suggestion has been made by Aggie here. Anyone volunteering to head out to the waters with nothing but a rowing boat and your wits?"

"I will go," Aggie said. "If I must." The islanders laughed at that, and when none volunteered to support her, they waved her away, and returned to discussing their original plan. Aggie sighed and returned to her seat, listening distantly. More trees would be cut down, rope woven, and a crew gathered to man the next journey. Fragile materials and even more fragile minds, Aggie thought, realizing her suggestions had been futile. No one would listen to her, a frail grandmother in mourning. Maybe she could use it to her advantage. It would guard her from their view as she set about her counter plan to hunt down the monster. Just as the Marool's beautiful lure would tempt a weary swimmer or sailor, Aggie could use her perceived weakness to her advantage. If she had to, she would set out to fight the Marool herself, and none on the island could stop her.

Aggie returned to her cave that night and sat with the bones as she looked out the cave's mouth to waves lapping on gray sand. And as the full moon rose high in the sky, casting its light across the pale white bones around her, she realized. There *was* more than just stone and wood on this island after all.

Aggie knew the dead wouldn't mind. The Marool had tried and failed to fully destroy the ship and regurgitated what it could not consume.

So, she began to arrange their bones in a different way—the forgotten and restless dead with their mismatched parts. First, she fashioned armor with the same care she had once crafted furniture. Wove femurs together to create guards for her aged legs, helping her stand upright without effort. A helmet she made from fingers tied side by side with leather and old fishing net, with two jaws hooked together to protect her face. Around her torso, she created a cuirass of ribs, curved around her shape so that she became twice her size. She felt powerful, fearless.

Sometimes, she worried the other islanders would try to stop her, but when she roamed the beach gathering the new bones, washing them in seawater, none paid her any mind. She was just a mad old woman with a penchant for dead things. They continued with their plan, and she continued with hers.

It was the rowing boat that took the longest. A vessel made from smoothed and hollowed out skulls and vertebrae, an oar made from shoulder blades and leg bones. Every night she worked on the structure, using anything she found discarded on the beach to strengthen it, to make sure it would take her where she needed to go.

Finally, Aggie crafted a long dagger from a sternum, sharp and light. In the handle, she carved the names of her fallen family, then as she held it towards the sea it shone as silver as a lure in the moonlight.

"Sea Mither, defy me," she whispered her intent to the waves. "I'm coming for him."

In her bone-clad armor, and her boat made from the remains of the dead, Aggie set out at sundown to seek the Marool's lair. The sea was calm for her, and she breathed in its scent. The only sounds were the waves sloshing against her boat, and her bone armor creaking with each stroke of the oar. She didn't look back at the island as it faded into a dot behind her.

She had been rowing for half the night when she finally spotted the soft light of the Marool in the distance. She rowed slowly, careful not to attract his attention, until her boat was above the source. He hadn't sensed her yet. But he soon would.

Leaning slightly over the edge, she took her oar and swished it in a round motion. She sang a soft song as she made a whirlpool in the waves, a mix of the Marool's and the counter song the islanders sung. His light moved upwards. Aggie steeled herself. She dropped the oar and picked up her dagger instead, moving carefully to the very back of the boat. When the Marool raised his ugly head above the water, his crest of flames glowing bright in the sky, teeth as sharp as glass, the light of the lure gleaming azure on her boat made of bones, Aggie shouted a battle cry and called the Marool forwards.

The Marool opened his jaw wide and let out a long gargling shriek. Aggie looked at the chasm within, the chasm her family had once faced and succumbed to. And she smiled, baring her teeth beneath her helmet of woven jaws. She waited a few long seconds as the Marool moved to swallow her and the boat whole. The force sucked the water down. The boat tipped forwards. She locked her legs in her armor and held onto the stern of the boat, then when the Marool was close enough to touch, she leapt forwards, dagger in hand, and cut off his glowing lure in one precise swipe. In reflex, the Marool's jaw snapped shut and the sound of teeth breaking against the boat of bones echoed amidst the thrashing of water. Aggie fell back and held her breath, imagined the faces of the islanders if they could see what she'd done. The Marool flailed blindly, the boat now stuck in his jaw, and Aggie, having done what she'd set out to, let herself fall into the cold stinging sea.

Her bone armor dragged her downwards with the lure, still casting its light in the grayness in a luminous blue. She watched as it entangled itself with a jellyfish swarm, and as the lure's light faded, the jellyfish themselves became beacons, blooming into vibrancy. A trade had been made, awakening new light in the dark. They followed her descent to the seabed, lighting her way. The Marool followed, sinking down and down, the boat of bones trapped in its jaw and throat, the light in his crest dying. His scales shimmered silver then dulled, eyes blinking out one by one. The creature sang in a warbled sorrowful echo, but Aggie felt no pity for him. She had done it. She'd faced the monster that had taken her family.

When all was done, Aggie lay in the sand at the bottom of the sea next to the Marool, cradled within her bone armor, jellyfish dancing in the moonlight around her. As the water wrapped itself warm around her, she let out a breath and closed her eyes.

In the new tales, soon to be old, it is said that in deep dark waters the Marool still lurks, half-living, half-dead, sunk into the seabed by the bones of those it killed. Around it, jellyfish swim with their new light, adorned by the Marool's lure. And, it is said, that an old woman made of bones lies beside the monster she slayed, a shrine for those lost and forgotten at sea, avenged, and finally laid to rest.

The Right Side

By Alex Langer

Wrapping himself tightly in his army greatcoat, Yossel shivered. The Radomsko woods were freezing so close to dawn.

"The forest is no place for a Jew," he muttered in Yiddish.

"What was that about being a Jew? Something about money sticking to your fingers?" Jan teased in Polish.

"Fuck off," Yossel said, grinning.

"Fair enough," Jan said, a matching smile on his face. They'd fought in the Great War, cannon fodder freezing in the Polish Legion's trenches. Both had watched friends die, should have died themselves, but Adonai or the Devil or dumb luck pulled them through. Despite Jan being a police officer and Yossel a Jewish Labor Bund organizer, they helped each other whenever they could. Yossel did off-the-books work for Jan, while Jan kept Yossel in the know about the Bund's adversaries. Daloy politzey—fuck the police—of course, but Yossel made an exception for Jan, and Jan for Yossel.

Which was why they were in the woods at this godforsaken hour.

It all started with nervous peasants reporting wild animals fleeing the forest, the frozen glades fallen silent. Then there were the horse thefts. No one had found the stolen horses, Jan said, which was normal, but the deaths of the horses not stolen weren't. Jan's face drained of color when Yossel had pressed him about how they died.

Badly, he'd said.

Then the night before last, two children had gone missing. Little Izabella and Lech Witek hadn't come home from a walk in the woods. Their father had come to the police station. *Her scarf,* Jan said their father babbled, pressing a photograph into the policeman's hands, *she was wearing a red scarf.*

You're the only one I can trust to help me, Yossel, Jan had said to him. He'd shown up at Yossel's rented room, hammering on the door. Yossel opened the door gripping his revolver, ready for a shootout. Instead, Jan collapsed onto a chair, stinking of vodka.

It hasn't gotten out, but you know what will happen when it does, Jan had said.

Now, far from his apartment, anxiety washed over him. Two little Christian children gone, and not long before Passover? Yossel knew what would happen once the rumors metastasized, knew it in his marrow. There would be blood and fire.

Behind him, Yossel heard the clomp of shod hooves. A well-appointed carriage trundled down the road, a liveried driver at the reins. The man tipped his cap, and Yossel returned the greeting while Jan flagged it down. Autos hadn't caught on yet so far from Warszawa or Kraków, their congested streets filled with the smell of burning diesel.

The carriage slowed to a stop. "Nadkomisarz Jan Ferenc. Have you seen two children, a boy and a girl?" he said.

The groom shook his head.

"Your name?" asked Jan.

"Piotr," the groom said. His voice was choked, and his square-faced grin showed too many teeth. He must be nervous, Yossel thought. So were the horses, it seemed. They pawed at the ground and whinnied, the groom pulling the reins to keep them in place.

"And who's in the carriage, Piotr?" Yossel asked.

The groom's blue eyes were bloodshot. "My master," he said.

"Anyone with him?"

The groom shook his head. "Not today."

The boy didn't seem very bright, and Jan was curt when he waved the groom along.

"That was Count Pustkowski's carriage. Coming home from the whorehouse, I presume," Jan murmured to Yossel, as though the nobleman might overhear through the carriage doors. "I hear he's in debt."

"Up to his ears. His American investments went bad," Yossel said. He was a unionist, and unionists always knew which of the bourgeoisie were financially embarrassed. Money problems for them meant money problems for their workers too.

"His manor's up the next hill. I'd love to ask a few questions," Jan said.

Yossel laughed, bitterness under his tongue. Even the police had to bow and scrape to the parasites. "They don't even let you boys do that, do they?"

Jan chuckled. "Not without a good reason, no," he said, then gestured to the trees. "Shall we?"

Yossel cracked his hands and nodded.

"Something devilish is afoot," the peasant woman said in Polish as she tramped through the snow. "Yet the count does nothing."

She crossed herself, and her stone-faced husband nodded. Yossel's gut tightened as the wind hissed against leafless branches. He fiddled with the kashket that covered his short-cropped hair, knowing himself to be an intruder here.

They'd wandered for hours, getting lost and finishing the flask of slivovitz Yossel kept in his coat for long days on a picket line. Finally, they'd come to the cottage. Squatting among the trees, its whitewashed walls and thatched roof reminded Yossel of a moldy block of cheese. The peasants had offered Jan a drink and to show them something.

"What have you seen?" asked Jan, his notebook open. "Any children wandering about?"

"We don't let our children wander," the woman scoffed, then grew dour again. "There are strange lights in the forest. And yet you're the first police we've seen!"

"Since around Christmas?"

"Yes, around then," the woman crossed herself.

Jan's pencil dashed across off-white paper. "Any strangers about? We suspect smugglers or horse thieves are involved."

"The gypsies, but they left in September." The woman's eyes slid over to Yossel, raking his olive skin with hostility. Yossel wasn't sure if the peasants knew he could understand them. "But there are other things that don't belong here," she said.

Jan, face in his notebook, didn't seem to notice her and her husband's glares, and Yossel winced. He loved the man, but this was Jan's country. He didn't understand. In his work with the Bund, Yossel had cared for survivors of the last round of anti-Jewish riots. People crowding into makeshift shelters in synagogue chambers and union halls, eyes vacant from the horrors they'd experienced at the hands of their neighbors.

It was supposed to be safer here now that Poland was free. A land of golden liberty and democracy, Marshal Piłsudski said. But Yossel could feel the old curse lingering, a hateful taint in the air and the soil.

The woman stopped. "Here," she said, pointing at the ground."

The snow was disrupted in a winding pattern—*tracks*, Yossel thought—as though something had scraped across the ground and against the trees. Tufts of mane hair and torn flesh were caught in a tree's bark along with a sticky fluid, too dark and viscous to be blood. As he knelt, a smell wafted from the frozen gore, like cider turned to vinegar and old grease left to spoil. He pulled back and gagged, trying to clear the taste from his mouth.

"What's that way?" he asked, spitting.

"Marshland, and then the Pustkowski manor," the peasant's husband said. "There have always been evil things in the wood. Things they once bowed to in the darkness. And now they bow to the Jews!"

The man spat, and Jan's face flashed with irritation, as though he'd stepped in shit. "Well, thank you for your time. We'll take things from here." As the peasants left, Jan made an apologetic face, but Yossel waved him off.

They followed the tracks in silence. Yossel kept his footsteps light, wincing at the crunch of snow under Jan's polished black boots. His friend walked like there was nothing in this world to threaten a Pole in a policeman's uniform. *You can't make a difference there*, he'd told his friend when Jan first joined the

State Police, to no avail. And Jan was decent as far as police went. But you couldn't be a good man and a komisarz. Yossel's hand, jammed into his pocket, tightened around his pistol. He hoped that when the day of reckoning came, Jan would pick the right side.

Yossel smelled the marsh before he saw it, the trees thinning as the ground descended. Frozen reeds peeked through the snow, ice coating the stagnant water like an oily film. Yossel spotted a mass among the reeds near the water's edge. Before Jan could stop him, he hurried down for a closer look.

It had been a horse, once. Its eyes were bloodshot and wide-open, and its swollen tongue lolled to the side.

Something or someone had hollowed the horse out.

The smell of the black gore, corrupt and overwhelming, walloped his senses. Yossel fell to his knees and vomited. As he retched, Jan clomped to a halt behind him.

"Mary, Mother of Christ," Jan swore, crossing himself.

Through narrowed eyes, Yossel saw a malevolent sheen underneath the dead creature. "Help me lift the horse."

"What?"

"There's something underneath. Help me lift it."

"Yossel…"

"Come on. Unless you don't want to get that fancy-schmancy uniform dirty?"

Jan sighed. "Fine, you'll pay to clean it then."

Shedding his gloves to avoid ruining them, Yossel grimaced as his hands squelched against dead flesh and gore. Together, straining and sweating in the cold, they pushed the carcass aside.

Underneath was a cracked orb, shining wetly like mercury. The irregular curves seemed to add up to more than was there, bending and twisting in the half-light. Curious, Yossel reached out.

what are you, another supplicant

what do you WANT

HUNGER MEAT BLOOD

The stone was cold to the touch, but Yossel yanked his hand away as though he'd touched hot coals. When he did, the buzz of rage and hatred faded from his mind.

"Yossel," Jan said, a tremble in his voice.

"What?"

"Look."

Jan pointed. Yossel followed his friend's hand, and felt his face drain of blood. There was a wool mitten lying against the bloody snow.

A child's.

The manor's furnishings were modern. Yossel had worked in enough textile warehouses to recognize Paris fashions when he saw them. The whole house was opulent—although Yossel spotted empty places on the mantle where the house's silver should have stood—but it was musty and cold, like an extinguished candle. It set Yossel's teeth on edge.

They'd spent another hour searching around the marsh to no avail, looking for the children and following the scant blood trails left by whoever or whatever had killed the horse. Running out of daylight, Jan had suggested visiting the manor. Perhaps the count and his servants had seen something. Only one way to find out. The groom they'd seen before—Piotr, his name was?—let them in when Jan showed his badge and asked to speak with Count Pustkowski. He'd shrugged at Jan's questions and pointed them to the parlor, warmed by a roaring fire.

Yossel flopped into an armchair while Jan paced, his black boots clomping against the ornate floor rugs. "Don't get comfortable there," Jan warned.

"Come on. You dragged me out here, and you know I don't like the woods," Yossel said.

"You enjoyed Galicja just fine," Jan said.

"No, I enjoyed your sister Gabriela just fine. Both Gs, easy to confuse them," Yossel said in a deadpan.

Jan laughed and made a rude hand gesture. Neither of them fondly remembered the forests of Galicja, dodging Russian artillery fire and watching their brothers-in-arms die in the bitter cold. Humor had kept them alive when nothing else did.

Piotr lumbered back in with a tea tray and a round of cheese. Yossel tried the tea—tepid and barely brewed—and grimaced before setting it down, still queasy. He'd seen his share of blood, in Galicja and now in Radomsko. Poland's factories—competing based on low costs and cheap life—were vicious places, and Yossel organized their workers to fight back. Strikes sometimes ended with gunfire. But what they'd found at the water's edge touched a nerve. It wasn't calculated. It was raw savagery.

Jan turned to the groom. "Is your master able to see us? I want to thank him for his hospitality," he said.

The groom shook his head. "Sick," he said, and no more. Yossel eyed the bob of his throat, the sheen of sweat on his brow. The groom was lying, but about what?

Jan's eyes narrowed, but he nodded. "That will be all," he said.

They watched him go. "Strange that the groom is serving us. With a count, you'd at least expect a serving girl," Jan muttered. "And where are the other servants? He wouldn't fire all of them, not if he had a nickel left. Must keep up appearances."

Yossel nodded his agreement. "There's dust everywhere, like the house hasn't been cleaned in weeks."

"Something's not right. We'll wait for the groom to forget about us, then poke around. You go upstairs, I'll search this floor and the kitchens," Jan said in a low voice, gray eyes distant. "Before we were Christians, the woods were a place for sacrifice. Still are, in a way. We dip Marzanna in the streams, and then burn her. It's all connected, but a piece is missing."

They sat in silence for an hour, until they heard no movement beyond the doors and the sky glowed orange with the sun's embers. As they crept through the manor's halls, Yossel noticed the sickly-sweet smell of the black gore. It was faint, obscured by the other smells of an old, corpulent home, but it was there.

They reached stairs clad in rich carpet. Yossel's eyes caught on a polished cavalryman's saber hanging on the wall. Count Pustkowski had served in Haller's Army during the war, burning his way through the shtetls. Yossel wondered grimly how many Jews had seen their last terrified moments reflected in its shine. Jan looked at it too, and their eyes met.

"Be careful, Yossel," Jan whispered after a pause, before disappearing down the corridor.

Yossel climbed the stairs. The smell grew stronger as he walked down the corridor. He passed oil portraits of the count's ancestors, heavily armored blonde men with sweeping mustaches, and women in gowns of silk and brocade and pearls, worth more than the lives of every peasant on their estate. Poland had been formed and destroyed and reformed, but those in charge stayed the same.

The bedchamber was the most opulent room yet, wallpaper flecked with gold leaf enveloping a four-poster bed with velvet curtains. It stank, expensive perfume covering up a corrupt smell. Yossel's neck tingled. He didn't belong in this room amidst the velvet hangings and tobacco smoke and tapestries, every nerve in his body screaming. Something evil lived here, and it didn't want him to see.

Yossel swept back the curtains.

Count Pustkowski looked older than Yossel remembered. The count had been healthy at the last Reunion Day celebration, belly straining against his wartime uniform as he paraded about. Now he was withered against his sheets, tangled hair gray-turning-white. He had weeping sores the size of chestnuts on his neck, a single black pimple in the middle of each one. His mustache was crusted with flakes of black. The smell from him, cloudy and rotten, was overwhelming. And clutched to his chest was a cracked orb shimmering like liquid silver.

Struck with horror, Yossel only just noticed the thump behind him. He turned, and saw the groom stepping forward, raising the count's sword over his head, grinning emptily, gums black and swollen.

Yossel let out a piercing cry and ducked aside, the saber slicing through the air next to him, missing by an inch. He dodged as the groom howled wordlessly. Another sword stroke missed, and Yossel toppled over. The groom raised his sword again. He was much too close to miss.

Crumpled on the floor, Yossel closed his eyes and began to say the Shema, the declaration of faith before death, before the bark of a revolver made him open them again.

"Go to the stable and saddle a horse!" Jan yelled, pistol smoking. The groom lay on the floor, blood and brains staining the wall behind him. Jan fired two rounds into his chest for good measure. "Go to the barracks, tell them what we've found."

Yossel huddled on the floor. Bits of skull and viscera dotted the rich carpet, and he failed to stifle a chuckle at the thought of the cleaning bill. Then, Jan hauled him to his feet and slapped his face.

"A horse, Yossel, you know what that is?" Yossel nodded mutely, and Jan pushed him towards the door. "I'll be on your heels. Go, Yossel!"

There was little light in the stables. Yossel found an oil lamp near the entrance, and lit it with the flint he carried in his coat. Flickering light and the greasy odor of burning tallow washed over the barn.

Yossel cursed. Despite having seen the groom's carriage earlier, there were no horses here. Yet, it reeked of manure and that horrid spoiled smell. The floors were crusted with blood and traced with boot-prints, leading to a spiraling staircase at the back of the stable. His chest heaving, Yossel followed them down, and down.

The dark of the basement weighed on Yossel. It felt a hundred generations old and smelled like a slaughterhouse. Burnt-out candles lined the places where the walls met the floor, dried wax seeping into dried blood. At the center of the floor was a stone altar, engraved with swirling patterns. There were nine divots in the stone. Six held orbs that glowed, untarnished and swimming in the air.

Then, Yossel felt a drip on his shoulder. He lifted the lamp, and screamed.

The ceiling, like the floor, was covered in blood. It hadn't yet dried. Splayed across the ceiling were what was left of at least two horses. And tangled among them was a red scarf.

Yossel hurried up the stairs. He needed to find Jan. They said there were no atheists in the trenches, although he'd made it through the war gently mocking Jan's rosary. Now, at least of the Devil, he wasn't so sure.

He reached the top of the stairs, and a familiar figure stood waiting for him near the entrance of the stable. Jan grinned, his mouth stretching to his ears.

"Jan! Thank God you're here. Below…" Yossel said, then trailed off. Jan wasn't listening. His smile was too wide, and his eyes were bloodshot.

"Jan?"

Jan stepped forward, and Yossel saw that his uniform was covered in blood, dark red marring the blue. Black ooze dripped from his nose.

"Jan, what happened up there?"

Jan kept smiling. His mouth worked to form words, but nothing came from it but a choking noise.

"Stop where you are," Yossel said. He set the lantern down and felt for his pistol, still stowed away in his pocket. He pulled it out, hand shaking.

This wasn't Jan. Yossel had lost friends and comrades in war, seen bodies shredded and faces beaten past the point of recognition. He knew too well what a dead friend's eyes looked like when the light went out.

Behind that empty grin, Jan wasn't there anymore.

The-thing-that-had-been-Jan raised the count's saber in his hand and shrieked, a high-pitched keen that felt like needles in Yossel's ears.

"Jan!"

It charged, and Yossel fired until the revolver clicked empty, sending Jan sprawling to the floor. Yossel hurried to his friend's side. Blood and black oozed from Jan's heaving chest. Yossel kneeled, putting pressure on the wounds. He knew there would be a day, someday, when he and Jan would be on opposite sides of a battle line. Jew and Pole, proletarian and bourgeoisie, it was inevitable. There are no good policemen, he'd always known that.

But not Jan, not yet. It wasn't time.

"Jan, come on," he whispered. He wept as he tried to lift his friend, his hands slick with blood. "You're going to be fine."

Jan turned his head to Yossel. There was no white to his eyes, only broken blood vessels and swollen pupils that swallowed his gray irises.

He choked, blood daubing his lips, and grinned that empty smile.

A tangle of black limbs, spidery and many-jointed, poured from his mouth, snapping the cartilage and bone of his jaw and tearing at Yossel. It gripped his arms with a terrible force, pulling him towards the wreckage of Jan's face. Yossel screamed and fell back, kicking his feet and shouting for help that wasn't there.

The thing scrabbled and Yossel writhed, trying to get away. As he struggled and kicked, the thing's needle-sharp teeth made contact, and Yossel was flooded with *hunger*

darkness and flame

the clamor of men's mouths, greedy and bilious

what do they want? gold and silver, diamonds and riches?

what they always want when they call us from the deep

they have erred and want our help to save themselves

but there is no gold here only BLOOD AND HATE AND

everything is wrong wrONG WRONG

Glass shattered and the world was on fire. The straw on the floor surged with flame from the broken lantern, and the many-limbed thing screeched. Yossel rolled aside, and the thing snapped at his feet. Smoke filled the air and he coughed as the creature followed him, trying to latch back on. He kicked again, and again, and finally the creature was flung fully into the roaring flames. It squealed, the sound like spikes against Yossel's eardrums as he fled.

Yossel scrambled out the door. Collapsing against the ground, he turned. Smoke poured from the doorway as flames engulfed the stables. He sat in a daze, watching the building be consumed by flames. He looked at his coat. He was covered in blood. Whose, he wasn't sure.

What would he tell the police? It's not like they would trust a Jew. Yossel would have to explain what happened without sounding like a raving madman. Jan could have.

Jan.

Yossel blinked away tears and stifled a racking sob. His head pounded, and he could feel the gorge rising at the back of his throat.

Dizzy, forehead beaded with sweat, he lay back and looked at the sky. The sky was pitch-black now, molten with stars. He shut his eyes tight, and the world spun.

hate them HATE THEM

He opened them back up. He touched his neck where the beast had bitten him, and his fingers came away wet. He looked at them. They were red with blood, but also something bright and metallic, like mercury in the vial.

A compulsion to jam the bloody fingers in his mouth swept over him *hunger STARVING* and before he could stop himself, he licked his fingers.

The iron tang of blood brushed against his tongue. Yossel felt a wave of nausea, but it was quickly overwhelmed by a feeling of euphoria. Frantic energy surged through his limbs, which felt pleasurably numb. His throat choked.

Yossel felt better now. He felt comfortable, like he was sitting in front of a roaring fire. His mind flickered like a guttering candle, confusion and horror twirling round and round to a sudden halting, pleasant nothingness.

A flash of a red scarf and the Radomsko Synagogue in flames were his last thoughts before his mind snuffed out.

Yossel stood and smiled wide. His eyes empty and bloodshot, he trudged down the hill.

Wick, Wax, and Tallow
By Kanishk Tantia

Wicks hang twisted and knotted from rocky walls.

Drip.

Wax falls from uncountable melting candles.

Drip.

Tallow runs in yellowing pools along an uneven stone floor.

Drip.

Shining yellow flames dance merrily, throwing the warm fragrance of melting wax into the cold night air. Candles line rough stone shelves—some long and thin, some short and squat. Some twisted, some straight, some simple, some ornate. They flicker with varying intensity.

The woman I've led here flinches in the blinding light before her senses adjust. I expect a gasp, but her fortitude surprises me.

A solitary creature sits in the dirt, a tattered, age-gray cloak hanging upon its frame. Jitters in the shoulder, tension in the back—the creature works furiously, incessantly. Its true name is a scrap of forgotten memory. In the village, we name it Candlemaker.

I have never known it to rest.

Lady Alyona's black veil shimmers in the candlelight. "May I approach?" She looks to me.

It is not for me to say. This meeting is between Candlemaker and Candleholder. I am neither.

She lifts the veil, and I see a face wet with tears, eyes shot through with blood. The face of someone who does not think they have more to lose. Good sense often falters before grief.

The creature pays us no heed.

"You are the Candlemaker." Alyona wrings her hands together, sweat beading on her forehead. "Please. A candle. Make me a candle."

The candles flicker as one, throwing her face into sharp relief. I see the hollows of her cheeks better now, the cracked lips expressing equal parts defiance and desperation. The Candlemaker continues to tease softened wax, lengthening and carving to its satisfaction.

"A candle. Just one." She moves closer, drops her voice to a whisper. "Bring my child back. Please."

Her hand clutches her stomach as she utters the words. Perhaps she truly has nothing left to lose.

Wick. Wax. Tallow.

It does not speak and it does not pause, but its words reach us all the same.

Alyona produces a twine-wrapped bundle and lays it on the floor. I am sure it contains the softest wick, the purest wax, the densest tallow. Dark tales of candlelight have brought her here, and she did not come empty-handed.

"This should be enough. For my child."

Wick. Wax. Tallow.

Alyona turns to me, confused, but the usher does not interfere in the sacred bond between Maker and Holder. I cannot tell her that the Candlemaker needs no earthly material.

Her eyes are drawn to the ocean of candles. More than the cavern could hold, should hold. A ring of waxen hearts melting into each other infinitely. A sphere of green and blue, burning from within. The chiseled face of a cherub, the melting wax forming deep furrows down its cheeks.

Alyona reaches into the sea of light, and draws forth a simple candle, as if it called out to her. Long and slender, lilac and lavender. The flame atop the candle sputters, too weak to melt the dense wax below. A candle saving itself for something else. For someone else.

"My candle then." Alyona kneels, offering it to the Candlemaker.

I see a flash of leathery gray skin, of blackened nails and varicose musculature. Then the cloak reasserts itself. The

Candlemaker tears out the wick, melts the tallow, skims the wax. In the end, only a lilac stub remains.

Fingers moving, muscles twitching, a new candle forms in its hands. Twin snakes upon a caduceus, each scale glinting in the waxen staff's intense flame. A candle destined to burn in greatness.

Twelve months. One child.

"Wick, wax, and tallow." Alyona whispers.

The lilac stub sputters to life, purple flame flickering merrily once more.

"Wick, wax, and tallow." I whisper back to her.

I carry her upon my back and lay her to rest. My bed has seen many a Candleholder recover from their trek up the mountain.

Throughout the night, her body burns with fever. Her skin is waxy to the touch, soaked in warm beads of sweat. I can only hope the nightmares which plague her now are preferable to the waking nightmare of her life before. I try to make her comfortable, but when I attempt to leave, her hands grip mine and refuse to let go.

There is a single phrase on her lips.

"Wick, wax, and tallow."

She mumbles it all night long, mantra and curse, until dawn breaks. As the first rays of morning fall on her face, Alyona stirs, and her eyes meet mine.

"Thank you."

Very few people thank me. Alyona is the first who seems to mean it. For most, I am just another part of their night with the Candlemaker, silent witness to their misery.

I'm not sure what to say, so I say nothing, extricating my hand from her grip and moving towards the kitchen.

"I have tea and bread." I open a clay pot of tea leaves for steeping. "Stew, if you can stomach it, though I suspect you cannot."

"Stew then." Her voice is weak, but firm. "A double serving."

"It was not meant as a challenge."

Alyona has no place to go. Her husband, a so-called lord, abandoned her when she failed to produce an heir. After breakfast, I can already see the question form on her face.

I shake my head. "You do not want to stay here. I am the usher, Alyona."

I leave the house and return to my post, sitting upon a flattened rock at the foot of Mount Fos, awaiting those who wish to make the trek to the Candlemaker. As night falls and thunderclouds gather, a lone figure approaches me.

"Do you wish to meet the Candlemaker?" The words roll out, rehearsed over centuries. "I am its usher, and I will guide you if you so choose."

"No. But it will rain soon, and I see you have no cover."

"I—What?" I look closer and see Alyona, a bamboo sheet bundled in her arms.

"A cover. For the rain." She drapes the cover over me with a defiant smile. "It would be a sorry sight were the Candlemaker's usher to catch a cold, would it not?"

"I—I do not succumb to mortal ailments." I suppress a laugh. "I am the usher, I cannot be killed by animals, disasters, or disease."

She looks a little put off, but her smile reasserts itself immediately.

"I never said a cold would *kill* you." She plants herself next to me and pulls the cover over herself. "Just said you'd look a sorry sight."

A few hours later, as the rain pelts down over us, I must admit the cover is comfortable. I look over to Alyona to tell her so, but she is asleep, her head resting on my shoulder.

Slowly, Alyona becomes a part of my life. I am not sure how, but in only a few weeks, I expect her at my cottage when I return home. Sometimes she sits with me, talking about her life before meeting the Candlemaker. Sometimes she visits the fruit pickers during the day and returns at night bearing gifts. Sometimes I find my cottage filled with the smell of roasting fish. The villagers fear me and give me space, knowing I am the usher. But Alyona is mortal, and they welcome her openly.

I take more travelers to the Candlemaker. They climb the jagged trail with me and make their way into the cave where the abject creature plies its unearthly craft. Many balk at the price of a candle and descend empty-handed. A few find the bargain amenable, and after their deals are struck, spend the night burning with fever, tongues rasping the call of the Candlemaker.

Wick, wax, and tallow.

Over and over, until morn breaks, and they come to their senses once more. All have places to go, and leave as soon as they can, sparing nary a glance. So Alyona and I live in my cottage, alone with each other.

"Will you raise my child?" The question is unprompted, asked as I eat a meal I do not need to eat but enjoy nonetheless. "I won't be around, you see."

I dismiss the notion entirely. "You must find someone better."

"Who would be better than you?" She pours another helping of soup into my bowl. "Or has someone raised a child borne of the Candlemaker's sorcery before?"

"I have never raised any child before."

"After centuries alive, perhaps you will learn." There is a quiet certainty in her eyes, the kind she often has when she proves me wrong.

Through the Candlemaker's blessing, her belly grows. The village physician pronounces the babe within her to be in excellent health, though his manner when talking about Alyona is more subdued.

"We could send you to the Capitol, if you wish." Like the other villagers, he has grown fond of her. "It would be a short journey, only a few days."

"I do not wish." There is no frailty to her manner, only her body. "I will stay here, at home."

The doctor says nothing more. He understands just as well as I do the deal Alyona made. We cannot speak of it, but we know nonetheless.

"Follow my instructions then, and you may yet hold your baby."

He does not say for how long.

A few months later, Alyona holds her son close. For almost an hour, I watch as his body rises and falls with his mother's breathing until at last, with a single exhale, Alyona's chest falls and does not rise again.

The boy Kerion sleeps, blissfully unaware.

At first, Kerion is a hindrance. I have no desire for a child, nor the ability to care for one. Alyona made no other arrangements.

The village takes him as their own, but his responsibility falls to me. I watch over him as he plays and crawls near my post, and during the night as he sleeps with nary a cry or sob. The tailor crafts a sling for me, unasked for but welcome nonetheless, to carry Kerion in when I walk the mountain trail.

As I guide Candleholders up the rocky path to the Candlemaker's cavern, Kerion's eyes remain fixed on the glowing cave. He makes no sound. When he sees the Candlemaker, he does not shudder. When the Candlemaker speaks, he does not flinch. In his eyes, I see the reflection of his own candle, twin snakes curled around a caduceus, bright and blazing.

Little wonder then, that after many such trips, he says his first words.

"Wick, wax, tallow."

He learns to walk soon, and then to run. He never calls me father, and I never ask him to.

"Why take them up the mountain?" he asks me one day, after an old man struggles through the trek. "To throw away their lives?"

"I am only a guide." I hoist the old man upon my back, though I know he will not make it through the night. The candle left behind is a sliver barely larger than my fingernail. "And those who come here give of themselves freely."

He is dissatisfied. I know because his eyes have the same defiance as his mother's.

The seasons change, and the village with it. The Candlemaker's cavern is the only constant. The young turn old, and the old turn to dust. Amid them, Kerion turns from boy to man faster than I anticipated.

"You could farm. We have land, though I have never tilled it." I stroke his hair as I say it, dearly hoping he will listen to me. "Or apprentice with the potter. She has plenty of work, and no students to teach."

But I know Kerion has already decided.

"I will mend flesh, not till land or shape clay. That is what I was meant for."

"The village doctor—" The words die in my throat. Kerion's eyes are fixed on the gate and his heart is set on the Capitol. "When do you leave?"

"Tomorrow."

As morn breaks, Kerion accompanies me one last time to the foot of the mountain. There is little left to say. I press a few gifts into his hand. Fruit for the journey, parchment to write home with, and a few bundles of paper money for trading.

"Wick, wax, and tallow keep you."

Kerion's absence makes itself known in the emptiness of my cottage as I wake, in the single plates of food I make, and in the silence that follows as I forgetfully call for him. It makes itself known in the presence of an emotion I have not felt in a long time: loneliness.

Even with centuries behind me, the years pass haltingly. The days have a familiar rhythm, interrupted only when Candleholders come and I assume the duties of the usher once more. I pay them little attention once we enter the Candlemaker's cave, for my eyes are busy searching for a candle I know well.

Twin snakes around a caduceus, a flame burning strong. Kerion sends no letters, but the intensity of his light never diminishes.

The night is uncomfortably warm, a thick blanket of heat and humidity that threatens to smother me if I breathe too close. An ailing Holder lies in my bed, a young man who has chosen to forfeit a long life alone for a few more years with his wife. He will leave in the morning and would likely have left tonight if his legs could bear his weight.

I watch over him as he sweats and shivers, as his mouth forms silent words. He is too weak to voice the words I know well.

Wick, wax, tallow.

"You should cool him off." A soft voice sounds out from the doorway. "A cold cloth over his forehead, perhaps?"

"You would tell the usher how to care for the Candleholders?"

"No, I would tell you what I learned in the Capitol."

It is an odd thing to feel such joy when a man lies trembling in my bed. Kerion embraces me, and even with that brief contact, I can tell he has grown. His frame is broader, his hair thicker, his manner more certain. We spend the night caring for the Candleholder, Kerion insisting on lowering the man's temperature and forcing ice into his mouth for hydration.

"His candle will neither lengthen nor shorten because of your efforts."

"Perhaps. Or perhaps it is already longer because the Candlemaker knows I will make an effort." He squeezes a poultice over the man's forehead, and for the first time, I see a Candleholder sleep peacefully.

Proving me wrong, just like his mother.

Kerion opens his own practice in the village, much to the relief of the old village doctor, who retires. He spends his days administering to patients and makes a habit of facing death and winning. His confidence in his own skill is at once remarkable and worrying. No mortal man ought to treat death as a foe to be defeated, and yet, Kerion insists. At night, we share our meals.

"No one should die before their time." He speaks with certainty embellished by the optimism of youth. "That is all."

Only the Candlemaker knows when it is time, I think to myself, but remain silent. It is not the usher's place to say, after all.

• • •

I should not have been surprised when he came to me. When he arrived at the foot of the mountain, hands covered in gore, eyes brimming with tears.

"I wish to meet the Candlemaker."

An usher can only guide. The climb is silent, and as we approach the Candlemaker's cavern, I hope Kerion turns back. But as the blinding lights envelop us, as he steps forward without looking at me, I know he will not.

From the countless flickering flames, he finds his candle. The smell of burning wax pounds into my head. Wax, and life.

"A child lies in my practice. I have stitched her wounds." His voice is firm, the steadiness of habit. I wish he were more fearful. "But she is foaming at the mouth. She will not survive the night."

Wick. Wax. Tallow.

"I know. A decade, simple and strong." He offers the candle, and I watch as the Candlemaker carefully grasps the wick between cracked yellow fingers and pulls at it. I watch as it carves waxen flakes off the twin snakes and boils them, as it cleans the melted tallow, as it pulls out a small, sputtering candle, mending it until the flame gleams.

The twin snakes look leaner now, their scales diminished. The caduceus is shorter, but the flame atop it burns as brightly as ever. And in return, the child's candle, a thin skein of yarn burning from the inside, has increased in size.

We leave and climb downwards in stony silence. It is only as we approach the cottage that Kerion speaks.

"I am sorry. But I must."

I say nothing and lead him inside. The usher must not interfere with the bond, only guide the Holders to the Maker. We both know that nightmares await him. I hold his hand through the night, reducing his temperature as much as I can, applying cool cloths and poultices to his forehead until he finally sleeps. He mutters the same words over and over.

"Wick, wax, and tallow."

When he wakes, he will not meet my eyes. I think he is afraid he will find disapproval or disappointment.

"I have tea and bread." I pause, and am reminded of a similar conversation I once had. He is so like his mother. "And stew if you can stomach it, though I suspect you cannot."

"Bread and tea please."

Perhaps not so similar after all, and for a moment I hope he will stay away from the Candlemaker and accept the necessity of death.

It is not so. Each time Kerion comes to me, I wonder if I should refuse him, but the usher can only guide.

With every visit, his candle loses splendor, the two snakes shriveling into worms, the caduceus shrinking to a stump. The flame sputters and spits, emitting a sickly light. At the same time, Kerion's frame recedes, clothes hanging loose upon his body as though they weigh him down. His eyes worsen until he needs glasses to tell night from day. His hair falls out in clumps on his pillows and sheets.

And all I can do is watch.

Kerion lies in my bed again, shivering, his paper-thin skin burning with unearthly fire. He moves to grip my forearm, but his hands fall limply to his side. His eyes do not see, and his mind does not comprehend.

He has sacrificed his remaining time to save his last patient. She will sleep peacefully tonight in his practice, and as morn breaks, will find there is no doctor for her to thank.

I should have stopped this long before now. I should have refused to take this trip. An usher only guides, but a father must protect.

Kerion's frame is light upon my back. He groans in my ear with each step I take, but as the cavern comes to view, I can feel his eyes fixed upon it once more. His skin burns fiercely, so warm it should scar even me.

I lay him upon the floor, turning his head so he may watch. I do not know how this bargain will be made, but no matter the outcome, I want him to watch.

"A deal, Candlemaker."

The cloaked figure continues to carve, unbothered by my presence. It has only ever acknowledged me once, to give me purpose. Now, I will make it acknowledge me again.

"Save my son." From within the expanse of candles and flames, I reach out to one I know well. A string of wick, a sliver of wax, a drop of tallow. A candle close to being extinguished, but I will not let it go out.

Wick. Wax. Tallow.

"You know I have nothing to offer." I sit on the floor, and though it should be warm, even burning from the heat of the candles, it is as cold as the air outside. "Save him nonetheless."

Wick. Wax. Tallow.

"I *have* none."

There is no voice. Hearing my plea, knowing of my years of service, seeing my son lying broken upon the cold stone floor, none of this will placate the creature. It cares only for candles.

"Answer me, Maker." My words sound distant. A pulsing fills my ears, punctuated only with the gasps Kerion makes behind me. "Will you save my son?"

It is madness born of love, but as the Candlemaker continues its silence I find I can do nothing but reach for its grimy cloak. The cloth feels rough in my hand, and with an aggression I had not known lay within me, I pull at the cloak. I do not know if I want the Candlemaker to fall, or to pay attention to me, or to reveal its true form.

As I pull, I find the cloak continues to lengthen, the cloth pooling around my feet. But I cannot stop now. Kerion's candle flickers weakly as I continue to tear away more and more of the ragged, never-ending cloak from the Candlemaker's form.

Wick. Wax. Tallow.

The cloak wraps around me, rags sticking to my skin. The threads bind me until my movements are not my own. Slowly, the cloak pulls me in, and yet all I can think of is the candle in my hand. The remnants of a caduceus and two snakes. Soon, even that thought disappears.

There is wick, wax, and tallow all around me. My skin is leathery gray, my nails cracked and yellowing. The cloak guides me, and I unmake Kerion's candle, preserving it in eternal stasis. My hands know what to do, my fingers blur.

Wicks must be twisted, wax must be melted, tallow must be cleansed. I must make candles, see them burn.

"Father?"

A candleless man speaks to me. But does he have something to offer?

Wick. Wax. Tallow.

"Usher? Father?" He kneels near me. But still, no candle, no wick, no wax, no tallow to give. Useless. I cannot stop working. The next candle will be my finest yet, a hundred candle shells within each other, burning and cascading for decades. "Father, can you hear me?"

It is best if he does not speak. It is best if ushers do not speak.

Wick. Wax. Tallow.

Story Eater

By Jean Strickland

Colossal coral reefs enclose the lagoon. Thousands of fireflies flicker, secreting honeyed beads of enchanted light into the water. Each drip glazes the surface with golden, viscous scum.

As Wago's ship drifts through the fireflies, his sucking tube collects them. The vacuum drones, and the fireflies buffet the sides of the tube, staining the glass.

Wago opens a hatch in the tube. The sounds inside, the bumping and buzzing, satisfy him as he catches a firefly between his long, grimy fingers, pulls it out, and admires it. It has black, bulbous eyes and an irresistibly confusing disparity between its chitinous exoskeleton and comforting light. He holds the firefly above his open mouth and squeezes gently until a globule falls onto his tongue.

A sour shiver shakes him. The texture is gummy, the taste disgustingly acidic, but as a result, his body illuminates with ethereal light. The illumination lasts only a moment, bursting through the threads of his coat, before it dies.

Satisfied with the quality, Wago returns the firefly to the sucking tube. The tube snakes below deck into a storage hold and deposits the fireflies into a pod. The bottom of the pod is spattered with expended fireflies while live ones weep into a dispenser. Along the hold's walls, the gelatinous light is stored in canisters, ready to be sold.

As Wago steers out of the lagoon and toward the first port town, the sky is a black canopy. At some point, the sun will rise for two hours, only one tomorrow, the onset of the dark season.

Wago turns off the sucking tube. The drone dies down.

In the darkness beyond the ship, sticks drag through the water. Eerie, gentle songs drawl.

Wago scratches behind his ear where the skin is dry. The things that row withdraw from light, and Wago has plenty of light.

On deck, his precious candles burn within a protective shrine. A trough catches the candles' seeping wax. Every now and then, a candle will melt entirely into the trough and its light will go out, but he has enough candles to give him time to recycle the wax to make new ones.

Wago wanders to his shrine. The low susurration of the licking flames helps him ignore the things. He thinks of them as things because they do not interest him. He cups a candle flame. Unlike fireflies' cold light, it strokes heat onto his palms. Wax milks down. It fights him, struggles against his closing grasp.

The resiliency of flame to spread and grow, despite how easily it snuffs, has always pleased him.

He hunches over the trapped, shrinking flame, and coos. It shivers beneath his breath. He chortles and accidentally blows it out.

The first port town is silent save swinging lantern frames.

In their homes, people huddle by dim canisters. The canisters, previously bought from Wago, contain firefly light that is weak unless ingested and weakens more over time. From the dock, Wago can hardly make out the people's silhouettes.

Wago rings his ship bell, the sound bellows, and people shock alert. They scurry, deciding who will go out, and pour their remaining canister light into old lanterns to carry. They creep onto the street and run toward the ship. Each one clutches creased papers: handwritten stories of tragedies they've suffered. Wago licks his lips.

The exchange rate is one story, one canister.

A woman grasping the hand of an eleven-year-old boy climbs aboard. Her grip looks painfully tight, but the boy shows no complaint in his expression. Instead, he gazes around the ship in wonder. Near the front, canisters are stacked in a pyramid: each glass faintly shining. The boy wanders past, captivated by the shrine of candles. The woman does not scold him. She only follows.

At the humans' approach, the flames tremble.

"Don't touch," Wago warns.

The boy jumps. "We want to buy them." He holds his papers as evidence.

Wago heads them off and closes the front of the shrine.

The dock darkens. People in line whimper.

"I only sell the magic light."

"You don't need them."

"I need them as well as you," Wago lies. "I have more ports to attend."

Lapping waves sound like rowing. The woman kneels down, whispers compromises.

The boy shrugs off the woman, and the story crinkles in his grip. He glares at Wago. "Why do you make us write these? My mom cried really bad for this one. She told me not to read it."

Something scrapes the hull. The ship rocks, weighed down on one side as if something climbs it. People on the dock shout to reopen the shrine.

Instead, Wago uncaps a canister and slurps down its light. He straightens to his full height and walks to the ship's side, his body a beacon. The sounds recede.

The boy trembles, leans into the woman. Wago walks back to them, stoops, takes the story, and exchanges it for a single canister of light.

The woman's expression is too complicated for Wago to interpret unwritten, but it makes him hungry.

"You're cruel," she says.

Wago leans forward, curious. His artificial glow gives a sallow color to the woman's complexion. "How is it cruelty if you cannot live without it?"

The woman stomps on his foot. His toes yelp. She sets her expression, and she and the boy hurry off the ship.

As they run home, Wago watches after them. That one canister might not last them to his return. If only they had come up with more to barter.

Additional sales follow. People do not linger on his ship, and the stories build up. Still, Wago does not reopen his shrine until after he sails off in case anyone else has ideas about taking his candles.

Alone, finally, Wago sits down to read. He takes a candle from beneath a floorboard, where he stores hundreds more, and lights it with one from the shrine. He settles on a carpet and sets the candle on a plate. From his sales box, he pulls the boy's mother's story.

The paper scorches into dust, and Wago breathes in deeper than his lungs: beyond his own weak senses and into the story.

The smell is moss, rotting trees. Wago stands in a swamp outside the fireflies' lagoon. The muck is uneven underfoot. *What do you mean?* he asks. His voice is a woman's: pitiful and helpless; confused and angry. A man answers, *I mean I don't know what happened. It's black out there. We separated to catch the fireflies. There are barely any left. The swamp water was higher than we expected. I guess she slipped. I heard splashes…* There is a thumping against glass, insects hitting the wall of a jar. *Before I could find her, the songs started. I heard the…the sticks in the water, the rowing. I didn't have enough light left to keep them away.*

Wago screams a name frantically. Mud sloshes. Arms wrap around him, dragging him back. His chest gorges on the cavernous pounding.

The story ends. Wago touches his cheeks, rubbery and sucked dry by the cold. His heart yearns, as it always does after he eats, to go into town and paint all the buildings and all the people with his magic light; to distribute his candles, his wealth, to every poor family; to keep them protected from the things that hunt them.

Instead, Wago takes the candle and places it on the shrine.

He offers a moment of silence.

Then, he lights a new one to burn another story.

Between ports, Wago looks over the water. In the dark, he can't tell the details of the things, but he can hear them. They row evenly, calmly, beside his ship.

He has always wondered what the things would sound like dying. But it is just idle curiosity. He won't kill them.

The things are necessary.

Just like him.

Each port further from the fireflies' lagoon has people more and more reliant on Wago for light. They swarm the dock before he even rings his bell. Their bodies are thin. They shade their eyes from the light of his ship, and when they climb aboard, they are desperate and deferential.

At the fourth port, a man pushes through the crowd and leaps aboard the ship the moment it docks. He clasps a thick pile of stories. Wago's candles reflect in his irises.

Wago moves around him and lays the gangway. The man's chin quavers.

Wago holds out his withered hand, and as the man hands the stories over, the man bursts into tears. On the dock, hushed arguments rise. Then, a teenager runs aboard. The man grabs him, holds him back, shouting, "No, Tas. We'll all die."

"We don't need him! Take his boat!" the teenager cries. He holds a fish hook. His knuckles are white.

Wago frowns. Distaste sits in his gut like tar.

"We don't know where he goes," the man reasons. "We don't know where he gets the light."

"The candles." The boy's arms hang at his sides.

Wago's fingertips crick, but the man's expression is resigned. "Candles don't last forever either."

Wago shuts his shrine. The wind blows, distorting the songs that are sung in the streets of the towns. The boy's head falls into the man's shoulder. People on the dock sob.

Wago looms beside the man. "Ten stories, ten canisters."

Alone, again, Wago sits on his carpet to eat. He singes one of the man's stories into inhalable ash and sucks it in.

The sounds are chants, rattling windows. *How many weeks until the merchant comes back?* As he speaks, the vibrations scratch his throat. Others rustle but do not answer. Something scrapes the wall. A canister—the only one—falls and breaks. The window shatters open. He dives for the goo and slurps it from the floor to his throat. As he swallows, shards of glass cut his soft palate. His body gleams, and he sees it: cloaked body, long, knuckled claws, black hole face. Its song echoes like it comes from deep inside a cave. The thing crawls back through the window. There are sobs. Plastic scrapes against the floor. The teenager asks, *How much is left?*

Wago grabs his chest, trying to hold onto the phantom heartbeat. It pulses with sensation, euphoric and nourishing. Then, it fades. The emptiness inside him growls hungrily.

At the final port, Wago cannot see into the town. The circle of vision granted by his ship's shrine shows the dock unattended. Wood crunches and something splashes as his ship hits empty rowboats. More than usual. A stick floats in the water.

Wago rings his bell.

No one comes.

He rings his bell again. A few more times.

Each unanswered chime digs a hole in his chest. The things. His customers. The delicate balance he curated with his magic light. There's been an upset.

He hurries down his ship's creaky stairs to a hold below deck where he keeps a vat of rare oil. He harvested the oil from sea slugs that sometimes stick beneath his ship. He's kept it a year now, with more riches in reserve. He dips a torch into the tub and carries it, dripping, to his shrine of candles. The torch catches. The flame blazes.

He goes out into the town, and his torchlight fills the first home. A coat is draped over a chair next to a writing desk. On the desk, there is a stack of papers. The top sheet is indented by harsh scribbles. There are no words.

Wago brings the page to his torch, burns it, breathes it in.

It tastes like nothing.

His chest moans: empty, wanting.

As he continues his search for customers, Wago ignites street lamps, the town grows brighter, and the things recede. Their pathetic black bodies are slow and satisfied. They have no fear, even when Wago waves the torch near their faces. They simply slink away from it.

He hates them. The useless, unfeeling, murderous things. They go too far.

He corners one of them. With walls behind it, it has nowhere to go. It faces him blankly. Blood is congealed in its claws. He tries to conjure the pounding heartbeat, the terror. He cannot. He presses the torch into the thing's empty mouth. Its song stutters. Its head bursts. Its body crumples.

What a waste.

Wago gets back on his ship. He douses his torch and after he returns it, he wanders into the hold where he kept his fireflies. He stares, conflicted, at their drained bodies. They too are dying out.

He crosses the port off his list for good. Only seven ports remain.

As he sails away, the town burns radiantly behind him. At the dock, the things skulk back to their boats. They sing softly, eagerly. Their sticks splash in the water. They row, following him.

Stories Between the Ribs of the Great Monster Tyron

By Carson Winter

1.

"He went there," she said, pointing toward the crumbled city.

The sky was scorched, thick with gray smog. Ash hung, suspended in the air.

The man said, "I don't think we can go there. I don't think we should go there."

She nodded and said, "No. We shouldn't. But we will."

On the hill they stood upon, where fungi grew in the twisted forms of the evaporated dead, they stared at the crater that swallowed the city. In its center was the final resting place of the great monster Tyron.

Its skull rested on its side, carnivorous and reptilian, empty socket staring up at the obfuscated sky. Its vertebrae extended two city blocks to a great ribcage, where Haley mentally imagined how many of her old houses could fit within it. From the ribcage on, more of the great beast lay, forever in repose. Charred spines lined its back and tail, arms and legs reached out and disassembled into the dust of the crater. Its great crown of horns lent it royalty, even in death.

Haley took a deep breath and tightened her grip on her rifle.

Wicks said, "I guess we didn't come here for nothing."

"No," said Haley. "We didn't." She gritted her teeth.

Ipcress Paul would die tonight.

2.

Wicks touched the skull, each tooth the size of his body. Even now, with the beast dead, he trembled. "Never thought I'd be this close," he said.

"Do you remember it?"

"Barely."

She didn't ask him to elaborate. They were about the same age; they'd have the same memories. A black shadow swallowing them up, parents pulling them violently into cover as the thing's hot breath singed the air. The silhouette of its reptilian head against the last blue sky they'd ever see. What Haley remembered most were the sounds. Tyron was uncomfortably silent now, where before its gargantuan blood vessels, flexing muscles, and churning stomach created a pervasive susurration distinct from its ear piercing cry.

Wicks backed away. "This is so wrong," he said. "I don't like looking at it. Why did he have to go here?"

Haley shrugged. "Because he thought no one would follow him."

They walked beside the column of bone that used to form a neck. They'd been following Paul for three days now. They'd watched him make his run from afar. Miles away, in another village, tucked between mountains and trees, they'd seen Ipcress Paul do his worst.

"Do you ever get the sense that he wasn't chased here?"

"What do you mean?" he said.

"I don't know," said Haley. "He seemed to know where he's going."

"Magnetic pull, of some sort, I imagine. How birds know where to fly. Paul also knows evil. He knows where to flee."

"Probably. Maybe."

In the dark skeleton of Tyron, she felt a sense of foreboding. Adrenaline coursed within her, she felt her hands tremble. But they went deeper still.

"He's killed children, I hear," said Wicks.

"Whole villages, so say the stories."

"I heard once that he was raised from the dead."

"Yes, like Lazarus."

"He was buried and he came back."

"Clawed right out of the earth, like a zombie. Remember zombies?"

"Barely."

The stories about Ipcress Paul spread like wildfire over what remained of the world. They knew he was a fearsome monster. A killer, of sorts. A sorcerer, of sorts. A boogeyman. But when she saw him for the first time, he looked nothing like any of those. He was a frail man who wandered into town with a chin that jutted too far from his skull. His hair was long and unkempt, but so was everyone's. He spoke in carefully chosen words, slowly articulating his thoughts as if he had a stutter. She hadn't liked him, necessarily, but she had not feared him.

"There's footprints," said Wicks.

"He's not careful. I heard he could fly. Why didn't he fly?"

Wicks shrugged. "He's a con man, that's all. He can't fly, not really. Right?"

Haley thought back to that day in the village, where she saw Ipcress Paul strip the flesh off a wriggling infant with his mind. "I don't think we should make assumptions," she said. "Shoot him, then burn the body. That's a sure-fire way."

Haley raised her rifle. "Did you hear that?"

Distantly: the sound of scuffling, a rat scrambling atop bones.

Wicks looked to Haley. They advanced carefully. Their fingers twitched as they stroked their triggers.

The great curved bones of Tyron's ribs hung over them and Haley felt a surreal sense of terror at being inside the thing that shaped her trauma.

An image flashed.

Black smoke, a body made of steel scales, toppled buildings. Fiery breath. A god on earth. A crown of curving horns.

It went as quickly as it came. A bright photoflash. She shook her head.

Wicks dropped the barrel of his gun temporarily and blinked.

"Paul?" she called, her voice echoing. "We know you're in here. You can't run."

The dark of the sky and the shadows from the bones made the area within Tyron nearly impenetrable, except for stripes of gray light.

Wicks said, "It's getting late. Maybe we should camp."

"In here?"

"Might as well."

"He might escape."

"I don't think he'll leave," he said.

She didn't say anything, but she didn't have to either.

3.

Haley rested against a vertebrae, Wicks against another. They'd chipped bone off Tyron's great fingers to build the beginnings of a fire. Both of them knew that this could attract Paul, but both of them also hoped that it would. Haley wondered if she would be so lucky to find their boogeyman approaching them timidly, looking for scraps of food like a hungry dog.

She figured not, but it was a nice dream.

They resolved to only sleep for a little. To only rest.

When they did, they heard the roar of blood and the heat of shimmering flames. They could look down on everything, all at once. In their dreams, they were more powerful than they could ever imagine. Out from the fiery pits of earth they came, old and enraged. They destroyed until the only thing left was to destroy themselves. Even as they slept, they could feel the heat kiss their skin.

When Haley woke, she gasped.

She blinked.

And then she stood up.

"Wicks," she said. "We need to go. We need to find Paul."

Wicks woke instantly. His face worn with consternation. "Yes, let's do it. Let's end this."

4.

They heard the noises near the bottom of Tyron's ribcage. First, a sort of joyous cackling, then: a long, low vibration. A psychic hum that sent electric shivers through them and the earth.

"Is that him?"

"It must be," said Haley.

They could not see more than ten feet ahead. Wicks shuddered. "Should we even go? We can turn around."

"He won't stop. We're supposed to kill him. That's our job," she said plainly. "There's nothing more to say."

Wicks nodded. "Yes, I suppose so."

They stuck to the edges of the spinal column, their guns raised, with the meager illumination of corroded flashlights. The noises continued, intensifying as they advanced. Haley reminded herself why she was here, a constant murmur in the back of her mind. *I am here to kill him because someone has to. I volunteered to kill Ipcress Paul. I am not good at farming but I can hold a gun. Someone has to kill him because he can't be going around doing what he's doing. It isn't natural.*

She chuckled bitterly. She could only faintly remember *natural*.

The vibrations continued. They rumbled through her bones, as well as the bones around her.

Ipcress Paul was near.

Wicks whispered, "Over there."

To their surprise, a voice answered back. "Yes, over here."

Wicks followed the words with his light.

Haley's heart fluttered. *We're here, we've done it. No more searching.* She wanted to cry, she was so happy. There he was, the boogeyman, hanging upside down from a rib, like a bat.

"Hello," he said. "You've come to find me. Here I am."

He was still thin, still scraggly. He wasn't smiling, but he looked as if he could laugh at any time. There was a sense of boredom in his expression, like he'd been waiting. He hung upside down, staring at her, vibrating with strained patience. As if to say, *yes, please, come on, go ahead.*

She did not wait to pull the trigger. Haley raised the rifle and quickly took aim. The gun kicked and Ipcress Paul fell heavily to the ground.

Wicks looked to Haley. He took his shot too, into the dead body. "Thank God," he said. "That was much easier than I thought."

"Yes, thank God," she said, suddenly uncomfortable with the words.

They approached Ipcress Paul's body, poking it with their feet. They were afraid of it, in some distant way. But no more than anyone is afraid of a dead thing.

Wicks said, "He's gone."

"We should burn him, though."

"Okay."

"If we don't burn him, they'll believe he'll be back."

"Of course. We'll make a pyre."

Haley breathed deep and fired twice more into the body of Ipcress Paul. He looked very normal like this, not like the stories at all. He was just dead.

5.

They dragged his body into a stripe of feeble light and left him to gather fuel for their funeral pyre. Wicks hacked at Tyron's bones with a machete. There were no leaves here, no wood. Only bones and dust. Each time they came back with handfuls of bones, they were relieved to see that Ipcress Paul was still there. He had not moved. He had not risen from the grave.

They built these splintered fragments high, into the shape of a triangular prism. The bones lit easily. They flashed green, igniting spectacularly, then hissing violently. In a moment, the flames settled into an orange glow. Haley and Wicks piled more and more bones on the pyre.

"We're going to burn Tyron. We're going to burn it all up!" laughed Wicks. "Wouldn't that be something?"

"A fitting reversal," said Haley.

Each piece ignited so fast that they had to wait before adding more to the pyre. They stacked the bones beside the roaring flames, slowly adding the fuel when it was safe to do so. As the fire strengthened, they arranged the coals in the shape of a man.

"Quickly," said Haley. "Help me with him. I want to be done with this."

Wicks grabbed the head and Haley grabbed the feet. Together, Ipcress Paul's body felt like nothing at all. He was wafer thin, airy. She wondered, as she swung his body to and fro, if his bones weren't hollow, like a bird's.

When they let go of him, they sighed in relief, once again, that, when his body touched the coals, he did not scream.

Haley and Wicks both grabbed an armful of Tyron's chipped bones and threw them onto Ipcress Paul's body. He was nothing but light now. The flames flashed electric emerald and then flushed with white-red heat. And once again, he did not move.

6.

Haley watched the fire, her rifle resting on her lap.

Wicks drank from a rusty flask.

"Do you hear something?" she asked.

"What's that?"

"Nothing."

He swished the drink between his teeth, feeling the heat on his gums. "He's dead. That's a good thing."

"Yes. That's a good thing."

There was a long pause. The fire crackled.

"Do you think it had a soul?" she asked.

Wicks adjusted himself. "A soul?"

"Yeah."

"Tyron? No." He cleared his throat. "But I don't believe anything has a soul. Not you, not me."

She nodded. "And yet, the great monster Tyron persists."

"We're inside of him. He's dead."

"We're old enough, barely old enough, to remember how our parents talked."

He looked down at the earth he couldn't see. "I remember. God."

"God. That's right. They called it God. They told me stories about God."

"And?"

"I hear the same stories as before. Only God is now the great monster Tyron."

"What's your point?" asked Wicks, his tone curt.

Haley pointed to the flame. "The boogeyman may burn," she said. "But he too will persist."

Some great shifting, a wind, or the creaking of bones filled the air.

"We should sleep," he said quickly.

The flames roared.

Haley didn't agree, but she didn't say anything either.

7.

The earth moved when it was touched. It screamed at the feet pounding it. A loud roar erupted from the belly of the beast. Suicide danced in the street and the towers. Bodies rained out of windows, splattering on windshields and other bodies.

The air smelled of roast pork and thick acrid smoke.

Tyron reared its head and its mouth filled with liquid light. Emerald flames coughed from his maw, engulfing blocks of wide-eyes frozen in terror.

Each city burned, just like the last.

8.

Haley woke with a start. She raised her rifle.

Wicks whispered, "Stop."

The fire had died down to glowing embers. She did not sigh in relief when she saw the body lain out on the white-hot bones.

Ipcress Paul had not burned.

His clothing was gone, but he was not.

His body flickered with light, shifting shadows that danced in circles around his flesh. So much so, that she was not sure if she saw his hand move or not.

"He's going to rise," Wicks said, his words barbed with inevitability. "He's going to get up."

"That's not how this works." Haley watched Paul's filthy body, unmolested by the heat. "Those are just stories."

"And yet they persist," he whispered.

Haley aimed down her sights. She watched the body carefully. She held her breath.

Wait.

Then, she turned her head away.

"Did you hear that?"

"Yes."

"What is that?"

"A growl. A moan."

"A roar."

"Maybe."

She returned her eyes to the rifle sights.

Ipcress Paul's head turned gently, as if he were waking from a long nap. His fingers twitched over the hot coals. He opened his mouth slightly, as if to let out a silent moan.

No.

She squeezed the trigger—once, twice, three times. Each blast screamed in her ears, echoing as violent throbs.

Ipcress Paul sat up on the hot coals, pink and nude, and turned to her, his eyes ablaze with a ring of neon. She hadn't missed a shot. But Paul was unharmed. The bullets had smashed against his skin, useless.

Wicks fired two more shots from his rifle, but Paul was already stepping off the coals, his glowing eyes two ominous pinpricks.

"I'm sorry," shouted Wicks.

Haley was up too, backing up in the opposite direction. Wicks was shaking his head at her and Paul was running toward him, the firelight sending black shadows shivering over the bony ribs of the great monster Tyron.

He ran.

She saw him disappear into shadows, the echoes of his heavy footsteps resonating with fierce vigor.

Ipcress Paul reared his head back and roared.

A cold memory dragged its claws along her brain.

He bounded forward, as if unused to his own gait, hunched slightly and taking ponderous steps. He opened his mouth again. A jet of green flame shot into the screaming blackness.

Haley blinked. She hadn't ever seen the world so bright. Not since—

Wicks.

He was far away now, down at the great monster's skull, when the blast hit him. She saw his body ignite instantly. It was as if his flesh had been soaked in kerosene. He went up like dry brush and the fire that touched him only kept working itself deeper, peeling him like an onion. Soon, his muscles were incinerated, then his organs, and before he could even fall to his knees, his bones became black dust.

Haley stepped lightly. She held onto a rib for support. She dipped between two of the bones and started to run.

Behind her, within the bones, was a low roar. Within the ribs of the great monster Tyron, where life and death held hands in tenuous continuity.

9.

She was sure sometimes she was being followed. In the dark-light of day, she thought she heard the thrumming blood of tragedy. But whenever she scouted for the source of it, she found nothing.

If Paul was there, he was nowhere to be seen.

A mile out from her village, her body began to fail her. She stumbled with each step. Her vision spun. Her stomach churned. She kept hearing people scream. Each time, she'd spin around with her rifle at her waist and fire wildly until the barrel was hot and the magazine was empty. Sometimes, she heard great footsteps, pounding behind her, shaking the earth with each step.

Just a little further. One step, then two. You can make it.

But when the ground vibrated, she lost her balance and fell. The last time it happened, she felt a shadow fall over her. She closed her eyes tight, and waited for an emerald kiss.

10.

Two boys found her curled up like a shrimp, cradling her stomach. She looked up with wild eyes at the people who came to help her. A doctor gently separated her from her gun, spoke to her while the others carried her into the village.

"What hurts? Is it your stomach? Did you eat anything?"

She shook her head.

"What happened to Wicks?"

"Gone."

"Have you had any water?"

"Yes."

After another dozen questions, he said simply, "Rest. Let her rest."

Haley was taken to a small structure with a warm bed. She was given water and food and left alone.

In the warm bed, she sweated feverishly. She tossed and turned. In her dreams, she was a child again, looking up at the great monster Tyron. She heard its thunderous footsteps. Every so often, she braced for impact, expecting that foot to smash her to a paste.

When she woke, she heard children playing. She felt better, for a moment. They laughed and giggled. One of them growled and the others reacted in mock terror.

"I have come to destroy you!" said a tiny voice.

Stories, just stories, she thought.

The children grappled outside. "I am taking your skin with my *mind*."

Stories, just stories.

She turned over on her side and held a pillow over her ear. This was much better. Much more peaceful.

She breathed slowly, counting as she did.

The earth shook.

Her breath hitched.

The children went quiet.

The air smelled of smoke.

Haley closed her eyes tight.

A great low rumbling reverberated through her flesh. And then, there it was, from outside: the first scream.

She shook her head, burying her face under the covers.

Stories, just stories, she told herself.

And yet they persist.

Acknowledgments

Monster Lairs, *A Dark Fantasy Horror Anthology,* was first conceptualized when Rob Carroll, Editor-in-Chief of Dark Matter INK, asked if I'd be interested in guest editing. I'm indebted to him for that wondrous question, and his trust and belief in the project to follow. Dark Matter INK published two 'monster' themed anthologies prior: *Human Monsters,* edited by Sadie Hartmann and Ashley Saywers, and *Monstrous Futures,* edited by Alex Woodroe. It's thanks to these incredible editors that I could see the path ahead of me, and I've certainly not traveled it alone.

For my family and friends, I offer my thanks for supporting me as I stepped in and out of stories, lair after lair, and for their gifts of patience, wisdom, encouragement, coffee, ice cream, and chocolate.

Thank you to the reading team and Dark Matter staff who offered up some of the most precious currencies: time and expertise. These beautiful souls are Kelsea Yu, Jena Brown, Marie Baca Villa, Marie Croke, Marissa van Uden, Peter Zuckerman, Samuel Poots, and Somto Ihezue. Thank you to the sharp eyes of Maddy Leary, Production Editor at Dark Matter INK, for proofreading the anthology, and to Samantha Carroll, who ensured emails and questions were answered promptly.

To the writers who heard the horn's call and responded so ardently: the truest, brightest, most potent magic I found in the submission pile came from the spellwork of your unique voices.

And what a journey it's been.

—Anna

About the Authors

Fatima Abdullahi is a Nigerian writer, poet and photographer. She was a second place winner in the 2023 Dreamfoundry writing contest, and was shortlisted in the 2023 Valiant Scribe Poetry Competition. Her works have been published in a variety of platforms, including: *Augur Magazine, Midnight & Indigo, Lunaris Review, The Decolonial Passage, Libretto Magazine, The Last Stanza Poetry Journal, The Poetry Nook,* and elsewhere. A lover of books and quiet corners, she believes firmly in the power of storytelling in all mediums and how it can be used to shape lives. She lives in Nigeria with her family.

J. W. Allen is an award-winning SFF writer from England. He holds a degree in Theological Studies and several diplomas in creative writing. A huge reader of science fiction and fantasy, John writes to explore our own world and its many cultures. He lives behind a pile of books on the east coast of England, creating new worlds and civilizations in his mind. You can follow John on Twitter/X @TheOnlyJohnnyA and via his website at johnallenwriter.com.

R. F. Anding is a reclusive writer and illustrator with a penchant for medieval marginalia, fountain pens, tarot cards, and loose leaf tea, who has lived in England, as well as the Northern Marianas, and now resides in the Midwest with a small menagerie and large collection of antique books.

Michael Boulerice is an active HWA member who hails from the wilds of New Hampshire. His short stories can be found in *Cosmic Horror Monthly, the Creepy Podcast,* and *Thirteen Podcast,* as well as anthologies by Tenebrous Press, Dark Matter INK, and Little Ghost Books. When he's not pouring his greatest fears into a keyboard, Michael is either snowboarding in the White Mountains or spoiling his pets rotten.

Kevin M. Casin (he/they) is a gay, Latine fiction writer, and cardiovascular research scientist. His fiction work appears in *If There's Anyone Left, Idle Ink, Medusa Tales Magazine, Pyre Magazine,* and more. He is Editor/Publisher of *Tree and Stone Magazine* (https://www.tree-and-stone.com), and an HWA/SFWA/Codex member.

Kaitlin Caul is a Canadian author, artist, and chef of Polish descent. By day, she works as a PowerPoint wizard and Sales Effectiveness Coordinator. By night, she splits her time between writing projects, video games, and Dungeons & Dragons. She can be found roaming the streets of Ottawa in search of adventure, or at home, doting on her two felines that are quite convinced they are descended from royalty.

Lyndsey Croal is an Edinburgh-based author of speculative and strange fiction, with work published in several anthologies and magazines, including Mslexia's *Best Women's Short Fiction 2021, Dark Matter Magazine, Shoreline of Infinity,* and *Orion's Belt.* She's a Scottish Book Trust New Writers Awardee, British Fantasy Award Finalist, former Hawthornden Fellow, and a Ladies of Horror Fiction Writers Grant recipient. Her debut novelette "Have You Decided on Your Question" was published in April 2023 with Shortwave Publishing.

Marie Croke is a fantasy and science-fiction author who won the Writers of the Future Contest with the story "Of Woven Wood" and attended the six-week Odyssey Writing Workshop. She has since gone on to have over thirty stories published in numerous anthologies and magazines such as *Beneath Ceaseless Skies, Diabolical Plots, Apex Magazine, Lackington's, Apparition Lit, Dark Matter Magazine, Cast of Wonders,* and *Fireside.* She currently lives in Maryland with her family, all of whom like to scribble messages in her notebooks when she's not looking.

Koji A. Dae is a queer American writer, living longterm in Bulgaria. Her work focuses on parenting, relationships, and neural technology, and can be found in places such as *Clarkesworld* and *Apex*, among others.

Oleander Dudek is a trans, queer, and neurodiverse writer based in North Carolina. They can provide you with as many trans gays in gothic fairy tales as you could possibly wish for, and quite a bit more cannibalism. When not writing short stories about his fellow queers transforming into monsters, he is writing books about them too.

Victor Forna is a Sierra Leonean writer based in his country's capital, Freetown. His short fiction and poetry have been published or are forthcoming in homes such as *Fantasy Magazine*, *PodCastle*, *Lightspeed*, *Strange Horizons*, and elsewhere. He is an alumnus of the 2022 AKO Caine Prize Writing Workshop.

L. P. Hernandez is an author of horror and speculative fiction. His stories have been featured in anthologies from Cemetery Gates Media, *Dark Matter Magazine*, and Sinister Smile Press, among others. He is a regular contributor to *The NoSleep Podcast* and has released two short story collections. His debut novella, *Stargazers*, was released by Cemetery Gates Media. When not writing, he serves as a medical administrator in the U.S. Air Force. He is a husband, father, and a dedicated metalhead.

Jordan Hirsch writes speculative fiction and poetry while living on the ancestral and current homelands of the Dakota people: Mni Sota Makoce. Her work has appeared with *Apparition Literary Magazine*, *Daily Science Fiction*, *Proton Reader*, and other venues. Find her overuse of Star Trek GIFs on Twitter/X @jordanrhirsch.

Andrew Leon Hudson is a technical writer by day, and is technically a writer by night as well. An Englishman resident in Barcelona, Spain, in addition to *Dark Matter Magazine* his genre fiction has most recently appeared in *Little Blue Marble, Cossmass Infinities,* and the anthology *Triangulation: Dark Skies.* Since April 2020 he has been editor of the spec-fic zine that lives at Mythaxis.co.uk. He blogs at AndrewLeonHudson. wordpress.com and tweets @AndLeoHud, but not so often that you'd notice.

Vanessa Jae writes horrifically beautiful anarchies, reads stories for *Apex Magazine,* and is poetry editor at *Strange Horizons.* She also collects black hoodies and bruises in mosh pits on Tuesday nights.

Ai Jiang is a Chinese-Canadian writer, a Nebula-, Locus-, Ignyte Award finalist, and an immigrant from Fujian currently residing in Toronto, Ontario. She is a member of HWA and SFWA. Her work can be found in *F&SF, The Dark, Uncanny,* among others. She is the recipient of Odyssey Workshop's 2022 Fresh Voices Scholarship and the author of *Linghun* and *I AM AI.* Find her on Twitter @AiJiang_ and online at aijiang.ca.

Wailana Kalama is a dark fiction writer from Hawaii, with credits in *Mother: Tales of Love and Terror* (Weird Little Worlds Press), *Pseudopod, The Maul, Apparition Lit, Rock and a Hard Place, Dark Matter Presents Monstrous Futures: A Sci-Fi Horror Anthology.*

Alex Langer is a Canadian Jewish writer and lawyer usually based in Brooklyn. He's currently on a sojourn to the Midwest, with his wife and fluffy mobster of a cat. His short fiction has appeared in *Apex Magazine, On Spec,* and the *Upon a Once Time* anthology from Air and Nothingness Press. You can find him on Twitter/X @AlexLanger1993.

Rajiv Moté is a writer and software engineering director living in Chicago with his wife, daughter, and a tiny dog. He's a member of SFWA whose stories appear in *Cosmic Horror Monthly, Diabolical Plots, Escape Pod,* and other publications.

Leah Ning lives in northern Virginia with her husband and their four pets. Her short fiction appears or is forthcoming in *Writers of the Future Volume 36*, *PodCastle*, *Beneath Ceaseless Skies*, and *Apex Magazine*, among others.

Damilola Oyedotun is a Nigerian who writes contemporary and speculative fiction, and non-fiction about pop culture. He was a winner in the 2022 PEN America Dau Prize for Emerging Writers, and a winner in the Inaugural Utopia Awards. He has works published/forthcoming in *Reckoning, Nightmare, Lightspeed, Clarkesworld, Solarpunk Magazine, Science Fiction World, Our Move Next*, and other places. You can find him on Twitter/X @dhamlex99, and on Instagram @dhamlex.

Zachary Rosenberg is a Jewish horror and SFF writer living in Florida. By night, he crafts horrifying and fantastical tales. By day, he practices law, which is even more frightening. You may find his work in anthologies such as *Nightmare Sky*, Air and Nothingness Press's *The Librarian, Shakespeare Unleashed*, and *Fiends in the Furrows III: The Final Harvest*. His upcoming books can be found from Brigids Gate, Darklit Press, and Off-Limits Press. Find him on social media at @ZachRoseWriter.

Abhijeet Sathe grew up in India and moved to Chicago for the weather. He is absolutely obsessed with causality, history, Faustian bargains, and low-grade evil. You can read more of his stuff at *Beneath Ceaseless Skies, Tasavvur*, and *Tales From An Unfamiliar Nation*. He can be reached at admin@tfaun.com

Jean Strickland received her BA in Writing from Loyola University Maryland, and her fiction has appeared or is forthcoming in *All Worlds Wayfarer, Strangelet Journal*, and *Literary Orphans*. She enjoys watching anime and convincing people to play games with her.

Kanishk Tantia is a BIPOC Immigrant from India. His speculative fiction often involves plants eating people. He currently lives in

San Diego with his partner and an adorable dog with a criminal record. His works have been published by or are upcoming in Dark Matter Ink, Flametree Press, and *The Dread Machine*.

Gretchen Tessmer is a writer/attorney based in the U.S./Canadian borderlands. She writes both short fiction and poetry (so much poetry), with work appearing in over fifty publications, including *Nature, Strange Horizons, Bourbon Penn, F&SF*, and *Beneath Ceaseless Skies*. Her poetry has been nominated for Pushcart, Rhysling, and Dwarf Stars awards.

V. F. Thompson is just compost in training. She can be found clowning around Kalamazoo, Michigan. Her poetry collection, *Shimmer*, is available from The Dionysian Public Library. Follow her on Twitter/X at @VF_Thompson.

D. Matthew Urban hails from Texas and lives in Queens, New York, where he reads weird books, watches weird movies, and writes weird fiction. His stories can be found in *Ooze: Little Bursts of Body Horror, Shredded: A Sports and Fitness Body Horror Anthology*, and *Annus Horribilis: An Anthology of Horror Set in 2022*, among other venues.

Emily Ruth Verona is a Pinch Literary Award-winner and a Bram Stoker Awards®-nominee, with work featured in *Under Her Skin, Lamplight Magazine, Mystery Tribune, The Ghastling, Coffin Bell*, and *The Jewish Book of Horror*. Her debut thriller, *Midnight on Beacon Street*, is expected from Harper Perennial in 2024. For more visit emilyruthverona.com.

Carson Winter is an author, punker, and raw nerve. His fiction has been featured in *Apex, Vastarien*, and *Tales to Terrify*. "The Guts of Myth" was published in Volume One of the *Split Scream* series from Dread Stone Press, and his novella *Soft Targets* is available from Tenebrous Press. He lives in the Pacific Northwest.

Lucy Zhang writes, codes, and watches anime. Her work has appeared in *CRAFT, The Spectacle, Redivider,* and elsewhere. She is the author of the chapbooks *Hollowed* (Thirty West Publishing) and *Absorption* (Harbor Review).

About the Editor

Anna Madden is a writer and Acquisitions Editor for *Dark Matter Magazine* and Dark Matter INK. Her fiction has appeared in *Apex Magazine, Orion's Belt, PseudoPod,* and elsewhere. She was the guest editor of the Ironwood *MYRIAD* zine, available from *Hexagon Magazine*. In free time, she makes birch forests out of stained glass.

About the Cover Artist

Oliver Jeavons (Olly) is a UK-based artist also known as *artofolly*. He works with many different medias and styles, and he is always pushing his creativity further. Comic book art, book cover art, and commissions of all types are included in his portfolio.

Permissions

"Karakonduzhul in Love" by Koji A. Dae, copyright © 2023 Koji A. Dae. Used by permission of the author.

"To Guard a Garden" by Kevin M. Casin, copyright © 2023 Kevin M. Casin. Used by permission of the author.

"The Last Guardian" by Fatima Abdullahi, copyright © 2023 Fatima Abdullahi. Used by permission of the author.

"Your Ballad from within His Gourd" by Ai Jiang, copyright © 2023 Ai Jiang. Used by permission of the author.

"A Journal of Strange Creatures and Beasts from Africa" by Damilola Oyedotun, copyright © 2023 Damilola Oyedotun. Used by permission of the author.

"Who the Sun Gets to Eat" by Oleander Dudek, copyright © 2023 Oleander Dudek. Used by permission of the author.

"In Pursuit of the Black Chuck Wagon" by Michael Boulerice, copyright © 2023 Michael Boulerice. Used by permission of the author.

"Moloch's Children" by Rajiv Moté, copyright © 2023 Rajiv Moté. Used by permission of the author.

"Patch Job" by Kaitlin Caul, copyright © 2023 Kaitlin Caul. Used by permission of the author.

"To Meld Flesh with Gown and Gown to Flesh" by Marie Croke, copyright © 2023 Marie Croke. Used by permission of the author.

"Said the Spider to the Fly" by V. F. Thompson, copyright © 2023 V. F. Thompson. Used by permission of the author.

EXPERIENCE *MONSTER LAIRS* IN AUDIO

Scan the QR code below to sample or purchase *Monster Lairs: A Dark Fantasy Horror Anthology* in audiobook, narrated by Cheryl May.